A TIMELESS Romance ANTHOLOGY

EUROPEAN COLLECTION

EUROPEAN COLLECTION

Annette Lyon
G.G. Vandagriff
Michele Paige Holmes
Sarah M. Eden
Heather B. Moore
Nancy Campbell Allen

Mirror Press

Copyright © 2014 by Mirror Press, LLC
Paperback edition
All rights reserved

No part of this book may be reproduced in any form whatsoever without prior written permission of the publisher, except in the case of brief passages embodied in critical reviews and articles.

This is a work of fiction. The characters, names, incidents, places, and dialogue are products of the authors' imagination and are not to be construed as real.

Interior Design by Rachael Anderson
Edited by Annette Lyon and Whitney McGruder

Published by Mirror Press, LLC
http://timelessromanceanthologies.blogspot.com

E-book edition released November 2013
Paperback edition release October 2014

ISBN: 978-1-941145-31-9

TABLE OF CONTENTS

War of Hearts	1
The Earl of Oaksey Takes a Wife	57
Gift of Love	105
A Lesson in Love	165
An Ocean Away	211
What Happens in Venice	271

OTHER TIMELESS ROMANCE ANTHOLOGIES

Winter Collection

Spring Vacation Collection

Summer Wedding Collection

Autumn Collection

Love Letter Collection

Old West Collection

Summer in New York Collection

Silver Bells Collection

All Regency Collection

California Dreamin' Collection

WAR OF HEARTS
by Annette Lyon

Other Works by Annette Lyon

Fiction

Band of Sisters
Coming Home
The Newport Ladies Book Club series
A Timeless Romance Anthology Series
A Portrait for Toni
At the Water's Edge
Lost Without You

Non-Fiction

Chocolate Never Faileth
Done & Done
There, Their, They're:
A No-Tears Guide to Grammar from the Word Nerd

ONE

December 10, 1939—Finland

Anna didn't realize she'd fallen asleep until the freezing, bumpy train screeched to a halt and jolted her awake. She opened her eyes and tried to regain her bearings. The sky outside was pitch black; she couldn't see anything through the windows, not even stars. She stared at the windows—blacked out to avoid detection by Soviet aircraft. A shudder went down her spine.

That's right. I'm in a war zone. Her mind came fully awake. This wasn't California. She'd traveled across the entire U.S., took a ship to Sweden, and finally, this train on her way to a non-combat encampment north of Lake Ladoga.

Dill, her boss at *The Star* had planned to send Keith, another, more senior reporter to cover Stalin's invasion of neighboring Finland, but his appendix ruptured, so he'd be in the hospital for the foreseeable future. While Anna would never wish bad fortune on a colleague, if Keith *had* to get sick, she was quite happy to take his place at the last minute. She'd convinced Dill she was the right reporter to cover the so-called Winter War in Keith's absence.

"I've worked harder than any of the other writers on staff," she'd told him. A staff of almost all men—just one other woman. "I deserve the assignment."

He'd agreed, so she'd gone home to pack, relieved to be traveling. She hadn't told Dill her biggest reason for wanting the job, because it had nothing to do with being a journalist. Simply put, Anna needed some distance from Pete, from the torrent of emotions that seeing him every day in the news room meant.

Now she had her distance. She was far from home in the dark and cold, and most definitely alone in this frozen wasteland. She'd done some research on the war so far and knew the basics, including the geography of cities she'd only just heard of. She'd build on that knowledge after she arrived in camp.

Stalin wanted to take over ports and other areas of land he viewed as strategically good for Russia as a whole and for Leningrad in particular, almost certainly taking over the country entirely in the process so it would fall to Communist rule. When he'd first invaded, he's planned for the exercise to be over almost as quickly as it began. A few days, ten days at most. About two weeks into the fighting, the Finns had proven to be far greater adversaries than Stalin ever expected from his miniature neighbor, and all the political experts now said that the war was just getting started.

Anna stood and buttoned her new coat as she waited to exit. She bought it in New York City en route for this assignment—no finding one like this in southern California. When the car door opened and a whoosh of frigid air swirled inside, Mother's voice came to Anna's mind. "You're leaving one kind of difficulty only to ask to enter another, far more horrible kind."

"I'll be safe," Anna had told her. "They aren't sending me to a conflict area."

What Mother hadn't known was that Anna wouldn't mind physical suffering; it would be much easier to endure than the emotional turmoil she faced every day. No, whatever this war held for her, Anna would much rather be near the Tolvajärvi battlefront in the deepest winter than walking through Santa Monica, seeing the palm tree beneath which Pete had first kissed her.

As Anna waited in the short line to get off the train, her mother's words repeated in her mind.

Perhaps I am a little crazy, but I had to get away.

Arctic weather, soldiers with powerful stories to tell, a foreign landscape; it would all help distract her from the bitter breakup she'd gone through the night before Thanksgiving. The humiliation of that evening still stung.

The humiliation part was your own fault, she chided herself.

In her defense, she'd thought Pete was going to propose that night three weeks ago—a lifetime ago. When he'd arrived at her parents' home to pick her up for their usual Friday date, his surprised expression said that he hadn't remembered her parents' offering to have him over for dinner, not until he saw them standing in the dining room beside an elaborately set table.

He'd leaned in and whispered, "Anna, there's something important we need to discuss. Can we go somewhere private?"

"Of course, darling," Anna had said, her heart speeding up at the prospect of wearing Pete's ring. "Come meet my parents first." Like a silly schoolgirl, she'd blushed with anticipation as she'd led him to the dining room and introduced Pete to her mother and father. Looking back, Anna remembered Pete looking a bit pale.

Turned out that Pete *was* nervous—just not for the reason Anna assumed.

Throughout dinner, he'd remained uncharacteristically quiet, even when Anna hinted that he broach the topic on his mind. "So what's the important thing you wanted to discuss?" she asked as she buttered a roll. She sent her mother a smile; they both just knew it would happen tonight.

Pete swallowed a bite of meatloaf, his eyes moving nervously from Anna, to her father, to her mother. He cleared his throat uncomfortably. "Could we speak alone?"

Anna set down the roll and patted his arm playfully. "Come now, Pete," she said, in hopes of easing his jitters. "If you have something important to say, you can say it in front of my family."

They'll be your family soon too.

He pushed away from the table, placed his cloth napkin beside his plate, and stood. "I, uh . . ."

Anna licked her lips and clasped her hands, ready to say yes.

"I-I need to go." Pete headed for the front door.

"What?" Anna said, her voice going up an octave as she flew to her feet.

Pete's step paused, and he turned around, but he avoided her eyes—and Father's, and Mother's—seeming unable to find a place to look until he settled on the rug. "I came to say good-bye, Anna. I'm not ready to be tied down." His eyes met hers briefly. "I'm sorry." His cheeks had spots of pink in them. Their gaze held, and she sensed pain and regret in his before he looked away, muttered "Excuse me," to her parents, and strode away. The front door shut hard behind him as if he couldn't wait to escape.

Now Anna stood in a train car with support staff for a battlefront a world away from that dining room. How could she have been so foolish as to think he cared about her—was about to propose to her?

You came here to forget. Stop thinking of him.

She hefted her suitcase and clutched her purse, making sure that her notepad and pencil were easily accessible; one never knew when one would find a golden nugget worthy of reporting. Along with the other passengers, she shuffled closer to the exit and peered outside but found almost total darkness, save for a few lamps and the light of the full moon reflecting off the snow.

What time was it again? She checked her wristwatch, tilting it toward the light inside the car. Ten o'clock at night. Of course it was dark. She'd heard of Finnish winters, how the days had only a few hours of sunlight. She looked forward to seeing that for herself tomorrow.

A plane buzzed in the sky overhead. For a moment, everyone in her car stopped moving and held their breath—a secretary, two nurses, a few soldiers, and others, all frozen as one. Only when the plane passed without a strike did they breathe a sigh of relief and keep moving toward the door.

The moment Anna reached outside air, the shock of the frigid air made her gasp involuntarily. One step outside the train car was miles colder than inside it. She descended the remaining steps and reached the platform, where she quickly lifted her coat collar to protect her face. Her nose was already starting to tingle with pain. She set down her suitcase and searched her pockets for the thick gloves she'd bought, also in New York, and put them on.

Heavens to Betsy. She'd known she was coming to a cold place, but she hadn't expected to be chilled to the marrow after only seconds. And men lived and fought in this weather?

The things we do for freedom and our families.

That's exactly what the Finnish soldiers were doing, against all odds. That's what she was here to do: show American readers of *The Star* what was really going on in this small nation.

I'll have to actually be able to see something first. She hated the dark already. This assignment would be a bigger challenge for a California girl than she'd assumed. On her way, she'd braced herself for cold, for pine trees instead of palm trees, for snow. For things to be different. But this was beyond *different*. Back home, even in December, winter, such as it was, mostly meant it wasn't hot out—not that your lungs felt as if they were freezing your body from the inside out.

"Miss Miller?" a deep voice called from behind her, one with a thick accent, making the I's sound like long E's, and rolling the R at the end of her name: *Mees Meellerrrr.*

She turned to see two men striding toward her, one much larger than the other. The taller looked to be in his mid-forties. The other was shorter and much younger, twenty at most. He wore civilian clothes—leather boots, a warm coat, and hat, but nothing official-looking, yet he was clearly a soldier. He carried a rifle and walked like he'd recently come out of military training.

With a start, Anna realized he probably *had* just come from training.

The two men stopped before her, as the elder shook her hand. "Welcome to Finland," the older one said in accented but clear English. "I hope we can make your stay comfortable." He spoke like a concierge at a hotel.

"Thank you." This was Anna's first chance to really see the young man up close, and she couldn't help notice his obviously worn coat and boots. Word was that the Finnish army was low on almost everything, but especially on ammunition, guns, and artillery. They had virtually no tanks to speak of, and their men had never been trained for what to do when confronted with them, which had been a disaster the first day of the war. They had a limited number of men, and even an even more limited number of uniforms. So the rumor about uniforms was true.

The young soldier reached for her suitcase, which she surrendered with a smile. She turned back to the older man. "Are you Colonel Talvela?"

"No, no. He is my commander. I'm Kuusinen. No relation to the fake president." He shook his head, clearly disdainful of the puppet government Stalin had erected for the Finns.

"I'll remember that," Anna said, and followed them through the snow, picking her way behind them toward a jeep. She could hardly see where she was stepping. If she reached the car without slipping and falling on her face, it would be a miracle, even though she'd bought a pair of sensible boots to go with the coat and gloves instead of the pretty boots with the high heels she'd eyed in a Manhattan department store. Even so, Anna had to scurry to keep up.

They finally reached the jeep, which was parked near a snowbank. The young man hefted Anna's suitcase into the back then hopped behind the wheel. Kuusinen gestured toward the back seat. "For you—the back is a somewhat gentler ride."

"Oh, okay. Thank you," she said, taking his hand as he helped her up.

Climbing up in a skirt was tricky business, but as she settled into her seat, she was extra glad for the thick long johns she'd put on underneath. Otherwise, her limbs would have frozen right off.

She clutched her purse on her lap and made sure her suitcase was steady. "Has my photographer arrived yet?" The magazine promised to send a photographer along, but they had different itineraries. As Anna was a last-minute replacement for Keith, she didn't know when the photographer would be arriving or even who it was.

"Yes. He came yesterday morning," Kuusinen said as he lifted himself into the jeep.

Whoever he was, he'd gotten almost two full days' worth of experience ahead of her. She hoped he was a team player, that he'd share his information so his pictures and her stories that went with them would be good—award-worthy good.

"Let's go," Kuusinen said after Anna scooted back in her seat. The younger man nodded and started up the engine.

They were off, bouncing along icy roads, the headlights looking like two slashes cutting the way before them. The darkness felt so all-consuming and unfamiliar that Anna wished herself back home in her apartment with a cup of chamomile tea.

At least someone from home was in camp; a little bit of the familiar would be welcome, particularly when the "little bit" was simply a fellow American. Not for the first time during this journey, Anna wished she'd gotten a chance to meet her photographer and get to know him so she could get a feel for how he worked and how best to utilize his skills.

The jeep slid around a corner, just missing an animal, which pranced off through some trees. "Was that a—a reindeer?" Anna stammered. Her arms shot out, griping the jeep for dear life.

"Yes," Kuusinen said. "We mustn't hurt the animals, of course."

Of course? How about we keep ourselves safe first? Her grip tightened. *Oh, I need a good laugh if I ever get safely back on solid ground.*

What she wouldn't give for her cozy bedroom with the yellow glow from her lamp as she read a novel under her comforter. She'd done so the night before she left three days ago, but it felt like another world, another lifetime now as the jeep hurdled her through the inky, never-ending blackness.

At least this will keep me from thinking about Pete.

"I hear it's this dark in the day as well." she called to the front seat, determined to keep Pete out of her head. The cold air bit her throat and lungs. "Is that right?"

Kuusinen turned to talk to her over his shoulder, one arm resting on the driver's seat. "This time of year, yes." He looked as relaxed as if he were strolling down Hollywood Boulevard. "We get a few hours of light each day. Three or four, maybe."

"Three?" Anna repeated, incredulous. People lived this way? How?

"Or four," Kuusinen said. "Oh, but just wait six months, and we'll have so much light, you can hardly sleep at night. That's when we have three or four hours of *darkness* a night."

"Goodness," Anna said, shaking her head as she tried to grasp what such a life would be like. She wouldn't mind seeing a Finnish summer, but she was rather glad she wouldn't be here anywhere near long enough to find out what they were like.

"It's a beautiful country and a beautiful life," Kuusinen said. His face grew more serious. "A wonderful life we *will not* lose to Russia."

She nodded. "I believe you." The intensity in his eyes said that no matter what, he and his people would never give in, even against the giant Soviet army.

"I don't know how you do it," Anna said.

"Sisu," Kuusinen said without missing a beat.

"I'm sorry. I don't know that word." Anna's forehead crinkled. "See-soo? What does that mean?"

"There is no good English word. Some say it's 'guts,' but . . ." He made a face and shook his head, showing his disdain for the translation. He pounded his chest. "Sisu. It's what makes us strong. Determined. Brave. We get through anything. We keep going no matter how hard. The Russians thought they could come take over with their tanks, cannons, and hundreds of thousands of men against our small numbers. But we don't surrender. *This* is what we learn from living with these winters and defeating them every year."

As he spoke, puffs of white escaped his mouth. He leaned closer to Anna and narrowed his eyes. "*That* is sisu."

Two

They arrived in camp perhaps ten harrowing minutes later. Anna had never been more relieved to have a car stop in her life. Kuusinen took his leave. The young soldier had lit a small lantern and carried both it and Anna's suitcase across the snow. She hurried along behind him.

"What's your name?" she asked.

"Me?" He paused in the snow, seeming hesitant to speak English. "I am—Antti."

"Nice to meet you, Antti."

He smiled at that then continued on, leading her to what looked like a hilly mass of branches and snow. Not until he stopped before it and knocked did she realize that this was a shelter of some sort—a camouflaged dugout. It blended in perfectly with the surrounding the forest.

Antti set the suitcase before the door. "Here is the women's place. I don't go in," he said, gesturing toward the dugout. He lifted a hand and gave a slight nod, as if he were tipping a hat—as he probably had to ladies on the street before the war broke out—and walked away with the lantern. Alone in the darkness, Anna felt even colder than before.

She lifted a hand to knock again, but the door opened before her knuckles made contact, revealing a pretty woman with a round face and blonde hair pulled into a tight bun.

"*Oi anteesk—*"

Anna shook her head, hands raised. "I'm sorry; I don't speak Finnish."

The woman looked up. "Oh, hello." She spoke the two English words with confidence. "American?"

"Yes. I'm a reporter. Antti says I'm to stay here?"

"Ah. You came to see the war and write for a newspaper, yes?"

"For a magazine, yes," Anna said. She pointed inside the dugout. "Do I stay in here?"

"Yes, yes," the woman said. "Come." She led the way inside. Anna struggled to drag her suitcase inside. She closed the door, and immediately felt better; the bitter cold was gone. She was enveloped by a highly unexpected feeling. Not warmth, exactly, but also not the freezing cold she'd stepped from. This was quite tolerable. She looked around. The walls were covered with hides with short hair. A glow spilled from a lantern in the corner, making the room lighter than Anna would have expected. She reached up and stroked one of the furs on the wall. "What animal is this from?"

"Reindeer," the woman said.

"Brilliant," Anna murmured. Drawing her hand down the wall, along the concrete, which gave her a feeling of security, although she had no idea whether it was a false sense of safety. Could a bomb or tank still bash it to pieces? Probably. But this area of the war was supposed to be quiet.

She heard a boom in the distance. Mortar fire or a bomb, surely. But how close? She swallowed back the nerves climbing up her throat, reminding herself that she'd asked for this assignment.

I will prove myself as equal to any other reporter on staff. Another boom, this one closer. It took Anna's breath away.

When the boom subsided, the woman crossed to a cot on the far side of the room, seemingly unfazed by the noise. "My name is Kaisa. I'm a nurse. And I believe this is your cot."

"Thank you," Anna said, following from behind and setting her suitcase beside the cot. The dugout had ten cots, with nine obviously in use; personal effects and clothing were stacked beneath them and on top of them. Each cot had a small shelf unit or other storage. Remarkably nice for an icy war zone.

Kaisa turned toward the door, apparently ready to leave, but Anna called her back, unwilling to be left alone with nothing to do. She pulled out her notebook and pencil and hurried toward Kaisa.

"Could you show me where my photographer is?" Anna asked. "Kuusinen said he arrived yesterday."

The nurse stopped at the door and turned around. "Tall man, blond hair, very handsome. Could pass for a Finn?"

Anna shrugged but smiled at the description. "I don't know; I haven't met him." She mentally went through the photographers she knew at the magazine, but that didn't do much; several were tall and blond, including Pete.

Ugh. Stop thinking about him!

"He's *very* handsome." Kaisa's eyes lit up. "He went on a ski patrol a few hours ago. They should be back soon. Would you like to wait in the mess hall for him?" She pushed the door open, letting a stream of frigid air into the dugout. "That's straight ahead about one hundred meters. You can use the flashlight on your cot to find your way."

Anna found the flashlight, which she hadn't noticed before, and flipped it on. The yellow beam was a strange comfort in this land of what felt like eternal night.

"I must go to my shift in hospital now," Kaisa said, making a move to leave.

Anna jumped at the opportunity. "May I come with you?"

Kaisa stopped in her step a second time and looked questioningly at Anna. "You want to see hospital?" Her voice sounded incredulous.

"I want to see the war from all sides."

Kaisa seemed to consider the suggestion for a moment before nodding. "Very well."

Anna quickly opened her purse, from which she snatched two extra pencils in case one broke, and followed Kaisa into the bitter cold. Even though she'd been outside only moments before, the sheer force of the winter was again a shock to her system, as if she'd walked into a wall of ice. She tried not to show her reaction to Kaisa, who tromped along, seemingly without noticing or caring about the temperature or the snow squeaking beneath their boots.

Along the way, Anna couldn't see tents, dugouts, or other structures until they were nearly upon them. Only their two small flashlights kept Anna from stumbling and running into things.

"I'm glad you're leading the way," she said to Kaisa, hoping to keep the heaviness of the darkness from pressing in on her like a heavy weight. "I'd be liable to wander into the trees and get lost in the snow without your help."

Slowing her step, Kaisa turned around, her face suddenly somber. "That is exactly what happens to the Russians. They aren't ready for our winters and don't want to fight anyway. Their leaders lie about why they've invaded our country."

"What kind of lies?" Anna mentally opened her reporter's notebook so she could remember this conversation. She couldn't take notes in the dark, but she wanted to hear what was on Kaisa's mind. Anna's journalistic instincts promptly overcame her desire to get out of the cold, and she felt no need to hurry, even though her toes burned with the cold.

"Stalin tells his soldiers that they are coming to liberate us poor, downtrodden Finns. Some prisoners we've captured say they can hardly believe their eyes when they see how we Finns live more comfortably than they do in Russia. We have everything we need. They have nothing to offer us." She shook her head wistfully. "Poor Russian boys . . ." Even though she spoke of her enemy camped somewhere in the dark in the distance, her face showed compassion. "Most of the Russians soldiers are hardly trained at all. So many young men are just sent to the border on trains and then they march. Many have died from the cold as they come across the border before they ever see battle. Those who survive are told that if they are captured, the Finns will torture them, pluck out their eyeballs, and then kill them. Of course we do no such thing."

Anna's stomach twisted. "How horrible. Why don't the soldiers refuse to fight?" Even as she asked the question, she knew the answer. Soldiers didn't disobey orders.

The faint glow of Kaisa's flashlight showed her pained smile. Clearly, the idea of suffering was hard for this nurse to bear, even if it meant the enemy. "The commanders give them no choice. Russian soldiers march toward us with guns at their backs. They are shot either by our snipers or by their own commanders." Kaisa nodded toward the forest behind Anna. "Or, if they try to escape into the trees . . . they get lost, as you said. It doesn't take long for them to freeze and die." She cleared her throat, shook her head as if to clear such sad thoughts, and turned toward the path in the snow again. "Come. I must report to my shift."

They entered one of two tents, both of which Kaisa indicated belonged to the field hospital. The other was for surgeries, this one for the recovering wounded. The tents were large and painted white as camouflage in the snow. Kaisa held open a heavy canvas flap, which, like the dugout, was lined with fur. Anna stepped inside. The temperature within the tent didn't feel quite as warm as in the dugout, but the sting of cold wasn't here. Cots lined both sides, more than half filled with wounded.

Kaisa consulted her superior as she began her shift, and Anna took in every detail, trying to commit it all to memory as she looked for a spot to sit where she could take notes. She spotted a chair the opposite side of the room from Kaisa, where she sat to jot down all she'd learned so far.

Low-toned Finnish was spoken in whispers, mostly by nurses caring for soldiers, but also by a surgeon and a few others. The language sounded nothing like French or German, or even Russian. It had a distinctive, beautiful quality to it, one she'd have to find a way to put into words when she wrote about the war. Through the hum and buzz of conversation, with rolled Rs and vowels Anna had never heard, a different voice pierced the sound, one that didn't match the others.

She lifted her head and found the source: a man three cots down on other side of the room. He groaned, seemingly half conscious, as his bandaged head moved back and forth and he clutched his arm, which was in a sling. The words coming from his mouth sounded strangely familiar—or rather, not the words, but the accent. He *wasn't* speaking Finnish; she was quite sure of that.

She took a step toward Kaisa, who was now consulting a clipboard at the base of the first cot on the left. She replaced the clipboard then removed her stethoscope from around her neck, blew on the metal end a few times—surely to warm it up—as she approached the head of the bed then listened to the man's heart. A blood-soaked bandage wrapped his leg, and he wore a glazed expression.

As Kaisa listened to the man's heart, she kept her eyes on her watch. Then she wrote a note onto the clipboard and replaced the stethoscope around her neck. She asked a question to the soldier, who shook his head and said something Anna interpreted as a thank you.

Kaisa moved to the next cot. Anna crossed the narrow room and touched the nurse's arm. Kaisa turned toward her, a question in her eyes. Anna nodded at the moaning soldier, who still mumbled in a different accent. "Is he Finnish?"

"No," Kaisa said simply.

"Swedish?" Anna asked next. Many Finns spoke Swedish natively, or so she'd learned in her research. Plus, some Swedes had volunteered to help their neighbor country.

Kaisa removed the next clipboard and consulted the information on it. She glanced briefly to her right, at the man Anna meant. "Him? Russian, of course."

The words froze Anna in place almost as much as the cold had before. Shouldn't a POW be kept elsewhere, or at least restrained? Had he not been moaning in Russian—saying what Anna now realized was probably *Stalin*—she would have assumed he was one more in a line of Finnish wounded.

Seemingly without noticing Anna's reaction, Kaisa continued her duties. She shook a thermometer then placed it under the second soldier's tongue then went on to change a bandage on his forehead.

Likely sensing Anna behind her, Kaisa said, "We see many injuries in the face." Her movements were gentle and precise, like a true professional. She didn't flinch at the angry red stitched-up wound, but Anna did. "We have many good snipers who grew up hunting. They can shoot while they hide in the trees at a great distance. But when they have to fight, it's often very close, with knives instead of guns."

Anna tried not to shiver. She opened her notebook and wrote furiously, grateful that she'd brought pencils instead of a fountain pen, which would be little more than a block of black ice here. "Did he . . ." She gestured toward the Russian. "Defect?"

Kaisa looked up from changing the dressing. "*De . . . fect*? I do not know that word."

How to explain? "Did he leave his army to join the Finnish army?"

"Oh, I understand." Kaisa set the bloodied bandage into a metal bowl then went to work cleaning what looked like an angry, swollen stab wound below the young man's eye. "No. We treat the few Russian soldiers we capture as our own. They are no longer the enemy then, simply another person who needs help."

Even though the soldier needed help because of wounds caused at the hand of a Finn? Being humane toward prisoners was one thing, but Anna had never heard of this kind of care toward a prisoner of war. "Surely your own men get medical care first."

Kaisa looked up, her brow furrowed in what looked like genuine confusion. "We treat wounds in order of how serious they are. I believe you call it *triage*?" She set aside a cotton ball she'd dabbed on the soldier's wounds and looked at Anna straight on to explain. "We are nurses and doctors. Our job is to help anyone who needs us. These poor Russians had the misfortune to be born where Stalin would one day rule and send them off to be slaughtered. We may have to fight them to stay free—and we will fight while Stalin ships endless numbers of boys to be killed, as if they were worth nothing more than bales of hay." She finished bandaging the wound then stood and returned to Anna's side. "What's hard for us is that we don't have as many men as the Russian do. The same men fight all the time, without rest, but the Russians keep coming in waves, always fresh, never ending." Her eyes looked weary.

Kaisa picked up the bowl and moved to dispose of the old bandage, leaving Anna standing there. Her mind whirled. The Finnish field hospital's triage put Russians ahead of one of their own if the wounds were worse? The world needed to know about these good people, living in a country roughly the size of California but with a far smaller population, fighting the single largest nation on the planet, which was run by a ruthless butcher.

She recalled political commentators saying this war could go for months. How was that possible, between one of the largest, strongest nations in existence, against a tiny neighbor? But if the Finns could hold out until spring or later, how would that affect the battle? Already the world was looking down on Russia, condemning the decision to invade its small western neighbor, and with good reason.

Anna looked around and found a chair, which she sat on to write easier. Her hand moved quickly on the page to capture her thoughts. Dill would be pleased with the first piece she'd send back. She'd have to interview a few more people to corroborate the information Kaisa had provided, but Anna was well on her way to having a solid story, assuming she'd ever meet her photographer and get a few good images to go with it.

Americans always did love rooting for underdogs, she thought as she wrote. Perhaps FDR would bend and send aid.

THREE

Lieutenant Haikkola glided to a stop beside Pete. "You did well," he said, stepping out of his cross-country skis. "What did you think of how we take care of the Reds? They don't know where we come from or how we slip away so quickly; it terrifies them." He grinned with obvious pride.

In the two days Pete had been at the Tolvajärvi front, he'd learned that the Finns had far fewer resources than the Russians but used what little they did have to their extreme advantage.

Will I be here as long as they say—for months? Pete almost hoped he would; being away had been the best thing he could have done to distract himself from thoughts of Anna. But better to stay in this eternal dark of winter. He didn't want to be here long enough to see spring, with blossoms and grass and chirping birds, things that spoke of life and happiness . . . of the love he'd given up.

I couldn't stay with her! He mentally yelled the words at the universe. He and Anna were both journalists, which was enough reason to not try to maintain any kind of relationship; they would both be forever going in different directions, rarely seeing each other as they traveled to cover whatever assignments they had next. What if she wanted a family? Would she stay home with a baby while he went gallivanting across the globe, putting himself in danger? That wasn't fair to her or a child.

As long as he'd stayed in California, his thoughts had kept returning to her, to the pained shock in her eyes when he'd said it was over between them. He hadn't been able to stop second-guessing himself, wishing he could go back to her, undo what he'd said, and start over, even though she deserved more than him.

He *couldn't* give Anna the calm, quiet life she deserved. He could be headed for a different state or country after one phone call. He'd learned to pack a duffle bag with the essentials in about ten minutes, and he could live out of that bag for weeks. He'd done so many times.

Pete handed his skis and poles over to an enlisted soldier as he'd just seen Haikkola do then followed the lieutenant toward a dugout for officers. "Your men are in great shape," Pete said, still huffing from tagging along on the ski patrol.

"My men could ski almost as soon as they could walk."

The cold was so oppressive, it limited conversation until they were inside the warmth of the dugout, where Pete sighed with relief. That's where the two of them took off their white snow suits, which were used to blend in with the snow. Pete had seen firsthand on the patrol how the Russians hadn't tried any kind of camouflage whatsoever. No wonder the Reds were terrified; they faced a smaller force, but one that was nearly invisible to them.

With their suits off and set aside, Haikkola patted Pete on the shoulder. "I hear we have a Russian POW, found in the forest wounded and nearly frozen. We think he got lost after a recent fight. He needed surgery on his leg and stitches on his face. You may find his views interesting."

Pete's eyebrows went up. "I'd love to talk with him. Is there someone here who could interpret for me?"

"I believe we could find someone," the lieutenant said with a nod. "Or perhaps you'll get lucky, and he'll speak English. But first, let's get some coffee, and then you can visit our POW before you go to bed."

"Thank you," Pete said. He tilted his wristwatch and shined his flashlight on it. Nearly eleven. Despite the hour, the mess hall would have food. He'd definitely want to go there for a late dinner, especially after such a rigorous time skiing on the patrol. Then he'd go to bed and sleep dreamlessly, if he was lucky. "On second thought, coffee might be a bad idea at this hour. I'd like to talk with the prisoner then have a small meal and go to bed."

"Trying to sleep at night, are we?" Haikkola said with a laugh. "Very well. You'll find him in the recovery tent."

"Thanks," Pete said. "And thank you for letting me come along today. I know I slowed you down."

"Our pleasure," Haikkola said, pausing at the door then heading out for his coffee.

Pete stayed back for a few minutes, writing notes about what he'd seen on the patrol and what he hoped to photograph his next time out. He glanced up, thinking of hot coffee warming him from the inside out. As tempting as the thought was, he shook his head and returned to his notebook.

So far, he'd managed to maintain a semi-normal routine, even though most schedules at the camp were rarely morning-to-night. Depending on the shift, a soldier could have "breakfast" at one in the morning or at three in the afternoon—whenever they woke up. Someone had to be patrolling and guarding and running the place around the clock. The few hours of sunlight they had per day made switching schedules around easy—as it was pretty much dark for the majority of everyone's shift, it didn't much matter when you slept. Yet Pete still preferred to stay on a normal schedule, if you could call anything *normal* in a war zone. Even though he was finally adjusting to the time difference.

Pete tucked his notebook into his coat pocket then turned on his flashlight before heading out of the tent and into the cold in the general direction he thought the field hospital tents to be.

The tents were, of course, completely blacked out, so any interior light didn't show, and they were white, making them hard to spot. Without the foot-trodden paths throughout camp, Pete would have gotten completely lost. He pushed open the tent door, and light burst through, and with it the relief that he'd found the right place. He wouldn't end up like the frozen Russian the patrol had come upon an hour ago.

The sharp smell of antiseptic and putrid stench of rotting flesh hit his nostrils. He forced his face to remain impassive, intent on not showing disgust to the healing soldiers inside. Time to earn their trust by showing compassion, not revulsion. He stomped his boots to get rid of the snow so he wouldn't track it inside then removed his hat and ran his fingers through his hair. As he moved to take off his coat and step inside, he froze at what had to be an apparition, a figment of his imagination.

Not twenty feet away, Anna sat with her back to Pete at the bedside of a wounded man. It couldn't be Anna. Pete had traveled across a continent, an ocean, and another continent to escape this heartache.

Yet there it was: Anna's red hair pulled back, her head tilted in a familiar way. At first he tried to convince himself it was another woman who just looked like Anna from behind, but his heart knew better. He stood there, unmoving, his heart pounding as he remembered running his fingers through flowing red hair, kissing her lips, holding her close.

How could I have been such a fool as to think I could walk away from her?

That question was answered as quickly as he asked it. *Because she deserves more than to be poor for life, with a photographer husband who's never home.*

He almost convinced himself it wasn't Anna, but then she spoke to the soldier on the cot. Her words didn't penetrate Pete's mind, because her *voice* was all he needed to hear. No question; this was Anna. He felt as if the wind had been knocked out of him.

What is she doing here?

A tiny seedling of hope whispered that maybe she'd come here to find him and win him back. He'd go back, willingly—eagerly—except for the fact that he refused to become a burden to her.

Pete stood there, debating what to do. His first impulse—to rush over, sweep her into his arms, and kiss her soundly—was obviously out of the question. He could try to whip around and walk right back out, pretend he hadn't seen her, but she'd probably see him leave.

Then again, she'd see him at some point anyway. As military camps went, it wasn't exactly huge, but it wasn't so large that he could avoid her. He might as well get the first contact over with.

His hands clenched his hat as he tried to come up with a greeting. How would she react to seeing him? Would she be glad? Angry? His palms started to sweat, and he swallowed against a dry throat.

As Pete mustered the courage to approach her, Anna soothed the young man by stroking his face and holding his hand. Yet the soldier, who couldn't have been more than twenty, continued to moan and thrash, his head moving back and forth from pain. Pete's eyes stayed on Anna's hands, gently touching, gradually calming the soldier. Pete knew exactly what that touch felt like and wanted to feel it again.

A nurse hovered nearby with a syringe, but the soldier flailed too much for her to use it.

The man cried out. "Anna. Anna."

The shock that this young man knew Anna was eclipsed by his accent. He was *Russian*. The man mumbled something unintelligible in his native tongue then reached for Anna's face. She took his hand and held it to her cheek, smiling and murmuring something surely intended to comfort him.

He doesn't know her. He thinks she's someone he left behind. Trust Anna to try to comfort those around here no matter where she was.

Pete found himself drawing deeper into the tent one step at a time. He reached a chair and found Anna's dog-eared notebook covered with her handwriting. The sight cemented the reality that Dill had really sent Anna here. Of course Keith would be replaced; Pete had gotten a telegram saying as much a few days ago, but no hint that it would be Anna.

He sat on the edge of the chair as she hummed. He didn't recognize the song, but it was soft, with a lilting rhythm. By the third verse, the soldier's intense grip began to relax, and soon he stopped thrashing and began breathing easier. Anna smiled up at the nurse yet kept singing, still holding his hand between both of hers.

After another minute, Anna looked up at the nurse and whispered, "I think he's asleep."

The nurse nodded. Whether she understood the English or not didn't matter; she took his left arm and injected whatever was in the syringe. The soldier grimaced in his sleep but then drifted away again. The nurse sighed with relief. "He should sleep several hours," she said to Anna with a thick accent. "*Kiitos*. I mean, *thank you*."

"My pleasure." Anna gently placed the soldier's arm across his stomach and stood. From where he sat, Pete could see her face and the expression of pain and angst crossing it.

Pete wanted to rush over and hold Anna, to comfort *her*

and get rid of that look of distress. This was no place for a female reporter. What had Dill been thinking?

Aside from Anna being put into harm's way, how was Pete supposed to keep his focus on his work, with her red hair flashing beside him, her scent hanging about him like a cloud whenever she passed, her voice haunting his mind and heart as they talked story angles and hooks?

This isn't going to work.

Anna stood, straightening her skirt. Pete instinctively stood as well. Her hands rose and smoothed back her hair, but then she saw Pete. Her eyes widened, and the movement of her hands paused. After a moment, they lowered, and her brows drew together in surprise. "Pete? Is that really you?" He didn't know whether her soft voice was to keep the Russian asleep or whether it was from shock. Maybe a bit of both.

He mustered a wan smile. Now that she'd seen him, he had no idea what to say or do. "I, uh, didn't expect to see you here." *Obviously.*

Was she pleased to see him? She didn't seem *displeased*, exactly, only shocked. A few more moments of silence could well make her reaction progress from shock to hurt or anger. As they stood there, looking at each other, Anna with an expectant look on her face, Pete knew he'd been wrong, so wrong, when he'd said goodbye. Not that he hadn't needed to leave; he had. But this wasn't a surface love he would ever move on from. This was a bone-deep need to have her in his life as she would always be in his heart.

He'd dreamed of her, fitfully, every night since walking away. Now here she was, in the flesh—in a war zone. A surge of protectiveness washed over him. He wanted—no, needed—to care for Anna, to have a life with her. To make her happy. Was that possible? Could he be with her yet? Or was he playing the fool, setting himself up for disappointment when he realized yet again that he couldn't be the husband she deserved?

How long had they stood here, just gazing at each other, silent?

Pete shook his head to chase away such thought; he probably looked like a dolt, gaping mindlessly. The antiseptic smell, the odor of infected limbs, and the moaning of the wounded all came back, but they were still overshadowed by Anna as if the sun itself were approaching him with its life-giving light.

Anna was close enough to hug, but instead she folded her arms, a clear signal that things were different between them now. Of course they were. He'd made them different. She narrowed her eyes. "Dill sent you." The simple statement came out as an accusation. "Why couldn't you have stayed home and taken a walk right off the Santa Monica pier?"

Ouch. They'd had more than one outing at the pier. He remembered eating hot dogs as they walked along the wooden planks then looked out at the Pacific and imagined their future together. He had to swallow to hold back the emotions threatening to break through.

"I doubt it helps, but I swear I didn't know you were Keith's replacement. I was already in New York by the time he made the decision."

"You're really my photographer." She shook her head. "Unbelievable."

He chuckled, the ludicrousness of the situation settling in on him. "What were the chances, right? You know how Dill pays no attention to anything the staff does aside from turn in stories. I don't think he realized that we . . . that you and I . . . well, you know." He cleared his throat and studied the opposite wall, unable to look into her eyes.

Pete searched for a way to fill the silence that felt like a giant void hanging between them. She stared at him, seeming to take in his features as if she hadn't seen him in years instead of days. What was she thinking? He'd give his best lens to know.

"Dill had his hands full just getting permission for

anyone to report north of Lake Ladoga," Pete offered. "I suppose swapping colleague names wasn't on his priority list."

She nodded, and as she spoke, she avoided his eyes. "I heard that Mannerheim himself refuses to let journalists anywhere near the most crucial fighting down in the isthmus. We're lucky to be this far south instead of up in Lapland."

"Or holed up in that hotel in Helsinki like most of the journalists," Pete said.

Too bad Dill got permission to send anyone to this sector. From a journalistic standpoint it was good for the magazine, but with Anna standing two feet away, Pete couldn't think like a journalist.

Yes, she had an inner strength of steel; he knew that she could handle tough situations, likely even war, although he didn't *want* her to have to handle such things. But she was also a small woman—scarcely over a hundred pounds, he'd guess—and this was a dangerous place. The hotel would have been a better choice.

Anna looked about the tent then back at Pete. "Let's go someplace else to talk. We need to discuss story angles."

Of course she could stay objective and professional. *I'll do the same.*

"Have you eaten since you arrived?" he asked. "We can go to the mess hall. I hear they're making sausage soup. I don't know if it's ready, but it's worth checking on; the soup is delicious."

"They're cooking at this hour?" From her pocket she pulled a small watch, which was attached by a ribbon.

"Schedules don't mean much out here. Someone is always coming off a shift and ready for food. Besides that, the field kitchen cooks for a couple of thousand soldiers in the area, and they have to deliver it to the various camps."

She tucked her watch back into her pocket and smiled— a little. Oh, how he'd missed that smile. And now he wanted to kiss the mouth that made it.

"Sausage soup sounds delightful." Anna stepped to his side, their arms brushing.

He sucked in a deep breath at her touch—silently, so she wouldn't hear it—and fought the urge to take her into his arms.

She gestured toward the door. "I don't know the camp yet. You lead the way."

He did, holding the hospital door open then releasing the flashlight he'd clipped to his belt and turning it on to light the boot-trodden path through the snow. As they walked in the darkness, his cheeks seemed to burn even with the sub-zero temperature. With any luck, by the time they reached the mess hall, she'd assume his pink cheeks were simply from the cold rather than from seeing her again, being so close to the woman he loved.

Four

The walk to the mess tent felt longer than Anna expected it to be; now that she knew what the scent drifting through the air was, her stomach rumbled with hunger.

Plus, the fact that she was walking beside Pete made the trip seem to last even longer. A charged silence hung between them like a dark cloud. Neither had said a word yet about their breakup or what happened between them before, or even what a dolt Dill was for not knowing better.

She wanted to grab her suitcase and head back on the first train. To go home and burrow under her comforter—and cry. To think she'd run away from her memories of Pete only to travel across the globe and end up in the same place as him anyway.

Like some horrid joke at my expense.

In spite of her twisting stomach and aching heart, Anna couldn't help but make a surreptitious glance at Pete's evening stubble, which had always made him look ruggedly handsome. The old attraction flamed in her chest, but she tamped it down, taking a deep breath of the cold air as if that could put out the fire still burning for Pete.

After a few minutes, the pathway narrowed to single file. Pete had the flashlight, so he went ahead to light the way. She couldn't help but notice his confident gait and broad shoulders. She knew all too well that beneath his coat were well-toned muscles.

Have mercy.

The only sounds were their boots on the snow and their steady breathing. After a moment, Anna girded up her courage to speak. She could—would—be professional through this. "You've been here longer than I have. Do you have any suggestions about things we should be sure to cover?"

Pete glanced over his shoulder at her, making her middle flip like a pancake. So much for professionalism keeping her from thinking about him as *her* Pete, of the two of them not as a journalistic team, but as the romantic couple they used to be.

The couple we still should be, if things had worked out as I'd expected them to.

But there was no sense in toying with romantic thoughts; they were sheer nonsense. He'd made that abundantly clear last month. The two of them were here with a job to do. An important job. And that was that.

"I've been here only two days longer than you have," Pete said. "I haven't had time to give stories much thought, but so far, I can tell you what my biggest challenge will be."

Sensing concern in his voice, Anna paused in her step. "What's that?"

Pete stopped, turned around, and sighed. "My equipment freezes solid within seconds of being out in the cold. All of it. Shutter won't even move."

"Then how on earth will you take any photographs?"

Instinctively, Anna put her hand on his arm. He looked at it, and she realized she'd crossed a boundary. She almost pulled away but couldn't keep herself from looking into his eyes, hoping to find something in them.

Pete shrugged, acting as if her touch meant nothing. She quietly removed her hand as he kept talking. "Any photographs will take planning and a lot of effort. I'll have to keep everything inside my coat until the last second. If I can whip out the tripod and camera and take a picture within, say sixty seconds, the equipment should stay warm enough from my body heat to work for one quick shot." He turned about and kept walking.

"Goodness." Anna walked on behind Pete, mind now firmly in journalist mode. She had much to write about; too bad she didn't have her notebook open or the light to scribble it all down right now. Yet even as the thought appeared, it was a whisper in her head compared to the thoughts and feelings about Pete crashing like cymbals inside her.

The path widened again, and Pete once more slowed so they stepped side by side. Did he still care? Why had he'd decided to walk away? It had to be because he didn't care anymore. He'd hardly noticed her touch. He hadn't shown the slightest inclination to hold her or kiss or even apologize for being so cruel. She supposed she could try to get him back—only she wouldn't, because if he didn't return the feelings, she wouldn't grovel in hopes of him simply giving in. No, she wanted a man who loved her—as she'd thought Pete did.

Instead of leaving a land of eternal summer, but where her heart felt dead and cold, she'd traveled to a frozen land, and now her heart was burning with the heat of emotion. This had not been the plan; she was supposed to have a break, time to heal. Yet her heart felt close to ripping in two all over again.

Pete resumed talking, for which Anna was grateful.

"One thing I learned the first night I was here was when some of the men were cleaning their guns. Turns out that equipment freezing is one of the Russians' big problems right now—they're still using regular oils, which freeze, so their guns freeze solid too, and they're left with nothing to fight with, no matter how many men and how much ammunition they have. Well, not all the Russians' guns have frozen yet, obviously. There are always new guns being sent, and not all have been cleaned. And they have plenty of artillery and tanks. But freezing guns has been a problem."

"I don't understand how they'd invade so ignorantly," Anna said, deliberately keeping her attention on the war effort. Her forehead wrinkled in confusion. "I thought the Soviet army was one of the most advanced in the world. How did Stalin send his men so ill prepared? It's not as if he invaded in the middle of summer. He had to know winter was coming."

Pete's arm brushed hers as they walked; Anna swore she could feel his touch through both of their coats.

"That's the golden question," he said. "I think it comes down to him being a pretty awful excuse for a human. A week-long skirmish meant that his armies wouldn't need anything special—not even winter uniforms, although this is already one of the coldest winters in decades, which he couldn't have predicted. I wouldn't be the least surprised to find out that Stalin is capable of cold-blooded murder. That's basically what he's done to his men over the past two weeks—when thousands fall, he sends thousands of replacements. No regard for human life—his men's or the Finns'. Who cares about strategy to spare his own men, when he has so many?"

"How awful."

In the distance, the sound of engines starting came through the darkness. Anna's chin came up, and she cocked her head, listening. "A nighttime patrol?"

Pete shrugged. "Possibly. But they're probably just

keeping the engines warm. You'll hear every vehicle run for a bit every fifteen minutes, around the clock. If that doesn't happen, the engines turn into frozen blocks of steel until spring. That's another thing the Russians are finally figuring out; they've lost several vehicles already because the engines weren't running often enough to keep from freezing."

"You've learned a lot more in two days than you give yourself credit for." Anna stared off into the woods in the direction of the sound. "So many things in this war I never thought of. And it sounds like a lot of these same things never occurred to the Soviets."

The scent of sausage soup grew stronger now; they had to be close to the field kitchen and mess tent. In their relatively short walk, Anna had grown colder than she'd ever been in her life. She wrapped her arms about herself and rubbed her hands up and down her arms through her coat. "Let's get some food."

"This way," Pete said, nodding forward.

They each took only one more step before shouts and running and other chaotic noises sounded from the rear of the camp. They halted to listen. At first, Anna assumed the noises were something easily explained, like what Pete had described with the men making sure to turn on a truck engine to keep it from seizing in the cold, or a training exercise, or perhaps something else she hadn't learned about yet as the army dealt with the Finnish winter. But the look on Pete's face made her heart grow cold.

"Pete? What is it?"

He stood there, stock still, listening. Wordlessly, he held out a hand, palm out, signaling for her to say or do nothing. Suddenly men were running in all direction, yelling and cursing. Shrieks of pain echoed through the night.

We're under attack! The thought came to her in a flash, and Anna knew it was true. *But this isn't a combat zone!*

The Soviets weren't in this area in great numbers—at least, that's what Marshal Mannerheim had predicted. The enemy was supposed to be stuck following the obvious narrow roads, unable to get through the dense forests with their tanks. The Finns protected the roads easily, throwing Molotov cocktails into tank air vents and setting the whole thing on fire. This was supposed to be a safe place.

Yet flashes of light lit up spots in the night. The simultaneous booms told Anna that it was rifle fire from both sides as Russian and Finn met. In the distance, soldiers seemed to be shooting blindly into the darkness, which made sense; they certainly couldn't see one another clearly. Groans and cries echoed, followed by the sound of a man—Two? Three?—crying out.

Were the fallen Finnish or Russian? Anna couldn't tell from where she stood, unmoving. Yet she found herself worrying, caring about the people she'd just met. These weren't nameless fighters, but men with lives, loved ones, and physical pains.

The fighting slowly spread, drawing closer and closer. At first Anna stayed alert, taking it all in, until Pete grabbed Anna's hand and yanked her off the trail and into some brush. They half ran, half stumbled into the thick trees, with snow halfway up their legs.

Pete stopped briefly, searched the landscape, and pointed. "There!" he whispered, indicating a snowbank and a cluster of trees a few yards off, lit only by the full moon reflected off the snow. They ran and hid, crouching behind the trees and snow as the fighting went on.

They were safe for the moment, but Anna's heart raced, hammering against her chest as the realization that this "safe" area was still in a war zone—and she could have been killed. Could yet be killed.

Together they stayed hunched down and waited. Anna breathed hard and fast, sending wisps into the air. Could the enemy find them by the fog of their breath? The snow began to seep through her boots, stockings, *and* long johns, while the booms and blasts continued, making her tremble.

Yet Pete was beside her, still holding her hand. She could feel his breath on her face. The idea that he was here, protecting her, made her want to weep. She wanted to kiss him hard, if only to thank him. Another cry of pain rang out, and another making her shudder.

This could be my last chance to tell Pete I love him. Stop thinking about him. You're a reporter!

Tears stung her eyes, but she forced them back; she couldn't be objective if her emotions got tangled up in her work. She hoped that whatever was happening would be over soon, but the screams, moans, and gunfire didn't ebb. Her feet throbbed from the cold. More shots boomed and flashed through the forest, and her body started to tremble. She found herself drawing nearer Pete for comfort; journalism could go hang. Pete must have sensed her anxiety, because he put an arm around her shoulders and pulled her close.

"It'll be all right." His embrace felt warm and comforting, familiar—right. For the moment, she blocked out the fact that they were no longer a couple, that they had no future. She closed her eyes and let his presence calm her, take her away from the war raging around them.

She found herself shaking uncontrollably, yet she couldn't blame more than half of it on the temperature. A constant parade of images marched through her mind: Russians finding them and dragging them away. Russians torturing them, shooting them. Fear and adrenaline pumped through her trembling body.

She grasped one of Pete's hands between both of hers and tried to breathe evenly. A voice in her head whispered that she should be taking in as many details as possible so she could write a great story about this battle—one she couldn't see even though she was in the thick of it.

"Anna, I—" Pete's voice cut off, but his eyes stayed locked on her, and even with the battle raging, a thick silence hung between them.

She had to know what he had been about to say.

"What?" It came out as a whisper. The moon lit one side of his face, casting the other half in shadow.

"You need to know that . . ." He glanced over his shoulder, in the direction of the fighting, took a deep breath, and tried again. "I left in a cowardly way. But I've never stopped loving you. I just had to leave, because you deserve so much more than what I can offer you."

Anna straightened and stared at him. Her heart felt as if it had jumped back to life. But the sad look on his face didn't give her the hope she needed. "What do you mean?"

"You deserve to be with someone you can count on, not someone who hops around the globe unexpectedly. You should be able to have stability, and a few kids, and a white picket fence and—"

She shook her head, cutting him off. "Who said I want all that?"

"You . . . don't want children?"

"Sure I do, but—"

He shook his head and interrupted. "And you talked about settling down."

"I didn't mean it that way—I meant being with one person, no more dating." Anna wasn't sure whether she wanted to know where this conversation was going. "What made you think that?"

"The way you talked about your parents made it sound like you wanted to stay near them, and have a house like theirs . . ."

"No, Pete." Anna put her hands on his chest to get his attention. "That's not it at all. I knew who you were when I met you. That's part of what I love about you . . . you have no fear. I loved hearing about your travels and seeing your eyes light up when you talked about it. I wanted to experience that *with* you."

Pete brushed a lock of her hair away from her eyes. "But you're so close to your parents."

"They are dear to me, but there is so much more of the world to see than California . . ." Her eyes searched his for understanding, for hope. "You never gave me the chance to choose. You just . . . left." Tears pricked her eyes, and this time they wouldn't stay put. One ran slowly down her cheek as if it were partially freezing on its way.

Pete lowered his head. "I didn't know it would hurt you like that."

"How could you *not* know? I love you, Pete Sorensen. And that isn't going to change, ever, even if you walk out of my life again." *But I hope you won't.*

He looked about to respond, but suddenly the noise about them dimmed. Both Pete and Anna turned their heads to see what had happened. Some voices—Finnish ones—called out orders and questions with an urgent tone. What was happening? Was it over? She didn't hear anyone speaking Russian. Did that mean the Finns had won the battle?

Pete gradually stood from a crouch, grimacing, his legs likely frozen in place. Anna's were stiff too didn't know if she could stand if she had to. Pete lifted a finger to his lips. She nodded, agreeing to stay silent.

He jerked his head to one side and mouthed, *I'll be right back.*

Again Anna nodded, this time sending a prayer heavenward that Pete would be able to return to her safely. He moved slowly, but Anna could hear snow crunching and squeaking beneath his boots, and she cringed with every step, waiting for another blaze of light from a Russian rifle taking Pete out.

Please, please, please. The single word repeated itself as the purest prayer she'd ever offered. She still loved Pete. Always would.

The freezing darkness pressed on her as she waited an eternity for Pete to return. She leaned against the trunk of a tree and closed her eyes, willing away the cold burning into her feet and hands. What she wouldn't give to see—to feel!—the sun again.

Five

Pete came upon the skirmish near the field kitchen and mess tents, not far from where he and Anna had been standing. Between a few lanterns on the ground and the bright moon, he could make out a bloody mess as men fought in hand-to-hand combat—something neither side was used to, he was quite sure; long-distance artillery and rifle shots were the norm.

A couple of cooks in white, stained aprons ran past Pete, nearly knocking him over. At the same time, several others—including Kaisa from the field hospital—surged into the fray with improvised weapons: chairs, pocket knives, metal drawers. Kaisa had a scalpel in hand, and the fire of hell in her eyes. In spite of their efforts, Finns kept dropping to the snow, bleeding, one after the other.

It's a bloodbath. Pete's stomach twisted with equal parts horror and terror. He looked over his shoulder in the direction he'd come, hoping Anna wouldn't be spotted behind the trees. No one seemed to be going anywhere near her. He crouched behind a jeep beside the mess tent and watched.

Suddenly, without any order or signal that Pete could tell, the Russians stopped fighting and went on the defensive, as if they were trying to run away. As if they were trying to run *to* some place.

The Russians quickly retreated toward the kitchen and mess tent, leaving panting, wounded Finns behind. Several slumped against the nearest supports or even dropped to the snowy ground to catch their breath.

That's when Pete really looked at the Russian soldiers as they rushed into the mess tent. Their faces were chalky white, likely from the cold. But some noses, chins, and ears had black spots—frostbite. Their eyes were sunken in, their cheekbones and jawlines jutting out, skulls visible through stretched, thin skin. The men, young and old alike, retreated, stumbling into the mess tent and field kitchens as if driven, haunted by something.

They're starving to death.

Quite clearly, the Russian attack had stopped as quickly as it had begun when the men smelled food. Cooking sausage soup was tantamount to a Thanksgiving feast for them. No doubt after they satisfied their bodies' crazed drive to eat, they'd come to their senses and resume the attack.

If the Finns were very lucky, this break would last long enough for reserve troops to arrive, and the Finns wouldn't be slaughtered by the Reds.

Better get back to Anna—fast, before they finish eating.

As Pete turned to go, he spotted a Russian coming out of the kitchen with a whole sausage in one hand. He wore a look of absolute contentment as he left the mess tent, oblivious to anything but the heaven in his mouth.

In that brief moment, at least this Russian became human for Pete. This poor young man—boy, really—had been forced far from home because of a heinous dictator.

Starved. Lied to. He'd suffered from cold and hunger and looked not far from death from both.

Yet the Finns had to fight back against men like this, destroy them all, or risk losing their very lives and liberty to the Soviet Block. Even with a best-case scenario, tonight wouldn't be pretty. One side or the other had to die.

The professional in Pete looked around, realizing that he'd never get any pictures of tonight; his equipment was too far away and in its cases. A strange sense of relief came over him at the thought, but the journalist side chided him.

Pete turned and scurried down the slight hill of snow and along the path to where Anna hid. She had to be near, but all the pine trees looked the same in the dark. "Anna!" he whispered as loudly as he dared. "Anna, where are you?"

"Pete?" she whispered back. Her arm stuck out from behind a tree, followed by her face—lined with pain. She grimaced with each movement; Pete wanted to get her a cup of hot coffee to warm her up then hold her close and kiss her all better. To tell her he loved her and always would. Maybe he'd been wrong all along. She was right about one thing; he hadn't given her the option to choose a life with him.

The first chance he got, he'd say so and pray she'd say yes. But with the fighting tonight, who knew when that would be.

Pete hurried through the snow to her. "We need to get you to a dugout before it starts again. Come on." He helped her to her feet—a much slower process than it should have been, as Anna's legs moved stiffly. "Are you in pain?"

"Some," she said with a forced cheerful tone and a half nod. "My feet feel like blocks of ice." She chuckled, but the sound fell flat, which only made Pete want to pick her up and carry her into a dugout, but he didn't trust himself to be steady while carrying her in the dark over thick snow and ice.

Instead, he put one arm beneath both of hers to support her weight. His other hand braced her from the front of her waist in case she pitched forward. That was the best he could do.

"I'm a bit stiff," she whispered, limping with each step. "Sorry."

"You're doing fine," Pete said. *But we do need to hurry.*

He didn't use his flashlight—too much chance of being noticed. Besides, both hands were occupied by keeping Anna upright. Their pace was much slower than would be ideal; every nerve in his body screamed to get her to safety *now*.

Anna tripped on a tree root and winced. He held her close it seemed her pain had subsided, smelling the faintest hint of lavender in her hair, a scent so Anna. A scent from before he'd been a fool. *Please give me chance to make things right.*

She turned her face and looked into his eyes. With their faces an inch apart, Pete almost forgot to breathe. Their lips were only a breath from each other; he could have easily closed the distance and kissed her.

I have no right to do that. Soon again, I hope. And we have no time for that now anyway. He gritted his teeth and nodded at the path. "Let's go."

What a chicken-livered, yellow-bellied ninny he'd been to walk away last month without telling her why. The night he'd left, he'd known that Anna would try to convince him to stay—and that she'd likely succeed if he gave her the chance, yet he'd done it anyway, thinking he was somehow being honorable. He lacked the fortitude to stick to his decision in the face of her eyes, her voice, her touch . . .

She still deserved an explanation. As he'd left her house that night, he'd felt as if his heart had died. He hadn't realized that hers had too.

I think she still cares, after what I did. He could hardly fathom it.

Pete had to distract himself from the havoc his emotions were wreaking on the situation. He'd tell Anna what had happened in the attack to refocus on why they were here in the first place. "Some Russians broke through and attacked from the rear," he said. As soon as the words left his lips, he realized that they were ridiculous; she'd surely figured that much out on her own.

"But why did the fighting stop?" Anna asked. "Surely Finns in a non-combat unit couldn't overcome a surprise ambush."

Trying to distract himself by telling her that the ambush had been an idiotic decision. Pete didn't want to put any haunting images of starving men into her head. He bought some time by deflecting the question. The women's dugout wasn't too far now. If he kept talking, then maybe they'd reach safety without her ever needing to know the details. He knew she'd find out soon enough, and that she needed to know to write about it, but not tonight.

"That's the irony. The Russians stopped attacking. Had they kept going, they could have completely broken the Finns' defenses here, circled around south, and attacked the Mannerheim Line from the rear."

"And the Mannerheim Line is the most important front. They lose that line and Stalin wins, right?" Clearly, she'd researched the war and geography.

"Right."

"Which brings us back to my original question." Anna put a hand on Pete's arm and forced him to pause in his step. "What aren't you telling me? I can tell there's more; your voice always gives it away when you're trying to hide something."

Curse the fact that she knew him so well. For a moment, he didn't answer; he stared forward where, only moments ago, he'd seen another unexpected horror of war.

Finnish staff members still buzzed about, rushing to and fro, collecting more objects they could use as weapons. He sent a silent prayer upward that the telephone lines hadn't been cut, so the call for backup troops had been received. They were the only hope of the camp, and, likely, of the entire Finnish nation.

Anna squeezed his arm. "Pete. Tell. Me. Why did they

stop attacking?" Her tone brooked no argument. He might as well tell her now anyway; she'd learn for herself soon enough.

Pete studied her and had a sudden realization that Anna could handle the information. She had more strength in her five-foot frame than he'd given her credit for, in character if not in body. As he tried to put the images into words, the horrors returned to the fore of his mind. If he'd doubted why the Russians had stopped their attack, the memory of their faces erased it.

"The Russians are starving," he said simply. "They stopped attacking to . . . eat soup." The words were true, yet they didn't convey—not remotely—what he'd seen in the haunted eyes of the Red army.

"Let's go," Anna said, shifting directions, pulling Pete away from the path leading to the dugout and back toward the mess tent—the battle area.

"No." Pete planted his feet and pulled her toward him.

Anna turned to face him, her eyes steely. "We're here to do a job. To witness and report. I don't know about you, but I intend to do my job."

She wrenched her arm from his and marched, stumbling a bit, into the darkness in the general direction of the mess tent. Pete stood there, debating what to do. Anna was a strong woman. He shouldn't treat her like some fragile flower. Yet he didn't want to see her put into a dangerous spot, especially if he could prevent it.

Yet she was right; reporting on this war was why they were here. One thing he loved about Anna was how determined she was to do a professional, top-notch job. He'd never known a more passionate journalist, whether her assignment had been to cover a library event or a city government scandal. She always did the best job possible, and she'd worked her way up to better, harder jobs—she'd earned a level of prestige.

Helplessly, he watched her slip into the darkness,

knowing that he had to let her do this. He still debated: should he go after her? They were a team, after all. Or, he could probably make it back to his dugout for his equipment so he could snap a few photos—although he'd need to use a flash, which would certainly draw unwanted attention from the fighters. But maybe it would blend in with rifle flares when the fighting resumed.

He looked to his left, in the direction of the dugout then back toward the path Anna had taken. The job could go hang; he wanted to be *with* her, at her side, if only to be sure she was safe.

He debated for only a moment, but it was long enough for the fighting to pick back up and become ferocious. Lantern, flashlights, and rifle flashes lit up the night like some kind of sick fireworks display. He spotted bayonets used to skewer men and leave them to die on the ground, gored like an animal. Pete brought a hand to his mouth, sure he'd be sick.

Several Finnish men running past him, carrying hand-sized bottles with liquid inside—Molotov cocktails, the poor soldier's grenade. Word said the State Liquor Board in Helsinki had sent cases of bottles to the front for just this purpose, and the makeshift bombs had done their fair share of incapacitating tanks and causing other chaos. All well and good on paper, and when soldiers were throwing them into those air vents. But not here, in the vast expanse of night.

A soldier at some distance lit a cocktail and hurled the burning bottle through the darkness. Pete wanted to yell at the man to be more careful; he could hit a tent. Or a dugout. The soldier moved to light another cocktail. Before he finished, Pete set off at a dead run in the direction Anna had disappeared.

But the bottle arced and exploded. Pete stumbled to a stop as a shocked cry rang out, and a cry that soon escalated into shrieks of pain—female shrieks.

Please, God, no!

Caring nothing for the fighting going on around him, Pete rush forward, dodging Finnish and Red soldiers locked in hand-to-hand knife combat, homing in on the sound of Anna's cries. This camp had plenty of other women around—nurses and secretaries and a typist, and Lotta Svärd—the female war support group members.

But Pete knew the inhuman cries didn't come from any Finnish woman. The next words he heard confirmed his fears

"Help! Oh, it hurts!"

A burst of energy went through Pete. He ignored the brutal slashing feeling that went through his lungs with every breath. He forgot the bitter cold, the darkness, and the reality that he could be on the receiving end of a bayonet. He had one thing as his focus, and one thing only: to reach Anna.

He found her a couple of yards from a tent, her skirts aflame from a Molotov cocktail gone astray. She half sat with one arm propped under her as she vainly reached for enough snow to put out the flames. Pete raced to a snowbank and scooped an armful of the white stuff, which he unceremoniously dumped it onto her legs, followed by another and another.

He dumped snow, and she moved it about until they were certain the flames were out. She sat there panting, face a mask of pain. He wanted to add more snow, knowing that the heat in her burns would still be there, but something stopped him—the memory of the frozen man in the forest.

Anna began shaking hard, whether from the pain, exhaustion, or cold, he couldn't tell. Perhaps all three. Pete knelt beside her and cradled her head against his chest, stroking her face and whispering, "You're going to be all right."

He knew now, as he never had, that he couldn't live without Anna. Break his camera and send him to live in a hut in the middle of the wilderness, and he'd be happy, as long as Anna was with him. He'd have to convince her to take him back, to give him another chance to prove himself. He give her any life she wanted.

Anna moaned in agony. Pete looked around frantically, trying to find something he could do to ease her suffering. "Pete . . ." Anna said weakly, and she slipped into unconsciousness.

Six

A heavy weight seemed to fill Anna's mind, as if she were at the bottom of the ocean, trying to break the water's surface. She blinked, in an attempt to gain her bearings. Where was she? What had happened?

Sharp pain shot through her legs and hand, making her suck breath between her teeth.

Right, I'm burned. That much came back to her, but nothing else seemed to make sense. She opened her eyes and saw her own breath. Why was the room so cold?

This isn't home.

The full truth came back in a horrid rush. She was thousands of miles from home. She was alone, except for Pete, who didn't want her. She remembered that moment behind the trees, when it seemed that maybe Pete did still care, that maybe he'd even kiss her there in the snow. But now she was burned. Would she walk again? Be able to travel with Pete after all? Was her face burned? She thought of the words they'd exchanged only moments before she'd been struck.

If he thought of reconciling before, he's surely changed his mind.

She was probably a cripple. How could a man—any man, let alone her beloved Pete, who climbed and hiked and traveled the world—want her now? She simultaneously wanted to see how bad it was and never wanted to look at her body again. The future rolled out before her, empty, desolate.

If I'm a cripple, even my career is over.

She found herself groaning from both physical pain and inner heartbreak. She turned her head on the flat pillow and saw several more beds in a long row, each holding someone injured. She grew more conscious by the moment; the hospital smells hit her in a wave as she fully comprehended where she was—the same field hospital tent she'd visited. Had it been only yesterday? Or was it today? What time and day was it?

"I think she's awake." She heard a feminine voice, tinged with a pleasant, familiar accent. Kaisa, perhaps?

Rushed footsteps sounded, followed by the legs of a wooden chair dragging on the floor. "Anna," came a soft voice. "It's Pete. Can you hear me?"

Her heart leapt at the sound of his voice, but fell almost immediately. She would not be the object of his pity. She turned her head the other direction.

"Go away." Her voice croaked. Speaking just those two words seared her throat, and she winced.

"Here." Pete reached over to her lips and pressed a moist sponge to them.

The drops of water trickling into her mouth felt like manna from heaven. She breathed deeply in relief.

"You gave us quite a scare," Pete said.

Anna ventured a look at him. He sat beside her bed, leaning close, his arms against his thighs. He swallowed hard, making his Adam's apple bob. He did pity her. He clearly felt obligated to stay with her now that she was ugly and wounded and . . .

Yet she couldn't look away; this might well be her final chance to look at him. She tried to memorize every hair—the cowlick by his right temple, every line—the crinkles by his eyes, even the tiny mole by his chin, so she could recall it all one day when she'd need the comfort.

Pete pressed the sponge to her lips again, soothing her parched throat. "Anna . . ." His voice trailed off, and he looked over his shoulder as if making sure no one was listening.

An ache went through her at that; he was embarrassed to be with her, but she knew he was too noble to be a "coward" again. He'd stay even though her legs were scarred, damaged—maybe crippled.

He leaned forward and whispered. "Kaisa says you're too fragile for me to talk to yet, but she doesn't know the strong spirit inside that I do."

Anna furrowed her brow. This wasn't what she'd expected. She braced herself for whatever was coming; it couldn't be good if Kaisa worried she wouldn't be able to tolerate it.

"The moment I saw you in the medical tent, I knew—*knew*—I'd done the most foolish thing a man can—I let you go. Pushed you away. I thought I was being noble and good, making sure you were free to have a life I assumed you wanted."

A tiny pinprick of hope flickered in her heart.

"Anna, I almost lost you last night," Pete said, his voice suddenly thick. "And part of me nearly died too." He shook his head vehemently. "I can't risk that ever again. If you'll have me . . ." He knelt before her bed and pulled out a small piece of granite with wire clumsily wrapped around it, formed into a makeshift ring. "I'll find something better when we're out of this place, but if you'll give me the honor of your hand and make me the happiest man alive by being my wife, I promise to make you happy, whatever and wherever that means." He held up the wire and stone and waited expectantly.

Anna blinked, sending tears into her hairline and onto her pillow. She wanted to cry out that yes, of course she'd marry Pete. But doubts made her hopes collapse like a falling house of cards.

"I can't be the wife you deserve." Even that much tore at her throat.

"Stop that right now." His jaw tensed, and his nostrils flared. "If anything, *I* don't deserve to have someone as amazing as *you*. Please."

Her heart fluttered in her chest, but she had to be sure. "Get Kaisa," she rasped.

Pete blinked and blinked again. That clearly wasn't the reaction he'd expected. "What? Why?"

"Just . . . please."

He slipped the ring into his shirt pocket and waved Kaisa over. The nurse came into Anna's view, leaning over the bed.

"Can I get you anything? How is your pain?"

Anna had other ideas. She glanced at Pete then looked at Kaisa again. Painfully, she managed to lift one burned and bandaged hand and motion for Kaisa to draw nearer. Finally, Anna could whisper into the nurse's ear without Pete hearing.

"Does he pity me?" It was a simple yet loaded question, but one Anna had to know the answer to.

Kaisa pulled back knowingly but stayed close, inches away. She shook her head as she whispered back, "Not as you mean. He has been—how you say—beside himself. Walking up and down hospital, praying, begging God to let you live so he could have one more chance."

"Does he stay because it would be bad to leave me . . . wounded and ugly?"

A warm smile spread across Kaisa's face. "English

doesn't have a strong enough word for *no* to answer that. In Finnish, I would say not just *ei*, but *eikä*. He cannot bear the thought of not being with you for always."

Warmth flooded Anna's chest and spread throughout her body. "Thank you," she said, more mouthing the words than saying them.

Kaisa nodded. "You are very welcome," she said, straightening.

Pete nearly jumped out of his seat at that. "Please don't tease me," he begged of Kaisa. "Do you mean Anna . . . that she . . ."

Kaisa just grinned. "Ask her yourself."

Flushed bright pink, and looking more alive than he had since Anna first saw him in this very room, Pete turned to her and got back on his knee. He held out the ring and silently pleaded. His eyes were ringed with red, and he looked ready to cry. "Please say yes."

Heart pounding near to bursting, Anna smiled and managed, "Yes, Pete. I'm yours. Always." She wanted to say so much more, but was too weak.

Her left thumb was the only digit on that hand without a bandage. So he took the "ring" and pried the wire open a bit more then eased it onto her thumb.

"You won't pity me?" she asked, needing to hear the words from his own mouth even as she looked at her ring.

"Only that you're tied to a sop like me." Pete grinned, leaned in, and kissed her long but gently on the lips.

"I'll follow you anywhere," she said.

"Even to war, apparently." Pete chuckled and looked around them. His voice lowered. "You won't be able to shake me. I'll follow you to the ends of the earth and back again."

With one more kiss, Anna's heart soared, and she knew there was nothing that would make her happier than being married to Pete. No matter where that might take them.

Author's Note

The Winter War began with a Soviet invasion and air raid on November 30, 1939. More Soviet soldiers crossed the border that first day than the Finns had in their entire army and reserves combined. Stalin claimed the action was in part to protect Leningrad (now St. Petersburg) if Hitler decided to invade.

On the night of December 10, Russians penetrated the Finnish line. As described in the story, the starving soldiers were distracted by sausage soup cooking in the Finnish kitchens. The delay in fighting, during which the Russians ate, allowed the Finns to regroup, get reinforcements, and fight back. Had the Russians continued their attack, the war would likely have ended quickly with a Soviet victory. The events of that night were later dubbed "The Sausage War."

Soon after the Winter War began, the League of Nations kicked the Soviet Union out, and the world's attention turned to cheering on plucky little Finland battling Soviet Goliath. The Finns held on, and refused to surrender as they waited for promised aid from many countries. No significant aid ever arrived.

The Finns paid a high price for resisting Stalin. Under the terms of the ceasefire, they lost hundreds of square miles, which to this day are under Russian control. But even Stalin couldn't call the result a victory. First and foremost, he lost the respect of the world at the expense of his people. Khrushchev later quipped that Russia got just enough land to bury their dead, and he estimated their losses at a million soldiers over the 105-day conflict.

Thanks to their *sisu*, Finland became the only country bordering the Soviet Union to retain its freedom and never fall to communist rule.

About Annette Lyon

Annette Lyon is a Whitney Award winner, a two-time recipient of Utah's Best in State medal for fiction, plus the author of ten novels, a cookbook, a grammar guide, and over a hundred magazine articles. She's a senior editor at Precision Editing Group and a cum laude graduate from BYU with a degree in English. When she's not writing, editing, knitting, or eating chocolate, she can be found mothering and avoiding the spots on the kitchen floor.

Find her online:
Website: http://annettelyon.com
Blog: http://blog.annettelyon.com
Twitter: @AnnetteLyon

THE EARL OF OAKSEY TAKES A WIFE

by G.G. Vandagriff

Other Works by G.G. Vandagriff

The Regency
The Taming of Lady Kate
Miss Braithwaite's Secret
Rescuing Rosalind
Lord Trowbridge's Angel
The Baron and the Bluestocking
Lord Grenville's Choice

Historical Romance
The Last Waltz: A Novel of Love and War

Women's Fiction
Pieces of Paris
The Only Way to Paradise

Suspense
The Arthurian Omen
Foggy With a Chance of Murder

Genealogical Mysteries
Cankered Roots
Of Deadly Descent
Tangled Roots
Poisoned Pedigree
The Hidden Branch

Non-Fiction
Voices in Your Blood
Deliverance from Depression

ONE

1817—England

Lady Melissa Burroughs, Countess of Oaksey, repeated her new name to herself as her husband's carriage bowled through the countryside on its way back to London from Gretna Green.

"Happy?" he asked, his gloved hand over hers, his luminous dark eyes warm with their new intimacy.

"Blissfully," she assured him, putting her other hand on top of his.

"You do not regret that you have not had a grand wedding in Town, but only an uneducated blacksmith's service over the anvil?"

Melissa thought about this before replying. "I think not, Thomas. If you knew my mother, you would understand why I have always dreamed of eloping." She smiled and teased his irresistible dimple with her fingertip. "Our marriage concerns the two of us, not yards of satin, Mama's megrims, or Papa's bombast. Besides, I am very put out with him for having tried to marry me off to Lord Trowbridge, who did not love me in the least. It will take me a long time to forgive Papa for that."

"Now *he* must forgive *you* for marrying me."

"That will not be a problem," she teased him merrily.

"Even though I am virtually a pauper?"

Melissa was startled. How could she not have known this fact? Probably because she had not spent time with the earl above three or four times before he suggested they elope, thus escaping her forced engagement to the man who wanted to marry her best friend. Lord Trowbridge had supposedly compromised her, but it had all been a misunderstanding, and Melissa could not bear to stand between him and Sophie.

All she *had* thought about was how vastly pleasant it would be to marry this man. His mere presence made her heart glad; his slightest touch enflamed her.

Now a horrible thought assailed Melissa. It surely should have occurred to her before now! *Did Thomas elope with me to secure my fortune?*

No. He could not have. Her father had kept the amount of her dowry a secret. There was no way Thomas or anyone among the *ton* could have known she had thirty thousand pounds.

Melissa released the breath she had been holding. "Papa sets a great store by rank. He pushed for a marriage to Viscount Trowbridge even before my supposed indiscretion. He will be thrilled that his daughter is a countess. I suppose it is too much to expect that you are a fire-breathing Whig?"

"I am afraid so. My family have been Tories for eons."

It seemed very odd to Melissa that she did not know such basic things about him, even though the night before had provided her with intimate knowledge of another sort. She began to feel uneasy. Had she been so elated to find a way out of the engagement her father had forced upon her that she had made a mistake? Taking another deep breath, she put the thought firmly behind her.

"Do you take an active role in Parliament?" she asked.

"I have not yet taken up my seat in the Lords, but that does not mean that I will not."

"Are you aware of my father's position in the Whig party? He is one of the leading lights."

"Yes, Lord Kent. He has taken up a stand for the repeal of the Corn Laws."

"I know this is a ridiculous question to ask of you at this time, but have you any strong feelings about the Corn Law Tariffs? I agree with Papa's stance. A tariff keeps the price of grain so high that poor people cannot buy bread."

"I grow grain on my estate, Melissa. If the tariffs remain in place, the price I get for my crops will be stable and adequate to make a profit. This benefits you and our future children."

Melissa swallowed but remained silent. *Yes, our children will have plenty to eat, but what about the poor?*

"Such talk is absurd," she said, forcing a little laugh and tightening her grip on Thomas's hand. "What matters is that I love you and you love me. Not the price of corn."

Her new husband took her in his arms and looked into her face. His eyes were remarkably expressive. The fires that had stirred within them when he was aroused were now banked somewhere in their depths. At the moment, they caressed her with a tender light.

"I do love you," he said.

He began kissing the nape of her neck. She quivered at the slightest touch of his lips, the quivers growing into shakes as he kissed her along her hairline until he met her ear. He whispered,

"You are my wife. Is it not wonderful?" There was a catch in his voice, but then he moved his lips to Melissa's closed eyelids, to the tip of her nose, and finally, to her mouth. His passion grew steadily until it engulfed her, warming her from the inside out. She was glad they had had at least three days together in wayside inns before returning to London and facing the consequences of their actions. There was bound to be scandal, and her mother, at least, would not be pleased.

On their wedding night, they stayed at the King's Arms in Lancaster. For dinner, they had shepherd's pie and wine then spent the night in each other's arms. The next day, by making an early start, they got all the way to Birmingham. For a bit of diversion, Melissa played cards with her new husband and won three guineas.

"I hope you are not a gambler, sir. Either you are letting me win, or you play very ill indeed."

He laughed and managed to look like a mischievous boy. His tanned complexion and sun-kissed hair, mussed from running his fingers through it, told her that he spent much time in outdoor sport. She ought to know more about him than she did. Was he indeed a sports-mad Corinthian? Melissa hoped that he avoided excessive addiction to betting and dangerous horse-racing.

Casting these thoughts aside, she put her head on his chest, and recalled the first time she had looked into those expressive brown eyes. Melissa remembered the delicious sensation of falling headlong into bliss with a man who seemed to see her innermost self. It had been during her first waltz at her come-out ball. That night, as she recalled the sensation from the warmth of her bed, she had written in her journal, "Our souls kissed."

Now, as his hand rubbed circles on her back, she asked, "What did you think of me when you first met me?"

He kissed her forehead. "It was uncanny, actually. There seemed to be no barriers at all between us when we waltzed. I thought you could see straight inside me. But later, I thought I must have been mistaken. It was several weeks before you even looked my way again."

The Earl of Oaksey Takes a Wife

"I felt the same way about you, but I convinced myself that it was only because I was such a green girl." She put up a hand to caress his face. "Thank heavens you were persistent. The night of the masquerade ball, it all came back to me. I think it was because of that daring Red Indian costume you wore."

He chuckled. "Planned with you in mind, my love. I was a peacock, fanning my tail for you."

"It worked," she said, initiating a burning kiss.

The following day, they arrived in London at ten o'clock in the evening. Exhausted by three long days in the carriage, Melissa felt her stomach grow increasingly tight at the thought of greeting her parents. They were certain to be angry about the scandal she had undoubtedly caused by running off to the Border with one man while engaged to another. By the time they pulled up in front of Kent House, she had a pounding headache.

Two

Papa was *not* pleased. Thomas stood beside Melissa, his arm securely about her waist, as her father bellowed, "This man may be an earl, but he hasn't a sou! I didn't think any daughter of mine could be such a ninnyhammer."

"Papa, please. Calm yourself."

"Your mother and I are not blind, Melissa. We know you had a preference for Trowbridge. Why do you think we made certain we secured him for you?"

Melissa could not stop the blush flooding her face so violently that she became dizzy.

Her husband withdrew his arm. "Is this true, Melissa? You had a *tendre* for Trowbridge?"

She could not be less than honest. "At one time. Before I found out that he was in love with Sophie." Turning to face Thomas, she looked into his somber, dark eyes and took both of his hands in hers. "You know I love you, Thomas. If I did not, I can assure you I never would have married you."

He stood tall and straight with indignation, his full mouth set in a grim line. Even so, she loved his aristocratic face with its noble forehead, cleft chin, and high-bridged nose. "I tumbled into love with you at my come-out ball. I stood in this very room and told Sophie about you. I even danced around, holding your posy of yellow roses as my partner."

His look softened. "I sent them because they reminded me of your hair."

Lord Kent grumbled. When it came right down to it, her father could deny her nothing.

"I guess we had better go to the library, my lord, and talk settlements," her father said. Turning to her, he murmured, "I certainly hope you know what you are about, Melissa. It is too late now to do anything about it."

She gave him her sunniest smile. "I love Thomas, Papa. Let there be no doubt of it."

During dinner, her mother's eyes were red rimmed, and Melissa could almost hear her thoughts. *I have but one daughter, and now I am to be denied seeing her married at St. George's in satin and lace. My beautiful girl. How could she be so cruel?*

Melissa dreaded the time they would spend in the drawing room while the men were at their cigars and port. Thomas had winked at her when he came out from the conference in the library, so she knew the money was all right. Papa would never let her live like a pauper.

She was right about her mother. When the two of them sat at opposite ends of the sofa in the drawing room, she let fly all of her complaints and recriminations.

"You thought of no one but yourself. It has always been the same. You are an unnatural daughter; that is what you are. A mother always looks forward to her daughter's wedding. Just you wait and see. I hope you will have but one daughter, and I hope that she will flee off to Scotland in the midst of a scandal!"

"Come, Mama. I know it was a disappointment to you, but my wedding is not the end of my life! And I shall be but two streets away in Grosvenor Square when we open up Oaksey House. There is nothing to say you cannot throw a ball, as elaborate as you please, for Thomas and me."

"I do not even know where his estate lies," her mother said.

"In Suffolk. Quite a beautiful old home, he tells me. Sixteenth century, and not far from London. See? I know you and Papa prefer to live here year round. We shall not go down to Bury St. Edmunds until the end of the Season, and it is only April. We have two more months together at least."

Lady Kent made a great to do of inhaling over her vinaigrette and dabbing at her eyes. Finally, the gentlemen appeared.

"Well, my dear," Thomas said. "You father has invited us to stay on here until we get Oaksey house opened up."

Melissa's heart sank. She had been hoping for Grillon's Hotel. What bride wishes to stay with her family when she is only just married?

Three

M elissa woke to find her husband no longer beside her in bed. Stilling her disappointment, she rang for her maid, quickly washed, and was helped into her turquoise striped muslin. She told Stella to style her thick blonde hair quickly in a simple chignon. Melissa yearned to see Thomas.

However, when she arrived at the breakfast table, she found only a note and a key awaiting her.

Dear One,
I had to go out to discharge some long overdue business. I shall doubtless be gone most of the day. Perhaps you and your mama would care to go over Oaksey House in my absence and determine what you would like to do to refurbish it. You may do whatever you like, with the exception of decorating in either

chartreuse or puce. I shall not be home for dinner, if you could kindly inform your mama.

Yours,

O.

What a very unloverlike letter! And what business could he have in such a rush? Why would he not be home for dinner? Melissa did not want to view Oaksey House for the first time without him. Decisions about the house should be made together. Not with her mama.

Melissa's brother, Lord Donald, entered the breakfast room and went to the sideboard. "What?" he said. "Is Oaksey a slug-a-bed?"

"No," Melissa said.

"Gone out and left you miffed, has he?"

Donald's most irritating flaw was his cheerfulness.

"He has business," Melissa said.

"I am certain he does. He has been pockets-to-let this age."

"What does that mean?"

"Debts, my dear sister. Surely you knew. He's in debt to everyone. Apparently, that estate of his eats money."

Melissa closed her eyes and bit her tongue. "You exaggerate. You always do."

"Not this time. When I told Oaksey about your dowry..."

"What!" Melissa exclaimed. "When you did what?"

Her brother shrugged. "It was by way of helping out. Knew you didn't want to marry Trowbridge. Thought of Oaksey. Knew he'd go for it in an instant."

"Because . . . because of my dowry? How *could* you, Donald?"

Melissa rose and dashed from the room, her heart lanced with pain. Tears burned at the backs of her eyes. She concentrated on attaining the one place she could escape discovery.

The Earl of Oaksey Takes a Wife

Clattering up the stairs to the third floor, she flew through the doors to the nursery. Sunshine flooded the rooms, which smelled of disinfectant and floor polish. At this moment, she welcomed the bracing smell. She closed the doors, wishing she could slam them without drawing notice to herself, and flung open the window leading onto the roof. Stepping out, Melissa watched her feet as she walked close to the nursery chimney.

Just as when she had been punished as a child, she hugged the cold stone to keep from falling off the slates. How could she have been so deceived as to think the man she married loved her?

His proposal to elope had come at the perfect time, so she had swept away all doubts about its obvious prematurity. Crying bitter tears, she wondered if she should have married Trowbridge instead. He had compromised her. Not intentionally, of course. He had needed her help, and she had given it willingly.

But how could she ever have married Frank when he loved Sophie deeply? So desperately that he convinced them both not to care about the consequences when he asked Melissa to show him how to break into Sophie's house in the middle of the night. He had been aflame with his need to see her when she was deathly ill.

Returning to the ball after their visit with her, Melissa and Frank had been discovered leaving the carriage together. Papa had declared her ruined. Of course, she was not ruined, and Papa's actions had only made the scandal worse.

He had wanted Frank for her the moment he met him. They had played right into his hands with their thoughtless behavior.

But she and Frank would have been dreadfully unhappy married to one another. And Sophie, who had never had much happiness, would have been bereft.

But now! Now, it was Melissa who was heartbroken. She had married a fortune hunter. Worse than that, she had thought he loved her. He had told her so for the first time on the balcony at the masquerade ball. And his kiss!

Looking back, she could see clearly why she had agreed to his idea of an elopement. She had been so blinded by the prospect of escaping her unwanted engagement that she had been thrilled at his idea. After such a short acquaintance, she knew nothing of his debts. Yet it was her fortune he wanted. It now made sense that he would not want to waste time courting in the normal way. She had been a fool.

She would not live in a sham of a marriage. Especially now that she knew in intimate detail what was involved. Melissa would rather be alone. Surely this new knowledge of his true nature would work to smother her own love if she kept away from him.

She would live in the townhouse on her own. Oaksey could keep his rooms or hire another establishment. With her money. She did not care about the gossip.

Let him get a mistress if he pleases. All I care about is that he never . . . touches me again.

༺❦༻

Melissa let herself into Oaksey House using Thomas's key. The house smelled of dust and mildew. She wrinkled her nose. How long had it been shut up? It would take a lot of work to make the place livable.

Walking through the hall, she came upon a downstairs sitting room, probably the morning room. She threw back the dusty drapes and opened the windows. She did the same in the other ground-floor rooms—a library smelling of leather and book paste, and a massive ballroom. Downstairs was a kitchen with no stove, but an open fireplace. Positively archaic.

On the first floor, she opened the windows in the drawing room, dining room, and two small saloons. She moved to the second floor and found the master suite. It was dark and brooding, with heavy mahogany furniture, dark blue velvet bed hangings and drapes, and matching carpets. Nothing opened from it but a masculine dressing room. So master and mistress were expected to share this room. She found four other bedrooms but no boudoir. The masculine dressing room would have to be converted for her use.

She went back to the master suite, where she yanked on the draperies and bed hangings until they fell in clouds of dust. She opened the windows, letting in the spring air and light. Yes, this would be a pleasant room when she refurbished it. Perhaps lavender and white stripes, with rose and leaf-green accents. The crown molding, now varnished wood, she would have repainted in white.

Melissa decided to begin her efforts in this room and the morning room on the ground floor. Those would be the most used while she lived here alone.

The very first thing to do was hire servants—a cook, a butler, a downstairs maid, and a chamber maid. She would bring her personal maid, Stella.

By the end of the day, with her mother's help, Melissa had hired servants from an employment registry to begin working the next day. With the help of Stella, her mother's footman, and the family carriage, she had transferred linens and all of her personal effects to Oaksey House. While Stella unpacked Melissa's things in the master suite, her mother gave advice regarding what she would need to modernize her kitchen.

"It is really appalling," Lady Kent said. "I do not know how long it must be since anyone has lived in this place. No cook today could be expected to prepare meals under such conditions! We must buy you a stove at once." She drew herself up and continued. "As for the mildew, we shall consult Mrs. Hutchins. I have never encountered a housekeeping problem she did not know how to deal with. In fact, I think it best if I lend her to you for at least two weeks until you get this place in order."

"Thank you, Mama. That will be most helpful. She can also organize my staff."

"The house will be grand when you have refurbished it. While it is being cleaned tomorrow, we will go to the drapers and look at pattern books." Melissa could not have chosen more wisely any activity guaranteed to cause her mother to be more resigned to her marriage.

She ate at home with her parents.

"So where is this husband of yours, gel?" her father asked.

"I have no idea," Melissa answered, trying to effect the manners of a tolerant spouse long married. "He left word that he would not be home for dinner. I do not expect him to live in my pocket."

After her parents had gone up to bed, Melissa and Stella left the house, accompanied by Stern, her father's footman, whom Papa insisted escort them for safety. They walked to Oaksey House in Grosvenor Square. When Stella had helped her mistress to undress, they said goodnight and retired.

Melissa lay alone in her freshly made bed, fighting tears after a long, arduous, and heartbreaking day. How could she have been so duped? Oaksey had deceived her utterly. Remembering the intimacies of her honeymoon, she still had difficulty believing they were not motivated by sincere feeling. However, she had often been told that men could indulge themselves in what seemed to her to be intimate behavior without any regard for the woman. Surely, if he loved her, he would not have left her their first day in London, going off to spend his newly acquired fortune.

Reviewing every word and every look that had passed between them in nearly a week's time, she felt terribly used. *How gullible he must have thought me! What a green girl I was to believe someone like him could have fallen head over heels for me! Likely the only reason for his desire to elope was that the bailiffs were camping on his doorstep. His debts must*

The Earl of Oaksey Takes a Wife

have been urgent indeed. But the worst thing by far is his acting as though he loved me—he was so tender, so passionate. As though I were the most desirable girl in the world.

All day, she had blotted out these realizations with action and then exhaustion. But now they would not leave her. She was appalled by her naiveté. Indeed, it seemed she directed as much of her anger at herself as she did at Thomas. He probably thought she knew he was at his last prayers, financially. According to Donald, all of London knew. He probably thought she was so desperate to get out of her unwanted engagement that she would welcome his marrying her for her money. At last, she gave into tears of humiliation and cried herself to sleep.

FOUR

Lord Oaksey was enjoying the novel sensation of having more than a feather to fly with. He had been to Lord Kent's man of business, obtained a draft for thirty-thousand pounds, and spent the better part of the morning staring at it, trying to take it in while waiting to see his bank manager. His days of poverty, of trying to maintain the stature expected of a gentleman, on a very thin stipend, were over. Bless Lady Melissa Aldridge, now his dear wife.

Finally, he was called in to see Mr. Judd. Placing the bank draft on his desk, Oaksey said, "There you have it. I'm certain you never thought you would live to see the day that I repaid my overdraft."

Judd stared at the draft. "Thirty thousand pounds. You must have married money!"

"And a very lovely young lady. Daughter of Lord Kent—Lady Melissa Aldridge. I thank you for your indulgence these many months."

The Earl of Oaksey Takes a Wife

"I don't mind telling you it worried me tremendously, seeing your inheritance dwindle as you restored your estate. How anyone could live on the stipend you allowed yourself, I don't know. Congratulations on your fortunate marriage."

Next, Oaksey went to White's, where he wrote out drafts to those friends who had lent him money and probably never expected to see it again.

Lord Russell said, "Congratulations, old man. That gel you ran off with had the dibs, eh?"

"Lady Melissa. She is a lovely thing. I am indeed fortunate."

"Billiards?"

He drew a long breath. No longer must he shun a gentleman's pastimes. He could afford to wager now. "Yes."

As luck would have it, now that he was possessed of money, he won more often. That same luck extended to whist and faro.

At dinner, he extended his hospitality the friends he had repaid that day. Four bottles of claret were consumed, toasts were made, songs were sung. It was very late by the time he made it back to the Kents'.

Surely Melissa would understand; she had a father and a brother and knew that gentlemen didn't spend their time hanging about hearth and home every night. For the better part of a week, he had spent all his time with her. Not that he regretted it. She was lovely and bright. Oaksey was very satisfied with his wife.

He was therefore surprised upon his return to find that she was not in their bed in her bedroom. The household was asleep. Where on the earth could she be? Had she taken a bed in another room for some reason?

Taking off his boots, he gingerly explored the hallway in the other direction from the Kents' suite. In one room, he found Lord Donald lying across his bed in his evening clothes, sleeping off his drink. There were two more bedrooms, but both were empty.

Where the devil has she got to?

It was only then that he remembered Oaksey House and the key he had given her. Luckily, he had another. But Oaksey house had been shut up since his father's time. Why would she choose to sleep there? It was a bit grim inside, to say the least.

He went back downstairs and put his boots on, glad that he had learned to do without a valet, and walked out into the night. It was a brisk ten-minute walk to Oaksey House.

Turning his key in the lock, he hardly knew what to expect. He had not been in the house in at least twenty years. Surely the last time had been when he was ten years old and the family had removed to London for the Season. Since inheriting, he had chosen to spend his money on much-needed repairs to his estate in Suffolk and had nothing to spare for this place.

It smelled horribly musty. Groping about in the dark, he located a candlestick on the hall table. After lighting it, he found his way upstairs.

There she was, asleep on the bed in the master suite. Melissa must not have been able to wait to be mistress of her own home, such as it was. He smiled to himself.

By candlelight, her eyelashes looked like fans on her smooth cheeks. Her bright blonde hair was in a single long plait. Desire stirred within him, and he bent down to kiss her.

FIVE

Melissa was awakened only slightly by a kiss in the middle of a dream about Thomas. Too deeply asleep to remember the revelations of the day, she brought her arms around her husband's neck and drew him to her for a lengthier, more satisfying embrace. The taste of wine on his breath gradually brought her to full consciousness. Breaking her clasp, she brought her hands down so they lay flat on his chest. She gave him a mighty shove.

"Go back to your own rooms or to my parents' house. You are not welcome here!"

"Melissa! You have had a nightmare, darling. I am your husband. We are married, remember? This is my house."

"From this day, we are married in name only," she said, pushing him again. "You are never to touch me again. Now, go!"

Thomas stood by the bed, fully dressed. "What is this?

Why are you behaving like a melodramatic schoolgirl? What has happened to upset you?"

"I found out that you have deceived me most cruelly. Please leave. I do not wish to see you or speak to you." Melissa rolled over so her back was to him. So she could not see his handsome face and athletic build looming over her. When she did not hear him move, she said into the darkness, "Leave me!"

"I will not. You are behaving most foolishly. In what way have I deceived you?"

Humiliated by the idea that he thought her unable to see through his actions, she refused to utter a word. Finally, she heard the floorboards squeak as he moved off. But sleep had deserted her. She had no idea of the time. None of the clocks in the house were wound. Aching freshly over Thomas's deception, she lay on her back and stared through the darkness, her happy memories of the last week blotted out.

Melissa kicked back her blankets in frustration. Going to sit in the window seat, she viewed the gray dawn. Thomas had been out very late. Drinking. Probably celebrating his escape from debtor's prison.

A step sounded on the bare floor. Melissa jumped.

"You did not really think I would go away, did you? This is my house."

"I have chosen to live here," she said, masking her fury with a low, calm voice. "Therefore, you must live elsewhere."

"Why?" There was a note in Thomas's voice she had never heard before. He had never been anything but kind and loving, but now his voice was sharp.

She gripped the seat where she sat and raised her chin. "Did you think I would not find out? My brother told me. How he went to you, told you about my dowry. You saw an opportunity to clear your debts. This was the reason you eloped with me."

"All of London knew of my debts. Of course that is why I married you."

His words cut clear through her. What she had expected, that he would deny it?

Anger sent blood to her head, and she shook with fury. "I have more than paid for this house. You will dwell elsewhere. I care not where."

"I thought we dealt well together, Melissa. We can continue on that path, or we can part, if you are determined. I think you are turning your back on happiness because your pride is hurt."

His words so inflamed her, she could not reply. For several moments, Oaksey stood, brows drawn together over his eyes, his lips in a firm, thin line. "Very well. As you wish." He turned and walked out of the room, his heels sounding loudly on the floor and the stairs. Even from the second floor, Melissa could hear the front door bang shut.

Angry tears flooded her eyes and coursed down her cheeks, over her chin, and down her neck. Against all reason, she had hoped that he would convince her of his love. And now he was gone. She sat like a statue, feeling her heart break.

Six

Lying in his bed in Melissa's parents' house, Thomas was more than a little annoyed. He had thought her magnanimous not to have brought up his debts before this, but it turned out he had married a foolish creature, indeed. She truly had not known of his debts. How, he did not know. Her father did. Her brother did. But she had not? And to think he had thought he was falling in love with the girl! He certainly desired her, though.

And now how was he to live? He would not stay in London and let her make him a laughingstock. No. He would go down to Oaksey Hall. Thomas loved his home, and now he had money to repair it. It was early enough in the season that he could still see to the planting.

His mind was soon busy with the long-delayed projects that he could undertake—draining the south field, mending the worker's cottages, experimenting with cross-breeding strains of wheat.

The Earl of Oaksey Takes a Wife

He would not dwell on the false enchantment of his honeymoon. Yet even as he made this resolve, his thoughts wandered to his wife, and he found that his grand plans were not sufficient to overcome the ache in his heart.

How could the woman go from loving him to despising him in so short a period? He had poured his limited means into saving Oaksey Hall with hopes that he and his wife would raise a family there. How ironic if he was to be forced to live there alone with all the money he needed but no family.

Giving up on sleep, he climbed from bed, dressed, and began to make preparations for a journey. He saw neither Lord nor Lady Kent at the early hour. After eating a poor breakfast, his was on his way to Suffolk.

Oaksey Hall was a hard day's ride from London to North Suffolk. Taking his black stallion, Magic, the lone extravagance he had allowed himself, Thomas urged him to a gallop, looking to ride out at least some of his disappointment in Melissa's declarations.

The many colors of green in the landscape did not soothe him in the way they normally did. His thoughts were all of dashed hopes. Despite the fact that she had proven to be childish and stubborn, he longed for Melissa's company. He had long dreamed of bringing a bride home to his estate. Family was the reason he had sacrificed almost everything to preserve his home.

His own mother had died when he was fifteen and away at school. His father had followed her only a year later. Thomas never had siblings. Fortunate to have a devoted mother and father, his warm memories of childhood had informed his adulthood. Though he had been financially strapped and had sown his share of wild oats, he had always intended to settle down. In this desire, he was influenced by visions of his lovely mother.

In the garden bower among the bees and butterflies, she had read stories of her own devising, of pirates and buccaneers, sultans and sheiks, duels and derring-do. Before he had gone away to Harrow when he was ten, she had been his teacher. A former governess, Mama had taught him in the cozy nursery below the eaves. He had learned to read, do sums, and explore the world through her inventive geography lessons. Thomas had even learned something of classical history and Latin, her favorite subjects.

Always calm and unruffled, his mother had possessed an unusual beauty, which reminded him of gardenias. His father, of whom Thomas was the perfect image, had worshipped her. She was a vicar's daughter and had brought no dowry. They had scarcely any servants, and the hall was literally falling down about them, but at ten, Thomas had not realized these things. His principal recollection was of listening to his father read to him in the evenings by the drawing room fire, or of the two of them listening to his mother play pianoforte. They were not social people. He had grown up in the circle of their contentment until a legacy from an uncle had given them the funds to send him to school.

He had dreamed of home during those hurly-burly school years. Then the death of his parents had left him profoundly melancholy and alone. And so, from that time to this, he had always fantasized about reconstructing his little family and its cozy felicity. Those dreams were behind all he had done to reconstruct the physical foundations of Oaksey Hall with what was left of his uncle's legacy.

Unlike his father, he had married money. But he had not married just anyone. He had been captivated from the first by Melissa's cheerful good humor and charm. Before he had even known the amount of her dowry, he thought he had seen the partner of his dreams.

He had been wrong. Now approaching his home, he felt more alone than ever. The first few days, he tried to compose a letter to express his love. Every time he recalled his behavior that first day in town, the more hopeless he became of convincing her. How could he explain how elated he had felt about being out of debt after so long, without underscoring what he had said about the reason he had married her? Looking back, he realized that he had taken her love for granted. He had behaved in a manner most unfeeling.

His acts nor his words spoke of a man in love, and no mere letter could convince her otherwise.

Seven

Melissa stayed awake after her husband had left. Still angry after the sun was fully up, she hoped to not see him again for a very long time.

Not only did she not see him, but she heard nothing of him. She did not speak to her parents about the reason for her estrangement with his lordship, and Sophie had gone to Vienna with Frank on their honeymoon. Melissa had no one else to confide in, so she kept her own counsel. She stayed busy enough. Before six weeks had passed, she had her home completely in order.

She tried to take comfort in the beautiful dark blue and gold theme carried through the downstairs, and in the handsome cherry-wood furniture that adorned the rooms. The upstairs featured lavenders, apple greens, and blush pinks. But when this project was completed, her lonely state was even more evident. She only shared this beautiful home with a handful of servants. Its emptiness echoed around her.

The Earl of Oaksey Takes a Wife

Melissa knew that gossip about her and her estranged husband was fierce. Because she had never been one to ignore a challenge, she began to go about in Society. Whenever she paid a call, talk ceased the moment she walked into the room. A few seconds later, it resumed—louder than before.

Her mother constantly badgered her. "Melissa, where has your husband disappeared to? Now that he has your money, has he left you and gone off somewhere to enjoy it without you? You should hear what the gossips are saying! I can hardly hold up my head."

"Do not worry, Mama. They will soon have something else to talk of."

She was planning her first dinner party, with her brother playing host, when she began to feel ill. At first it was just a malaise, a dip in spirits. She could not stop her mind from returning to the scenes of her honeymoon.

Melissa's anger began finally to cool, and she wondered if she had made a terrible mistake in sending her husband away. Truth to tell, she had really never thought he would oblige her by staying away from Oaksey House. The fact that he had found her so easy to leave was another private grief.

One day, she steeled herself to go to his rooms and leave him a note.

Dear Thomas,
I know I was very angry when last we spoke. I still do not feel that you behaved in an upright manner towards me, but I should like to see you, nevertheless. Will you please call upon me?
Your wife,
Melissa

For days, she waited for him with increasing eagerness, but he did not come. It was then that the exceeding exhaustion began. And she felt nauseated at all hours of the day. Thinking she had some sort of rheumatism, she gave up on the idea of a dinner party and spent her days in her dressing room, her low spirits and poor health combining to make her exceptionally cross.

Her mother paid a call after missing her visits for several days. "My dear, have you gone into seclusion? We cannot have that. People will say you are pining for your husband! What is amiss?"

"Oh, Mama, I am afraid I am indeed pining for Thomas. It is making me quite ill. I have no desire to do anything."

"Can you not make up your quarrel?" her mother asked.

Lying on the daybed in her dressing room, Melissa brought up her forearm to cover her eyes and the tears that were starting. "I wrote him a note asking him to call, but he has not seen fit to do so."

"I shall have your father go see him."

"No, Mama. I do not want that. I desire him to come of his own accord."

"Are you never going to tell me what all this is about, Melissa, dear? You were so happy when you came home from Scotland. Even though I was very angry, I could still see that."

Melissa felt so emotional that she decided it would be a relief to finally confide in someone. "Donald told me the morning after we arrived that he had gone to Thomas. The elopement was Donald's idea. He knew that Thomas had debts, ones so pressing that everyone in London knew. Except for me. Donald told him about my dowry. He did marry me for money."

After a silent moment, her mother said, "Well, dear, your father married me for mine."

Melissa stared at her mother. "He did?"

"Indeed. And I must say, even though it was not a love match, he has treated me very well, and I have no regrets."

"I am glad you are content, but when you were young like me, did you not wish to have a love match?"

"Of course. Every young girl does, no matter what she says. But I have seen that what starts out as a love match does not often endure past first attraction, though it be strong. I know you think me silly at times, but I do know a few things by virtue of my age. It takes more than desire to make a solid marriage, you know."

"I know you have helped Papa in his Parliamentary career."

"Yes, though I knew nothing about politics when we were married. I decided we needed a common interest if we were not to become one of those couples who never speaks to each other."

Because of her mother's overly emotional nature, Melissa had never really given her credit for having formed a healthy marriage. Her own intemperate emotions had virtually ended Melissa's marriage before it had properly begun.

Mama continued. "I have always thought that because of my support in his career, your papa was closer to me than the average husband and wife when I had my children. That is when love began to grow between us. We both loved you and Donald so much."

Had Melissa not chafed at that love, thinking it was perhaps too weighty, too manipulative? Thinking of Sophie's parents, she wondered how she ever could have complained. Sophie's mother was wildly unstable, manipulating her daughters quite shamelessly with physical and emotional mistreatment. Her father, though he claimed to love her, never did anything to restrain his wife. He lived quietly behind his library door.

"I am sorry," Melissa said. "Perhaps I have taken your love for granted and been a very spoiled, willful child. That is how Thomas sees me, I am convinced."

"That will change when you have your own children," her mother said, patting her knee. "We have perhaps overindulged you, dear, but you have a good heart. You will make a wonderful mother."

"I will never be a mother. I told poor Thomas that we would live separate lives. I was so hurt, Mama. I thought he loved me."

"Judging by the way he looked at you, I thought so, too. Are you certain he does not?"

"If he did once, he does no longer."

After her mother left, Melissa wept.

EIGHT

Thomas had not lived at Oaksey Hall by himself for any length of time since it had been refurbished. Thanks to his uncle's legacy, its ivy-covered gray stone walls were now secure. The slates on the perpetually leaking roof had been replaced, and the damage the leaks had done inside the hall was repaired. From his library window, he could see the lake, now full and free of weeds and scum since he had cleared the streams that fed and drained it.

He labored in the sun alongside his head gardener to restore the extensive flower gardens. Of course, this was ungentlemanly labor, and he could easily have hired more gardeners, but it gave him peace to his mind to be working thus. This garden had been his mother's pride and joy, and he felt close to her as he trimmed back overgrown perennials, tamed the tangle of rose branches, and planted flats of new varieties of English country flowers.

Each evening, he sat on his terrace and looked over the

results of that day's work. He drank ale with a simple dinner of fish or fowl. The next project would be the succession houses, which hadn't been used for nearly a century. He longed to fill them with all varieties of citrus, colorful orchids, and grapes.

In spite of his work, or maybe because of it, he fought a deep melancholy every night as he fell into bed. He lay for long hours, looking at the stars outside his window. Thomas had a wife. She did not want him, so there would be no child. Who was all of this for? The more beautiful and sturdy he made his surroundings, the deeper his melancholy grew.

One day in June, he was surprised to see a lone rider coming up the gravel drive.

He hastily raced to his dressing room to make himself clean and presentable. In a very short time, a footman entered to tell him that Lord Kent was below.

Does he bring tidings of his daughter?

Thomas entered the drawing room with his hand outstretched. "Lord Kent, how good it is to see you! How does your family?"

The parliamentarian looked stern but nevertheless took the offered hand. "Oaksey."

"Do you have news?" Thomas asked again. "Please have a seat."

Melissa's father seated himself in a massive red velvet chair. "My wife and son are well. Melissa, however, is in low spirits."

Despite himself, Thomas was glad. Was it possible she missed him? He managed to keep an impassive face as he said, "I am truly sorry to hear that."

"Now that you have her money and have deserted her, I doubt that very much."

Thomas swelled with indignation. "I don't know what she has told you, but she made it abundantly clear that she would not live in the same house with me. Nor did she ever wish to lay eyes on me again."

"Only because she found out you were after her fortune. You broke my gel's heart." Lord Kent's face set in a forbidding scowl, his thick, wiry eyebrows nearly covering his eyes.

His declaration gave Thomas pause. Had he really broken Melissa's heart? Or was this merely the interpretation of an overly fond parent?

"She gave me rather the impression of a spoiled shrew. I did not imagine it should come as any surprise that her money was welcome. You knew it, certainly, and so did Lord Donald."

"Was she never more than a bag of money to you then?"

"Of course she was! And well she knows it. For my sins, I fell in love with her. She knows that. But she chose to disregard my feelings. And, if she was honest with me on our honeymoon, she has since disregarded her own feelings as well."

Lord Kent raised his eyebrows. "Is that so?" He squirmed a bit in his chair. "Women can be the very devil! Unless you are constantly flattering them, they take offense over the littlest thing."

"To be honest, she thought I had deceived her, and that is no little thing. She led me to believe she no longer cared for me."

"That, my dear Oaksey, is a complete and utter whisker. She is very low in spirits. My wife tells me that Melissa lives like a recluse in her dressing room. Doesn't even venture to any other part of the house. Eats nothing but a little fruit. Sleeps through her days. It is not like my gel, not like her at all!"

Thomas stared at his father-in-law. Melissa, depressed to such an extent? His chatty, vivacious Melissa? The idea was almost as strange to him as it was to her father. Could she really be mourning him? He felt as though his heart had flipped inside his chest.

"How do you know her behavior has anything to do with me? Perhaps it is the gossip and scandal rendering her spirits so low."

Lord Kent rose and paced about in a circle in front of the fireplace. "What you say is possible. She has always been Society's darling. Her future may appear to her to be devilishly flat."

"Will she confide in you, my lord?"

"Possibly. I will tell her I have been to see you. I take it you never received the letter she left at your rooming house in Town?"

He stared. "What letter?" Confound it! Had she thought twice about the scene she had forced on him? "I left Town straightaway and came down here. I never received any letter."

"She thinks you did—and chose to ignore it."

"I wouldn't have done so, my lord."

"I will tell her so."

Thomas paced in front of the fireplace, impatience and hope combining to make his movements abrupt. "See here. If she has changed her mind and wishes to reconcile, have her write another letter, and I shall return to her. We will try to do things over and see if we can make a happy life together."

"That seems a most sensible suggestion. Let us hope she will not be stubborn about it." He remained standing. "Now I should like to see over your place here. Word has it that you spent your inheritance bringing this place up to snuff."

"I did. Come, I will show you everything. I confess, I hoped to make Melissa happy here."

For the rest of the afternoon and part of the next morning, Thomas showed his father-in-law completely through the hall, the park, and the farm. They dined and played loo in the evening.

"I can see that Melissa could be very happy here," Lord Kent said.

The Earl of Oaksey Takes a Wife

"I have always meant to raise a family here. I experienced great happiness here as a boy."

"May God grant your desires, Oaksey."

NINE

When her father came to call, Melissa was very ill indeed. She had not even risen from her bed to dress that day.

"Well, miss, I have paid that husband of yours a visit. I asked if he had received your letter. He said he had not, and I believe him. He has not been in Town all this time, but on his estate in Suffolk. A very fine estate it is, too. I think you would be most happy to be its mistress."

"Papa, you should have spoken to me. He will think I sent you. I assume he is spending my money like water?"

"No, as a matter of fact. He is taking great pleasure setting the gardens to rights with his own labor and that of his head gardener. I own, I was impressed with the man as well as with the estate."

Melissa groaned. Had her rashness and pride cost her any chance of happiness? The idea brought her to tears. If only she did not feel so wretched! Her weakness caused her to cry at the slightest thing. But was this really a slight thing?

Wiping her eyes, she said, "I let my temper and disappointment get the best of me, Papa. Mama says you married her for her money. Did you love her?"

"Love came to our marriage, but it was not there to begin with, no. However, young Oaksey says you should know that he does love you. He told you so."

She thought back to the time when they rode in the carriage the first day out of Scotland. He had told her so amid fervent kisses. But she had discounted the words afterwards, believing he had only said them to sway her senses.

A heavy burden settled in her chest. "I have made such a mistake, and I fear it is too late to make it right."

"Too late? Whatever do you mean?"

"I fear I am dying. I lose strength daily, and my spirits are most horribly depressed."

"Has Mama called the physician?"

"No. She does not know how ill I have become. I have not wanted to worry her. I was afraid of bringing on her palpitations."

"That was an unwise decision. We shall have the physician now. And while you wait for him, you will write your husband a letter, this time to his estate, welcoming him home. I believe all that ails you is a bout of low spirits brought about by loneliness and the knowledge that you are responsible for your own misery."

Melissa disagreed but took the calling card with her husband's country direction written on the back. While she waited for Dr. Kerry to come, she wrote a letter.

> *My dear Thomas,*
> *I am so terribly sorry for all the unhappiness that my surly temper has brought upon us. I should have remembered your words in the carriage, or rather, I should have believed them. I have had much leisure to*

consider the error I made in letting you think I wanted us to live in separate establishments. I was hurt, and I struck out at you. I honestly did not know I possessed such a temper.

I only hope it is not too late to beg you to forgive me and come to me. I am quite ill, but the thought that I may see you soon will sustain me.

I do truly love you,
Melissa

TEN

When Thomas first received Melissa's letter, he was greatly relieved by her profession of love and honest desire for forgiveness. However, the news that she was ill sent him from the breakfast parlor, flying up the stairs to his dressing room, where he pulled open the cupboards and shouted for his valet.

"Have I enough clean shirts for three or four days?" he asked. "And cravats?"

Winston assured him that he did. "Let me pack for you, my lord. You seem a bit agitated."

"My wife is quite ill. I wish to bring her out of London's filthy air and take care of her here in the country. Please tell Mrs. Abernathy to prepare the countess's suite and see that the beds are properly aired."

"Mrs. Abernathy is all that is capable, my lord. She knows well how to ready a room. You are working yourself into an unnecessary lather."

As he packed, he added further instructions. "And ask her to see to it that the most beautiful flowers in the garden be cut and arranged throughout the house, but particularly in the countess's suite."

"Yes, my lord."

"Have her tell Cook that we shall be returned, hopefully in four days, but that she is not to prepare anything rich. The countess is ill, remember."

"Yes, my lord. I remember."

Finally, with the aid of his staff, Thomas was off on his stallion, glad he had left his carriage in London so he could travel post haste. Galloping through the countryside, he wondered why Lord Kent had not told him of Melissa's illness. Thomas would have gone straight to her side, regardless. His mind went back to one of its favorite dwelling places: the memory of the carriage journey from Gretna Green to London. Three perfect days and nights.

He recalled Melissa's vitality, her passion, her playfulness. And her soft, soft skin. He remembered seeing her with her glorious fair hair down across her shoulders. And the sparkle of delight in those cornflower blue eyes. Thomas prayed they would have a chance to make new memories and that his beloved would not shortly be consigned to the cold earth as his parents had been.

Upon his arrival in London, he went directly to Oaksey House. Going straight in, he informed the astonished butler, "I'm Oaksey. Is my wife abed?"

"Uh, yes, your lordship. I understand the countess to be in her dressing room."

Galloping up the stairs, Thomas scarcely noticed the new look and fresh smell of his home. He raced through the countess's bedroom into her dressing room.

Melissa was asleep. His heart froze for a moment as he looked at her wan face and the dark circles under her eyes. He didn't remember her cheekbones being so sharp. Kneeling at the side of her bed, he placed his hand gently on her forehead. No fever. Nevertheless, he pulled up her blanket so it covered the hands which lay over each other on her waist.

Drawing a small stool away from the dressing table, he set it by the daybed and sat down, intending to wait until she woke. Almost immediately, her eyes flickered open.

To his surprise, she gave him a radiant smile, "Oh, Thomas, I am so glad you are here! I have such news."

"You are pale, and you have lost weight . . ."

"Thomas, we are to be parents! I am increasing."

For a moment, he was breathless. He could not take it in. "Then why are you so ill?" he asked. "Is there a chance you may lose the baby?"

"I do not believe so. Some women get very ill, is all. I have decided that the sicker you are, the more likely you will be to have a successful confinement."

For a few moments, Thomas remained silent, confused by contradictory feelings. "I have always wanted children, darling. But not at the cost of your health. Not if I may lose *you*." Kneeling by her side, he ran the back of his hand down her smooth cheek.

"I am taking very good care of myself. Presently, I shall walk about the house for some mild exercise. And Papa has found me the best physician in Harley Street."

Oaksey grinned. "He would. We are agreed that you are the most precious of women. Please, please forgive me." He took her hand in his and brought it to his lips.

"Of what do I have to forgive you?" she asked.

"For staying away my first day in London. I was eager to pay my debts to my faithful friends. But if I had been here, I do not think you would have mustered up such fury. I would have been on hand to convince you of my love."

She brought a hand up and ran it through his hair. Her eyes were earnest as she said, "I am so sorry for my dreadful temper. It is fitting that I should be struck so low. It has given me time to think. Thank you for coming so quickly."

"I want you to know that I fell for you at your come-out. I knew nothing of your dowry then. Your good nature sparkled from those beautiful blue eyes, and I was enslaved by every graceful move you made. I had been looking for a lady like you for a long time." He cupped her chin and leaned down to kiss her.

"But I am so ordinary," Melissa said.

"*Extraordinary.* Have you any idea how rare it is to find a good nature coupled with such beauty?"

"My nature is not so very good. I threw you out of your own house. And when I am old, I shall have thirteen chins."

He laughed at her solemnity. "I do not believe it. As for throwing me out, any woman with a speck of self-respect would have done the same. But you will be the perfect life's partner for me," he said. "I adored my parents, and for years I have had the dream of restoring domestic felicity to the hearth of Oaksey Hall. They died while I was away at school, and my home has never felt the same. But you will give it new heart."

"Papa said it was very grand, but very comfortable as well."

His heart swelled with happiness he had never thought to feel. "It is all ready for you and our child."

"I love you, Thomas. And I'm so very, very glad you were poor and had to marry me."

Leaning down over the daybed, he kissed his wife again then ran his index finger along her jawline. "I shall take the very best care of you," he murmured. "I want you to last."

Epilogue

It was a winter evening, and the snow was piled deep outside Oaksey Hall. But within, there was rejoicing. In the countess's chamber, a new infant's lusty cry could be heard. Little Lord Richmond Burroughs lay in his mother's arms. His wailing soon stopped as his suckling began. His papa, the earl, stood over his wife and son, tears trickling down both cheeks.

"You have an heir," his wife said, satisfaction evident in her voice.

"He is bone of our bone and flesh of our flesh," Lord Oaksey said. "Thank you for bringing him into the world, my love. That was a splendid effort."

"Thank you giving me the chance to mother this little mite. I think he is impressive, do you not think so?"

"Of course I do. Look how large his hands and feet are!

And those shoulders. He is so loud, I venture to say he will outshine your father in Parliament."

"Yes, he will make a grand Whig."

"Tory, my dear."

"I have heard that a mother's influence is greatest," Lady Oaksey said, her smile serene.

Remembering his own dear mother, Lord Oaksey wondered if she were not present somehow at this wonderful scene where a new generation had begun. He hoped so.

"You may be right, my love."

About G.G. Vandagriff

G.G. Vandagriff is the author of seventeen books, including six Regency romances. The most recent of these is *The Baron and the Bluestocking*. She loves the Regency period with all its absurd eccentricities.

Vandagriff is at home with historical fiction, her novel, *The Last Waltz: A Novel of Love and War,* having received the Whitney Award for Best Historical Novel of 2009. Her other works include a genealogical mystery series, women's fiction, suspense, and two non-fiction offerings. Visit her online at: http://ggvandagriff.com

Vandagriff studied writing at Stanford University and received her master's degree from George Washington University. She and her husband, David, have three children and four grandchildren.

Her favorite indulgence is travel, and she goes to Florence every year to stimulate her creativity—and eat gelato!

GIFT OF LOVE

by Michele Paige Holmes

Other Works by Michele Paige Holmes

Counting Stars

All the Stars in Heaven

My Lucky Stars

Captive Heart

Saving Grace

ONE

1760—Northern Ireland

Ethan Moorleigh wore a path over the hall rug. Seven paces, sharp turn. Seven paces, back again.

Lucky seven. His hands clenched at his sides. He wasn't usually a man given to superstition, but just now he was in need of luck, or heaven's blessings—a miracle.

"Please God," he said aloud for what was surely the hundredth time over the past eighteen hours. He didn't often pray, but he promised he would from this day forth if God would grant him this one wish. He'd pray, give more to the Church—build a new chapel if that's what was required. Anything for this one favor.

Please save Mary.

He didn't ask for the child's life to be spared as well. For a man known to breed misfortune as he did, that was too much to hope for. He'd feared for weeks that all would not go well as he'd watched Mary grow weary, as he'd seen the stress that carrying the babe was causing her.

And now she'd grown so weak she couldn't even cry out in her suffering. The past hour had been silent—worse even than the screams of agony that had preceded it.

Ethan stopped before the door, resting his forehead against the polished wood, listening for any sign of life from the other side. He'd stayed with Mary as long as he could, finally kissing her gently when the midwife shooed him from the room, telling him that men had no business at a birthing.

He'd thought that maybe if he stayed he might somehow help, might see Mary through the event he'd worried over for months, since the bittersweet morning she'd rolled to face him in bed and whispered, "Ethan, we're going to have a child."

He'd been half asleep and certain at first that he was dreaming. But her fingers tickling across his chest had fully wakened him. He'd captured her hand, stilling the movement as he raised his head, looking in her eyes. "A child?"

She'd laughed. "Is it so impossible to believe? You've scarce let me out of this bed the past six months."

"Now I'll have to keep you in it another nine." He'd kissed her then, long and slow and luxurious as most of their kisses were. From the first night of their marriage, Mary had made it clear that she adored him.

For years, she'd lingered in her cousin's shadow, always near when Ethan came to visit. He'd scarcely noticed her, busy as he'd been, carrying on in his father's footsteps as he maintained his numerous holdings and accumulated enough wealth to care for them.

But Mary had noticed him. And unlike the other women in the province who thought him cursed, or a murderer, or both, she hadn't avoided him as if he were the reaper himself. She'd made a point to welcome him in Stuart's home, and she'd made it clear that she had no qualms about marrying a man who'd already had two wives, both of whom had suffered untimely deaths.

Ethan's throat constricted when he thought of her courage and the unwavering love and devotion she'd shown him—a previously broken man.

Mary had healed him. She loved him, and he returned that love with more fervor than he'd thought possible. He couldn't let anything happen to her. The kiss he'd given Mary just before the midwife sent him away yesterday morning would not be their last.

Ethan banged on the door. "Mary? Are you well, Mary?" He'd brought this upon her, and he was the one who ought to see her through it. The devil take anyone who told him otherwise.

No reply came. He tried the handle—locked. Alarmed, he pounded harder, demanding entrance. He shoved his shoulder to the door, but the solid wood didn't budge. He turned away, intent on retrieving an axe to break down the door, when it suddenly swung open.

The midwife stood before him, her ashen face a sharp contrast to her bloody apron. "They are dead." Her red-rimmed eyes were wide with fright.

Ethan pushed past her to the bedside, to Mary's still body. He knelt and touched her hand, already cold. Her face wasn't peaceful, but troubled. She'd died in agony.

He turned to look at the midwife. "How long—why didn't you call me? I should have been with her!"

He fell forward, his cheek against Mary's silent chest, struggling for breath. All the hurt he'd felt before—after Clara's accident and Abigail's drowning—paled against this pain. He pressed his lips to her hand. "I'm so sorry. My sweet Mary."

Tears fell, and he had no care who saw. Behind him he heard steps and turned to see Stuart, whom he'd sent for when Mary's labor had begun. Ethan looked at his friend, the man who had trusted him with his cousin's life. "I'm so sorry."

Stuart's look was grim, but he placed a comforting hand on Ethan's shoulder.

Ethan bent his head as more tears fell. This could not be happening. Not to Mary. *Not my Mary.*

A tiny cry pierced the air, and his head jerked up. He'd given no thought to the infant. Hadn't the midwife said—

He met the woman's large, frightened eyes; she glanced from Ethan to Stuart and back again.

Stuart ran around to the end of the bed, to the cradle. In shock, Ethan watched as he lifted the baby. It cried again.

"It lives." The midwife's voice was astonished. "Impossible. She was—"

"She is very much alive. In spite of your poor care." Stuart's tone was scathing. "I shall personally see that you never deliver another child." He carried the squirming bundle to Ethan. "Your daughter."

Ethan reached out and took the child. He looked at its face, hoping to feel something—some instinctive parental joy. None came. Only numbness and disbelief, his scarred heart growing cold already. His gaze slid back to the bed, to Mary.

He had no love to give their child.

Two

1763—England

"Dear Lord," Amelia began. "Most humbly I thank thee for thy bounties, for the good sisters who care for me, for this abbey, for the vows I am shortly to take. Help me be ready—oh—ooh!" Unable to stand it any longer, Amelia pushed off the side of her cot and bent to rub her knees, frozen with cold from the hard floor.

Shivering, she continued her prayer silently. *Help me be grateful, Lord. And to understand why we cannot have rugs beside our beds.*

As soon as the blasphemous thought left her mind, she felt guilty—but not so much that she was willing to make her knees suffer again. After jerking the scratchy wool blanket from her bed, Amelia dropped it to the floor and knelt once more, hands clasped in front of her, penitent for her unruly thoughts.

"Help me be good, Lord. Forgive my selfish thoughts and desires. Help me be ready." She stayed there some time, arms wrapped around herself in an attempt at warmth as she contemplated all that being ready entailed. Though she'd had many years to prepare for her final vows, now that the time was upon her, she didn't feel as certain about taking them as she ought.

The idea of sharing this uncertainty with the abbess or any of the other sisters was too awful, so she turned instead to God. He knew her heart, and surely He would calm it. *And my chattering teeth.*

As if Amelia's thoughts had been overheard by the abbess, her voice rang loudly through the hall. "You cannot simply remove her."

Amelia ended her prayer but remained on her knees, listening, her curiosity more than piqued at the elderly matron being up and about and agitated at this time of night.

"This is her home. This is what she knows," the abbess continued.

"She'll have another home now. And I most certainly can remove her. It was I who brought her here to begin with."

Stuart! Amelia's eyes flew open as she recognized the second voice—her half-brother's. She'd not seen him in nearly three years, since the day he'd come to tell her their cousin Mary had died in childbirth. Before that, it had been a two-year stretch—since that lonely day he'd first deposited her here for safekeeping on her thirteenth birthday.

Amelia quickly bowed her head again. "Dear Lord, whatever misfortune has befallen Stuart, please bless him and any who suffer. Be thou with them in their time of sorrow."

"Amelia." Light slanted across the floor into her dark room. Amelia looked over her shoulder at Stuart standing in the open doorway, silhouetted in lantern light. The abbess's aged hand swayed, the light swinging behind him. Stuart stepped into the tiny room.

Gift of Love

The abbess followed. "You *cannot* do this." She nodded toward Amelia. "Look at her. See how ready she is. This is the life she knows. You are the one who brought her to it. Removing her now would be most cruel."

"I cannot see how." Stuart glanced around the bare room, distaste evident in his face. "She won't be leaving much," he muttered, half under his breath, but Amelia heard it all the same. She doubted the abbess had, near deaf as the old woman was.

Amelia rose, shoving the blanket beneath the cot so the abbess wouldn't see her weakness, and addressed her brother. "What has happened?" No doubt it was something dreadful to bring him this far, this late at night.

"Nothing, my dear Amelia." His face broke into a smile, and he stepped toward her, clasping her hands. "Only that you are needed elsewhere."

Though she'd overheard their conversation in the hall, his words still took her by surprise. Stuart wanted her to leave. A thrill of fear shivered down her spine as she recalled his words when he'd first brought her here.

The world is an evil place, Amelia—especially for a woman. I promised your mother that I would keep you safe, and safe you'll be here. This will be a good life for you, one filled with peace.

He'd been right, mostly. The sisters were kind, and she was surrounded with goodness—music, prayers, and devotions. Peace had been harder to achieve. She was still striving for that: calming her spirit, curbing her curiosity about all that lay outside the abbey walls, and being satisfied with the life of quiet service chosen for her.

Chosen for me. That's it. That is my problem. Stuart chose this life for me. I didn't. The revelation was startling in its simplicity, yet she sensed that in it lay the peace she'd so yearned for. *All I must do is choose for myself.* Which, it appeared, was the opportunity presented to her this very moment.

She looked Stuart squarely in the eyes. "This is my home. This is what I know—and love." Her conviction deepened as she spoke the words she knew to be true. There was much to love about the abbey.

Behind Stuart, the abbess smiled approvingly.

"I know this is sudden—and unfair," Stuart conceded, glancing behind him at the scowling nun. "But the situation is urgent. I've thought it through many times, and you're the only one who can help. You're the one he needs, Amelia."

"He?" The heartache and loneliness she'd wrestled with many times over the past years burst to the surface. "A child?" This insane desire, as she'd once heard another nun describe it, was the greatest thing holding her from her vows: to be a mother, have a child of her own to love.

Stuart shook his head, and his unkempt hair fell across his eyes. Amelia noticed the condition of her usually well-groomed brother—dusty breeches, wrinkled and soiled shirt, bags beneath his eyes. Even his movements seemed stiff and sore and tired.

"The *he* is a man, my good friend, Lord Moorleigh."

Amelia tamped down her disappointment. "Mary's husband." A child might have tempted her away, but never a man. It was that species Stuart had brought her here to be safe from in the first place. She turned away, but Stuart caught her arm.

"He's been our neighbor and my friend for years. You may remember him."

Amelia shook her head. She'd worked hard to forget her childhood, those years of being in a family before she'd come to the convent. It was easier that way.

"Ethan was a good husband," Stuart continued. "He still grieves Mary. He loved her dearly."

"What has any of this to do with me?" Amelia asked.

"Nothing," the abbess cut in. "This is a fool's errand, and you'd best be on your way now, Lord Peyton."

Gift of Love

"Ethan Moorleigh must remarry," Stuart said. "Else his title and property stand to pass to another line. Even now he is considering giving up his title and holdings. His grief is that great."

"Giving up one's wealth is no sin," Mother said.

"It will not heal him," Stuart predicted. "Amelia, I believe you're the one person who can. Your heart is pure enough to mend his sorrows, to let him live a life again."

"A life, Lord Peyton, is not a title or possession." The abbess held the lantern close and looked at him pointedly. "Be honest in what you are asking your sister. You wish her to marry your friend so he may produce an heir to retain his title. Am I correct?"

"I wish her to marry him so he may retain his heart." Stuart met her gaze steadily. "It has broken into a hundred pieces and requires another heart equally tender to heal it."

"Humph," the abbess scoffed. "Is it so terrible that he still mourns his wife? I think not. In this world, we must all suffer. If your friend experienced a bit of joy before his sorrow, all the better for him. He is one of the fortunate."

"I'm sorry, Stuart." Amelia turned away, hoping he'd take his leave and ease her conscience. While she didn't feel the least amount of guilt in rejecting Lord Moorleigh's suit, she hated telling her stepbrother no. With Father, her mother, and Mary gone, he was her only family. Being Lord Moorleigh's bride might allow her to see Stuart more often. She would have liked that.

It might also have allowed me to have a child. Though that was her dearest wish, Amelia found that her fear of the unknown Lord Moorleigh was greater.

Perhaps that is my answer, she reasoned. *Though I long for what I cannot have, I am too afraid to seek it. The best path for me is right here, and has been all along.*

But the empty place in her heart, the spot that had begun hurting when Father was killed and had nearly consumed her after Mother's death, felt torn open again.

Amelia closed her eyes, angry at her inability to overcome the past. This loneliness, this desire for family, kept her from her vows. Stuart showing up tonight, reminding her of all she longed for, was most unfortunate.

"There is something else." Stuart's voice was quiet.

"It doesn't matter," Amelia said. God was testing her. That was all. He'd heard her prayers and wanted to make certain she was ready to take her vows and was willing to give up all her fanciful notions about what might have been. She steeled herself against anything Stuart might say. It wouldn't matter. No luxury he might offer, no proximity to him and the home she'd grown up in. Nothing could change her mind.

"Mary's child," Stuart said. "The babe she died birthing is three now. The little girl hasn't known a mother's love, and her father has barely been a presence in her life. She needs you, Amelia."

Five years at the abbey and all her preparations toward becoming a nun—it all seemed to fall away at his words, simply vanish, as so much vapor in the air. Though Amelia hadn't said a word, wasn't facing Stuart, had not so much as blinked, there was a palpable change in the room's atmosphere.

A little girl! The peace that had always eluded her seemed to swirl into and fill her soul. On its heels came a rush of joy.

Stuart was offering her a child. Amelia couldn't help but smile, and she thought that God might be smiling down on her too. Even the abbess had taught that there was more than one noble calling on earth, more than one way to serve.

And I've found it.

She turned around and saw that they both already knew her answer. The abbess's lined face wrinkled in defeat. Stuart's smile was triumphant, if not a little smug. Amelia didn't care, and though they already knew her answer, she spoke anyway.

"I will come with you. I'll marry your Lord Moorleigh, and I'll love his little girl."

Three

"The church is so—full." Amelia's grip on Stuart's arm tightened, and she hesitated at the back of the overflowing chapel. More people than she'd seen in her lifetime spilled from the pews, lined the walls and—she glanced behind her—waited on the steps outside.

Keeping his gaze straight ahead, Stuart whispered, "Ethan Moorleigh's estates are vast, more than five times greater than Papa had. He practically owns the county."

"And the people wanted to see him wed again?" Amelia asked.

"Something like that." Stuart stepped forward, pulling her with him. They walked down the aisle, the elegant gown flowing behind her. With the silk swishing about her feet, Amelia grasped for the confidence she'd felt a short while ago, when the maids had stood her before the tall glass.

It had been years since she'd seen herself properly in a mirror, and having the first occasion be her wedding day—

when she was done up in finery, hair arranged, Mother's pearls at her neck—had been quite a shock. She hadn't looked at all like she remembered, like the scrawny, freckled, straight-haired, puffy-eyed child who'd entered the abbey five years ago. Instead, a stranger, a *woman* had stared back from the glass.

Now Amelia held her head a little higher. *If the people have come to see their lord and his new lady wed, then they shall.* Two weeks ago, she might have been insignificant, a lone girl locked away in a nunnery for safekeeping. But today, she at least looked the part, looked worthy of this moment that likely many women in attendance would only dream of.

I am marrying well. Papa and Mama would be pleased. Stuart has kept his promise to care for me.

"Like a lamb to the slaughter, poor thing."

"And giving his *own* sister."

"Took her straight from the abbey, I heard."

The whispered words reached Amelia as she passed the benches midway through the chapel, giving her fragile confidence a sudden dent. Much more than seeing their lord wed again had brought such a large congregation to the church.

"There's such a thing as loyalty, but I'd never—"

Never what? she wondered as Stuart hurried her along.

"What must she be thinking right now?"

"Three wives dead before her."

Three? Amelia felt suddenly faint. "Stuart," she whispered urgently.

"Shhh." He cut her off and continued towing her down the aisle.

Her steps grew heavy. *Three. Three wives before me and all dead.* Stuart had only told of Mary's death. He'd never mentioned that Lord Moorleigh had been married more than once before.

Did they all die in childbirth? There was only one way to

ensure she never suffered that fate, but Lord Moorleigh needed a male heir—likely the only reason he was marrying her.

Fear gripped Amelia as she grasped for understanding, for the calm she'd felt minutes ago. Hadn't Stuart said that Lord Moorleigh still loved Mary? That he ignored his only child?

If so, perhaps he won't care for me at all. Maybe he doesn't really want an heir. Perhaps he's marrying me as a favor to Stuart. With all of his estates to oversee, surely he would be gone much of the time. *Let him go out of the country tomorrow. Let him be lost at sea. Let him . . .*

"Bless her bravery," someone near the front whispered.

Amelia didn't feel brave at all. She stared straight ahead at Lord Moorleigh's back. Through her veil she could tell that he was tall, his hair dark, and his bearing stiff.

They were nearly there, and he hadn't yet turned to look at her. She took this as a good sign. If he'd really wanted to marry her, if he had the least bit of interest, he would have turned to her, wouldn't he? She pulled her gaze to the priest, hoping to find comfort in a man of God, but his face was dark and solemn.

There is no joy in this occasion.

She thought of her yearnings while living at the abbey and remembered the abbess's saying about another man's field not being more plentiful than one's own. Amelia had always felt differently. She'd been quite certain there was more joy and color to life outside the abbey walls.

Perhaps I was wrong.

Two steps more and she was at Lord Moorleigh's side. What at first had seemed a daunting journey—passing all those people—was over quickly, and Stuart released her, depositing her at the side of the man who would now be her caretaker, the one she would have to listen to and obey.

A complete stranger.

Three dead wives.

What have I done?

The feeling she'd faint returned, and she swayed a little on her feet. Stuart grabbed her arm, and in a move likely not traditional ceremony, placed her hand into Ethan Moorleigh's.

His palm was warm against her cold one. Surprisingly, he gave her a quick, reassuring squeeze. She glanced up at him. His face was still forward, eyes glued to the priest. But she'd felt his offer of comfort, and she accepted it as one would a lifeboat in the midst of a storm. So simple, yet somehow, it calmed her frantic heart.

She dared a squeeze back, a thank you. He turned to look at her, and in that brief second, his eyes were kind, if not sorrowful, and he was young—younger than Stuart even. Ethan Moorleigh didn't look old enough to have had three wives already.

Nor old enough to cope with their loss.

Her heart softened, and instead of fear, she felt compassion for the man beside her who had suffered so much. What was it that Stuart had said at the abbey? *You're the only one who can heal him. He needs another tender heart.*

How easily she'd dismissed that—the man she was to marry. Her thoughts had been all for his child. Amelia felt her face flush with guilt, and a second later, when she realized the priest had addressed her and she hadn't responded, she felt even more abashed.

She gave her answer, acknowledging her name and the purpose for which she was here.

I am marrying Ethan Moorleigh. According to Stuart, he'd loved at least Mary dearly. Her brief glimpse into his eyes had confirmed that he was a man who *could* care. Minutes ago, she'd hoped he'd ignore her completely. But now, with her hand nestled in his warm one, her shoulder brushing his arm, she wasn't so sure that she wanted to be ignored.

Her heart beat faster, but this time it wasn't from fear. Warmth seemed to radiate from Lord Moorleigh's hand to her own, up her arm and into her heart. Feelings she hadn't at all anticipated took root.

There may be more to be gained from this arrangement than the opportunity to love a child. Perhaps—someday—he may care for me as well.

Her face had to be flaming now. She silently rebuked herself for such unholy thoughts about her marriage. How had she gone in a matter of days from preparing to take a vow that would keep her chaste forever, to giving herself to a man with something akin to eagerness?

The priest droned on. He seemed to be coming to the important part, so she refocused her attention. When she was called upon to speak her vows, her voice was loud and clear, so all the gossips in the pews could hear.

Three wives. Fear still nagged at her, but she pushed it away and faced her future squarely. When Lord Moorleigh's turn came to answer, his voice was rich and melodic—and soothing, as his touch had been.

At last their vows were accomplished. They turned to face each other. He slipped a weighty band on her finger and gave another gentle squeeze to her fingertips. Then he released her and reached for her veil.

She stood perfectly still as the gauzy fabric lifted. Their eyes met, and she'd started to smile when he gasped. His eyes widened in shock, and his face drained of color. She might have reached out to steady him but for the spark of anger she glimpsed in the depths of his blue eyes. The veil fell back, and he turned away.

Amelia stood frozen in place, listening to the horrified whispers of the congregation as Ethan Moorleigh—her husband—rushed out the front doors of the church. Bells pealed wildly, signaling what was supposed to be a celebratory departure. To her they signaled disaster. Somehow, she'd ruined things already.

Four

Humiliation colored Amelia's face, but utter panic made her tremble. She searched the front pew for Stuart and was further dismayed to see him running down the aisle after her husband. Amelia looked about for another exit and noticed a forlorn figure on the front bench, kicking her legs in and out, sucking her thumb and twisting in her seat, looking toward the back of the church.

There was no mistaking her cousin's child. A riot of blonde curls adorned her head, and her large brown eyes looked just like Mary's. *Abandoned as I am.*

Amelia lifted the veil from her face as she walked to the bench. She knelt before the child. "Lizbeth?"

The little girl looked at her curiously, and for a moment, Amelia feared that whatever flaw in her features had sent Ethan Moorleigh running would also frighten his child.

"Mama?"

Amelia smiled with relief. "Yes. I'm to be your new mother."

The little girl threw her arms around Amelia's neck, nearly sending them both sprawling backward. Only just managing to keep her balance while holding the child, Amelia stood, Lizbeth's hands still clasped firmly around her.

"Papa's gone." Lizbeth's tone was so forlorn that Amelia was reminded of the day her own father had disappeared. The terrifying feeling of being left behind wasn't something she'd wish on any child.

"We shall go too." She followed Lizbeth's gaze toward the chapel doors—so far away now from this end of the aisle. There was no help for it; she'd have to walk past all the staring people again. She could only imagine what the gossips would whisper this time.

She hoisted Lizbeth to a more comfortable position and squared her shoulders. Head held high once more, she retraced her steps down the aisle, doing her best to ignore the stares and comments.

They were nearly to the doors when Lizbeth began to squirm. She arched her head back, looking up toward the ceiling. "Papa said the bells would play when we left."

They already did. Amelia would not soon forget that burning moment of humiliation and panic, but she pushed her misery aside and thought of the little girl. She knew from experience how a father's broken promise could hurt.

"Excuse me," she said, addressing the priest standing near the doors. Apparently, he, too, had started after her husband. "Might you ring the bells once more? This little girl was promised they would ring upon her exit, and she shall be greatly disappointed if they do not."

The solemn-looking priest paused a moment, likely taken aback by her forwardness, but finally nodded his acquiescence. Without a word, he turned away, disappearing through a side door.

"Now we've only to wait a minute," Amelia said,

hugging Lizbeth to her. A warm smile was her reward, and it seemed filled with such love and trust that for a fleeting second, Amelia felt true happiness.

Then she remembered the man who came along with the gift of this little girl. Perhaps Amelia's first wish was being granted already—that he intended to leave her alone. Though she wouldn't have wished him to leave her quite so fast.

He might have escorted me from the chapel, at least.

"Mistress Lizbeth!" An elderly woman with a severe bun and a reprimanding voice descended upon them. "You'll be the death of me yet, you naughty girl, leaving your seat like that."

"She is with me," Amelia stated, offering no apology. By right of her vows, the child was hers.

"I am her governess," the woman said, seeming not the least cowed by Amelia's statement.

"Would you be so kind as to fetch Lizbeth's cloak?" Amelia asked. "I'd hate for her to catch a chill before the festivities." She had no idea what, if any, festivities were planned. She couldn't imagine that a man marrying for the fourth time could be expected to celebrate the occasion.

The governess's mouth opened and closed like a fish— wanting desperately to protest, Amelia guessed. At last the woman nodded curtly and turned away.

Governess, indeed. Those Amelia had growing up had been kind and gentle, characteristics she could already see lacking in that woman. No matter. Lizbeth no longer required a nanny. Henceforth, Amelia would see to her care. It was the least she could do to honor her cousin.

And to fill my lonely heart.

The bells rang once more. Amelia wrapped her arms tightly around Lizbeth and exited the church. Delighted by the sound, Lizbeth lifted her face to the gray skies and giggled.

Amelia looked around desperately. Neither Stuart nor

Lord Moorleigh were anywhere to be seen, and she suddenly wanted nothing more than to be away from this place and the people spilling out behind her, looking forward—no doubt—to a continuation of the drama.

With brisk steps, she descended the stairs and marched down the walk toward a line of waiting carriages. She focused on the largest, sleekest, shiniest of the lot, guessing it must belong to her husband. When she was still a few paces away, the footman opened the door and put down the step.

Relief swept through her, but she worked hard to keep her face free of any emotion other than a commanding authority she didn't quite feel.

"Thank you," Amelia said as she marched past the footman and deposited Lizbeth inside the carriage. She followed quickly, seating herself and settling the child upon her lap before the door had fully closed.

"Will Lord Moorleigh be joining us?" the footman asked, staring at her in a manner that bordered on rudeness.

"He'll be coming later," Amelia said, wondering yet again what was so terribly wrong with her appearance. Truly, she'd felt most satisfied upon seeing her reflection this morning. But perhaps in the five years she'd spent in the abbey, fashion had changed. Perhaps the stain on her lips or the curls at the side of her face were dreadfully outdated and made her look a horrid old spinster.

She did her best to brush aside her insecurities. "Lord Moorleigh and my brother have some business to attend to," she said, hoping the footman might find her words both believable and convincing.

"Very well." He nodded and at last pried his gaze from her face. "Home, then?"

Amelia was struck with sudden inspiration. "There has been a change of plans." She straightened her back and did her best to look authoritative. "We'll be going to Lord Moorleigh's estate in Bamburgh."

Home. Five long years since I've been there.

"But milady—" The footman faltered, clearly struggling to keep his place. "It's midday now. It would be well after nightfall before we arrived. His Lordship said—"

Amelia nodded. "I am aware of the distance. All the more reason not to dally. His Lordship will follow shortly." She wasn't exactly certain of this but guessed it was probable, as she was taking his daughter with her.

The footman hesitated a second more and then nodded. "Very well. We'll be off at once."

Amelia dismissed him with a nod. As she reached for a blanket folded on the seat opposite, she glanced out the window and spotted Lizbeth's distraught governess on the top step of the church, scanning the crowd for her charge. Amelia slid to the far side of the carriage and pressed back into the seat.

Lizbeth squirmed, protesting her lost view of the bells.

The footman secured the door and mounted his perch, muttering, "Like seeing a ghost, his bride is."

Amelia brought a hand to her cheek. Had the ordeal in the chapel caused her to look overly pale? She glanced at her hands, certain that fair skin hadn't gone out of fashion. If anything, she had more color than most women, from her days spent laboring in the abbey gardens.

"Miss Lizbeth!" The governess's screeching voice carried through the window at the same moment the carriage lurched forward.

Not a second too soon. Amelia dismissed her worries over her appearance and tucked the blanket around Lizbeth as the wheels turned, carrying them away toward her childhood home and her new life.

Five

Ethan walked briskly, placing a good amount of distance between himself and the church *and the woman inside*. Just thinking of her sent a jolt through him again, forcing him to stop. He placed a hand on one of the large oaks growing behind the church and leaned forward, breathing deeply, trying to steady himself as the second set of bells continued to ring and Stuart came up behind him.

"The devil take you," Ethan said.

"Devil take *me*?" Stuart asked, his breathing labored from running to catch up. "You just walked out on my sister!"

Ethan turned to face him. "You might have mentioned beforehand that Amelia is the exact image of Mary."

"She is?" Stuart's brows drew together in consternation. "I hadn't noticed. At the abbey she looked like all the other nuns, and it was dark when we traveled. I haven't seen her the past few days, and this morning, her face was veiled."

"Humph." Ethan waved a hand dismissively. What did it matter now? Their vows were spoken. What was done was done. He had two choices: avoid his new wife completely or steel himself against the painful reminder of what he'd lost every time he looked at her. He was leaning toward the former. Amelia was his fourth wife; what expectations of their marriage could she possibly have, after all? He certainly had none.

His chest hurt when he recalled lifting her veil. Like Mary, she was so young—so innocent. Then she'd looked up at him with something between hope and promise in her big, brown eyes. It paralyzed him just thinking about it. Almost four years earlier, her cousin had looked at him in almost the same way.

Perhaps Amelia did have expectations.

"She's not Mary," Stuart said. "She's nothing like Mary. Amelia's practically been raised in a convent, for heaven's sake."

"Heaven's sake, indeed," Ethan muttered. She'd about sent him to heaven with the way she'd practically made his heart stop today, first squeezing his hand boldly, something so like his Mary. And then looking so much like her.

"What I meant," Stuart said, "is that Amelia won't behave at all like Mary. She's been sheltered. She knows nothing of men. She'll be neither bold nor forthcoming."

"Really?" After two minutes of marriage, Ethan could tell that he knew more about Amelia than Stuart did after years as her brother.

"She's timid," Stuart said. "Right now she's probably huddled on some bench inside the church, distraught and sobbing." He turned back toward the building and was nearly bowled over by Lizbeth's governess running toward them, waving her hands and trying to speak.

"Gone," she finally wheezed. Unbound from her bonnet, her gray hair was blown askew. "She took her."

Ethan grabbed her arms as if to hold her up. "Lizbeth is missing?"

"With your new wife—in the carriage."

"Oh." Ethan relaxed his grip a little. "They'll have gone home then." He sighed with relief. Though he was not surprised to learn that Amelia was *not* withering away, making a scene on some bench in the chapel.

"Impossible," Stuart said, seeming genuinely shocked that his sister had managed to get into a carriage of her own accord.

"Aye," the governess said. "Impossible they've gone home. The carriage took a sharp turn at the fork, headed toward the north road."

Ethan released her so suddenly she stumbled backwards. He glared accusingly at Stuart. "Timid, you say? It would appear your family breeds only women who are the *complete* opposite."

Six

"Which one do you like?" Hands behind her back, Amelia strode up and down the stable, pausing every so often to admire the fine horses. Lizbeth trailed behind her, mimicking a similar stance and expression each time they stopped.

According to the servants, Lord Moorleigh rarely visited Bamburgh anymore. He'd frequented it during his marriage to Mary—her childhood home was here as well—but since his wife's death three years ago, he'd come only a handful of times.

Amelia was pleased to see that, in spite of his infrequent visits, he still kept many fine animals. "This one, I think," she said, stopping before a horse with a white patch on its nose. The animal bent to nuzzle her outstretched hand. "She looks gentle."

The stable boy, who'd been frowning at her since she'd entered the building, stepped forward between her and the stall. "I can't saddle her for you."

"Can't? Or *won't?*" Amelia asked, half expecting more trouble; she'd been meeting it at every turn since her arrival last night.

Lizbeth wasn't to feed herself—she might choke. She wasn't to play in the gardens—some of the flowers were poisonous. And they both were *absolutely* not to go anywhere near the beach.

As if collecting seashells involves great peril.

The stable boy cleared his throat. "Lord Moorleigh won't let his daughter or any of his wives ride."

Amelia arched her brow. "Wife. He has one. And I am she." It rankled her to be reminded of those who'd come before. Especially when Ethan Moorleigh had filled her dreams the whole night through. "Very well," Amelia conceded. Arguing had proved pointless several times already. As it was, she'd had to sneak Lizbeth out the conservatory window. "Come along, Lizbeth." Amelia took the little girl's hand and walked briskly out of the stable and toward the gardens.

She'd spotted a gardener's shed there earlier, and where there was a shed, there would likely be a cart. One of the many skills she'd mastered at the abbey was pushing a cart full of vegetables. Lizbeth couldn't weigh much more.

"I want to ride a pony," Lizbeth said, dragging her feet.

"I know, darling." Amelia turned and knelt in front of the child. "I promise we'll ride a pony today, but first, you get to ride in a cart."

Lizbeth's face brightened. "Will it be fast?"

"Terribly fast," Amelia said, thinking of the sloping hill separating the Moorleigh estate from her brother's. She wondered if Stuart was home yet and which of his homes Ethan Moorleigh was at. While he was away, she had more freedom, but remembering the feel of his hand upon hers, Amelia wasn't entirely certain that freedom was what she wanted.

"What do you mean, they're not here?" Ethan tried to curb his temper as he listened to his butler's halting explanation of the events that had unfolded at his Bamburgh estate in the past twenty-four hours.

It seemed that his new wife and Lizbeth had arrived in the middle of the night, risen early this morning and breakfasted by themselves in the kitchen downstairs, had attempted to have a mount prepared, and had last been seen heading toward Stuart Preston's estate, Lizbeth riding in a *gardener's cart*, which Amelia was pushing to and fro as if she were intoxicated.

"I see," Ethan said, and he did. Stuart's sister was mad. No wonder she'd been locked up in an abbey. No wonder Stuart had been so willing to give her in marriage.

Some grand gesture. Some friend.

Ethan left the house and headed toward the stables. He'd only just arrived, but there would be no resting until he saw Lizbeth safe and sound—and saw Amelia rebuked for the danger she'd placed his daughter in.

Lizbeth . . . in a cart . . . down that steep hill.

I may become a murderer yet.

He chose the fastest horse and left the yard at a gallop, hoping Amelia wasn't too far ahead. If she'd obtained a horse and she and Lizbeth had ridden out, she could be anywhere on Stuart's estate.

When the slope at the bottom of the hill leveled off, Ethan reined his mount toward the stables. As he came around the side of the building, he caught sight of a horse and two riders in the adjacent field.

He rode closer, hobbled his mount, and stood watching them, his bride and his daughter, riding astride a horse—the oldest he'd ever seen. Likely the only danger lay in the possibility of the animal suddenly dying.

But the fact remained that Amelia had taken Lizbeth, convinced his coachman to drive hours to the home Ethan frequented the least, and explicitly disobeyed his standing orders by riding a horse.

He should have been furious, but at her gumption, he found himself fighting something akin to admiration and amusement—emotions he'd not experienced for a precious long time. Perhaps Amelia wasn't completely mad, just different.

Different from any woman he'd ever known.

Except Mary. She had been like this—well aware of what she wanted and resourceful enough to get it every time.

And look what it cost her.

Amelia would have to be punished or at least put in her place. He'd never been an overbearing sort with any of his wives, and he didn't wish to start off that way now. But something must be done before matters grew completely out of hand.

With purposeful steps, Ethan strode across the field, working up what he hoped was a ferocious scowl. He reached the gate, undid the latch, and stepped inside the paddock, knowing there was absolutely no danger of being trampled by the animal. The poor beast barely moved as it labored beneath its light load.

They came around again, and he stepped in front of the horse. It snorted a weary breath and looked at him in what almost seemed gratitude for being forced to stop.

"Papa!" Lizbeth held her arms out to him, and Ethan stepped closer, pulling her from the horse. With concerted effort, he refrained from smiling and greeting her with equal enthusiasm.

"What have I told you about horses?"

Her lips drew into a thoughtful pout. "That they're fast and uncontrollable and I may be killed if I ride one," she recited perfectly. "But Mama's old horse wouldn't hurt a flea." This also sounded like a recitation, and Ethan looked suspiciously at Amelia.

For a fleeting second, he questioned Lizbeth's free use of the word *Mama*, but he pushed his uneasiness aside. Surely his daughter had been referring to Mary. She couldn't possibly have taken to Amelia so quickly.

Could she?

He set Lizbeth down and took a step closer to Amelia, who'd dismounted on her own, and felt unnerved once more by her uncanny likeness to Mary.

"You rode, explicitly against my order." They made eye contact, and her other offenses temporarily fled his mind. Upon closer inspection, Amelia's eyes were different than Mary's—deeper brown. Her hair was a shade darker as well. And when she smiled, a tiny dimple formed on the left side of her mouth. She was *smiling* at him.

He remembered at once that he was supposed to be angry. "What did you mean by riding?"

"I meant to bring Lizbeth a little joy," Amelia said. "It would seem," she added drily, "the poor child has been sorely lacking that in her young life. What did *you* mean by leaving me at the altar to face a room full of strangers?" Her smile grew pert, and her brows lifted as if she actually expected him to answer.

"You reminded me of Mary," he admitted before he could think of a better excuse. "I hadn't expected that." *And it hurt.*

She must have discerned that anyway. "Oh." A sigh escaped her lips. "Well, then—"

"I'm sorry," he said, for the first time contemplating the embarrassment she must have felt. "I shouldn't have left you."

"No," she agreed. "You shouldn't have. It was quite awful." For a second, her face looked pained. "Let's start again, shall we?" She extended her hand as a gentleman about to strike a business deal, and Ethan found himself taken aback yet again.

He stuck his hand out as well, taking her slender fingers in his larger ones. Out of mere curiosity, he gave her hand a gentle squeeze, as he'd done at the altar to calm her obvious fear. Back in the chapel, he'd felt something tug at him, as she took her place at his side then almost immediately began to sway. He'd felt a hint of admiration for this unknown girl, his soon-to-be wife, who must have been terrified to be marrying a man who'd buried three wives.

He certainly hadn't expected her to squeeze back. Nor the havoc her simple touch had caused. Ethan found himself hoping to feel that again, the surprising warmth her affection had sent coursing through him. Emotions he'd long believed forever cold had stirred at her touch, and he wanted to see if he could feel them again.

As if she knew this, Amelia returned his grasp and furthered the damage by bringing her other hand over the top of his and patting him affectionately. Inward havoc flared to life.

"I'm sorry my appearance startled you," she said. "It was never my intention to remind you of Mary. Stuart has said how tender your affections for her remain."

Ethan was speechless. Amelia had married him knowing he still loved her cousin? What kind of woman would endure such a thing?

One desperate enough to escape a nunnery. A distant memory stirred, of Stuart telling how Amelia had cried dreadfully when he left her at the convent.

Had the convent been terrible for her all this time? Perhaps so much that she was willing to risk marrying a man rumored to have murdered three women.

Amelia's hand had stilled, though she did not release her grip on his hand. She cocked her head, eyeing him curiously. She'd likely think him mute if he didn't speak soon.

"About riding . . ." He cleared his throat. "My first wife was thrown. She struck her head and died."

"How terrible," Amelia said, eyes wide with dismay.

He nodded. "You see why now why I cannot allow you or Lizbeth to ride."

"But *you* ride." Amelia looked past him to the horse grazing on the other side of the fence.

"I'm not afraid of dying." How many times had he thought that very thing would be a blessed relief?

"Neither am I," Amelia said. "But I am very much afraid that you'll allow none of us to *live*, to experience the joy life has to offer. Don't you want Lizbeth to know the feeling of a fine animal beneath her, and the wind blowing in her hair? Would you deny her the opportunity to sit atop a mountain at sunrise or to ride along the beach as the tide washes in?"

Yes! He wanted to shout it. Any one of those things could prove fatal. The combination of the ocean and riding particularly frightened him, where there was both the danger of being thrown and the danger of drowning.

But he couldn't argue with Amelia's logic. Looking at it from her point of view, he was the insane one. He might as well have been dead the past three years, for all the joy he had felt. And Lizbeth . . . He glanced down at the child, arms flung wide as she spun in circles around them, giggling with each turn. When had she last been allowed outside to run and play as a child ought?

Never.

"It is difficult to expose Lizbeth to dangers," he managed to say, neither denying Amelia's request, nor affirming it.

She lifted her face to his. "I imagine it must be *extremely* difficult." Her words were sympathetic, yet he didn't feel at all that she pitied him. He took a step closer, looking into the depths of her brown eyes, so full of intrigue. Only one day into their marriage, and she fascinated him. Ethan hadn't expected that. Or to feel anything at all for his fourth wife, other than gratitude that their vows gave him the possibility—in years to come—of producing an heir.

But at this moment, gratitude paled against the other emotions warring inside him. His head bent toward hers, and he wondered if she would mind very much if he kissed her, as he ought to have in the church yesterday.

Amelia's eyes never left his. He saw her swallow and heard her quick intake of breath. She knew his intent and did not flinch. Her lips curved up in the slightest smile.

Permission?

Ethan placed his other hand on Amelia's shoulder and closed the gap between them just as Lizbeth crashed into his legs. Her outstretched arms wrapped around his breeches and Amelia's skirt, cinching them together in a threesome.

Amelia laughed. It was a beautiful sound.

Ethan looked down at his daughter and noted a smile brighter than any he'd ever seen.

"Papa. Mama," she said, looking up at them.

Instead of hurt, he felt a tiny corner of his broken heart begin to mend.

Seven

Amelia stood beside Ethan in the doorway of the nursery, watching as the planes of his face softened and a tender expression came to his eyes as he looked upon Lizbeth, barely asleep.

"This is not how things are done, you know," he said.

"Perhaps it is how they *should* be done." Amelia's arm brushed against his, reminding her of that moment in the church. But this one felt infinitely better, the happiest of her life that she could recall. Together, she and Ethan had helped Lizbeth get ready for bed and had sat upon either side of her, telling stories until she fell asleep.

Thank you, God, she thought, sending a silent prayer heavenward. *And bless you, Stuart, for the gift of this family.*

"You are quite unusual." Ethan spoke without taking his eyes off his daughter. "Most women in your position have little to do with their own offspring, let alone another woman's."

"Most women miss out on a great deal," Amelia answered softly. "I would like to think I'd feel the same if I'd been raised as most nobles are, but I cannot deny that my time at the abbey made me yearn for a child and family to care for—and taught me a great deal about the satisfaction of doing for one's self. Nuns sew their own clothes, cook their own meals, and grow their own food. Taking care of a child is far more fulfilling than those tasks."

"And I have it on good authority that you are quite skilled with a gardener's cart." He looked down at her with a mischievous smile.

Amelia's stomach flip-flopped, and she felt a little off balance in an entirely new and delightful way. "Do I sense envy?" she asked. "Perhaps I should offer *you* a ride next time."

Ethan laughed—and looked as surprised by the sound as Amelia felt. Lizbeth stirred, so Amelia brought a finger to her lips and shushed him. He quieted, but his grin remained in place as they backed out of the room and he pulled the door partially shut behind them.

"No more cart rides," he said when they were in the hall.

She frowned. "Must you decry all amusement?"

He studied her a moment as if weighing his next words. "There are far *better* ways to be amused."

Show me, she wanted to say but dared not. He might have recited how unusual she was, but no woman could be so bold as to ask for affection.

No matter how much I long for him to hold my hand again or to kiss me.

So she said nothing but sighed inwardly and moved farther away so they would not accidentally touch again. Attempting to curb her wayward thoughts, she decided to bring up Mary—a risky proposition at best, as she'd learned the past few days at Bamburgh.

"I think Mary would be happy to know you've dismissed that horrid governess and that you're the one tucking Lizbeth in at night."

Gift of Love

Ethan's expression darkened, and Amelia caught a fleeting glimpse of pain etched in the lines on his forehead and even deeper in the blue pools of his eyes.

Stuart had been right in one thing, at least—Ethan Moorleigh still suffered from a broken heart. Less certain, Amelia thought, was her ability to heal it.

"Must you always bring her into our conversations?"

How long would it be before he was willing or able to speak of Mary—the invisible barrier between them? Amelia hadn't much hope of overcoming it, but perhaps, with time, his past with Mary might not be so intrusive.

"She was your wife and Lizbeth's mother. And my cousin. It would be difficult *not* to speak of her. But if that is what you wish . . ." They walked down the hall.

"I'm sorry." Ethan shook his head. "You're right, of course."

Amelia smiled. "Not many a husband will admit such to his wife."

He glanced at her sideways, his wry grin returning. "I've had a bit of practice."

She winced. "So you have." She said the words carefully so as not to reveal the hurt they caused. How would it be as Ethan's first wife, to have earned his affection without others to compete? When she agreed to the marriage, she hadn't expected to care for him. But she'd found very quickly that she did, and it seemed there was no hope of her feelings being reciprocated. Her fondness for Ethan grew daily, hourly—by the minute. The more time she spent in his presence, the more she craved it.

"Will you tell me about each of your wives?" A painful question, to be sure, but perhaps it would get her yearning under control.

Ethan stopped walking and turned to face her. "You're unlike any woman I've ever known, Amelia."

"Is that supposed to be a compliment?" Of course she

didn't want to be like his other wives, did she? Amelia wanted him to see her, to want her for who she was, not for a resemblance to Mary or for the possibility of passing his title, or even because she loved Lizbeth.

"It is most definitely a compliment." He began walking again, Amelia at his side until they reached the end of the hall. Ethan hesitated, and she waited for him to bid her good eve as he had the past two nights.

"Would you care to walk in the gardens?" he asked. "The moon is full tonight, and it isn't too cold out."

Amelia's heart beat faster. *He's requesting my company—without Lizbeth.* Somehow she managed to keep her composure. "Your gardens are lovely, but I long to visit the shore. It's been over five years since I walked near the ocean. I've missed it so." Again, Ethan hesitated. Amelia prayed silently that she hadn't ruined her chance.

"I've not been to the shore for many years myself," he said, his tone more subdued than before. "Abigail, my second wife, drowned there."

"I didn't realize—I'm sorry." Amelia meant it with her whole heart. Already she couldn't imagine the grief she would feel were something to happen to Ethan.

"What was it you told me the other day when you'd gone riding?" he asked.

"I don't remember." Amelia felt her face color. She'd been far too bold that day, and she'd let her imagination run so wild, that for a moment, she'd almost thought Ethan had meant to kiss her.

"Something about missing the joy of life." Ethan held out his arm. "I've missed the ocean too. I'd say we're both overdue for a visit."

Amelia took his arm, and they started down the stairs. She'd missed living near the coast but feared she had almost missed out on much, much more when she'd nearly refused to marry Ethan Moorleigh.

Gift of Love

"Have you ever been there?" Amelia craned her neck, looking up at Bamburgh Castle towering above.

"A few times. The views from the top are magnificent, but other than that, it's just an ordinary castle."

Amelia snorted. "There is nothing ordinary about a castle. Someday you must take me. I should like very much to see the inside and the view."

They'd picked their way through the rocks to the beach below, where she stopped, leaning against a boulder while removing her shoes.

"What are you doing?" Ethan asked, looking back at her.

"I intend to get the most from this experience," she said, wresting a boot from her foot. "I want to feel the sand between my toes and the water lapping against my ankles."

Did I really just say that? Amelia berated herself as she looked down, concentrating on the second boot. *Ankles.* A body part no respectable woman spoke of.

"You're going to freeze," Ethan predicted. And when she continued to tug at her stockings, he added, "You'd best hold your gown up, or you'll really be soaked."

"Of course," she said, as if such a thing weren't shameful. The harm was already done.

In for a penny... She pulled the stockings from her feet and stuffed them into one of her boots, all the while telling herself that she wasn't twelve anymore. She could no longer skip along the beach as she had as a child. *I'm a married woman now.* But just this once, this first time in so long, she wanted the freedom she used to have.

Amelia tied her cloak strings tightly then gathered a handful of gown and cloak in each hand, lifting the hems so they wouldn't drag along the shore. She sashayed past Ethan toward the water.

He shook his head in mock disparagement. "I'd have thought that, coming from a nunnery, my wife might show a bit more decorum."

"Am I a disappointment, then?" Amelia laughed, making light of the question that had worried her since the moment he'd left her in the church.

"Not at all." Ethan caught up with her, taking her arm and looking into her eyes. "You are a miracle—to Lizbeth and me."

His sincerity made her breath catch and her eyes smart. Ethan stepped closer yet, and Amelia tilted her head back, certain this time that she didn't misunderstand—he intended to kiss her.

He shouted instead, as the icy cold tide washed in, drenching them both. Her hem wasn't nearly high enough, and his breeches were wet above his boots. She hopped around madly, trying to restore feeling to her frozen feet. Ethan swore as he poured water from one of his soaked boots.

Amelia burst out laughing. "I do find this a *better* way to be amused."

"You want amusement, you say?" He reached for her, and Amelia ran, shrieking along the shoreline, sand squishing between her toes, and the water lapping at her feet. The cold was soon forgotten in her haste to get away—and again in his nearness when he caught up. Ethan grasped her from behind, holding her firmly around the waist. "If you're going to laugh at me, you may end up swimming."

She was about to beg mercy when he released her and stepped back. She whirled to face him and caught his stricken expression.

"I shouldn't have teased. People drown—"

His wife. "Oh Ethan, I'm sorry. I didn't mean to remind you." The tide washed in again, but this time, neither reacted. Amelia's frozen feet were nothing to the anguish he must have felt, to the cold that must have enveloped him when death dealt him a second and then a third blow.

Amelia stepped forward and reached for his hands. She took them in hers and held tight. "I promise to never go swimming." He didn't respond, but she didn't give up. "You must tell me of each of your wives. It will help us both. I'll understand. I'll know how to be more careful."

He met her gaze finally, and the stoniness of his seemed to crumble a bit. Amelia moved to his side and tucked her arm into his. She began walking, dragging him along until his steps were sure and silent beside hers. She didn't ask again. He would tell her if he wanted to. And if not, she would understand. Some memories were simply too painful to recall. She had a few of her own buried deep inside.

They walked a long time, until the rock sloped to the water and they were forced to climb or turn back. Silently, Ethan steered them the way they'd come; sometime in the past several minutes, he'd become the lead and she the subdued follower.

As I ought to have been to begin with, Amelia thought, regretting her childish behavior had reawakened his sorrow and ruined their evening.

He spoke suddenly. "Abigail and I were married for exactly one month—twenty-nine days longer than I was married to Clara, my first wife."

Amelia considered her words with care. "Clara was thrown from a horse—on your *wedding day?*"

Ethan shook his head. "The day after. She hadn't wanted to marry me; she was in love with another. But as is the lot of most women, she hadn't much choice."

What would have happened at the abbey if I had persisted in refusing Stuart?

"Clara had a large dowry," Ethan continued. "I had a title and holdings that needed upkeep. As everyone else saw it, we were a perfect match."

"Did you realize—before, I mean—that she didn't want to marry you?"

"Yes." Ethan looked out across the moonlit sea. "But I didn't realize the depth of her feelings until our wedding night. By then it was too late to do anything about it. I tried to be kind. I told her I'd be patient and give her time to adjust to our marriage . . . Early the next morning, she fled."

"Do you think . . . Did she take her life on purpose?" Amelia bit her lip, knowing she shouldn't have asked the question. Ethan wouldn't want to think of his wife burning in hell. Amelia had the hardest time curbing her thoughts around him. He was so easy to speak to, and he didn't tell her to keep her peace as the nuns oft had.

"She didn't take anything with her," Ethan said. "But I believe Clara was running away to meet with her lover; she'd threatened as much the night before when I bid her goodnight and left her alone in her room. I think her accident was truly that. In her haste to get away, she was careless and fell."

Amelia didn't know what to say, so she placed her other hand on his arm, as if that might somehow comfort him and convey the sorrow she felt on his behalf. The hurt she'd experienced when he'd left her at the church seemed insignificant when she imagined what Ethan must have felt at being left by his wife.

"Nine months later, I married Abigail. We were friends, at least, and I believed we were compatible. I was away for a few days, and the very night I returned, her body was found washed up on the beach. People began to talk, saying I'd killed two wives in less than a year. I was some kind of monster and murderer." Ethan glanced at Amelia as if to see what she thought of him now.

"Utter nonsense," she said, stamping her foot in the sand. *Painful nonsense.* How he must have hurt during that time.

He shrugged as if it didn't matter, but Amelia guessed it did; it must. The rumors still abounded. She'd overheard them on her march up the aisle. "I hadn't much hope of a future until Mary suggested we wed."

"*She* asked *you*?" Amelia's mouth hung open in astonishment.

"She did." A smile played at the corners of Ethan's mouth, and Amelia felt stung. She swallowed back her own hurt. *He still loves Mary. He will always love Mary.*

Ethan stopped, turning Amelia to him. "Every time I speak of her, I wound you. I'm sorry."

She shook her head, dismissing what must be the obvious truth on her face. "It's all right. She was your wife. You love her."

He didn't deny it, but before speaking again, he took a deep breath and looked out at the ocean a long minute. "The past is painful—yours as well, I'm guessing."

Amelia gave the barest nod. She'd no desire to speak of it. It wasn't worth revisiting—ever.

"That time is also behind us," Ethan said. "And it would serve us well to keep it that way. We've the present, and that's—"

"A gift from God," Amelia said. How many times had the abbess shared that same sentiment? Often, that first year or two at the abbey, when Amelia's longing for the home and family she'd lost had been all consuming.

"A gift," Ethan said, brushing his fingers along her cheek, "only becomes such when it is accepted."

Accept me, Amelia longed to say. Strangely, she felt he was asking the same of her. She closed her eyes, savoring his touch and wishing it would never end.

"Look at me, Amelia."

She obeyed, lifting her face to his.

Ethan placed his hands on her shoulders and bent closer, hesitating until she gave the barest nod. Her eyelids fluttered closed as his lips touched hers, warm and gentle. She stood perfectly still, hardly daring to breathe as his mouth caressed hers lovingly.

Heaven, she decided, *could be no better than this.*

After a moment, he stepped back. Disappointed that he'd stopped, Amelia opened her eyes and saw a slightly amused grin on his face. Worry surfaced through her haze of desire.

I've muddled something. Stricken, she gazed up at him, wishing she knew what to do, but feeling too weak to do it if she did, and still intoxicated by the desires his lips had awakened.

Ethan took her arms and looped them over his shoulders. "Hold on tight," he instructed, a rakish gleam in his eyes.

His lips found hers again, this time not as gentle. His kiss felt possessive, as if he was claiming her for his own. Amelia had a sudden urge to claim him back.

The past is behind us. She belonged to him now, and he to her. She wanted him to know that. Tentatively, she moved her lips against his. He groaned, and she pulled back, afraid again that she'd done something wrong. But he wouldn't let her go.

He wrapped his arms around her waist and whispered in her ear. "It's all right for you to kiss me too." She hesitated, still unsure. He leaned back, searching her eyes. "*Please,* Amelia."

The intensity of his request and his use of her name proved her undoing. Keeping her eyes locked with his, she placed her hands on the back of his neck, holding tight as he'd instructed. Rising up on her toes, she brushed her lips against his softly at first then more forcefully as she gave in to her passion. He followed her lead, mimicking her movements, drawing ever closer and deeper until she thought she'd faint from lack of breath.

At last they pulled apart, but Ethan kept an arm around her, and with his other hand drew her close to his heart.

The rapid beat made her smile. *She* had done that. No doubt her heart beat as frantically. He'd done that to her.

What a wondrous thing. She lifted her face to his, silently asking for more. The pain she'd seen in his eyes earlier had diminished, replaced by what she deemed a tentative hope. He bent to kiss her again. Amelia clung to him.

The moon was high by the time they finally started home. The air was colder, but every few steps along the beach found them in each other's arms again. Amelia felt perfectly warm. When they reached the lane that led from shore to the street above, Ethan knelt before her, replacing her stockings and shoes, his touch on her ankles a new pleasure in and of itself.

He drove the carriage with one hand, his other arm wrapped securely, possessively, around her. They left the carriage to be attended to then made their way to the house and upstairs, never once letting go of each other. At the doorway to her room, Ethan kissed her yet again then looked past her through the open door to the bed beyond.

Amelia wasn't certain what to do. She didn't want him to leave. But neither was she completely ready for him to stay.

As if he sensed her uncertainty, Ethan bent his head to hers, placing a tender kiss on the top of her forehead. "Thank you," he whispered. "For *much better* amusement." His gaze held hers for a moment, the intensity of his look reassuring her that the evening had been about much more than seeking amusement. They were putting their pasts behind them and embracing a future together. And they would proceed at her pace.

"Goodnight, Amelia." Ethan brushed his fingers along her cheek once more. "I think—" The heat in his gaze softened, turning to merriment. "—that you would have made a terrible nun." With a grin, he turned and left her, going down the hall to his own room.

Amelia watched until he'd gone inside and closed the door. She retreated to her room, where she flopped across the bed, ignoring the nightgown laid out for her.

With hands flung wide, she looked up at the ceiling and uttered the happiest prayer of her life.

Eight

Amelia woke to someone snuggling next to her—though not the person she'd been dreaming of.

"Are you ready?" Lizbeth asked, crawling over Amelia and peeling back one of her eyelids.

"To tickle you?" Amelia teased, staring one-eyed into Lizbeth's excited face that nearly touched hers.

Lizbeth giggled. "No. To pick berries. You promised."

"Did I?" Amelia marveled at the child's memory. An outing to pick berries had been mentioned only once, over a week ago. At the time, it had sounded like great fun, but this morning, Amelia's thoughts remained on a moonlit beach. She and Ethan had walked its shores again last night. Nothing she did today could prove better amusement than that.

Light flooded the room. Amelia rolled to her side, where her maid had drawn the curtains and was setting a breakfast tray on the night table.

I could grow accustomed to this. Amelia sighed, snuggling deeper into the covers, though Lizbeth did her best to pull them back. How lovely to wake in a big, comfortable bed with a fire already burning in the grate and a soft rug to walk on.

How delightful to have Lizbeth seeking my company. How amazing that her father does the same.

"Has Lord Moorleigh breakfasted yet?" Amelia sat up, deciding to forgo the tray in favor of a family meal in the dining room.

"Hours ago, ma'am. He left early this morning."

"He's gone?" Amelia tried to keep the alarm from her voice as she assisted Lizbeth in throwing back the quilt.

The maid nodded. "Hocksley may be able to tell you more."

Amelia turned away from the maid and held her arms out to Lizbeth. "We shall have to pick berries on our own." Amelia's voice sounded overly bright as she worked to conceal panic similar to what she'd felt when Ethan had left her at the church.

It was what she'd felt at twelve years when her father hadn't returned for her and she'd hidden a day and a half by herself before she was found and told that he was dead.

She'd experienced it again just months later when Mother fell ill and died suddenly and again when Stuart had brought her to the abbey and drove off, leaving alone her at the gates before the nuns had even come to open them.

Amelia set Lizbeth on the ground and hurried to dress.

Ethan did not abandon me. He'll return soon.

She repeated the sentiment throughout the whole morning they spent outside. The sun shifted overhead and stretched into the afternoon, and still she didn't allow herself to doubt.

But when evening came—and a storm with it—and she was still alone, her fears began to win.

NINE

Amelia looked up from the book she'd been reading, in what she'd come to think of as her chair near the fire. Stuart entered the library, and, without greeting her, went straight to the sideboard and poured himself a generous glass of brandy.

She stood quickly. "What has happened? Where's Ethan?"

"Dreadful weather outside." Stuart shook his head, and drops of water flung outward.

"Stuart." Amelia crossed the room and stood before him, certain he had terrible news. He reeked of alcohol, and his eyes were unfocused. "You're drunk." She reached for his glass, but he jerked it away.

"What is it about Ethan Moorleigh that women find so attractive? Is it because he owns everything for miles around?"

Amelia frowned. "You wanted me to marry Ethan."

"Didn't mean I wanted you to throw yourself at him," Stuart said, his words slurred. "I've seen the two of you at night coming home from your trysts on the beach."

She fought the urge to slap him. "We're *married*. I enjoy walking along the shore, and Ethan is kind enough to take me."

Unnerved by the anger in Stuart's eyes, she stepped back. "What's wrong with you? Ethan's your best friend. You ought to be worried—as I am—that he isn't home by now."

"I am home." Ethan appeared in the open doorway, Hocksley trailing behind, attempting to remove Ethan's overcoat and hat. Before he could, Ethan crossed the room, swept Amelia into his arms, and kissed her thoroughly.

She emerged from his embrace feeling slightly damp, ridiculously happy, and as if she were the one intoxicated.

"I missed you," he said. "You and Lizbeth were all I could think of today. I couldn't wait to get home."

"What kept you?" Stuart had set his glass aside and looked more like himself.

"Haven't you heard?" Ethan stepped back to allow Hocksley access to his coat. "One of my tenants lost an entire flock of sheep last night. Slaughtered. Every last one of them."

"How terrible," Amelia said. "The poor sheep."

"Poor shepherd." Ethan handed the butler his hat. "Thank you, Hocksley. That will be all." He turned to Amelia. "I'm sorry I didn't tell you I was leaving. You were asleep, and you looked so peaceful. I didn't want to disturb you."

"Next time, see that you do," she scolded, though inside she was swooning; he'd come to her room to see her. "What happened?" She stayed close to Ethan, placing distance between herself and Stuart, whose unaccountable mood seemed to have changed again. He leaned against the fireplace, feigning interest in a crystal figure on the mantel.

"Just another attack on Ethan and his property," Stuart

said, as if such a thing were of little consequence. "It's become somewhat of a—tradition."

Ethan sighed. "I'd hoped—now that I've married again—that this would stop."

"What would?" Amelia asked, some of her worry returning.

"'Monstrous acts against the monster.' Or something of that sort, we think," Ethan said. "It started before I married Abigail and then again just before I married Mary." He looked at Amelia apologetically. Since that first night at the shore, they had not spoken of Mary. "And again before we wed," Amelia guessed.

Ethan nodded. "Believing me a wife killer, people protested me marrying again."

"Though Ethan always comes out the hero," Stuart said. "I imagine come spring, your tenant will find himself gifted a new flock of sheep."

Amelia couldn't understand his sarcasm and found it unbecoming his status as Ethan's long-time friend.

"As is my responsibility," Ethan said. If he sensed anything amiss with Stuart, he didn't show it.

Did her brother often behave like this? Had she simply not been around him enough to notice?

"Any other problems?" Stuart asked casually.

"Just one," Ethan said. "An accident with the carriage."

"What?" Amelia took his hand.

"Nothing serious." He drew her closer, circling his arm about her waist. "How was Lizbeth today?"

"Delightful," Amelia said. "We picked berries."

"I'm sorry to have missed it." Ethan's face grew thoughtful. "When I think of the time I've lost—what a gift she is . . ." His eyes met Amelia's.

"You are fortunate," Amelia said. "You've many years left to share with your daughter."

Behind them, Stuart began a slow, steady clap. "Such a speech, dear sister. Have you told Ethan yet how it was you came to agree to marry him?" His gaze shifted to Ethan. "She was not willing at first, you know."

Amelia frowned at him, but she felt no shame when she spoke to Ethan. "It was the promise of Lizbeth that lured me," she admitted. "I wanted to care for her then, and I have enjoyed every minute of it. But I didn't realize—"

"That she would adore you the way she does." Stuart pushed off the fireplace and walked to the door. "Hocksley!" he called loudly. "Would you be so kind as to retrieve the parcel inside my coat? Take care with it. It's a gift for the newlyweds, and it is fragile."

Stuart pulled his head back into the room and turned to them with a smile. Amelia watched her brother warily. Something was definitely amiss, but she couldn't quite determine what it was.

Ethan seemed to sense it as well. "What brings you here tonight?" When Stuart peered out the door again, Ethan exchanged a curious look with Amelia.

"Overdue congratulations," Stuart answered. "On your wedding day, I wasn't certain if you two were going to suit at all. Happily, my fears were unfounded." He took a cloth bag from Hocksley. "Here we are. I acquired this some time ago and have been saving it for the right occasion." He withdrew a bottle from the bag and presented it to Ethan. "The finest from across the channel."

Ethan took the bottle, removed the cork, and sniffed. "Well-aged Merlot." He clapped Stuart on the shoulder. "A fine gift, though not so fine as the one you brought few weeks ago." Ethan winked at Amelia.

Hocksley stepped closer. "Would you like me to pour out?"

"No need," Stuart said, dismissing the butler as if he were his own. "Amelia can do it. She's used to serving."

"Be civil," Ethan warned, his hand dropping from Stuart's shoulder. "Amelia is my wife now, *Lady* Moorleigh."

"It's all right." Amelia took the bottle from Ethan. "He

isn't well," she mouthed before turning toward the sideboard.

She took out three new glasses then lifted the bottle to her nose and inhaled. Instead of the rich, sweet scent she'd expected, her nostrils flared and burned. This was a much stronger wine than she was used to making on the small press at the abbey. Much too strong, for Stuart, at least, who had drunk too much already.

Too strong for me, as well. She'd no desire to fall asleep early tonight but rather looked forward to a long evening with Ethan. Amelia glanced at the men, but neither was looking her way.

Quickly she switched out the bottle for another red wine, hiding Stuart's in a lower cabinet. They could have it another night—one that may not matter as much as she felt this one had the potential to.

Later tonight, when she and Ethan lingered outside her door, she would not release his hand. She wouldn't watch him walk to his room. Nor did she intend to enter hers alone.

If only Stuart would leave.

Amelia set the glasses on a tray and carried them to the chairs near the fire where Ethan and Stuart had taken seats opposite each other. She offered a glass first to Ethan then to her brother.

He held up a hand. "None for me. As you pointed out earlier, I'm already too far into my cups."

"First sensible thing I've heard you say tonight," Amelia said, returning the tray to the sideboard. She lingered there, wondering how she might get Stuart to leave or retire to one of the guest rooms, at least, now that he'd admitted he wasn't fit for travel.

She sipped from her glass and caught Ethan staring at her with such intensity that a burst of heat flared inside her. Their eyes met, and she knew he wanted the same thing as she—to be alone together.

Stuart droned on while Ethan's gaze shifted from her face downward, appraising her openly. Only days ago, she would have felt mortified to have him look at her so, and an embarrassed blush would have stained her cheeks. But now . . . Amelia knew that any color to her face had to do with an entirely different set of emotions.

Desire. Passion. Love.

Better amusement, too. She smiled coyly and returned Ethan's appraising look, allowing her eyes to roam over him possessively.

His smoldering look faltered, and he choked on the drink he'd just taken, coughing, until some came from his mouth.

Stuart rushed to his aid. "Should have warned you it was strong."

Amelia bit back a laugh and turned away, pretending to refill her glass. How she loved being able to affect him like that. How wonderful to make him feel something other than the sorrow he'd dealt with so long.

How wonderful he makes me *feel.*

After composing herself, Amelia glanced Ethan's direction again and caught him using his handkerchief to wipe at a spot on his trousers. When he discovered her watching, his eyes narrowed in a rakish stare that told her she'd pay later.

She couldn't wait.

She stood and walked over to stand behind Stuart's chair, hoping to break into their conversation and suggest that he retire for the night.

Ethan started up, staring at her again, tempting her more subtly, but obvious to her, nonetheless.

He drank from his glass—successfully this time—then ran his tongue over his lips so seductively she felt a little giddy and lightheaded just watching. She reached for the back of Stuart's chair, accidentally knocking the glass from her hand. It fell to the floor and shattered.

Amelia gasped, and Ethan jumped up. Only Stuart didn't react.

"Feeling unwell, sister?" he asked, as if he'd expected as much. "Don't fret. Ethan's not at his best either, though the poison may take a bit longer to get to him. He wasn't supposed to drink the wine. He was supposed to die earlier, in the carriage accident."

"What are you talking about?" Ethan's gaze snapped to Stuart; all traces of teasing and humor vanished.

"The end of the Moorleigh dynasty, of course," Stuart said casually.

Behind him, Amelia reeled. *Poison? Stuart, a murderer.* It couldn't be. And yet . . . Long-buried memories stirred. Her hand shook on the back of his chair.

Thinking fast, she made an exaggerated show of staggering toward the door. Ethan started toward her.

"Don't." Stuart withdrew a pistol and leveled it at Ethan's heart. "She'll be dead in a minute or two anyway. That's how long it took her mother."

Mother. Amelia crashed into the sideboard, partly on purpose, partly from shock. The half-empty bottle teetered then tumbled to the floor. She fell across the marble top, her arm reaching inside for the wine Stuart had brought.

"Why?" Ethan asked, his voice a mixture of bewilderment, pain, and anger.

Don't do anything foolish, she prayed, not daring to look at him.

"Why did I wait so long, you mean?" Stuart said.

Amelia put the bottle behind her and straightened.

"It's the least you deserve after stealing Clara," Stuart said. "One night with you, and she came to tell me we were over. She no longer wanted to leave you. Of course, I couldn't let her go back. And I couldn't let you keep Abigail."

His murderous statements hung in the air. Amelia felt truly sick, though she'd had none of the poisoned wine.

"Then there was Mary," Stuart continued. "I wanted

her, and she knew it. Yet she threw herself at you, so I couldn't claim her as mine. It took a while, but I got her in the end. The midwife was supposed to kill your brat, too."

Ethan's hands clenched into fists at his sides. Behind Stuart, Amelia inched closer.

"Why bring Amelia into this?" Ethan kept his gaze focused on the gun pointed at him.

"You were supposed to die before her," Stuart said. "Then I, the ever-loving brother, would step in to care for her—and the fortune you left."

Amelia lunged toward Stuart and smashed the bottle over the back of his head. The pistol fired into the opposite wall, and Ethan wrested it from Stuart's hand.

"Good gracious!" Hocksley entered the room.

Ethan used the back of the pistol to ensure Stuart's unconsciousness, and Stuart slumped forward, sprawling on the floor.

"We shall require some rope," Ethan said, addressing Hocksley. "And send for a carriage."

Amelia's hands came to her mouth as she looked at Ethan standing over Stuart's body. Her gaze shifted to the broken pieces of bottle and the poisoned wine pooling on the floor. She thought of what might have been and burst into tears.

TEN

"I thought you were going to show me the *inside* first," Amelia protested, as Ethan hurried her through the main hall and up the stairs of Bamburgh Castle.

"Another time," Ethan said. "I know the owner. Returning won't be a problem."

"Would that owner happen to be—you?"

He grinned. "Guilty, I'm afraid. Now come. There's a storm rolling in, and I want you to see this first."

She laughed and ran up the stairs after him. There wasn't much in Bamburgh that Ethan didn't own, as she'd learned in the month and a half since their wedding. But that wasn't why she loved him. Since the night Stuart had tried to kill them both, their bond had been unbreakable. Ethan had been her personal pillar of strength as she'd dealt with her brother's treachery and uncovered the truth about her parents' deaths.

By the time they reached the top of the steep, winding

staircase, she was breathing hard. Ethan opened the door and led her outside to very top of the castle. Amelia turned a slow circle, drinking in the breathtaking vistas stretching in all directions—the quaint town, sail-filled harbor, and windswept sea. But it was what she caught sight of on her last turn that sent her heart racing.

A four-poster bed—minus the canopy—had been placed atop the castle.

"Whatever were you—" Her question turned to laughter as Ethan swept her up in his arms and carried her toward the bed.

"An extraordinary woman like yourself deserves an extraordinary experience." He set her down gently. "One that *no other* has had."

Amelia's laughter died out, replaced by a fierce love for the man before her. She reached for him, pulling him down beside her, accepting his gift and its meaning.

She was not his first love, but his last, and they would take each day given them and savor it for the gift it was.

About Michele Paige Holmes

Michele Paige Holmes spent her childhood and youth in Arizona and northern California, often curled up with a good book instead of out enjoying the sunshine. She graduated from Brigham Young University with a degree in Elementary Education and found it an excellent major with which to indulge her love of children's literature.

Her first novel, *Counting Stars* (Covenant Communications, 2007), won the 2007 Whitney Award for Best Romance. Its companion novel, a romantic suspense titled, *All the Stars in Heaven* (2009), was a Whitney Award finalist, as was her first historical romance, *Captive Heart* (2011). *My Lucky Stars* (2012) completed the Stars series.

When not reading or writing romance, Michele is busy with her full-time job as a wife and mother. She and her husband live in Utah with their five high-maintenance children and a Shitzu that resembles a teddy bear, in a house with a wonderful view of the mountains.

You can find Michele at MichelePaigeHolmes.com, on Facebook, and Twitter @MichelePHomes (preschooler permitting).

A LESSON IN LOVE
by Sarah M. Eden

Other Works by Sarah M. Eden

Seeking Persephone

Courting Miss Lancaster

The Kiss of a Stranger

Friends and Foes

An Unlikely Match

Drops of Gold

Glimmer of Hope

As You Are

Longing for Home

Hope Springs

For Elise

Timeless Romance Anthology series

ONE

1813—London

Lucy Stanthorpe had every intention of taking London entirely by storm. She was returning in triumph, having survived two Seasons as a debutante and ultimately securing for herself a husband any lady would be proud to call her own. She had her darling Reed to go with her to balls and musicales, and to drive her about Hyde Park during the fashionable hour. She wouldn't spend the entire Season sitting alone in the parlor, or unclaimed for dance after dance at the fashionable balls. She could go to every event with her husband at her side. And she would love every elegant minute.

This Season would be simply wonderful.

"I wonder what will be playing at the Theatre Royal," Lucy said as the carriage rolled over the cobblestones toward their London home. *Her* London home. It was a wonderful thing to have a place of her own, one she and Reed would come to every year, where she could host her own at-homes and balls, where they would one day have children in the nursery and years of memories. "Lady Parvell will, I am certain, host her annual musicale. And I have missed the British Museum. We must visit it this summer."

Reed nodded as he flipped a page of the newspaper. "I understand the Egyptian collection has been recently expanded."

The first thing they'd found in common was their love of history and the museum. She wouldn't have to spend the Season begging her father to take her to see the exhibits.

"Ooh, and Gunter's for ices." Lucy grinned at the reminder of one of London's greatest treats. "And Hyde Park during the fashionable hour." Reed had taken her for a drive in the park more than once in the final days of their courtship. She'd come to love going to the park with him for company.

Reed gave her a quick smile. She hoped that smile of his would always make her a little giddy.

The carriage pulled to a stop in front of the tall, columned Stanthorpe family London residence. Reed's mother was spending the Season in the country with her sister, so they would have the house entirely to themselves.

"Welcome home, darling," Reed said, leaning in to press a quick kiss to her lips. One corner of his mouth twitched upward, his eyes twinkling. "What I wouldn't have given to say that to you this time last year."

She shook her head at his comment. "We didn't know each other yet this time last year."

"Oh, I assure you, I knew exactly who you were long before we were formally introduced."

That was a bouncer if ever she'd heard one. The Stanthorpes sat on a more elevated rung of Society than her family could claim. She doubted Reed had taken even a passing notice of her before being all but forced to dance with her at the Parvells' ball the Season before.

Lucy gave his shoulder a playful shove. "You are an unrepentant flirt, my dear."

"I speak only the truth."

The carriage door opened. The footman put down the step. Reed folded his paper and tucked it under his arm then stepped out of the carriage. He turned back once his feet were on the walk and held his hand out for her. He never failed to offer her that courtesy, just as he always offered his arm when they walked together and kissed her farewell every time they parted. Was it any wonder she adored this thoughtful, loving man?

Reed pulled her arm through his and walked with her up the front steps, where the butler held the door for their arrival. "Welcome home, Mr. and Mrs. Stanthorpe."

Lucy only just held back a giggle. Even after seven months, she still loved to hear herself addressed as Mrs. Stanthorpe.

"We are most happy to be back in Town again, Taylor," Reed said. "I trust our rooms are ready for us?"

"Of course, sir."

"Perfect. Would you send word to the kitchens to have our dinner brought to Mrs. Stanthorpe's sitting room?"

"Of course, sir."

She and Reed walked up the elegant front staircase. "Oh, darling," she said. "This will be the very best Season I have ever spent in London. I am certain of it."

He lifted her hand to his lips and pressed a light kiss to her knuckles. "Indeed. I find myself looking forward to the next few months, something I don't usually feel at this time of year."

Musicales. Balls. Soirees. The theater. Her mind simply spun with all of the wonderful things they would see and do. And they would see and do them together.

It would all be perfect. Positively perfect.

Reed Stanthorpe couldn't imagine a better prospect for a London Season. Days at his club. Afternoons at Gentleman Jackson's Boxing Salon. Quiet evenings at home. Heaven knew he'd spent more than his share of Seasons forced into the social whirl. If there'd been any other way of undertaking a courtship, he'd have jumped at the opportunity.

But he was a married man now. No longer would he have to run from one social engagement to another, or stay up until all hours of the night, or drag himself through the interminable evenings at Almack's. He wouldn't need to endure the tiresome company of Society every single evening. He'd have Lucy's companionship, which was all he really wanted. Most everyone else grew tedious after a few encounters.

"What do you think of this gown, dearest?" Lucy leaned closer to him. They sat side by side on the sofa in her sitting room, having finished the fine meal Cook sent up for them. Lucy pointed to a sketch of a gown in her copy of *La Belle Assemblée*. "This style is a bit bolder than any I've worn before, but I'm a married woman now, so I'm permitted more options."

Reed didn't know much about ladies' fashion and couldn't say what exactly was different about the gown she pointed out from those she'd worn before. "I think it's lovely."

"So do I."

He adored the way her eyes danced about when she was excited. Society had such a dampening effect on the natural exuberance of a debutante. He'd seen that in her face when they'd been introduced. She was bubbling over with life and enthusiasm. He'd known from that moment on that he simply had to know her better—that the woman behind those dancing eyes was worth the aggravation of endless

A Lesson in Love

social calls and balls and trips to the theatre.

"And, thank the heavens, I am no longer confined to pastels." Lucy groaned dramatically, as if her previous color palette had been a most excruciating form of torture. "I have decided I absolutely must have a dress in a vibrant shade of blue."

Reed nodded his approval. Though he knew little about fashion, his lovely wife already had a dressing gown of blue. When she wore that shade, her eyes looked like sapphires, and her hair shone like gold.

"I am sorely tempted to buy myself a matching silk turban with a very tall feather to wear at balls," she declared firmly.

"Good gracious, no."

His immediate objection brought a wide-eyed look of surprise to her face.

"Darling," he said. "Only the oldest and dreariest of matrons wear feathered turbans."

"Doesn't your mother wear one?"

"Yes, which is—" He stopped short at the overly innocent look in her eyes. She was funning him, the little minx. Two could play at that game. "Which is, come to think of it, actually a very convincing argument. A feathered turban, yes, but don't neglect a powdered wig to complete the ensemble."

Her smile spread until her dimples reappeared. "A powdered wig for you as well, my dear. And knee breeches and heeled dancing slippers with great gold buckles."

"And shall I sport yards and yards of lace as well?" he asked.

"Of course." She looked ready to burst with laughter. "We will be quite the fashionable couple amongst the older set."

He slipped his arm around her shoulder and pulled her closer to him. "As much as I complain about the ridiculously close cut of today's jackets and the tedious nature of having my cravat tied in the latest style, I do not for one moment wish to trade that for the cumbersome fashions of our parents' generation."

Lucy set her magazine on the seat beside her and shifted so she knelt on the cushion facing him. She reached up and touched his face. "Even in the most ridiculous fashions, you would be the most handsome gentleman I've ever known."

"Flattery, my love?"

"I speak only the truth," she said, repeating the declaration he'd made in the carriage earlier. Her teasing tone indicated she'd chosen the response on purpose.

Reed kissed her well and deeply before pulling her fully into his arms. Yes, a Season spent quietly at home, away from the hustle and bustle of Society. Just the two of them. The perfect London Season.

Two

"Reed." Lucy stood in the doorway of Reed's bedchamber, looking with dismay on her husband in his shirtsleeves, his cravat tossed aside, and his feet shoeless. "You cannot go out dressed the way you are."

Though none of her new, fashionable gowns had arrived from the *modiste*, she had chosen the most modish of her older gowns to wear that night. Her abigail had threaded ribbons through her hair and quite artfully tucked tiny white flowers throughout. And Lucy had chosen to wear the amber necklace Reed had given her at Christmas. She'd taken great pains in her preparations, and there Reed sat in his shirtsleeves.

He kept his gaze on the paper held unfolded in front of him. "I mean to stay in tonight."

Lucy stepped inside. Surely Reed was teasing. He'd required prodding each evening since their arrival in London, but tonight was different. They were scheduled to attend the Parvells' ball, the event at which they had first been introduced the year before. On that night a year earlier, she'd arrived nervous and unsettled, so afraid of spending the evening as a wallflower. But then she'd met him, and everything in both of their lives had changed for the better. The Parvells' ball would always be special to the two of them.

Lucy stepped inside. "Tonight is the *Parvells' ball*, dearest," she reminded him.

"We have been out every evening this week," he said. "I am too weary to go out again."

They had indeed attended several functions over the past few nights, but Reed had insisted on returning home long before the events were over. They'd not been out late; neither had they attended more than one function in any given evening. Furthermore, he'd spent the day at his club. How could he be too tired for a ball, especially *this* one? This was their special anniversary.

"We replied to the invitation already, Reed. The Parvells are expecting us."

"The ball will be exceptionally crowded." He turned a page of the paper, slumping down in his chair a little more. He was the very picture of a gentleman settling in for a long, leisurely read. "The Parvells will not notice our absence, nor will they care."

"I will care," she answered. "I have been looking forward to this evening. And I am already dressed to go."

"But, as you pointed out," he said, "I am not."

"I cannot go without you," she said, her voice quieter than before. Married women had more freedom than unmarried, but to attend a ball without her husband when they were only newly married would be not only noted, but fodder for the gossips. More than that, she *wanted* him to go with her. "We needn't stay beyond the supper dance."

He lowered his paper and looked at her over it, his expression one of near exasperation. "The supper dance isn't until one o'clock in the morning. I have no desire to be out that late."

"But we would be out together. And we could dance with each other."

"We have been out almost every night since arriving in Town."

She stepped to his chair, unsure what to make of the annoyance in his face. "Have you not enjoyed the Season thus far?"

"I would enjoy the Season far more if I were permitted to spend it in peace and quiet." His sincerity could not have been more apparent. He didn't seem angry, simply determined to remain home.

Lucy held back the immediate protest that sprang to her lips. Perhaps he really was tired. He had objected the evening before, and she'd pleaded with him until he agreed, just as she had the evening before that and the one before that. She didn't want to argue with him again. If he didn't wish to go to their special anniversary ball, she wouldn't press him to.

"I won't pester you to go. There will certainly be other balls." She managed a bit of a smile.

"Yes, there are always other balls," he said dryly, a touch of a smile on his face.

Lucy pondered that a moment, even after Reed raised his paper once more. He'd always seemed to enjoy balls while he was courting her. Not only balls; he'd eagerly sought her out at musicales and soirees, and he'd visited her family box at the theatre every time she was in attendance.

So why was he chafing so much at the social whirl now? While they were yet unwed, he could only have enjoyed her company for the brief moments allotted a couple with no understanding between them. But now married, they would have each other's company the entire night at whatever event they attended.

Perhaps that is the difficulty. He has grown weary of me.

Lucy refused to ponder that idea more deeply. "I'll leave

you to your paper, then." She leaned down and kissed his cheek.

He gave her a fleeting smile then returned to his reading once more. She returned to her room. There was no need to tug the bell pull; her lady's maid hadn't left yet.

"Were you needing something else, ma'am?" The maid's look of confusion was more than understandable.

"There's been a change of plans," Lucy said, keeping her expression and tone light. "We will be staying in tonight."

And they stayed in the next night, and the night after that. For an entire fortnight, the pattern repeated. She dressed for the evening's engagement then attempted to convince him to join her. Sometimes he did. Most times he did not.

The night of her dearest friend Fanny Alistair's ball, Lucy stepped into Reed's room once more, a feeling of dread settling on her shoulders. She'd lived this moment so many times over the past weeks, never sure if Reed would agree to an evening out. He'd not once agreed to attend a ball.

Her heart dropped at finding her husband in his usual nightly state of half-dress. They'd spoken only that morning at breakfast of Fanny's ball and Lucy's desire to attend. He couldn't have forgotten.

"Reed?"

He looked up. She could see in his eyes that he knew immediately what she'd come to ask. "I suppose this means you don't wish to stay in tonight?"

"Tonight is Fanny's ball," she reminded him. "I have longed to attend a ball."

His shoulders slumped. "There will always be others. We needn't to go to all of them."

"*All* of them? We haven't gone to any of them."

"But balls are so tedious. Wouldn't you rather have a quiet evening—"

"A quiet evening at home?" She repeated the phrase she'd heard from him more than any other the past two weeks. "There wasn't a single Society function last Season you didn't seem to make an appearance at," Lucy said. "You danced with me at every ball, sat beside me at every musicale."

Reed rose from his chair and crossed to the doorway. "Of course I did, Lucy. Every unmarried gentleman knows what is required of him. We dance that dance because we must."

"I don't understand."

He took her hands in his. That familiar gesture set her thoughts more at ease. No matter their different preferences of late, he was ever tender and kind. She disliked feeling at odds with him.

"I attended the balls and soirees and everything else last Season because you were there," Reed said. "I was courting you, dear. A suitor is required to do all those things. A husband is not."

A husband is not. The pieces began to fall into place. "Now that you've secured yourself a wife, you aren't obligated to squire her about to all those 'tedious' affairs."

"No, thank the heavens." He smiled as if being excused from accompanying her to those same entertainments they had once enjoyed was the greatest of escapes. Had he feigned his pleasure the Season before? Or did he simply not wish to be bothered to take her about?

"You don't wish to go to Fanny's ball tonight?"

He slipped a hand beneath her chin and gave her a quick kiss on the lips. "No gentleman ever wishes to go to a ball. We only go when we absolutely have to, but once that obligation has passed we happily leave the chore to those gentleman still neck-deep in the Marriage Mart." He gave her a lopsided smile then walked back to his chair.

This was her future then. She would either be forced to attend balls alone and be a wallflower as she'd feared during her time as an unwed young lady, or she would spend her nights in Town gazing out windows, wishing her husband had enjoyed dancing with her as much as he'd pretended to.

A suitor is required to do all those things. A husband is not.

She had been worth the effort of a courtship before they married. Now that he'd secured her hand, going about with her was seen as a chore, a distasteful bit of effort he'd rather not make.

Lucy returned to her bedchamber as she had so many times over the past two weeks. Her maid had taken to simply waiting for her. In silence, she helped Lucy undress then pulled the many pins from her hair.

Why did I even bother?

She felt rather like an old pair of slippers. She wanted to be worth the effort to him again. She wanted the feeling of being cherished and treasured, the joy of dancing with him, of watching for him to appear at her theatre box. She wanted him to do all those things, not because courtship *required* it of him, but because he wished for her company.

Her "perfect" Season had crumbled. She had looked forward to the coming months with eager anticipation. Then Reed declared going about with her a "chore." Her heartache began to give way to frustration then a surge of determination.

Perhaps it is time Reed discovered what life is like without his comfortable old slippers.

Three

Lucy occasionally took a breakfast tray in her room, so Reed thought little of it when she didn't join him for the morning meal. He spent a leisurely few hours at his club then an invigorating afternoon at Gentleman Jackson's. He fully expected to find Lucy up and about when he arrived home. The sitting room, drawing room and back gardens, however, were empty.

Lucy wasn't in her rooms or his. He made a quick check of the guest bedchambers and nursery, on the off chance she might be there. But in the end, he returned to his wife's bedchamber baffled.

Perhaps she was out making morning calls. The hour was only a bit late for that. She might simply be on her way back.

He moved toward the door, intending to spend some time in his book room, catching up on a few matters of business. He stopped, however, before stepping out of Lucy's bedchamber. Reed looked back at the room. Something about it was different, odd. But what?

The furniture was all the same and in the same places. He didn't think the curtains were different or the coverlet on Lucy's bed changed.

Where are her perfume bottles and her hairbrush?

Lucy kept more knickknacks on her dressing table than anyone Reed had ever known. But the dressing table was empty. Utterly. He pulled open the doors of her wardrobe and found it as empty as her dressing table. His wife and all her belongings had vanished.

What in heaven's name? Reed tugged on the bell pull. Someone in the house had to have seen her that day. Someone must know what had happened.

A moment later, one of the chambermaids stepped inside.

"I had hoped to speak with Mrs. Stanthorpe's abigail," Reed said.

"Begging your pardon, sir, but she's gone with Mrs. Stanthorpe."

Ah. Someone did know something. "And where did Mrs. Stanthorpe go?"

"I don't rightly know, sir. But she left in the carriage."

The driver would know where he'd taken Lucy. "Thank you," Reed said.

She gave a quick curtsey and scurried from the room. Reed waited but the briefest of moments before walking to the entryway. After inquiring of the footman whether or not the carriage had returned and learning that it had, Reed sent word to the stables that he wished the carriage brought around.

While he waited, Reed had ample time to ponder the odd turn of events, as he couldn't make sense of it. Where could Lucy possibly have gone, and why would she have taken her clothes, perfume, and jewelry with her?

With the precision Reed had come to expect from ever-efficient Taylor, the butler arrived at the front door in time to open it just as the carriage came to a stop in front of the house.

"What instructions do you wish me to convey to John Coachman, Mr. Stanthorpe?"

"Ask him to take me to the same destination he took Mrs. Stanthorpe earlier today."

"Very good, sir."

Reed settled into the carriage, his curiosity growing by leaps and bounds. He couldn't make heads nor tails of Lucy's departure, especially with her belongings missing, but felt certain the mystery would be clear soon enough.

The carriage wheels rolled over the cobbled streets, keeping to the finer areas of Town. At least Lucy hadn't wandered into dangerous corners. He recognized the house where the carriage at last stopped.

Why would Lucy bring all her belongings to her parents' home?

Reed climbed out of the carriage and made his way to the door. A moment later, the very proper butler welcomed him inside. As a member of the family, Reed wouldn't be required to stand on ceremony the way a visitor would.

"Good afternoon, Graves." Reed gave the butler a quick nod of acknowledgement.

"If you would, please, sir your calling card." Graves held his hand out, his bearing as haughty as any proper butler's ought to be, but with the smallest hint of apology in his eyes.

Reed didn't immediately comply. He was family. Family didn't generally present their cards when visiting. But Graves didn't give over.

Perhaps old Graves is beginning to lose hold of his faculties.

Reed pulled his card case from his jacket pocket and took one out. He handed it to the butler, unsure what to expect. The butler dipped his head and disappeared up the stairs.

Poor man must be feeling off today. He left me waiting here as though I were a presumptuous mushroom rather than a member of the family.

The grandfather clock near the door loudly counted off the seconds as Reed stood in solitary silence. Even if Lucy had left already, Reed's parents-in-law should have welcomed him in with none of the formality generally required of a caller.

Lucy's mother appeared at the top of the stairs. "Mr. Stanthorpe. What a pleasure to see you again."

She didn't come toward the entry way, but stood looking down on him, her bearing regal and unfailingly polite. And she'd called him "Mr. Stanthorpe," a formality they'd done away with not long after he'd married her daughter.

"Mother Harrison," he greeted, trying to clamp down his growing confusion. "I had hoped to speak with Lucy. I understood she was here."

She gave him a patient smile. "Now, now, Mr. Stanthorpe. Our at-home day is Friday. Today, as you must know, is Thursday."

What the deuce did their at-home hours have to do with the matter? He'd come for his wife. He wasn't some hapless suitor or socially inept neighbor.

"Do come by tomorrow during our at-home," Mrs. Harrison said. She gave him a quick smile and turned about, walking away with no further explanation.

What the blazes was that about? A few of his cronies had spoken of their mothers-in-law in terms one generally reserved for rabid and difficult dogs, but Reed had never seen Mother Harrison act the part of a dragon. She'd always been kind and affectionate toward him.

"Psst."

Reed glanced about but couldn't identify the source.

"Psssst." The sound was louder, more urgent than before. "Reed, my boy. Up here."

A Lesson in Love

He followed the voice and spotted his father-in-law on the first floor-landing above. Mr. Harrison waved him up.

"Quickly, son, before the ladies spot you."

Reed heard in Mr. Harrison's voice the promise of an explanation and didn't hesitate. He took the stairs two at a time then followed Mr. Harrison down the corridor. He'd never before thought of his father-in-law as spry, but the gentleman was making short work of their journey.

Mr. Harrison pulled open the door to his book room, a room Reed had been in more than once. "Inside. I don't think they've seen you."

Why was not being seen so important when Reed had come specifically to see someone? He stepped into the book room and found it wasn't empty. His brothers-in-law, both of them, sat near the fireplace, watching his entrance.

"Robert," he said. "Charles."

"Good afternoon, you twit," Charles greeted him with a smile. He was married to Lucy's older sister and was the closer of the two gentleman to Reed's age.

Mr. Harrison had taken his place in a leather armchair near his sons-in-law. All three watched Reed with looks of almost comical concern.

"What is this?" Reed asked. "A council of war?"

"We are staging a daring rescue." Mr. Harrison's tone was utterly serious, though his eyes twinkled with a bit of mischievousness.

"And whom are you rescuing?" Though he asked the question, he suspected he knew the answer.

"Have a seat, son." Mr. Harrison motioned to the empty spot on the sofa. "We are here to save you from yourself."

Reed looked at them each in turn. "Save me from myself?"

"Apparently, brother," Charles said, "you told your wife that husbands aren't required to squire their wives around, and that attending social functions is a distasteful chore."

"But it *is* a distasteful chore."

"Oh, we all know that," Robert, Lucy's brother, replied. "But we have the sense to not say as much to our wives."

"I—" Reed had a sudden realization. "How do the three of you know about that conversation?"

"Lucy arrived this morning with a bee in her bonnet," Mr. Harrison said. "She and her mother closed themselves up in the sitting room for a full hour. Then the flood of Harrison ladies began."

Robert took up the tale. "Mother sent notes to Clarissa and Amelia, insisting they were needed 'immediately' to sort out a problem of 'unparalleled urgency.' Your fateful error was revealed, and here we all are."

"So Lucy *was* here." He hadn't managed a straight answer from Mrs. Harrison.

"*Is* here, my friend." Charles looked ready to burst out laughing. "Lucy *is* here."

"Perfect." Reed stood up. "Nice to see you all again."

"Sit, you muttonhead." Charles went so far as to roll his eyes. "You are in far too deep to get out that easily."

He slowly lowered into his seat. "I think you had better tell me the whole story."

"First," Charles said, "you never tell your wife that time spent with her is a 'chore.' She'll think that means you don't care for her company."

"But that's not what I said."

"It doesn't matter what you say," Charles insisted. "All that matters is what she hears, and the two are often very different from each other."

"Furthermore," Mr. Harrison said. "There is nothing a husband is permitted to believe he is no longer required to do once he is married. Though the list of things we'd *prefer* not to do is long and detailed, we keep that list to ourselves."

"Are you trying to say that I'm in trouble with Lucy?"

"You have moved far beyond *trouble*," Charles said.

All three men were clearly laughing at him. Either Lucy wasn't as upset with him as they were letting on, or they were enjoying the thought of his apparent impending doom. "And I am in my wife's black books because I told her that gentlemen don't actually enjoy balls?"

"Yes," Mr. Harrison said. "And that spending time with her was unpleasant."

"I never said that."

"Again," Charles jumped in. "What you *said* is of little importance."

Mr. Harrison continued with his explanation. "Lucy told her sympathetic female relations that you haven't attended any balls with her since arriving in London. You have refused to attend any number of Society functions—most of them, in fact."

Reed leaned back, eyeing them each in turn. He could feel something like a smirk tug at his mouth. "So you are all envious, that's what this is. You have been forced to attend those things and can't believe I managed to get out of the obligation."

"Envious?" Robert actually chuckled. "Our wives aren't in the sitting room conspiring against *us*, Reed. I think you are the one who ought to be jealous."

"Conspiring against me?"

Mr. Harrison's grin only grew. "The ladies of this family mean to teach you a lesson, son. And if I know them as well as I think I do, they will succeed."

"What is it to be, then?" Reed asked. "Am I to be stretched on the rack or locked up in the dungeon?"

"Worse even than either." Mr. Harrison's eyes danced with amusement. "You are to be forced to court your own wife."

"Oh, good heavens," Reed muttered, beginning to understand what his father-in-law was hinting at.

"You are to be subjected to at-homes and requesting permission to dance at balls and visits to the family box at the opera. And I have been instructed to make it difficult for you." Mr. Harrison's look of empathy clearly indicated he would do nothing of the sort. "Never tell your wife that you're not required to court her unless you are fully prepared to do so."

Reed shook his head in disbelief. "Where in the world did this come from? Lucy didn't seem upset last night."

Charles and Robert exchanged knowing looks. Reed eyed them both. Charles took pity on him and explained.

"Considering the number of social functions we have not seen you at this Season, I am certain Lucy has been stewing over this for some time. She might not have seemed upset last night, but I can guarantee she was."

Robert nodded. "And since all of our wives have, at one time or another, been upset with us over our disinterest in squiring them about, Lucy has found an entire house full of sympathizers."

"I will have to go through with this, then?" Reed slumped lower in his seat. This Season was supposed to have been simple and easy.

"*Yes.*" Mr. Harrison pulled the single syllable out long. Spoken in that way, his yes sounded far more like "in a manner of speaking."

Reed's companions looked at him pointedly, their expressions growing instantly conspiratorially.

He leaned forward. "What do you have in mind?"

Four

Lucy sat in her parents' drawing room, chatting amicably with many visitors, as she had the previous two Seasons. And, as she had the year before, she found herself watching the door, hoping each new arrival was her Reed. A flutter of anticipation seized her with the very first visitor and only grew as time passed.

I have missed this.

Though last Season, not knowing if he would visit or dance with her, or invite her to ride out with him had been a source of worry, every time he had come by or had spoken to her or sent her flowers, she'd known with absolute certainty that he cared about her. She'd known he thought her worth the effort. *That* was what she'd missed—the little things that said he valued her.

Their at-home hours were nearly gone. Lucy caught her mother's eye, silently asking the question on her mind. *Where is Reed?*

Mother's eyes softened, and she gave a quick nod of reassurance. She had insisted, along with Lucy's sister and sister-in-law, that Reed would most certainly come call on her. Husbands grew lonely for their wives, they said. Having not seen her in a day and a half, Reed would realize how much he enjoyed her company and would do whatever he must to see her.

That was the crux of their plan, at least. Reed took her for granted. Requiring him to make even a minimal effort would show him how fortunate he was to have her as his wife. Perhaps he would decide that dancing with her and accompanying her to Society functions were not such chores after all.

Only a moment more passed, and there he stood. Reed greeted Mother first, as was proper, she being the hostess of this at-home. He smiled and nodded at the others in the room, a quick and unexceptional means of acknowledging everyone without taking time to do so individually.

Which will mean more time for the two of us to converse.

Reed took the empty chair nearest her. She kept her eyes trained on him, her smile feeling more natural by the moment. He was here. He had come.

His eyes met hers. She held her breath, excitedly anticipating the twinkle of mischief she'd so often seen there. But his gaze was little more than polite.

"Good afternoon, Mrs. Stanthorpe," he said, his voice low enough to not be overheard by those conversing with her mother and sister. "Fine weather we are having."

Mrs. Stanthorpe? They had on occasion resorted to formal address with each other when in public, especially amongst the older set, who were quite particular about that. But it was decidedly odd for him to not call her by her Christian name in her own parents' house, when they were the only two taking part in the conversation.

And had his first words to her after more than a day apart truly been a comment on the weather?

A Lesson in Love

"Yes," she managed to reply. "It has been very dry."

Reed wore the same smile as when he'd first stepped inside. There was nothing particularly personal in it. "I understand the Hombolts' ball is this evening."

Now they were getting somewhere. "It is indeed." She didn't entirely manage to keep the eagerness from her voice. "Are you planning to attend?"

He shrugged a bit as he reached for a cucumber sandwich. "It will, no doubt, be a terrible crush. Any gentleman with a modicum of sense will stay home."

"Oh." What could she say beyond that? He didn't mean to attend. Perhaps he thought she wasn't attending. That would certainly explain it. "I am quite looking forward to the Hombolts' ball."

He made a vague sound of acknowledgement. "This cucumber sandwich is excellent." Reed turned his attention to Mother. "An exceptional sandwich, Mrs. Harrison."

"Why, thank you." Mother's eyes darted to Lucy, a look of triumph in her eyes. Did she honestly think Reed's complement of her tea offerings was a sign of success?

"Well, ladies." Reed stood and took in the room with a quick sweep of his gaze. "It has been a pleasure visiting with you all."

And with that, he left. Two days apart, and Reed visited with her only for two minutes and spoke only of the weather and cucumber sandwiches. What an utter disappointment.

She rose from her chair. "If you will excuse me, Mother," she said quickly, and left the drawing room with as much dignity as she could summon.

The moment she reached the corridor, she took up a brisk pace, rushing up the stairs to her bedchamber. She hurried to her window, drew back the curtains, and looked down at the street below. Reed walked from the house at a leisurely pace, swinging his walking stick as though he hadn't a care in the world.

She pressed her open hand to the glass, watching him

leave her behind without a single backward glance. "Haven't you missed me at all?" she whispered.

***

"I am not convinced this is a wise course of action." Reed resisted his brother-in-law's efforts to nudge him into the Hombolts' ballroom.

"Nonsense," Robert insisted. "Everything is working perfectly."

Perfectly? If everything was so perfect, why was he keeping company with his brother-in-law instead of his wife? Reed considered that a significant step in the wrong direction.

"Stick with the plan, Reed," Robert said. "You'll not only settle your current contretemps, but you'll save yourself a great deal of misery down the road." Robert gave him a significant look. "You're a married man now. If you don't put your foot down, you'll soon become extremely well-acquainted with misery."

"That is a fine thing to say about your own sister."

"You are the one who married her and turned her into a *wife*. She was a fine, sensible sort of lady before that." Robert gave him one final nudge, forcing him into the ballroom. "Time to face down the dragon."

Reed straightened the cuffs of his jacket. "First she's a wife, and now she's a dragon. How much worse can this get?"

"Your mother-in-law is approaching," Robert answered.

"So quite a bit worse." He shot Robert a grin.

Robert laughed as they walked around the edge of the ballroom. "Mother isn't so terrible as some."

True. He was exceptionally fond of Lucy's family, even if its ladies were currently making life difficult for him.

A Lesson in Love

"Mrs. Harrison," he said. "It is indeed a pleasure to see you again."

She smiled. "I know the look of a suitor when I see one. I daresay you've come to ask permission to dance with our Lucy."

Robert pierced him with a significant look. Reed gave a subtle nod. He knew his part. "I am promised already for the next several dances," he said. "But should I have dance free before I quit the ball, I will be certain to seek your daughter out."

Mrs. Harrison's eyes pulled wide with shock. Reed offered a very appropriate bow and took leave of his mother-in-law. He glanced back only briefly. Robert, who still stood by his mother, gave him a firm nod of approval. Their plan was moving along nicely.

Why, then, do I feel so utterly dissatisfied?

He saw her in the next moment—his Lucy. She stood amongst a group of her friends, chatting away. Even from a distance, he could see the sparkle in her eyes. The first time he ever saw Lucy was at a ball, like this one. She'd been standing, as now. At first he'd taken only a passing notice of her. But then she'd smiled, and Reed hadn't been able to look away.

He hadn't managed to summon the courage to pay her court until the start of the next Season. Fortunately, he'd not turned coward then. He'd asked her to dance, and she'd agreed. At the end of that Season, he'd asked her to marry him, and she'd agreed.

What went wrong? Why has this Season been so miserably disastrous?

She hadn't been satisfied with his company any longer. Every evening, it was the same complaint—she didn't want to be at home with him. She wished to be out with Society and her friends.

Mr. Harrison appeared at his side unannounced, "You're not turning lily-livered on us, are you?"

"Not lily-livered. I only—" His eyes returned to Lucy. "I was only wishing things were different between Lucy and me."

"They will be, my boy." Mr. Harrison slapped a firm hand on his shoulder. "Your marriage'll be happy and loving again, just as soon as you've ignored your wife properly."

"I am beginning to suspect, Mr. Harrison, that your entire family is a bit touched in the upper works."

"Nothing mad about it, Reed. It's a fine plan."

He was attending a ball, something he generally did his utmost to avoid, and his wife, whom he'd not really seen in two days, was there. This "fine" plan required him to not dance with her—indeed, to not even talk to her. That seemed a little daft.

But he had only been married a few months. His father-in-law and brothers-in-law had more than forty-five years of marriage experience between them. They understood the issues better than he did. And if their plan worked, and he and Lucy could have the happy and contented stay in Town he'd anticipated, the entire ordeal would be worth it.

That was what he told himself as he tore his gaze from Lucy and walked away.

Five

Lucy's patience was nearly spent. She had sat through four nights of Society functions waiting for Reed to rush to her side and declare he couldn't bear to be away from her another moment. She had even seen him at most of the gatherings, but he never said so much as a word to her. He smiled and made friendly conversation with any number of people then left without ever noticing her.

She stepped into her parents' sitting room, where her mother and sister-in-law, Amelia, bent over their needlework, discussing someone's choice of gown the evening before.

"This is not working," Lucy declared with all the authority a youngest child could manage.

"Nonsense, dear," Mother said. "Our embroidery is coming along nicely."

"Not the embroidery." Surely her family had noticed her dilemma. "This plan we've concocted to remind Reed how lonely and miserable he was as a bachelor so he'll come running back to me and declare he'll never neglect me again. *That* is not working."

Mother looked at her over her needlepoint. "Why in heaven's name do you think that?"

Lucy looked from one of them to the other. Surely they weren't so blind as to have not noticed the lack of results their scheme had produced.

"Reed is living as a bachelor and couldn't be more pleased about it," she explained. "I have never seen him look happier at a ball or musicale as I have this past few nights. He pokes his head in, chats amicably with a few people here and there then gladly leaves with his cronies, no doubt to spend the night at their club. He's gleeful."

Mother and Amelia exchanged knowing looks.

"Clarissa said Lucy's determination was flagging," Amelia told Mother.

As Clarissa was not currently present, Lucy could only assume her "determination" had been a previous topic of discussion among them.

"This is not a question of determination," Lucy insisted. "I miss my husband. I miss seeing him each day and talking to him. That isn't a bad thing. I love him enough to have married him, after all. Wishing he were with me is to be expected."

"Of course it is," Mother said, but she didn't sound as if she actually agreed.

"He may not like to attend balls and soirees and such, or perhaps he doesn't like attending them with me—he has, after all, made more appearances at social events these past few days than in the weeks prior—but I would rather have his company quietly at home or doing something he enjoys than to not have it at all."

Amelia gave her a commiserating look. "And are you prepared to make that sacrifice every day for the rest of your life? You would be telling him that his preferences are the only consideration in your marriage."

"But by staying away, aren't I insisting that my preferences are the ones that must be bowed to?"

"Come sit, dear." Mother patted the space beside her on the sofa.

Lucy sat beside her, feeling more confused and frustrated and tired than she had in some time. Nothing about this Season had gone as planned. She longed for Reed's company. She missed the little gestures of kindness she received from him—his arm when she walked, the way he adjusted her wrap when they were out, their shared excitement over antiquities and ices. She missed his smile and his laughter.

Mother set aside her embroidery. "Reed has been in consultation with your father, Robert, and Charles." She made that fact sound like a terribly ominous thing. "They realize we mean to teach Reed a lesson in valuing his wife, and they mean to teach us a lesson in return."

"What lesson is that?" The only thing the past week had taught Lucy was that being a wallflower as a debutante is being a wallflower as a married lady. The former was disheartening, while the latter was simply heartbreaking.

Amelia, sitting in a chair facing them on the sofa, leaned forward. "The gentlemen mean to show us that we are the ones who cannot live without *them*, that we are more miserable in their absence than they are in ours. They are determined to prove that we will give over first and go running back to them, begging for their company. To make us admit that we miss them when they are gone."

Mother nodded her agreement with Amelia's explanation.

"But I don't know that I can live without him," Lucy said. "What is so wrong with telling him so?"

"And deal a blow to ladies everywhere?" Amelia scoffed. "No, dearest sister-in-law. Your victory in this battle will give hope to your fellow wives. You will be a revered warrior."

"'A revered warrior'? How utterly ridiculous. I only wanted Reed to take me to balls and such. When did this turn into a war?"

Mother waved off the question. "When? Adam and Eve, darling."

Lucy felt unaccountably exhausted. "How much longer do I have to keep 'teaching Reed a lesson?' This has been a long week for me. I don't get to go home to my husband as you do. I am alone every night and every morning and most of the day. I haven't danced at any balls, nor have I had the man I love to whisper with at the theatre. Your endurance may be endless with those things buoying you up. But mine is quickly running out."

"Do not fret," Mother said, retaking her embroidery. "The tide will turn tonight. We have it all in hand. You'll see."

That night, Lucy watched her mother and sisters assume their positions at the ball and couldn't help thinking that the undertaking rather resembled the positioning of troops on a battlefield.

Reed had arrived, flanked by the Harrison men. As they had during the past few evenings, the gentlemen quite obviously headed in the opposite direction of Lucy. But the Harrison ladies had anticipated the maneuver. Mother was waiting for them. They were too far distant for Lucy to overhear their conversation, but she could easily guess at it.

Mother offered a greeting, doing a poor job of pretending to be surprised at having bumped into Reed. He made some kind of polite reply, all the while glancing at his companions for some indication as to what he might do to counter the ladies' strategic victory. Before anyone could speak to the contrary, Mother had her arm threaded through Reed's and was leading him rather forcibly in Lucy's direction.

How utterly humiliating. All I wanted was for him to accompany me to Society functions, but here I am now watching him be bullied into even talking to me.

Reed reached her side a moment later. He wore the same vaguely polite expression he had at Mother's at-home a week earlier. "Mrs. Stanthorpe." The same emotionless greeting as before.

Oh, Mother. This had better be worth the heartache. "Mr. Stanthorpe," she replied, as her female relations had advised her to.

"As luck would have it," Mother said, "Our Lucy has this next set free. How fortuitous."

Reed hesitated for just a moment. Would he truly turn down such a pointed request? "I—"

Father interrupted whatever Reed was about to say. "Oh, dear, ladies. I do believe Mr. Stanthorpe told me he didn't mean to dance tonight."

Lucy kept her gaze on her husband. "Is that true?"

"I . . ." His eyes darted to Father then to Robert and Charles gathered nearby. "I am not particularly in the mood for dancing, and if would be unfair in the extreme for a person to be forced to do something he did not care to do." Something about the declaration felt practiced.

Reed has been in consultation with your Father and brothers. This, then, was what Mother meant. They were combatants. Indeed, Amelia and Robert seemed almost gleeful at the prospect of debating the topic.

"By that logic," Amelia said, "a lady who does not care to be left at home evening after evening shouldn't be forced to remain there by a husband who refuses to take her out."

Robert answered his wife's argument point by point. "Requiring a gentleman to undertake something he finds truly distasteful is hardly comparable to a lady spending a quiet evening at home."

"Distasteful?" Amelia clearly objected to the word. "If you found squiring me about all these years so torturous, why did you even bother?"

"I didn't have a choice," Robert answered. "I was never given the opportunity to stand up for myself and for husbands everywhere. But Reed here does. And I, for one, applaud him."

Lucy looked to her mother. Was this truly the great victory she'd promised? This was "having it all in hand?"

Mother didn't seem swayed in the least. "If Mr. Stanthorpe does not mean to dance, surely he would have no objection to taking a turn about the room. You would have been doing precisely that as it was."

As far as logic went, that was rather water-tight. Reed made a nod and small bow of acknowledgement. Lucy stood and took the arm he offered. They stepped away from her family, looking for all the world as though they were taking an unexceptional turn about the room. Inside, however, Lucy was tangled mess of emotions.

She had missed him, missed him to the point of misery. But he didn't seem to have suffered at all in her absence. She didn't want to spend the remainder of her Season without him, but neither did she wish to dig up this old argument every summer, having to beg and plead for every outing. She didn't want them to bicker in public the way Amelia and Robert were, or secretly conspiring against each other the way her parents were.

She held more tightly to Reed's arm, grateful for his presence even in her uncertainty. He set his hand on top of hers. That light touch took her back a year to their courtship when that was all they were permitted. Her heart pounded at the feel of his hand on hers. Lucy settled herself into that fleeting connection, finding a wonderfully welcome helping of peace by having him at her side again.

He broke the silence between them. "We are having very fine—"

"Don't you dare speak of the weather, Reed Andrew Stanthorpe."

He abruptly stopped. His eyes pulled wide and his mouth hung the tiniest bit open. She didn't apologize for her vehemence, didn't take back her words. An entire week they'd been apart, not seeing each other, not speaking. She would not endure a stilted and insincere conversation on topics neither of them cared the least about.

He seemed to fumble about for the right thing to say. "Weather is a commonplace topic between two people."

She pulled her arm free, shaking her head in frustration. "We've not seen each other in a full week, yet you have nothing to say to me beyond 'commonplace topics between two people'?"

"Lucy—"

"Either you are wounding me on purpose, or you really are utterly indifferent to me." The thought brought a fresh threat of tears. "I had thought you were as miserable as I was, that you missed me as much as I missed you. But Mother was right. You didn't. Not at all."

"Lu—"

She couldn't bear more empty words. Not caring that she was likely making something of a scene, Lucy hurried away toward the doors. The Barringtons lived but a few doors from Lucy's parents' home, and therefore, she could return there without waiting for the carriage to be summoned. The Barringtons' butler insisted on sending a footman to accompany her. Lucy didn't object, but neither did she wait.

The footman caught up to her a moment later. He accompanied her in appropriate silence, leaving her thoughts ample opportunity to turn and twist about. Her parents' butler opened the door to let her in and sent the Barringtons' footman off. Lucy was grateful the butler didn't inquire after her early return. She had no desire to explain.

She rushed up the stairs and to her bedchamber. Tears flowed by the time she dropped, exhausted, onto her bed.

Their plan had seemed so ingenious at first: some time away would show Reed how much he really enjoyed their time together. He would appreciate her company enough to be willing to take her to all the Society events she'd longed to attend. Though she knew she would miss him, she'd thought he would come to his senses quickly, that they wouldn't be apart for long.

And he doesn't even care. He hasn't missed me at all.

Six

By the time Reed reached the front of the Barringtons' home, Lucy was gone. He stood looking out into the dark night, worry tying his insides into knots. How had things come to this?

"The scales have tipped decidedly in our favor." Mr. Harrison slapped a companionable hand on Reed's shoulder. "We'll have the ladies agreeing to let us stay at home every night of the week soon enough."

Robert and Charles had come as well, both looking pleased as could be.

"Another evening or two, and we can declare this a decisive victory for the gentlemen," Robert declared.

"No." Reed snapped out the word.

"What do you mean, 'no'?" Robert smiled, even laughingly elbowing Charles. They all thought this a great joke.

"I mean there will be no more evenings like this. No

more." Reed stepped back into the entryway. "My hat and outercoat," he instructed the butler. "And send for my carriage."

A moment later, the items were in his possession and he was waiting in the vestibule for his equipage.

His in-laws closed in on him. "You are quitting the field?" Robert asked in a tone of surprise. "But we are winning."

Reed eyed them each in turn. "Gentlemen, this has gone too far. I saw tears in my wife's eyes tonight, and that is something I will never abide. Not ever. This ends now."

They looked at him as though he had lost his mind. "If you give in now, Lucy will be leading you about by the nose the rest of your life."

"So be it."

His carriage pulled up, and Reed was grateful for the escape. He preferred staying on friendly terms with his wife's family, but if they continued insisting he treat her with less kindness than she deserved, he would be hard pressed not to call each and every one of them out.

He'd gone along with the plan because he hadn't expected it to wound Lucy the way it obviously had. They'd convinced him she was playing along, that it was a friendly bit of rivalry between them. A bit of lark was all. In the process, he had hurt his wife, his darling, wonderful Lucy.

To his surprise, Mr. Harrison climbed in the carriage with him.

"If you mean to try to change my mind—"

But Mr. Harrison held up a hand. "Actually, I mean to admit to you that you're right. We took this game too far."

"That seems a very abrupt change of position." Reed wasn't generally a suspicious person, but he'd seen an underhandedness in his in-laws over the past week, albeit it a good-humored underhandedness, and it made him wary.

"Robert, Charles, and I were thoroughly enjoying this little rivalry with the ladies. And I know from speaking of it with my wife that she, Amelia, and Clarissa have been amused as well."

"Forgive me if I haven't found it overly amusing."

Mr. Harrison acknowledged Reed's position with a quick nod. "I am not at all happy with how things have turned out myself. We didn't mean to hurt Lucy's feelings."

"I need to apologize to her," Reed said.

"Oh, son, you must do far more than that."

The declaration was not a promising one. "Did you have something particular in mind, because I am currently at a loss."

Mr. Harrison's expression turned ponderous. "I might. I just might."

Seven

Lucy's tears dried by morning, though she kept to her room all the next day. She didn't want to hear any more of her family's schemes nor see the glint of triumph that would, no doubt, be in her father's eyes. The gentlemen had scored a decisive victory, with Lucy's broken heart being the spoils.

Over the past months, when something worried or upset her, she'd turned to Reed, and he'd listened as she talked it through. That always made her feel better. But he wasn't here, and he'd made it quite clear over the past week that he didn't really care to be.

She could go to their house not many streets away, ask if she could come home, and they could forget the rivalry they'd been entangled in the past few days. But there would always be the knowledge in the back of her mind that he hadn't asked her back and didn't really wanted her there.

When the dinner bell sounded, Lucy instructed her

A Lesson in Love

abigail to have her meal brought up on a tray. She simply wanted to be left alone. But the minutes stretched out, and her food didn't arrive. After nearly thirty minutes had past, Lucy began to suspect something had gone wrong.

She opened her bedchamber door a crack and peeked out. The corridor was empty. The family would be at their meal already. She tiptoed down the stairs, not wishing to draw attention to herself. They would want to talk, but she had no desire to. The corridor where the dining room stood was silent.

Now that is *odd.* She glanced around, trying to sort it out. It was the dinner hour, and her family was not one to miss a meal. She was nearly certain that Robert and Amelia, and Charles and Clarissa intended to take dinner with them that night. With six people sitting down to a meal, there ought to have been quite a bit of chatter.

Perhaps they had decided to eat elsewhere. The staff always seemed to know more about the comings and goings of the family than anyone. She stepped into the dining room, intending to tug the bell pull, but the sound of voices down the corridor stopped her.

She listened. Definitely voices. Lucy moved toward the sound. *The drawing room?* Why were they gathered in the drawing room? She pulled the door open a bit and looked inside. Seven pairs of eyes darted toward her. Then the room seemed to spring into action.

"Oh, no you will not, you lying blackguard!" Father declared in ringing tones, pointing an accusatory finger at Reed, of all people.

Lucy opened the door more fully.

"I will not be deterred, old man," Reed replied, in stilted and overly dramatic tones. "Resign yourself."

Mother pressed the back of her hand to her forehead and dropped against the sofa. "Whatever shall we do?"

Amelia and Clarissa rushed to Mother's side, waving smelling salts and patting her hands as if consoling her.

Robert rose and stood next to Father. Though his expression was serious, Lucy knew the look of laughter hovering in the back of her brother's eyes. "You will not get away with this dastardly plan, Mr. Stanthorpe."

"Oh, but I will," Reed said. "You will not keep us apart a moment longer. If I must move mountains or cross oceans, I will. For true love always wins in the end!" He spun about, facing Lucy. "Never fear, my lady, I have come to rescue you from this vile place of imprisonment."

"What in heaven's name—"

Reed stepped up to her and wrapped his arm around her waist. He looked back over her family, assembled in an obviously preplanned pose. "Do not attempt to follow us," Reed warned. "For I will allow nothing to come between me and my true love again."

"Reed, what is going on?" Lucy asked.

He looked down at her, and her heart nearly stopped at the intensity of his gaze. "Our long nightmare is over, love. I've come to take you away from this place."

"Have you really?" The words emerged as little more than a whisper.

"I have, indeed, and should have long ago." To her family he said, "Au revoir!" then swept her from the room and down the corridor.

A footman waited at the front door, clearly anticipating their departure. He held the door, and they stepped out. Reed's carriage sat in readiness, the driver already perched atop. They were quickly settled inside—Lucy on the forward-facing bench and Reed on the rear-facing—and the carriage lurched forward.

Her mind was in a whirlwind. What had just happened? Reed came for her, that much was certain. Though why he had remained a mystery. She would not allow herself to believe he had missed her and longed for her, when so much silence had stretched between them.

And, yet, he *was* here.

"Lucy?" His voice was a bit uncertain. "I need to say something, and I hope you won't take it the wrong way."

She braced herself. Heaven only knew what he meant to tell her.

"I have always liked your family; you know that. But darling, they aren't very bright."

"What do you mean?"

Reed moved and sat directly beside her, taking her hands in his and looking into her face. The streetlamps they passed illuminated his expression enough for her to see the earnestness there. "I realize you first came to your parents' home because I was being an utter featherhead and you needed someone to listen to you. By the time I realized where you were, your mother and sisters had already convinced you that this miscommunication we were having was worthy of a drawn-out battle."

That was true enough.

"Upon arriving, your male relations pulled me aside and convinced me of the same thing. Though I would have far preferred to simply bring you home and talk it through, I bowed to their years of matrimonial experience, thinking it gave them insight. But, Lucy, darling, they are idiots, the lot of them."

She actually laughed out loud. She knew Reed really did like her family, but considering the turmoil of the past week, she had to agree with his assessment of their mental faculties.

He brushed his fingers along her cheek. "We should never have listened to them, my love. And I am sorry their schemes hurt you and sorrier still that I had any part of it."

"We were both rather blinded by them," Lucy said. "We ought to have simply told them all how bacon-brained they were being and fixed the problem ourselves."

"Indeed." He cupped her face gently in his hands and placed a tender kiss to her forehead. "And now that I have rescued you from the dungeon of despair they were keeping you in—"

She smiled at the theatrical tone he had adopted once more.

"I think we had best set our minds to resolving the difficulty that caused all of this trouble."

Lucy leaned into his embrace, resting her head on his shoulder and her hand against his chest. "I know you don't care for Society functions," she said. "And I don't want to force you to endure them all the time."

His arms held her ever tighter. "And I know how much you do enjoy them, and I don't want you to miss them all."

"Perhaps . . ." She pressed a kiss to his cheek. "We could pick a few events each week I would particularly like to attend, and on the other nights, we could stay home."

Reed kissed her temple. "I believe that is an excellent solution."

Lucy shifted enough to more fully face him, brushing her fingers along his jaw. "And if there is ever anything you desperately wish to avoid attending, you tell me, and we'll stay home."

His hand slipped behind her neck, his fingers weaving into her hair. "And if there is anything you desperately wish to attend, you tell me, and we will make certain we are there."

"And"—she feathered a kiss on his lips—"we will never"—another light kiss—"ever"—and another—"listen to my family again."

"Agreed."

Reed pulled her firmly into his arms and kissed her thoroughly. The heartache and loneliness of the past week simply melted away. He did love her. He always had. If not for the poor advice and insistence of meddlesome relations, they might have resolved this difficulty very easily.

But, she told herself as he continued kissing her and holding her, that without the argument, they'd not be enjoying a reconciliation.

A Lesson in Love

The carriage came to a stop in front of their house. Reed pulled away, letting down the window.

"Circle the block a few more times, man," he called out to the driver. "And drive slowly."

He put up the window once more and drew the curtains. She felt his arms slip around her and his warmth settle over her once more.

"Now, my dearest Lucy, where were we?"

About Sarah M. Eden

Sarah M. Eden is the author of multiple historical romances, including *Longing for Home*, winner of *Foreword* magazine's IndieFab Gold Award and the AML's 2013 Novel of the Year, as well as Whitney Award finalists *Seeking Persephone* and *Courting Miss Lancaster*.

Combining her obsession with history and affinity for tender love stories, Sarah loves crafting witty characters and heartfelt romances. She has twice served as the Master of Ceremonies for the LDStorymakers Writers Conference and acted as the Writer in Residence at the Northwest Writers Retreat. Sarah is represented by Pam van Hylckama Vlieg at Foreword Literary Agency.

Visit her website at www.sarahmeden.com
Twitter: @SarahMEden
Facebook: Sarah M. Eden

AN OCEAN AWAY
by Heather B. Moore

Other Works by Heather B. Moore

Historical

Esther the Queen
Heart of the Ocean
Daughters of Jared
The Out of Jerusalem Series
Abinadi
Alma
Alma the Younger
Ammon

Contemporary

Finding Sheba
Beneath
The Aliso Creek Series
The Newport Ladies Book Club Series
The Fortune Café
A Timeless Romance Anthology Series

One

1841—Bordeaux, France

Gina Graydon tucked a deliciously romantic gothic novel under her arm and stepped onto the hotel balcony of her second-floor room. That the hotel balcony perched over a shadowed garden, and the sun had yet to rise, didn't deter Gina from hiking up her wrapper and nightgown and climbing over the rail.

In her twenty years, she'd had plenty of experience climbing from balconies. Doing so was her favorite early morning pastime back at home in New York City. Of course, her parents would not be happy if they knew what she was doing now.

Currently, it was dark enough to avoid detection by her parents, who slept in the next room over, should they awaken unexpectedly. And it was light enough to climb down the protruding stones without falling into a heap.

This was Gina's third early morning foray that week into the Bordeaux garden, and she'd become quite expert at scaling the now-familiar wall. She'd found, after a bit of slipping on her first attempt, that going barefoot gave her the needed grip, and the only tricky part was keeping her book from falling out of her bodice.

It was no ordinary book, but one by a female author who published under a nom de plume. Full of intrigue, dark English moors, a mysterious hero, and intricacies of kissing, which Gina had never before experienced, this was a book to be read in the wilds of the garden—a French garden, to be exact. The pristine order of her rented room would not do for this story. The words on the page had to be savored and mulled over in an atmosphere worthy of both the characters and the setting.

Gina took her literature seriously, and if truth be told, she'd rather read a delicious novel than do much else . . . with the exclusion of eating; Gina didn't wont for much in life. Except for the fact that her parents, namely her father, had scared off any eligible suitor for the past three years. She'd experienced no romance, no courting, and hardly even a conversation with an eligible gentleman since she had become of age.

Because of this, Gina had been driven to desperate measures, such as hiding in gardens, and reading forbidden books. As the only child of the esteemed Mr. and Mrs. Graydon of New York City, she was expected to act properly at all times, marry a wealthy man who'd add his fortune to her father's, and produce at least two grandchildren—preferably a boy and a girl—to be considered of value to the family name.

She let out a long, heavy sigh as her feet touched the ground. She made her way to the garden, entering through the arched gateway topped with thick vines. How could she ever secure a proposal with her father's intimidation toward other men? As a powerful and wealthy shipping tycoon, he believed no one was good enough for his little girl.

As Gina followed the twisting path outlined by tall rose bushes, she wondered if she'd ever have the chance to fall madly in love—a rare occasion even under the best of circumstances and without a tyrant for a father. But falling in love was entirely possible if she knew anything about her best friend, Eliza Robinson. The week before they'd left for France, Gina had attended Eliza's wedding in the coastal town of Maybrook, Massachusetts. Eliza had gone against great odds to marry the man she loved.

Gina stopped at a bush in full bloom with exquisite white roses. In the growing light, the white looked ethereal, reminding her of the flowers at her friend's wedding. Eliza's ceremony had been terribly romantic—so quaint and simple, with only the closest family and friends present. Far from society's prying eyes and ears, the wedding had been almost secretive, daring, one step from an elopement.

She bent down to smell the roses, letting the divine scent wash over her. Eloping sounded like the most fantastic thing in the world, but of course, she'd never admit that to anyone. They'd all think she was batty, and the only men who'd be interested would be the ones with sordid pasts to hide. Who, of course, her father would never approve of.

Gina straightened and continued on the garden path until a bench appeared before her. She sank onto the cool wood and brushed her hand across the cover of the delightful novel, pushing all thoughts of her hopeless circumstances out of her mind. She waited a moment before opening the pages. From her position, she had a good view of the hotel she and her parents were staying at. Their window was dark, as was hers, but the window on the other side was lit.

Odd. She remembered it being dark during her climb, which meant the man who occupied those rooms had just awakened. Had he heard her? Her pulse quickened. She hadn't actually seen the man, had only heard his deep voice a time or two.

The sky grew lighter behind the hotel, the early dawn softening to a golden hue. Gina's heart rate sped up as she opened the book at her marker and flipped back several pages to reread the intimate kiss described before her stopping point. Kisses were always a good place to begin.

Something drew her gaze back to the hotel windows next to her own. Gina froze as a man walked out onto the balcony. His dark form told her he was tall and well built. The fact that she could determine that from this distance meant that perhaps she had read one too many romance novels. Although she would never admit to it. She couldn't see him clearly, but surely he wasn't French. She'd towered over every French man she'd met. In New York, she was considered tall for a woman, but here she was practically a Viking.

The man stood still in the subtle morning glow, and she couldn't tell what he was looking at. Hopefully she was too far and too concealed for him to see her upon the bench, even if her wrapper was pale yellow.

I hope I'm not a beacon of light. The realization that he might be able to see her made her heart thump into her throat. What if he saw her and told another person? She wasn't doing anything scandalous, but she was in a foreign hotel garden by herself, wearing a wrapper, and reading something her mother would be irate about if discovered.

Gina slowly stood, watching the man's reaction. His head turned slightly, as if he was looking out over the garden, and not directly at one spot. He probably didn't see her. She could slip into a group of trees until he left. But before she could take a step, his head turned toward her, and his eyes met hers.

Even with the distance, she felt his gaze. She didn't dare move and bring attention to herself. Minutes passed, or perhaps only seconds, but finally, he turned away and disappeared inside his room. Gina let out the breath she'd been holding.

An Ocean Away

Would the man discover who she was? Who her father was? The gossip columns in France were not as formidable as New York's, and besides, they were in French, and what American paid attention to them anyway? Certainly not her parents.

Then Gina froze. Her grandmother read the French paper each afternoon while taking her thick hot-chocolate drink in front of a cheery fire. Grandmother Graydon had almost stayed home from this trip, but at the last moment had decided to visit Europe "one more time." The woman wasn't all that elderly, though her knees had been giving her a bit of trouble. Thus sleeping all morning and not reading the morning paper until afternoon.

Everyone else in the hotel seemed to sleep through the morning as well after attending late-night functions. Her parents enjoyed their wine, and being in Bordeaux, they took advantage of testing every vintage. This gave Gina uninterrupted hours each morning to enjoy her novels. But those hours would come to an end if any of her ventures made it to the French columns for her grandmother to read.

Gina kept a wary gaze on the deserted balcony for some time, and when her heart rate finally slowed she sat down again and turned to the novel.

Her lips curled into a smile as she read about a mysterious stranger grasping the heroine by the shoulders and leaning down to kiss her. Apparently the man couldn't help himself. The heroine's presence alone had tortured him far too long, although they'd barely spoken. They didn't even know each other's names. Words weren't needed for this couple.

Gina's skin tingled as she imagined herself as the heroine. Of course, she would add thunder in the distance and give the man a Spanish accent. He could say something very romantic . . . in Spanish. His hair would be dark, of course, and a bit wavy. Were Spanish men tall? She thought hard. Surely it wouldn't do for *her* to stoop down when kissing *him*.

She had to imagine someone taller . . . a British man. An infantryman, perhaps? No, too base. A commander? One with the favor of Queen Victoria and a large estate on the coast, with plenty of moors and blowing wind? Might the commander be crippled from battle? Would he be able to hold her tight in his arms, or would he be too exhausted and call for a quilt to put on his lap while he sat before a fire and recalled his famous victories? No, a British Commander would be tiresome.

She turned the next page, realizing she could not imagine anything more romantic than being kissed during a storm beneath a gazebo with the sound of thunder rumbling across the hills and rain gently tapping on the roof above.

Perhaps her first kiss could be from an Italian—they were known for romancing their women . . .

No, Italians were not known for being faithful. Would he kiss her then be off to his other woman? Gina probably wouldn't even guess about his unfaithfulness, because she couldn't understand the language anyway. He could murmur another woman's name while kissing her, and Gina would be none the wiser. She sighed, dismissing the Italian hero.

Better for the man to remain completely and utterly mysterious; thinking about the ways of a real man was just too . . . well, *real*.

Two

Mr. Edmund H. Donaldson chuckled as he parted the heavy drape separating his room from the crisp morning outside. The girl with the sunset-red hair still sat outside in the garden reading some infernal book. Granted, she was no mere girl—at least nineteen in his estimation—but it was easier to think of her as a young girl.

He needed to keep his thoughts where they should be—on the mess his late wife's estate had become upon her premature death and how to sort it all out. If matters weren't sorry enough, right before leaving America, he'd been notified of a lawsuit brought against his import/export company by an established shipping company. If there was one thing old-time New Yorkers were suspicious of, it was new blood. He had to return home as soon as possible to set things right.

The problem was, his wife's estate was in France and he had little knowledge of French law, and every turn he made, he was seen as a braggart American seeking his dead wife's fortune. Which was far from reality. But Jacqueline—God preserve her soul—was not there to testify to his good name.

Edmund admitted his marriage to Jacqueline had been one of convenience. He hadn't exactly loved Jacqueline, but he'd found her to be companionable, at least when she was in the mood to be. She'd had her pet friends and intimate parties, which Edmund rarely attended. It seemed they'd both been happy living their lives apart.

The marriage had been beneficial to them both. Jacqueline had wanted children, and Edmund had wanted a respectable wife to raise him above the blasted bachelor status he so despised. He'd long ago tired of dinners and balls, in which a half-dozen mothers threw their simpering daughters at him.

He'd been fed up with being treated like a prized bull, constantly prodded and gossiped about. So he married Jacqueline—exotic, foreign, French—everything the typical American woman was not. But then she'd died.

Damn carriage accident.

Jacqueline had suited him perfectly. Edmund had spent his days with his ledgers, inspecting cargo for his shipping company, doing what gave him the most satisfaction. And Jacqueline never complained about his long work hours. She had surrounded herself with luxuries and eclectic friends.

He'd never seen Jacqueline read a book or do anything remotely solitary. Perhaps that was why the young girl, who was apparently housed in the apartment next to his, had captured his attention. The morning before, the noise of the girl climbing down had brought him to the balcony, but he didn't dare step out for fear of startling her. But this morning, after she'd safely landed on the ground, Edmund had stolen onto the balcony to see if he could learn anything about her.

Leave her be, his mind told him. Just because she was unlike any woman he'd ever observed meant nothing.

Edmund drew the drapes wide, letting in a stream of sunlight. He wondered what book she read—what could be so fascinating as to make one scale down a wall in the early hours of dawn to hide and read it?

And in her wrapper at that. Yes, he'd noticed her clothing—unusual for him. It had been hard not to notice it, or that her hair tumbled about her shoulders as if were some sort of fire-haired faerie in a Shakespeare production.

The smile playing on Edmund's lips stayed put as he gazed out the balcony door. He had not planned on going to the hotel ball tonight, but perhaps he would. If nothing else, he'd be interested to learn where the girl was from. She wasn't French—she was too tall for that. Maybe she was Russian or Norwegian—one of those Viking women.

He stepped back from the door to prepare for a busy day of certain frustration and running into complications with settling his wife's estate. Surely when he returned to the hotel, he would be exhausted and have forgotten all about the tall redhead next door.

He dressed quickly, wanting to be the first to arrive at the solicitor's office so they would have no excuse of turning him away—and before he knew it, he was at the front of the hotel, waiting for a carriage to be brought around. His gaze moved to the north, by one of the garden entrances. Was the girl still reading on that bench? Or had she climbed back up to her room?

The thought made him smile, and without considering his actions, he found himself striding toward the garden's main gate. Once inside, he found the morning shadows were pleasantly cooling. It was too early for the bees or other insects to be about, and the dew brought out the fragrance of the roses in force. The girl's preference for the garden made sense now.

"Oh," a woman said.

Edmund stopped short, almost running into her. When he shifted his gaze, he looked into a pair of amber eyes. Up close, Edmund could no longer fool himself. The girl was no child, but a beautiful woman. Her eyes were wide as they stared at him, framed with thick dark lashes. And her lips were full and pink as they formed an O. He had the strangest urge to reach out and touch her hair, perhaps brush it back from her shoulder or slide his fingers through its soft waves. Her skin was slightly freckled, adding to her charm.

"Excuse me." The woman spoke again, because apparently, Edmund had been rendered mute. She hid her book behind her back.

"Sorry, miss, I wasn't . . ." he started. Her skin pinked. Was she blushing?

He had come upon her unawares, and she wasn't properly dressed. Of course he had embarrassed her, and she probably wanted nothing more than to flee to her room.

He made to move out of her way as she side-stepped at the same time, each in the same direction. Again they were in an identical predicament, facing each other, but now on the other side of the garden path. The woman laughed, startling Edmund. And she blushed even more.

THREE

*O*h laws, Gina thought. *I'm laughing like a ninny in front of a perfectly handsome man who must think I've lost my mind.*

She always laughed when she was nervous—a lot—and she was nervous now. She didn't know why. This man was certainly not mysterious, and this wasn't the thundering, stormy day of her imagination. There was no gazebo overhead, and not a speck of rain to be felt. And he was most definitely not romancing her. Gina's face flamed again as she realized why she was so nervous—she'd just imagined kissing a strange man with dark hair, and here one stood.

Most likely a married man. Her eyes flicked to his hands, subconsciously searching for a wedding band, making her berate herself even more. He wore no ring, but that didn't mean anything. Gina clutched her novel more tightly behind her back, wishing she'd waited a moment longer before leaving her bench so she would have avoided this embarrassment.

The man's face was somber, even in the face of her laughing. Yet she saw something change, however slight, and his deep-blue eyes seemed to sparkle—something gone so quickly, she must have imagined it.

She stepped deliberately to the left, making a wide berth around the stranger, who she realized was quite tall—at least a head above her. Remarkable. He definitely wasn't French, nor likely a Spaniard, for that matter, although his hair was dark.

"So sorry," she mumbled before she clasped her book to her breast and hurried past him.

She'd blushed far too much to be decent, without considering what she must have looked like to him—a wild urchin, that's what. She was only a few steps down the path when she realized the man had spoken with an American accent.

Why hadn't she ever considered an American in her kissing fantasies? Because those men knew her father, which meant there was nothing mysterious or romantic about them.

Something drew her to peek behind her as she neared the wall leading to her balcony. The American stood in the same spot, looking right at her. Gina took a deep breath, feeling her pulse go crazy. There was no account for why he stared. Did he have no other business to attend to? He was dressed for something serious in that black suit of his.

Gina hesitated below her balcony. If he didn't leave, he'd be witness to her scaling a stone wall in her wrapper. She had two choices: either walk around to the front of the hotel and enter like a proper lady, or return to the room the same way she'd left it.

In only a moment, Gina decided. She looked over at the American. She could have sworn he smiled as if urging her on. It didn't take much else. After tucking her book into her

An Ocean Away

bodice, she lifted her wrapper above her ankles and started to climb.

At the balcony rail, Gina didn't dare look back. Her behavior was very unladylike, and the sooner she was inside, the better. She didn't know whether she should laugh or cry about it all. She barely made it inside before her emotions collided and gasps of laugher consumed her. Collapsing onto her bed, she covered her mouth, laughing so hard her eyes watered. This morning's outing was even too fantastical for a novel. No one would ever believe it.

What if he *hadn't* been smiling? Gina shot up, perching on the edge of the bed, sobering at the thought. Perhaps he'd been grimacing . . . Maybe he was speaking to the hotel monsieur right now, filing a complaint about renegade women climbing the walls of the hotel.

"Oh!" Gina's stomach pitched with nausea. The only solution was to not leave her room at all, for the next five days, until they departed for London. She could only imagine the American describing the incident to the hotel concierge. How many red-haired women were at the hotel?

I must dye my hair. Right away.

Gina flopped onto her bed with a groan. Her parents would know something was going on if she suddenly appeared with hair dyed black.

Instead, I will be ill. But not so violently indisposed that Mother fetches a physician. Just slightly ill—too ill to attend the ball, but not too ill to cause worry.

No, that wouldn't work either. Last year when she'd had a bit of a fever, her mother practically walked a path in their Turkish carpet from pacing so much.

I'll have a headache. One that allows me to be left alone to sleep.

Gina closed her eyes, deciding when her headache should begin. Surely after supper, or else she might be restricted to soup only. She didn't want to miss one morsel of the French cuisine. But if she went to the hotel dining room, she'd be spotted—possibly by the American.

While she mused over the best timing for her pending headache, something brushed against the door. The sound was faint, but Gina could swear that someone had touched the door handle. It was too early for her parents to be moving about. She rose from the bed and crossed to the door. She wouldn't fling it open, intent on catching someone in the hallway. A lady's beaded bag could have brushed against it, or one of those pesky miniature dogs so popular in France. Or . . . might it be a letter slipped beneath the door?

Gina looked down and found a folded piece of ivory paper. She grasped the door handle and pushed it open, only to realize that it was locked. She fumbled for the lock, and then she tugged the door.

By that time, whoever had slipped her the note had disappeared. With one hand bracing herself against the door frame in case she had to make a hasty retreat, she leaned into the hallway and looked both ways. No one was in sight.

"Hmm." Gina straightened then shut and locked her door. She picked up the note, walked to the balcony, and stepped outside. It wouldn't do to read a mysterious note in the confines of her room. She needed fresh air and a fragrant breeze. It would be ideal if twilight had descended and a violinist were playing a mournful tune in the garden. But Gina couldn't wait until twilight to read the note. That would be the death of her, and who knew if the French were any good at violin music anyway?

She gazed at the folded paper in her hand. Anything could be written inside it. Anything. Her heart thumped. Maybe she'd been notified of some wealthy and unknown-until-now great aunt who had left her a fortune from a diamond mine in Africa. Or perhaps a lost sibling her mother had never told her about, a younger sister who'd just discovered the family's whereabouts. The heavens had conspired to bring them to the same hotel at the same time, and she and her newfound sister would be reunited and spend the rest of their days together, traveling and flirting with mysterious men.

Gina laughed at the thought then sobered immediately. She really should stop reading so many novels. Sometimes it was difficult to tell what was real and what wasn't, and she had no one to blame for that but herself . . . and a few novelists. With a barely steady hand, she opened the note. The inked scrawl was definitely a man's, so she at least had made one correct assumption: it was certainly mysterious.

Don't worry; your secret is safe with me.
—E. D.

Who was E. D.? She turned over the paper, but nothing else was written on it. She held it up to the sky in case a watermark would reveal the sender's identity. Nothing. Not another clue.

Something turned in her mind, and she realized who wrote the note. *The American.* Gina crossed to the wicker chair on the balcony and sank into it. E. D. was the American man who'd stared at her in the garden.

Your secret will be safe with me.

He was referring to her scaling the wall in her nightgown. She groaned, wishing she could take back the entire morning and stay in bed like any normal pampered American lady on vacation in France.

E. D. . . . Edgar Davids? Emile Dupaix?
Earl? Eli? Dorchester? DeMille? Darcy?

Hopeless. All thoughts of faking a headache fled. Gina would be going to the ball, if only to discover what E. D. stood for. She wouldn't sleep a wink tonight otherwise.

Four

Her laughter was unmistakable, even across the room. Edmund forced himself not stare in her direction. He'd never heard a laugh so unfettered, carefree, or joyous. In the garden, it had sounded a little nervous, but now it was freedom itself.

Confound it. Edmund looked over at the red-haired woman standing near a man who bowed, obviously asking her for a dance. Edmund's gaze narrowed. The man was exactly her height. Surely she'd rather dance with someone taller, someone who could properly lead her about the dance floor. Someone like him.

Edmund tried to dispel the thoughts. He'd only been a widow for a few months, yet he was acting like a drooling puppy. He'd been acquainted with plenty of beautiful women—Jacqueline had been strikingly so. What was it about this redhead that intrigued him? Her sense of adventure? Her laugh? Her amber eyes? Her apparent climbing abilities?

All of it.

Instinct told him she would be too much work. Too much involvement. He couldn't disappear for days inspecting ships or staying in his office, balancing ledgers, placing cargo orders. This woman would demand that he be a part of her life.

Edmund let out a sigh. The waltz had ended, and as another piece struck up, he found himself walking toward the woman from the garden, the one to whom he'd spent nearly ten minutes trying to decide what to write in a note.

Just as he reached her, she turned from her partner.

Her eyes widened, and then she smiled. To another man, the smile may have seemed confident, but something told Edmund she felt a bit wary. He'd hoped his note would have allayed her worries. He didn't think he'd ever seen any person, man or female, scale a wall so easily.

"I'm sorry I didn't introduce myself before," he started. "I'm Edmund Donaldson, of New York City."

"Hello," she said. "*Oh.* You are . . ." Her mouth clamped shut.

Beneath the chandelier candlelight, she looked different from that morning in the garden. Her hair was expertly coiffed, not falling about her shoulders as if she were a garden nymph. But both looks were equally charming. Edmund realized she'd stopped speaking. "Is something the matter?" he asked.

"It's just . . ." She took a step closer, providing Edmund with a whiff of whatever perfume she wore. Roses, perhaps. Her voice lowered. "I think I know you."

"Yes." Edmund wondered how she could have forgotten their encounter so quickly. He'd thought of little else, even during an argument with the estate solicitor earlier. "We met in the garden this morning."

"Not that," she said. "You see, I'm from New York City too."

Surely he would have met her then . . . This beauty

couldn't have gone unnoticed for long, even if her mother had been one of *those* mothers who pressed their daughters on wealthy men. Maybe she lived on a country estate outside of the city and didn't frequent the elite social circles.

Her gaze steady on his, she said, "My name is Gina Graydon. And if I'm not mistaken, sir, my father is suing you."

Edmund's mouth fell open. If she was *the* Miss Graydon, her father was definitely suing him.

Graydon Enterprises had a monopoly on imports and exports along the New York coast, but that had all changed a few years ago as Edmund's company had gained more and more prestige. Edmund paid his workers well. Even though his profits were leaner than other cargo importers', he enjoyed better employee retention and loyalty. Several of Mr. Graydon's top employees had quit and moved to Edmund's company. Graydon was plainly upset at the losses.

This could either be very fortunate . . . or very foreboding. Edmund's mind raced. "Would that fact preclude you from dancing the next set with me?"

One of her eyebrows lifted as if she was considering, but Edmund could plainly see in her eyes that she'd accept. A thrill coursed through him. Dancing with the enemy's daughter might seem foolish to another man, but Miss Graydon had risen in his estimation. Edmund never backed down from a challenge, and it seemed this red-haired woman wasn't about to either.

"I'd be happy to save the next waltz for you." A smile tugged at her mouth.

Edmund had to stop himself from staring, especially because she'd offered a waltz with him above other, less-intimate dances. "Excellent." He gave a small nod then turned away.

A plan formed neatly in his mind. Now he understood why he'd been drawn to her, and it wasn't because he was a lovesick school boy. It was fate that they meet and fate that they dance. He'd have the opportunity to explain his business practices to her. She could put in a good word to her father, introductions would be made, and Edmund would share a brandy with Mr. Graydon . . . They'd become friends, and the lawsuit would be dropped.

Gina Graydon was not a temptress, but a fortunate tool to get his company out of an unfortunate mess.

FIVE

Gina took a slow sip of the pale pink punch—strawberry or raspberry-something. It made her feel a bit heady. Plainly there was more than fruit in the drink. Her mother had to be on her third or fourth glass by now, judging by the way she leaned heavily on her husband.

Mrs. Anne Graydon was the epitome of elegance and finery, with her auburn hair piled on top of her head, glittering diamonds about her neck, and delicate hands and feet. She was classic in a way Gina wasn't but should have been. Gina might have inherited her coloring from her mother, but her height came from her father.

Thankfully, Gina's grandmother had kept to her room tonight. Being watched by one matriarch was enough. The more her mother enjoyed her drink, the less she'd pay attention. As it was, Gina would spend a good part of the next day discussing who had asked her to dance and what their prospects might be because her mother would barely remember. Not that her mother expected her to find a husband on vacation, or that her father would *ever* approve, but since all of the New York City gentlemen had seemingly steered clear of her, France could very well be her only chance to meet someone on her own accord.

Gina's gaze moved to Mr. Edmund Donaldson, who stood on the other side of the room. Observing him in such a formal setting was quite different than in the wilds of the gardens. First, she felt more comfortable with social norms keeping them at arms' length and dictating their conversation and actions.

With so many people around, surely she couldn't say something embarrassing or do anything foolish like scale a wall. They could talk about their homes, their families, the French countryside—all very tame topics. Mr. Donaldson seemed to converse easily with those around him. He stood with two other gentlemen, both of whom appeared very interested in what he had to say. A blonde woman joined them, linking her arm with one of the men—her father, perhaps?

Mr. Donaldson smiled at the blonde, and the lady blushed. Something in Gina's heart twisted. The blonde was about Gina's age, without the awkward laughing Gina found herself in the middle of all too often. By the way the lady kept her gaze on Mr. Donaldson, it was plain she considered him a catch—and available.

Gina knew more about Mr. Donaldson than she'd first believed. The more she thought back to what was said in the newspaper and what her father had spoken about, the more she remembered. He'd recently been widowed.

She remembered one morning when her father read aloud from the paper over breakfast. Her mother had admonished her father to perhaps hold back on the lawsuit out of respect for Mr. Donaldson's mourning.

But her father had pressed forward, with no thought but to see his business continue to grow, no matter who he pushed out of the way in the process. It was why he was such a successful business owner, Gina supposed.

The lady with Mr. Donaldson twittered . . . was it possible for a person to truly twitter? It fit the blonde perfectly. Gina's neck warmed, and then the warmth traveled to her face. What was wrong with her? How could she be affected by some strange woman speaking to a man she'd officially met only moments ago?

She must do something to stop herself from watching, like refilling her punch glass. Before she could turn, Mr. Donaldson's gaze locked on hers from across the room, and Gina found she couldn't move.

Surely now her face was a decent pink, perhaps cranberry red. Just when she realized she hadn't breathed for several seconds, Mr. Donaldson's gaze slid from hers and locked onto something else, changing into a cautious gaze.

What ever could he be looking at?

Gina turned to see her father standing beside her, with her mother hanging on his arm. Her father was also staring across the room at one Edmund Donaldson.

"What is that man doing here?" her father said in a low voice.

"Who are you talking about, dear?" Her mother hiccupped. "Oh. Pardonnnn me."

Gina felt mortified. Her mother was drunk, and the evening wasn't even half over, which meant that it would be Gina's duty to take her mother back to their rooms. Her father would likely stay throughout the ball and play cards or chess with some poor opponent. He was a skilled gambler, although he'd scaled back somewhat due to his wife's threats of tying up her money.

Her father said nothing to his wife's question, his jaw tight.

"Is that . . . weren't youuuu speaking to that man earlier, Gina?" her mother said. "He is handsome. Mmm-hmm." She giggled. "I think he's . . . ohhhhh, he's coming over to talk to ussss."

Gina snapped her head to look. Mr. Donaldson made his way through the crowd, his eyes still locked with her father's. Not only were the two rivals about to meet face to face, but her mother had started to giggle uncontrollably.

SIX

It took only a few seconds for Edmund to assess the situation. Gina looked ready to flee to the nearest window and shimmy off a balcony. Mr. Graydon appeared as startled as Edmund felt when he'd learned Gina's identity, and Mrs. Graydon . . . well, she was a socialite with little to do but fret over her husband and only child, but the boredom had gotten to her, so she dulled it with excessive drinking.

She leaned forward, and Edmund almost blushed at the display of her spilling bosoms. The woman laughed, and by the look of her flushed cheeks and glistening eyes, one more drink would do her in—if she wasn't done in already. Unfortunately, he was well-acquainted with this situation, due to his own marriage to a pleasure-loving wife.

He extended his hand to the man who looked like he was about to draw a pistol on him. "Mr. Graydon, I wanted to introduce myself. I'm Edmund Donaldson." If it hadn't been for the comedic woman at the man's side, Edward might have felt intimidated. But Mr. Graydon was human after all, and had his own difficulties. Ironically, that meant the two of them had something in common, or at least *had*.

As it was, he felt Gina's gaze, and the tension in the air thickened.

Mr. Graydon said nothing for a moment, but kept his narrowed eyes on Edmund. Finally, Edward dropped his hand. Would Graydon refuse to speak with Edward after all? Had the bold introduction infuriated him?

"Father," Gina's said, her voice cutting through the thoughts whirling in Edmund's mind. "This is Mr. Donaldson, out of New York."

"Yes, I know," her father muttered.

"My dearrrrr," Mrs. Graydon said, her voice trilling an octave too high. Edmund was familiar with that as well. "Don't be rrrude. He's a fellow American, even if you are suing himmm." She burst into laughter.

Edmund glanced at Gina; her face flushed scarlet with mortification. He wanted to tell her he understood her embarrassment, that he didn't hold her accountable for either of her parents' actions.

"Strange meeting you here, of all places," Mr. Graydon finally said, his hand remaining at his side.

"I was surprised to learn that you were staying at this hotel." Edmund's gaze strayed to Gina. When it moved back to Mr. Graydon, a marked frown creased his face.

Mrs. Graydon lurched forward, and Edmund caught her arm to steady her. She laughed. "You *are* handsome. I'm glad you've chosen my daughter."

"Anne!" Mr. Graydon said in a tight voice.

Edmund released the woman's arm and slipped his hand in hers, squeezing it. "I don't know if your daughter will choose me, but I hope she'll dance with me." He could almost feel darts jab into his skin—ones Mr. Graydon would have thrown if he'd had them on hand.

Mrs. Graydon smiled sloppily and leaned so close that Edmund caught a full whiff of her flowery scent mixed with wine. "Oh, she'll dance with you."

With that, Mr. Graydon couldn't really protest unless he wanted more people watching than already were. Edmund turned to Gina, holding out his hand and ignoring her father.

Her eyes widened as she glanced from him to her parents. But when her gaze met his again, something passed between them—an understanding, a camaraderie, as if they were in this together. Whatever *this* was.

"I'd be happy to dance with you, Mr. Donaldson," Gina said in a surprisingly steady voice. Not that Edmund thought she'd be nervous, or drunk, like her mother, or anything other than the elegant woman she was tonight.

Then she said something most extraordinary. "As I promised earlier."

Edmund heard the unmistakable intake of air from Mr. Graydon as Gina placed her hand in Edmund's outstretched one. He felt the eyes of the older man on his back as he led Gina onto the dance floor. Edmund guided her around several couples, her hand light in his, until they reached the center.

They were soon surrounded by other couples and out of the direct view of her parents. It was the best he could hope for. He took her into his arms, settling into the waltz position, and as they started to move together, he made the mistake of looking into her amber eyes.

Which made him forget everything he'd planned to say.

Seven

Gina was on fire. And she wouldn't be surprised if she burst into actual flames. First, the embarrassment with her mother's drunkenness and how she'd practically shoved her bosom against Edmund Donaldson. Second, even from dozens of paces away, Gina could feel her father's vehemence. Although he was no longer standing next to her, his anger wove through the crowd and struck her to the core.

The only thing keeping her from leaving this ruined ball was the man looking down at her with his deep blue eyes. At the moment he'd held out his hand out to her stubborn father, and her father had refused to take it, she'd decided that Mr. Donaldson was better than any hero she'd read about in any novel.

And she wanted him to kiss her.

That might provide a third reason she was on fire, but she couldn't ask him to kiss her. Not after he'd endured such a cold reception from her parents. Rather, from her father. Gina wished her mother's greeting had been less exuberant. Especially since her father was suing him, and apparently hated him as well. Couldn't a person sue another, yet be civil and friendly?

Not likely. It was too bad, really. She was enjoying her time with Edmund, and she couldn't stop the smile that appeared on her face.

"I'm glad you're feeling better," Edmund said, his tone warming her further. Winter couldn't come soon enough.

"Better? I haven't been ill." *What am I saying?*

"I meant . . ." He hesitated as if unsure, or perhaps even at a loss for words. "I meant that you didn't seem happy while standing by your parents, but now you're smiling."

"I hadn't realized it, but you're right." A small laugh escaped her. "Sorry, I don't mean to laugh. I often don't mean to; it just happens."

His eyebrow lifted, and Gina hurried to say, "It's a trait I share with my mother, I suppose—the only trait we share."

"With the exception of the red hair and a few freckles?" he teased.

"Don't ever let my mother hear that word." She tried to keep her laughter at a minimum.

"*Freckles?*"

Gina gave a mock gasp. "She'd be mortified to think she has even one."

"But she—"

"Hush." Gina placed a finger to his lips. Then, realizing what she'd done, she quickly dropped her hand to his shoulder again.

He looked as stunned at the bold move as she felt. His recovery was much quicker, however. "What else should I know about your mother?" he asked.

Gina narrowed her eyes. "Why? What are you planning?"

An Ocean Away

"Nothing." But the sides of his mouth quirked. "I thought if I could impress your mother, perhaps I could impress her daughter."

Gina's heart nearly stopped. Edmund Donaldson wanted to impress her? Certainly it had something to do with the fact he was trying to save his company from an ugly lawsuit. Her feet floated back to the ground. She exhaled. "She enjoys her wine."

Edmund didn't flinch or act surprised in any way. "My wife enjoyed her wine as well."

His eyes stayed on hers, and Gina caught a glimpse of their depths. For a moment, their gazes held, saying what didn't need to be said.

"I'm sorry about your wife's passing," Gina said. "I realized after talking to you at the beginning of the ball that I'd read about it in the paper a few months ago."

Edmund looked past her for a moment, and when their eyes met again, he said, "It was a tragic accident." He let out a sigh.

Was he grieving deeply? Did he miss her?

They continued to dance in silence for a few more moments. She edged closer to Edmund at the same time he moved toward her. It was as if they'd shared something intimate—an understanding that drew them closer.

"So, Miss Graydon, what were you reading in the garden this morning?"

Gina inhaled. Surely if he knew the truth, he'd see her as some silly girl. Perhaps she should tell him that she was reading . . . "Shakespeare." Her lie made her blush. She needed something cold to drink, but the waltz wasn't over yet.

One of his eyebrows arched. "Which play?"

She did not want to say *Romeo and Juliet*, although it was the one she was most familiar with if he should want to discuss it with her. "*A Midsummer Night's Dream*."

Amusement filled his eyes. "Are you sure?"

A small jolt of panic swept through her. "What do you mean?"

"You seem a bit hesitant."

Gina laughed, if only to cover her embarrassment. *How does he know? He doesn't. He couldn't.* "Some may not think reading Shakespeare is entirely proper, so I didn't know if I wanted to confess it—" She cut herself off when she realized he was stroking her hand.

"Are you afraid to tell me what you were really reading?"

She fell silent as her thoughts tried to organize themselves for an answer.

"Ah. So you weren't reading Shakespeare this morning."

Gina opened her mouth then shut it.

"Don't worry. I won't reveal another of your dark secrets," he whispered. "Would you care for a stroll in the gardens?"

Gina's heart thundered. What might it be like to walk in the gardens with only the moon to light their way? She had never been alone with a man before, at least a man this handsome and intriguing. One whom she wanted to kiss her.

But if Edmund learned even half her fantasies, he'd think her a silly school girl. She absolutely had to turn him down. She was about to come up with an excuse when her father strode toward them.

"I'd better not." She stepped out of Edmund's arms.

He turned his head, and she felt him stiffen before releasing her. But he didn't back down or step away. He stayed close as her father stopped in front of them.

"Gina," her father said. "Your mother wishes to retire for the night."

Which meant Gina would have to leave the ball. Her father hadn't asked whether she wanted to stay. It was understood that Gina would help with Mother. Without a glance at Edmund, her father turned and strode away. Gina wanted to disappear. Her father could be abrupt, but she'd never seen him so outright rude.

She turned to Edmund. "Mr. Donaldson, I—"

"Call me Edmund."

His voice was so low, she wasn't sure she'd heard him right. But then he spoke again. "Perhaps I'll see you tomorrow... morning. In the garden?"

Gina stared at him, knowing that her father was waiting impatiently, but she couldn't help taking another moment with Edmund. "Perhaps." She cast a glance over her shoulder.

One side of Edmund's mouth lifted in a smile, and then he took her hand and pressed his lips to her fingers. "I hope so."

The heat of his lips traveled along her arm, raising the hairs on her skin. She knew she should pull away, but she lingered. If her father happened to turn and watch, Gina wouldn't hear the end of it.

"I may be able to find a ladder," he said. "And perhaps I can carry your mysterious book for you."

Gina laughed, completely breathless, her hand still in his. How could this near stranger have such an effect on her? If she leaned in a little, would he kiss her?

Gina pulled her hand back abruptly. Had she lost her senses? Kissing in public would amount to being forever disgraced.

"I'd better help my mother, Edmund," she said then quickly turned so he wouldn't see the full blush on her cheeks.

Eight

E*dmund* . . . She'd said his name. Edmund had to force himself not to stare at her as she walked across the room to join her parents.

It took only seconds after Gina linked arms with her mother for her to glance back in his direction. He was glad he'd waited for it. Her skin still held a bit of her earlier blush. Edmund's mind spun. He'd never been tempted to throw away convention, but now he wanted to stride across the room, and capture her in his arms.

This is insane. Truly insane.

He didn't know if he could wait until tomorrow—until dawn, when, he hoped, she'd slip into the garden again. Perhaps he should kiss her tonight and get it over with. Surely it would satiate whatever boiled over inside of him now. He'd heard of ridiculous crushes but had never thought he'd be caught in one.

Edmund exhaled as Gina moved away with her mother

toward the double doors of the ballroom. He had to focus and calm his racing heart. He needed a drink.

Crossing the room, Edmund kept one eye on Mr. Graydon. The man was clearly keeping track of Edmund too. One drink, maybe two, and then Edmund would be ready to face the tyrant. Old money was still favored over new money, but the difference between Edmund and Mr. Graydon was that Edmund had worked for every dollar. Mr. Graydon had inherited his.

Of course now, Edmund had come into a healthy inheritance, but he wouldn't let Mr. Graydon know that. For Edmund's strategy to work, he needed Mr. Graydon to think he had the upper hand for as long as possible.

Edmund stopped at the refreshment table and accepted a glass of wine. He gulped it down then reached for another. They needed to serve something stronger at these blasted events.

With a smile, Edmund watched Mr. Graydon slip into the gentleman's lounge. Perfect. Edmund brought the second glass of wine to his lips and drank the rest. Then he made his way to the lounge, stopping a couple of times when someone greeted him. Having been in Bordeaux for a few days, he'd made a several acquaintances during meal times.

When Edmund stepped into the lounge, it took a moment for his eyes to adjust to the dim lighting. A fire burned low on the far side of the room, and the low-hung chandelier was much dimmer than the ones in the ballroom. Cigar smoke was already in abundance, causing Edmund to blink against the sudden stinging in his eyes.

He quickly spotted Mr. Graydon, who was settling at the card table, a cigar in one hand, and a generous helping of brandy in the other.

Edmund smiled as he saw the bills laid out on the table. It looked like the stakes would be high tonight. Just what he needed.

NINE

A rapping on the door thundered into Gina's room, startling her awake. For a second, she couldn't remember where she was. The room was pitch black, so she couldn't have been asleep long. The knock came again, this time accompanied by her father's voice. "Open up, Gina! Right away!"

Gina scrambled out of bed then had to take a moment to steady her swimming head by bracing herself against the bedpost. What time was it? She'd left the drapes halfway open, and moonlight still streamed through. By the black color of the sky beyond, it had to be the middle of the night.

She crossed to the door, unlocked it, and opened it a crack. "Is something wrong?"

"Let me in and light a blasted lamp," her father barked.

Gina opened the door wider and stepped aside. "Is it Mother? Or Grandmother?"

"No." He moved to the windows as Gina lit one of the

oil lamps. The low light was feeble at best, but the fire had died hours ago.

Her father pulled the drapes closed with a snap. Turning toward her, he narrowed his eyes. "That man is a fraud, through and through. You're to have nothing to do with him."

"Who are you talking about?" Gina stalled, although she had fairly good idea.

"Edmund Donaldson, that's who." He scrutinized her carefully.

Gina's face grew warm, and she clasped her hands in front of her. She'd danced with him only once; why the concern? Curiosity burned through her.

"How is he a fraud?" she asked.

Her father crossed to the dark fireplace. "You wouldn't understand."

Gina's thoughts tumbled. Her father's worry was surely about the shipping business, or the lawsuit, which she didn't completely understand. "Is it the lawsuit?"

"He set me up," her father said. "He placed a high stakes wager in a card game."

Mother hated him gambling. "What happened? Did you . . . lose?"

His face reddened, and he took a couple of steps forward. "He might have won his wager, but I'm going to crush everything he's ever built." He stopped in front of Gina, so close she could smell brandy on his breath and see that his eyes were bloodshot. "If I see you speak to him or so much *look* at him, you'll be cut off—do you hear me?"

Cut off? Gina took a step back. What had the wager been? And what had she done to deserve her father's threats? Her life had become a scene in a novel.

"Father . . ." she started, wanting to ask him about the wager, but he brushed past and opened the door.

He turned to look at her. "If that infernal man isn't gone at first light, we'll be leaving on the morrow." Before she could formulate anything remotely intelligent to say, he left, slamming the door behind him.

A shudder passed through her body, and tears threatened, but she kept her emotions in check as she locked the door and extinguished the lamp.

Gina stood in the dark room for several moments, too stunned to do much else. Then dread coursed through her as she realized her neighbor on the other side of her wall had surely heard the shouting. A door shut down the hallway. She hoped her mother was sound asleep and would miss her father's tirade. She stood, listening, but all was quiet.

She let out a groan as dismay then anger took ahold of her heart. She didn't know what had happened exactly between the two men, but it wasn't *her* fault. What had her father lost? What would her mother say about it—especially since she was the one to bring the fortune into the marriage?

Gina crossed to the windows in thought. Her mother might rant for a while. Predictably, she'd then finish off the nearest bottle of wine. Gina drew open the drapes, and moonlight flooded the room. With the aid of extra light, she grabbed a wrapper from the chair near her bed and slipped it on. She wouldn't be sleeping, knowing she might never see Mr. Donaldson again.

Gina stepped out onto the balcony. Only that morning, her life had seemed much simpler. She had not met the man in the room next to hers. Her gaze slid to his darkened windows. Was he in bed, or still in the card room? Perhaps he'd already left the hotel like her father hoped.

Something inside her felt profoundly sad at the thought. Mr. Donaldson was the one being sued, he had been recently widowed, and now . . . he'd incurred the wrath of a powerful man—her own father.

If the people of New York had to take sides, her father would win. He'd been established in the business longer, and her mother came from a long line of society's elite.

Gina's heart raced as she considered what she could

An Ocean Away

do . . . and what she *wanted* to do. Another glance at the darkened windows of Mr. Donaldson confirmed her decision—nothing short of what a heroine might do, although this might be a bit more risqué, since this was . . . well, *real life*. She gripped the balcony rail and climbed over the edge. The moonlight gave enough light to get to the ground safely. Now she only had to climb up again.

She arched her neck, looking at Mr. Donaldson's balcony, her heart responding with more thumping. This was beyond anything she'd done before. Gina thought about her father's harsh words and threats . . .

It was now or never. Tomorrow she'd be separated from Mr. Donaldson.

She grabbed for the first protruding stone then lifted her foot to find purchase. By the time she climbed over Mr. Donaldson's rail, she was out of breath. If this had been in a novel, the hero would be waiting for her, and of course he'd declare his love the moment she knocked. Perhaps passionately kiss her. Then he'd request her hand in marriage from her father, and the two men would become the best of friends.

As it was, this wasn't a novel, which was made clear when she knocked softly on the window but no one answered. She knocked again, despite her pounding heart. Still, no answer. Something moved below the balcony. Her heart nearly stopped.

"Miss Graydon?" a voice whispered from below.

Gina wanted to disappear. With her pulse racing, she turned and peered over the rail. Edmund Donaldson stood below, looking up at her.

"Hello," she said in a quiet voice. "I seem to have climbed the wrong balcony."

His mouth quirked into a smile, and it was then Gina noticed he wasn't wearing his suit coat or a tie, and that his collar was open, his shirt a bit rumpled, his hair disheveled . . . He looked every bit the romantic hero.

"*Juliet?*" he said.

Gina stared at him for a moment before understanding. He was teasing about her lie about reading Shakespeare. "I don't think this is how it went," she whispered.

"No? Romeo didn't call up to Juliet on her balcony?"

"Oh, that happened in the story, but this isn't my balcony, and my name isn't Juliet... It's not even close."

Mr. Donaldson laughed softly. "However could you mistake my balcony for yours? Mine has the hedges."

Gina played along. "Perhaps because they look identical when one doesn't notice the hedges, and it is quite dark out here."

"Darker than when you usually visit the garden, eh?"

"Much."

"And why, may I ask, are you climbing balconies in the middle of the night?" he said. "Has your nocturnal eyesight become good enough to read with only the moon as a guide?"

"No."

He laughed again, and not only had Gina's face warmed, but her entire body.

"Mr. Donaldson, if you would please turn around, I'd like to come down now."

One of his eyebrows lifted, but he turned and walked a few paces away.

Gina climbed over the railing. She descended slowly, highly aware that one slip would be witnessed, and might send her tumbling into his arms. At one point, she nearly lost her grip, earning a scraped palm for her efforts. When she was nearly to the bottom, two hands grasped her around the waist and lifted her the rest of the way down.

She gasped and turned around, coming face to face with Mr. Donaldson. Her hands rested on his arms, and she was suddenly glad he wasn't wearing a confining suit coat. It was a new thing for her to feel the warmth and strength of a

An Ocean Away

man's skin through his shirtsleeves—a realization that made her blush furiously.

"What are you doing out here?" she said, her voice not quite steady. She hoped to cover the fact that being in his arms made her feel faint, because of note, he had not yet released her. And the intensity of his gaze told her he wasn't about to any time soon.

"I was thinking about where I might find a woman on a balcony."

"You seem to have a lucky streak tonight . . . You find a woman on a balcony as you desired, and earlier, you won my father in a card game."

His face sobered, and he released her.

Gina regretted bringing up her father, but she knew it must be so. She might never see Mr. Donaldson again. "What happened?"

"How do you know about the game?" His eyes searched hers, and she didn't like what she saw in them: mistrust and doubt.

Could she trust *him*? She would take the risk to learn the truth. "My father was upset, said it was a high-stakes game. He came to my room and declared I am never to see you again."

Mr. Donaldson didn't answer, his gaze intent.

"What was the wager, Mr. Donaldson?"

"Edmund," he whispered, leaning down. "Call me Edmund."

Her heart hammered, he was so close. He wasn't even touching her any longer, yet her body seemed to yearn for his.

"Edmund, what was the wager?" Her head felt light, her body weak, as if she'd had champagne.

His fingers brushed against her arms, ever so lightly, then one hand moved to her cheek, like touching a porcelain doll. "*You* were the wager."

Ten

Before Gina could question him, his hand slid behind her head, cradling hers as he angled his face. His lips brushed hers, so softly at first that Gina wondered if it could possibly be a kiss. But when his kiss deepened, and his mouth moved against hers as if he was only focused on one thing, there was no doubt.

Fire spread through her from his touch, his hands on her face and neck. His scent enveloped her, and she wondered if this was what a heroine felt like when kissing her hero. Gina sighed against Edmund, and her lips parted, kissing him back.

Then both his hands tangled in her hair, and she wrapped her arms around his neck, pressing her body against his. As far as first kisses went, nothing much seemed amiss. At least, Gina found concentrating on something other than Edmund Donaldson difficult, and she quite forgot any of the romantic plotlines she'd read.

His kisses were urgent, yet gentle, as if he savored each taste of her, and she wanted to taste him back. His fingers skimmed her neck, causing warm shivers to course through her body. Then his fingers trailed her collarbone and rested on her shoulder.

"Are you all right?" he whispered.

She felt too dizzy to reply for a moment. "Kissing me was the wager?"

"No." His breath was warm against her ear. "Becoming acquainted with you."

"So you went straight to kissing me?"

He chuckled softly. "I'm sorry. I am taking advantage." But he didn't release her. "Ever since I first saw you scale the balcony wall, I haven't been able to stop thinking about you."

"You don't even know me," Gina said.

His arms stayed around her as he looked at her. "I intend to remedy that. Thus the wager."

Her mouth still tingled from his touch. "I don't want to be a wager."

One side of his mouth lifted, and he touched her jawline. "Your father was backed into a corner. The wager was that if I won, he'd drop the lawsuit. He lost, then demanded we play a second game for a chance to win back the lawsuit. But he had nothing else to offer, so I threw out your name, and he grabbed onto it." His low voice resonated through her.

She gazed into his eyes, her heart pounding at his nearness. "And you won?"

"Of course." One of his hands trailed down her arm then caught her hand in his. "They call my fortune new money because I won a couple of gold mines in a card game. I sold them and started the shipping company."

Gina's skin went cold. "You're a *gambler*?"

One of his brows arched. "Retired."

"It doesn't sound like you've retired."

His other fingers threaded through hers; they stood

nearly toe-to-toe. "I was until someone with a beautiful daughter decided to sue me."

Gina's mind tumbled. She didn't know what to think. Maybe her father was right—she should stay away from Edmund Donaldson. Here he was, a professed gambler, with his wife dead only a few months. She drew her hands away.

"Your father wanted to play again," he said, not seeming aware that she was keeping her distance. "He said all or nothing . . . and I asked what he meant by 'all.'"

Gina found herself holding her breath.

"He said 'my fortune for yours' and when I asked him the amount of his fortune, I could tell he thought he'd bested me." Edmund paused, moving closer to Gina. "My wife's property is worth twice that of your mother's and father's assets combined. I told him I didn't want his fortune, but I would wager my own in exchange for becoming acquainted with his daughter."

Gina gasped. "You risked all of your wealth for *me*?" Her face burned . . . with what she wasn't sure. Anger? Pleasure? Embarrassment? Then she realized . . . "You knew you'd win, didn't you? You cheated."

His expression turned to stone. "I'm not a cheat." His eyes narrowed. "Is that what your father said?"

"No," Gina breathed.

He grasped her arms. "I knew I would win because your father's face is as easy to read as a naughty toddler's."

"It was still a great risk. Why would you make such a wager?" she asked, unsure if she should be flattered or angry.

His grasp fell away, but he didn't give her any space. His tone softened. "There was no other way your father would let me near you."

The man was a flatterer. She'd only met him the day before, had danced with him once. How could he be so interested? "Surely you seek my company because it brings angst to my father."

He showed no hesitation in his answer. "No. But I won't deny the challenge."

Gina didn't know what to make of his answer. "Despite the wager, my father is determined to keep you away," she said in a quiet voice.

"Then, my darling." He moved close again. "We'll have to keep him to his bargain." He kissed her cheek, lingering, and Gina wished for more, though she feared this was all some sort of game to Edmund.

She was a challenge; he'd said so himself. Was the wager for her really a way to get back at her father as part of a revenge plot? Or worse, was she a passing fancy, someone to dally with while he got over the death of his wife?

"I know what you're thinking." His scent seemed to steal some of her common sense.

"You can't possibly know that."

"This is not about the lawsuit, and I'm not a man of idle convictions," he said, holding her gaze. "I would like to get to know you better . . . with or without a wager."

Her breath left for a few seconds. "Edmund." She felt her resolve to stay away from him weaken. She had to think this through. This man had been a gambler. Could he be trusted? Would she listen to her own father, or a near stranger who happened to make her pulse race wildly?

His fingers slowly traced her jaw, and then they moved to lightly brush her lips. "Tell me about yourself, anything and everything. Do you like music, painting? What books do you love?"

Her body trembled in response to his touch; she wanted to cling to him, to kiss him again, to ask him to hold her. But if this was anything real, if it had any potential at all, she must tell him the truth about what she read before she lost herself to him completely. Then she would know if he'd ever fully accept her. She took a step back.

"I read romance novels," she whispered. "Constantly. And without my parents' knowledge. I will not apologize for it, and someday I may write one myself." She had never admitted to herself that she was interested in writing novels, but with blurting it out, she realized it had been a hidden desire for years.

"Will you use a pen name?" he asked.

Gina straightened, getting some of her determination back with their new distance. "I haven't decided. Whether or not I do, I wouldn't be fit for marriage. Society frowns upon a married woman with an occupation. Especially a female novelist."

His gaze held steady for a long moment. "Whichever way you choose, I'll read your books."

Eleven

Edmund chuckled to himself as he remembered being with Gina in the garden. If her worst flaw was reading romance novels, she was a like a dove in the eye of a storm—innocent, to be sure. Her life had been more than sheltered.

He turned from the window and the rising sun to start packing. They'd reluctantly parted after another kiss or two and had returned to their own rooms—Edmund through the front doors of the hotel, and Gina back up to her balcony. Perhaps one day, he'd try balcony climbing himself.

He thought about her family as he unlatched his trunk, getting ready to pack. Gina's mother was a society drunk, and her father was ruthless; life was not all roses at the Graydon household. The man's reputation was callous at best, and if Edmund took the time, he'd probably uncover several questionable transactions made by Mr. Graydon to keep his company afloat. There was no secret about Mr.

Graydon's gambling history, and though it seemed to have lessened in the last few years, the financial sting would likely be felt for decades. If anyone knew the false promise of gambling, it was Edmund. Which is why he'd sworn to retiring the habit after starting his shipping company; wagering against the old man had been the single exception.

As Edmund loaded his shoes and trousers into the trunk, he realized that the fact he had no trouble hiring some of Graydon's top employees was a distress signal indeed. There might be more issues with Graydon's company than Edmund knew. No matter the outcome of the lawsuit, Edmund determined to court Gina. He'd had marital complications before, but now he'd rather enter into a love-filled marriage and deal with difficult in-laws, than marry for convenience—which he'd already experienced.

Marriage. Was he really thinking it? As unbelievable as it might sound to others, it wasn't to him. Would marrying Gina be so farfetched? He didn't think his interest would wane anytime soon. His marriage to Jacqueline had not been all it seemed. It wasn't something he readily admitted to anyone else, but it was hard to deny those who attended his wife's funeral—the most notorious bachelors in New York City.

Edmund had never caught Jacqueline cheating on him, but that hardly meant a thing. She enjoyed her drink as much as she enjoyed mixed company, and they often stayed at her parties far into the night. So late he'd found men and women sleeping throughout his home the next morning, not all of them in full states of dress.

Being married to a novelist would be like exchanging a lion for a lamb.

He smiled, which happened almost every time he thought of the red-haired woman in the rooms next door. Edmund started to fold his shirts and set them in the trunk. He'd leave the hotel, but he wouldn't be leaving France until things were completed with Jacqueline's estate. He hoped, perhaps beyond reason, that he'd be able to see Gina before returning to New York.

What would happen once they were both in New York? He honestly did not know.

When Edmund finished packing, it was still early, and he doubted anyone else in the hotel stirred. All the better. He wasn't much in the mood to run into Mr. Graydon, especially after a night without sleep and time spent kissing his daughter. The guilt would be plain on Edmund's face.

He left his room and went to the front desk of the hotel to request that his trunk be brought down and a carriage ordered. Soon he was on his way to another hotel. By the time he was settled into a new set of rooms, he was famished.

Once in the dining room with eggs benedict before him, he inquired of the waiter where he might find a bookshop with English translations. It didn't take long to find the bookshop, although he had to wait half an hour for the place to open. His first question to the shopkeeper was where the ladies' romance novels were shelved.

"This way, monsieur," the shopkeeper said in a curious tone, leading him down a narrow aisle.

The man stopped at a shelf of cloth-bound books in varying colors of burgundy to brown. He eyed Edmund up and down, as if assessing what type of man made such a request.

"Which is newest?" Edmund asked.

The shopkeeper reached for one and handed it over. He was quick to scurry away. Edmund leafed through the novel and decided to read a few pages. The author had identified themselves by initials only, making him suspect that it was a female writer. He leaned against the shelving and opened to chapter one. By the beginning of chapter two, he was smiling, not because of the light, humorous prose, but because an idea had formed in his mind.

An idea of how to win over Gina Graydon.

So what if it meant stealing a fictional plot?

TWELVE

Three months, Gina thought, turning over in her bed. It was after midnight, but she couldn't sleep. It had been an insufferable three months since her return from France, and the fact that the air was turning from autumn to winter didn't help at all. New York didn't have the kindest of winters, yet usually Gina looked forward to them because she could spend long hours by the crackling fire, curled up with a book.

But that wasn't to be this winter. The night before, her parents had declared that her father was having the credentials of a few potential gentlemen suitors investigated.

Investigated! Humiliating. Her father had hinted that her future husband needed to be mature and dependable. The *mature* part had her worried. At least they'd given her some warning, but Gina had yet to read a romance novel where the hero was twice the age of the heroine.

In truth, it made her sad that her marriage prospects

had come down to this. Sad because the one man she thought could even remotely imagine sharing her bed and raising a couple of children with, had disappeared . . . completely.

Mr. Edmund Donaldson had packed and left the Bordeaux hotel without so much as a note slipped under her door. Not that Gina hadn't known he was leaving—he'd told her—but she thought he'd at least keep his promise to stay in contact, to hold her father to the wager, to become better acquainted with her . . . to possibly court her.

But there had been nothing.

When she had inquired as discreetly as possible as to the progression of the lawsuit between her father and Mr. Donaldson, she'd been immediately told to stay out of "matters that don't concern you."

Hours before, she'd read in the evening paper that the lawsuit had been settled, and it seemed Mr. Donaldson had come out better, while her father had been ordered to pay damages. That might explain his glowering nature the past several days. It also might explain his new demand that she find a husband . . .

Gina burrowed deeper into her bedcovers. It didn't matter now. Mr. Donaldson had kissed and then abandoned her. He'd used her. She'd been a pawn in his game. Now he sat high in society, having bested his rival. No matter who her father's friends were, they all admired power and money.

Let Mr. Donaldson be admired. He would not be admired by her.

Gina let out a sigh, willing her tears to be gone. She was done pining over the man; crying wasn't an attractive thing anyway. If she was going to attract a husband, she needed to be back to her agreeable self.

She closed her eyes, but a moment later, opened them again. The early winter sun glowed against the outline of her drapes. Had she slept? She wasn't sure, but the dawn called to her. Much as she'd done in Bordeaux, she often rose early to go out into the garden. Except she hadn't been reading lately. Romance novels hurt her heart. Reading about love and kissing and daring heroes only reminded her of the man she'd thought might be her hero but had turned out the opposite. He'd become the villain.

Gina climbed out of bed and pulled on her warmest wrapper. She left her room, went down the back stairs, and out the kitchen door. No one was awake yet, and she was careful to close the door without a sound. She walked in the chill of the cold morning, certain it would snow any day now. The garden, once green and full of blooming flowers, now only had a few hardy rose bushes left to add any color, with the rest of the plants and bushes wilted to a dried brown.

She stopped at her favorite bench. Surprised to see a book left there, she bent to pick it up. Surely the cold and damp would damage the fine leather. The book wasn't familiar though; whose could it be? Who had left it out? None of the maids read, and she hadn't seen her mother read anything but gossip columns for a decade.

Curious, Gina turned the book over. It was a novel. Her heart pounded to think that one of her parents might have discovered it and thought it was hers. Opening the inside cover, expecting to see the name of the owner scrawled inside, she was startled to see an inscription written to her.

And signed E.D.

Dear Gina,

I have stopped by each morning for three days to see if I could glimpse you in the garden, reading upon this bench, much like you did in Bordeaux. Perhaps your vacation habits don't carry over to your home?

When I received no reply to the flowers I've sent weekly for two months, I realized that what happened between us in France was purely my imagination. I beg your forgiveness for being so presumptuous. Now that things are settled between your father and me, I wish to make one more attempt.

I do not think your father would welcome me as a gentleman caller, but if you would, I will face his ire. If I don't hear from you by tonight, I will know that you have forever moved on.

Yours,
E.D.

Gina re-read the words, disbelief pulsing through her. He'd sent flowers? Every week? He'd been in her garden? And... which night did he speak of? Last night?

She sank onto the bench, holding the book against her chest, trying to comprehend the note. Edmund had not rejected her. He had not turned his affections away. She stood, pacing back and forth on the path in front of the bench. What had happened to the flowers? Had her parents known about them? They must have. They must have kept the flowers from her.

Gina hurried inside the house. As she stood in the empty hallway filled with family portraits, she knew she had to make a decision, one with consequences for the rest of her life.

In moments she determined what she'd do, and when she climbed the stairs to her room, her heart beat in anticipation. She dressed quickly and pulled her hair back into a simple twist. She didn't want to waste another moment; too much time had already been lost—three months!

Gina sat at her desk and wrote a letter to her parents, hands trembling as she did so, but it had to be done. When they awoke, they would be livid, yet it would be up to them if they decided to accept their daughter into their home.

Just in case, Gina packed a satchel of her most precious personal belongings.

Leaving the note outside her parents' bedroom suite,

her nerves multiplied. What if Edmund rejected her? What if she'd misread his intentions? Perhaps he didn't intend to marry her, but simply to court her. What if she was about to completely embarrass herself?

With her satchel over one shoulder, she left the house through the front door, closing it firmly behind her. She made her way up the street, drawing a few curious glances from early risers. Once she reached the corner with the post office, she waited until she saw a carriage for hire.

If the driver was surprised at a lady requesting such an early ride, he was too polite to show it. That was one of the advantages of belonging to the upper class; you were rarely questioned on odd behavior. But Gina was sure the driver took special note of her appearance should he have to answer for his actions later on.

Gina gave the driver Edmund Donaldson's address. The minutes seemed to drag, and more than once, Gina wondered if she should turn around, rip up the note to her parents, and forget about Edmund Donaldson. But she kept thinking about the flowers. He'd sent some each week. Surely that meant something. Surely that meant he loved her.

Edmund Donaldson's house was elegant but not overstated. Gina was familiar with the outside, having driven past it a time or two in the first week since returning from France. All seemed quiet now, as it should be with the morning sky only a dusky pink.

She paid the driver and waited until he pulled around the corner before she approached the step. The double doors were imposing, but there was no turning back now. Gina knocked boldly then stepped back to wait.

Seconds passed, and more, until Gina was sure it was a full minute. Her heart pounded, and she wasn't sure if she dared knock again. Perhaps she'd made a mistake after all. Perhaps this was part of a twisting plot she hadn't expected. Nothing had been as she'd expected it this morning, not since she found that book left by Edmund.

The door opened, and her eyes flew to the man standing there.

Edmund said nothing at first, and it was clear that Gina had awakened him. He wore an ivory-colored shirt, untucked, which looked hastily donned. His trousers were long, but his feet were bare. As much as she regretted that, she was glad it wasn't a butler who'd answered. In fact, she was surprised it was Edmund himself.

"Gina . . ." His eyes were bluer than she remembered.

For a moment, she didn't speak. There was a depth to his eyes she hadn't seen before. When she'd only seen interest, amusement, and kindness previously, now she saw wariness, and perhaps even pain. He made no move to open the door wider, as if he were waiting for her to tell him why she stood on his doorstep.

"I—I found the book." She looked down; it was hard to look into his eyes. What if he rejected her? "I didn't know about the flowers." Tears pricked her eyes, and she lifted her gaze. "I don't know what happened—or who hid them from me. I . . . I'm sorry."

"You never received them?"

"No," she whispered.

His expression hardened. "I knew your father despised me, but—" He shook his head as if to rid his thoughts of something deplorable.

"I can't excuse his behavior," she said, her voice gaining momentum. "He wouldn't talk about you with me, and I only found out who won the lawsuit in last evening's paper. To tell you the truth, I was glad of the outcome."

He blinked as if surprised.

"Then today I found the book and read what you wrote inside, and I felt awful." She took a step closer. "Mostly because of the terrible things I've thought about you. I thought you'd forgotten me."

His jaw was set; she wasn't sure if he was angry. Perhaps he hated her now. To be ignored for three months would be a blow to one's ego. She knew exactly how that felt.

"Edmund," she began again. "I don't know how to tell you how sorry I am. I knew nothing of the flowers. It was as if you had disappeared. I thought I'd never hear from you or see you again."

His stance relaxed against the door frame, his eyes less hard.

Gina clasped her trembling hands together and took a deep breath. "I wrote a note to my parents this morning and left the house to come here. I told them that if they didn't accept you, they'd lose a daughter."

Edmund's eyes searched hers. She blinked back tears but kept her gaze on his, not willing to look away. She wanted him to know she was in earnest, about the price she was paying, and her regret over her parents' actions.

"Come inside," Edmund said, but Gina couldn't read his tone. Was he being courteous? Would he call his groomsman to take her home?

She stepped inside. If her eyes hadn't been blurred with tears, she might have taken time to inspect the grand hallway. As it was, her heart beat irregularly, and she wasn't sure how much strength she had left to stand any longer. Edmund shut the door, and they were left in the dim interior.

"What's in your bag?" he asked in a quiet voice.

Gina had almost forgotten she held it. "Some mementos in case I'm not welcomed home."

Edmund's brow arched at that. "You came at the risk of your parents' displeasure?"

Gina couldn't help it—she smiled then gave a little laugh. "They will be more than displeased." She exhaled. This wasn't going well. Edmund hadn't swept her into his arms and declared his undying devotion. "I suppose I can hire myself as a school teacher. They're in great demand out West. I have enough money for a train fare, at least."

Edmund folded his arms, one corner of his mouth

lifting. Gina hoped that was as good sign, but perhaps his smile was derisive. "You'd make a fine teacher."

Disappointment flooded through her, but there'd be plenty of time to cry about it later. If she was to have a broken heart, Wyoming sounded like a better place than New York to suffer it. "Do you know of a position out there?"

Edmund's face broke out into a smile. "You're incorrigible, you know."

It wasn't exactly a compliment, but the fact that he thought of her that way wasn't surprising. Her parents would agree. Tears stung her eyes.

"I have another idea." He stepped toward her and lifted his hands to cradle her face. "Why don't you marry me?" he whispered. "What's the worst that could happen? You've left your home, and now you're at mine. I can take care of you."

She nodded, hot tears forming. His touch was what she'd dreamed of, though perhaps he was simply being a gentleman to a distressed woman. "But . . . could you love me?" It was her deepest desire, though admitting it left her heart to be trampled upon.

His thumb brushed at the tears falling on her cheeks, making her heart ache more. "I already love you." His arms went around her, pulling her tightly against him, and his mouth found hers.

Warmth traveled the length of Gina's body as she clung to him and kissed him back. There was no doubt of his feelings now. He backed her against the door, pinning her between it and his body, as if he intended to make up for three months in a few minutes.

"Edmund," she gasped between kisses. "Won't your servants discover us?"

He chuckled. "I suppose we'll have to get married right away. How does this afternoon sound?"

"Impossible," she said as his lips sought her neck. She

was grateful she held onto his shoulders, or her legs might have given out.

"Not impossible." He lifted his head to grin at her. "It happens all of the time in novels. You should read one."

Gina laughed. She had no doubt if anyone could pull off a same-day wedding, it would be Mr. Edmund Donaldson. Even if the idea came from a novel.

To read about Gina Graydon's friend, Eliza Robinson, check out the *USA Today* bestselling novel *Heart of the Ocean*.

About Heather B. Moore

Heather B. Moore is the *USA Today* bestseller and award-winning author of more than a dozen historical novels set in Ancient Arabia and Mesoamerica. Heather attended the Cairo American College in Egypt, the Anglican International School in Jerusalem, and received her Bachelor of Science degree from Brigham Young University in Provo, Utah. Heather writes her historical thrillers under the pen name H.B. Moore. She writes romance and women's fiction under Heather B. Moore. It can be confusing, so her kids just call her Mom.

For book updates, sign up for Heather's email list: hbmoore.com/contact

Website: www.hbmoore.com

Blog: MyWritersLair.blogspot.com

Facebook: Fans of H.B. Moore *or* Heather Brown Moore

WHAT HAPPENS IN VENICE

by Nancy Campbell Allen

Other Works by Nancy Campbell Allen

Isabelle Webb Series

The Pharaoh's Daughter
Legend of the Jewel
The Grecian Princess

Faith of Our Fathers Series

A House Divided
To Make Men Free
Through the Perilous Fight
One Nation Under God

One

1894—Venice, Italy

Evangeline Stuart stood alone on the Doge's Palace second floor *loggia* and looked out over Venice's Grand Canal. She wished she could freeze the moment in time; it wasn't so much that she disliked people—just the ones with whom she lived and currently traveled. At twenty-one years, she was quite the spinster, and her step-father and his two daughters seemed loath to allow her to forget it. They were unpleasant in the extreme, although subtle about it, which somehow made it worse.

Moonlight glinted off of the wide body of water, and a soft breeze blew a few stray, golden curls away from Evangeline's face as she closed her eyes, enjoying the muted sounds of singing gondoliers and people in the courtyard behind the building, gathering for the pending masquerade ball.

Evangeline adjusted the purple silk, jewel-encrusted demi-mask that covered her eyes, wondering if she dared take it off for these few moments she was alone. Her view of the water wasn't encumbered by the adornment, but she wanted to feel the breeze upon all of her face, not just the lower half. Her younger step-sisters, the twins, had insisted it would be bad luck to remove the masks before the night was over, although Evangeline doubted nearly everything that came out of the girls' mouths.

Before leaving the inn, Evangeline had decided it was to be a magical night, so the mask would remain in place. She had dreamed of Venice for so long that she could hardly believe her good fortune; since her mother's passing the year before, her stepfather had denied her all but the simplest of pleasures. That he had allowed her to accompany him and the twins on their holiday to the floating city had been more a matter of keeping up appearances, but she had grasped the opportunity with both hands before he could change his mind and had breathed a bit easier when they left London behind.

Evangeline felt, rather than heard, someone watching her. She turned her head to see a man whose upper face was hidden by a black mask, which matched the rest of his dark attire, down to the shiny black of his boots. The only contrast to the dark night, and his equally dark suit, was the snowy white of his shirtfront, collar, and cravat. He leaned against one of the Byzantine arches gracing the *loggia's* outer wall to Evangeline's right and studied her with a silence she found unnerving.

Straightening, she lifted her chin. My, but the man was tall. And broad. For a moment, she felt a stab of fear and glanced at the doors leading back into the palace.

"I mean you no harm, *bella*," the man murmured, his tone low. The corner of his mouth lifted in a wry smile. "You may escape back into the crowd if you wish." His English was accented, but otherwise flawless.

"What are you doing?" Evangeline asked, feeling slightly stupid.

"I am a patron of the arts, you see, and I am admiring the exquisite."

Evangeline felt a blush steal across her face and was grateful for the mask. She knew well that the purple gown accentuated her figure to its best. She had enjoyed two Seasons in London while her mother was still alive but had spent little time recently in the company of gentlemen, as the twins now were the focus of the household.

The man made no move toward her. In fact, he remained quite still. He was compelling, though, and his intensity had her feeling overwhelmed. Warm. Evangeline was very near to fleeing the *loggia* when a small voice in the back of her brain reminded her that she wore a mask and a beautiful gown. For the evening, she could be whomever she chose, even if she decided to simply be Evangeline for the first time in a very long while.

She smiled a bit. How long had it been since she had allowed her joy to surface? How long since she'd *felt* it? For one night, just one night, she wanted to be the woman she might have become if circumstances beyond her control hadn't altered her existence completely.

"You are Venetian?" Evangeline asked. "Or visiting for the Biennales?"

He inclined his head. "I am here for the art show," he said. "From Florence."

"You are an artist, then?" she said, and bravely took the smallest of steps toward him.

Again, that smile—a wealth of information contained in it. Wry, self-assured, perhaps jaded. "Regrettably, no. But I do enjoy art. I am on the Biennales selection committee."

"Oh? Well then, you are acquainted with my stepfather's work. We are here because of it."

"His name?"

"Robert Montgomery."

The stranger leaned forward slightly. "Robert Montgomery is your stepfather? I should very much enjoy meeting him. His paintings are exceptional."

Again Evangeline was grateful for the mask. She hoped that it, combined with the darkness of the night, covered her dubious reaction. Robert fancied himself an artist, but Evangeline thought his work amateur, pedestrian. That he had been invited to showcase his work in Italy's first annual Biennales art show had come as a shock. Perhaps the selection committee was not so well-versed in what constituted quality.

"You do not agree?"

Drat. He had seen through both the mask and the dark.

"But perhaps you are not familiar with art, then?" he said. "You are merely here to enjoy the Venetian splendor?"

"I know good art," Evangeline said, hearing the bite in her voice. She had drawn and painted since early childhood, had begun formal lessons at eight years of age and had continued them until her mother's death. She knew, without any sense of guile, that her talent was special. That her stepfather should have his ridiculous efforts showcased on a world stage, while hers sat unnoticed in her attic room in London, grated against her nerves.

A chuckle from the stranger had her flushing again, and he pushed off from the arch, stepping closer. "You 'know good art,' do you?"

Hopes for a magical evening or no, Evangeline felt her temper snap. She turned to leave the *loggia* when the stranger moved quickly and caught her arm.

"*Bella*, no. Do not leave me so soon."

His long fingers were warm; he did not wear gloves. Trying not to feel scandalized, she looked up at him, taking in the dark curls just brushing the top of his white collar and the equally dark eyes behind the black mask. "You must join me," he said and pulled her hand gently through his arm. "Have you seen the gallery on the third floor?"

Evangeline shook her head, her heart thumping at either the man's proximity or his suggestion that they visit the gallery—she wasn't certain which. "I would love to."

"Your name?" he said, looking down at her, holding her eyes with his own. "Your Christian name."

"Evangeline," she whispered.

"*Cara mia*," he murmured. "Of course the name would be as exquisite as the body housing it."

Warmth at his bold compliment coursed through Evangeline as they walked toward the double doors leading into the palace, which had long since ceased functioning as a palace and now housed government offices and official receptions.

"And am I to have the pleasure of your name, sir?" Evangeline asked as they entered the building and the stranger led her through the reception room and to a staircase beyond it.

He hesitated and looked down at her for a long moment, pausing at the bottom of the staircase. "Matteo," he finally said.

She raised a brow. "You haven't a surname?"

The smile again. "You did not give me yours."

"You did not request it." Evangeline smiled in return as she looked up at Matteo and paused as the eyes behind his mask widened slightly.

"*Cara mia*, you should smile always."

Evangeline shook her head as they began climbing the stairs. "Something you undoubtedly say to all of the women you meet. I have heard of the Italian man's ability to charm."

Matteo covered her hand with his own as they reached the next landing. "In this, *bella*, you are mistaken. I do not waste time saying things I do not mean."

Evangeline glanced up at him again as he led her down a long hallway. In the cozy light of the wall sconces, his boldly handsome face with its well-defined Italian features quite took her breath away. What were the odds that he was actually unencumbered? The thought that he might not be involved with another woman was ridiculous.

"What of your wife?" she ventured. "Or your . . . your . . ." Drat. Could she truly not bring herself to use the word *mistress*?

He paused with her outside a set of large double-doors. "My . . ." He gave her the benefit of his full regard again, and it quite unnerved her. Which she found immensely irritating.

"Your *courtesan*?" she said and raised a brow, although he wouldn't see it beneath her mask.

"The position is currently vacant," he said with a twitch of his full lips.

"Which one?" she ventured, wondering if her blush was spreading down across the expanse of skin not covered by her dress.

"Both," he murmured and smiled before tugging her into the room.

Anything she might have been brave enough to say in response was completely lost as she looked at the walls in the splendid room, which were lit to showcase each beautiful piece of art to perfection. She placed a hand over her heart, her breath stolen.

"Oh!" She dropped her hand from his arm and moved more fully into the room, feeling her eyes burn. "A Vincini! Three of them!" Evangeline stood rooted to the spot, her mouth open. She moved slowly and approached the paintings, realizing it shouldn't have come as a surprise that the government seat of Venice would house masterpieces. "They are originals," she murmured and blinked back tears, suddenly remembering she wasn't alone. It would be awkward indeed to be forced to lift the mask to wipe her eyes.

Matteo approached and stood beside her, and she felt him watching her. "It would seem you do indeed know good art, *cara mia*. These are some of his lesser-known pieces."

"I would have thought to find these in the state

museum," she said and looked up at him.

"They were, originally. They came here two hundred years ago, when the doges still claimed this building as a home."

"Incredible," she whispered, turning her attention back to the paintings. "The use of light, his signature preferences for gold and deep green, the lifelike appearance of the mother and child..."

"And yet you care not for your stepfather's work? His style is similar, albeit more modern." Matteo's voice held confusion, and she had to admit to a certain amount of her own.

"My stepfather's work looks nothing like this," she said, frowning. "And he wouldn't know to blend these hues if I mixed the paints for him."

Matteo's face registered surprise. "You are an artist, *Evangelina*?"

Evangeline bit her lip and looked away, focusing instead on the far wall where she saw another artist of some renown, but nothing compared to Vincini. The urge to deny her talent was on the tip of her tongue, to downplay her efforts as she had become accustomed to doing as a means of defense at home. She glanced up again at the man who watched her as though he would learn her every last secret and relish each one, and remembered she wore a mask, which, ironically, allowed her to be herself.

"I am an artist," she admitted quietly, and felt a surge of the joy she'd missed since losing her father nine years earlier.

"And you are good."

"Yes." She nodded and felt the sting behind her eyelids again. "I am good."

"Did you not think to enter your own work in the Biennales?" He smiled at her, and it seemed, oddly, tender. Compassionate. He ran a fingertip along her cheekbone at the edge of her mask. "I am on the selection committee, after all."

Her lips quirked into a wry smile. "And interested in my art only after seeing me in a purple masquerade gown on a *loggia* in the moonlight."

He laughed, revealing a sense of unguarded, genuine humor. "Come," he said, smiling still, and led her to a small desk in the corner of the room. "I want you to draw something for me."

Evangeline sat and arranged her skirts as Matteo opened a drawer and produced a piece of parchment along with pen and ink. After uncapping the bottle and placing it in the inkwell, he took her right hand, tugging at the tip of each gloved finger and then stripping the length of the glove from her elbow. "You draw with this hand, yes?"

She nodded, speechless, as he released her hand and gave her the pen. She held it for a moment and looked at him as he drew a chair alongside the table. "What would you like?"

"Ah, *cara mia*, I should hate to shock you."

"You already have," she answered, wondering if she would ever stop blushing.

He laughed again and gestured toward the paper as he sat back, relaxing in his chair. "Surprise me."

Evangeline felt a stab of uncertainty under his close regard.

"Perhaps you should remove your mask, Eva."

She glanced at him and then sat closer to the desk, focusing on the paper before her. "No, thank you." Little did he know, the mask was keeping her honest. She could see well enough to accomplish her task.

Without giving it much thought, she dipped the pen into the ink and trailed it across the paper with sure, defined strokes. As always happened when she drew or painted, the world around her disappeared and became the work itself. In a matter of minutes, she created a rough sketch, pausing only briefly now and again to examine the subject.

With a quick flick of her wrist, she signed her name at

the bottom right corner and handed the paper to Matteo. He remained comfortably sprawled in his chair, but the very air about him had taken on a stillness, which she registered as her mind came back into focus. He looked at the paper for so long, she began to wonder if she'd done something he found offensive.

"You find me handsome then, *Evangelina*?"

She met the dark eyes behind his mask with her own gaze. "Of course," she said. "I doubt there is a woman anywhere on earth who would not."

He looked again at the picture for a very long time, his lips tightening fractionally. "Tell me about your stepfather."

Two

Evangeline tipped her head in some surprise. "I'm sorry?"

Matteo rose and held out his hand, brushing her other out of the way when she tried to replace the glove. Holding her bare hand in his, he led her to a seating area in the center of the room and sat by her on a soft sofa that was easily the most comfortable piece of furniture she'd encountered since sleeping on her own fluffy bed in her former bedroom in London—the bed she'd not slept in since her mother's death because her new attic bedroom was too small to accommodate it.

He settled beside her and, after meeting her eyes for a moment more, leaned forward and placed his fingers alongside her mask. "I must see you," he murmured, and after tipping his head slightly in question, she nodded. Evangeline leaned forward and allowed him to untie the ribbons from the back of her head, looking up slowly as it fell away.

She felt exposed and cold, and wished she'd not allowed it. When she turned her face away, he placed a finger beneath her chin and gently nudged her attention back to him. He leaned forward and placed her hands upon the ribbons at the back of his head. She hesitated for only a moment before untying it and meeting his dark gaze unadorned. Her breath caught in her throat. He was every bit as exquisite as he'd claimed her to be.

"Why did you not enter your own work in the Biennales?" Matteo asked as he traced his fingertip along her forehead, brushing a few stray curls from her eyes.

"I did not even know of the exposition until my stepfather told us he had been invited to enter and that we would be traveling with him." She held his mask in her hands, feeling the warmth of the fabric where it had lain against his skin.

"And 'we' are?"

"His twin daughters and me. My mother passed one year ago."

"And your father?"

"Died of consumption when I was twelve."

Matteo studied her again in the intense manner she was coming to recognize. "Did your father leave behind an estate?"

Evangeline refrained from rolling her eyes at the futility of her situation at home, but only just. "I am not allowed to access it until I am married or thirty years of age. I suspect it will be gone by then."

His eyes narrowed. "Your stepfather is your trustee then."

"Yes." It was grossly unfair. Had she been a boy, the estate would have been hers at eighteen, and she could already be living independently, entirely on her own.

"Does he know you paint?"

Evangeline allowed herself the eye roll that time and settled back more comfortably against the sofa. What did it matter if she told a stranger about her life? It wasn't as though she would see him again. "He does know, and painting is the one thing he hasn't forbidden me to do. But I am not to display my work anywhere except for my own room—my pieces that once hung in the house were removed when my mother died."

"And why do you suppose he would allow you to continue? I gather he is not a kind man."

Evangeline shrugged a shoulder. "I've asked myself the same question a thousand times. Perhaps he has a shred of humanity in him."

Matteo threaded his fingers through hers. "And he brought you here."

Evangeline shook her head and looked away, settling her gaze on the hearth. "Robert is concerned about appearances. One week ago, we had tea with some neighbors he wanted desperately to impress. When the topic of this vacation was brought into discussion, they assumed he would be taking his twins and me. He wants the world to believe he loves and cares for me as much as his own daughters. As he could hardly explain why he would leave me behind, I was suddenly part of the excursion."

"For that alone, I am in his debt."

Evangeline looked back at him with a smile. "You, sir, are incorrigible. And if we were in London right now and someone were to come upon us here, unchaperoned, I would be utterly ruined."

"Ah, but *bella*, this is not London." He paused for a moment. "When I found you on the *loggia*, you looked very much like a woman who did not wish to be disturbed. Dare I hope you are planning to attend the masquerade ball, though? The music has started; can you hear it?"

Evangeline sighed. "I had not intended to if I could avoid it," she admitted. "The twins were . . . quite upset when they realized I would be accompanying them to Venice. I am doing my utmost to stay away from them, although I am curious enough to eventually want a peek at the ball." A thought crossed her mind, and she quirked a brow at him. "You were also wandering the *loggia* alone. Perhaps you were avoiding the ball as well?"

He tipped his head in acknowledgement. "I have very little use for occasions such as these, *Evangelina*. I am here only because I must be."

"Are you here alone? No family with you at all?"

"Regrettably, I am here with my parents and three brothers."

Evangeline laughed. "You seem as thrilled as am I."

Matteo sighed and smiled at her. "There are expectations—my mother wishes for me to marry and bless her with grandchildren, and my brothers are irritating in the extreme."

"You have no wish to ever marry?"

"I have yet to meet a woman who does not annoy me once she opens her mouth and begins to speak."

Evangeline grinned in spite of herself, her mood lighter than it had been in ages. "Methinks you have been looking in the wrong places, dear sir."

He brought her fingers to his lips and placed a kiss upon the back of her hand. "Something tells me I ought to have been looking in London."

She laughed. "Truly, I suspect many women in London society would also annoy you dreadfully. But all I have heard my entire life is that a man does not want a woman's opinions, that he has no need for intelligent conversation with her. This is why he has gentlemen's clubs."

Matteo winced. "My kingdom for a woman with more on her mind than fashion."

"You are most singular."

He looked at her for a moment, opened his mouth and then closed it again.

"What is it?"

"Forgive me, *bella*, but how is it you are not spoken for, yourself?"

Evangeline felt heat suffuse her cheeks and she suddenly wished the floor would open up and swallow her whole. The humiliation would likely never leave.

He cupped her cheek with his hand and inched closer to her. "It is indelicate of me to ask, but I must know. Has someone hurt you?"

She shook her head and briefly closed her eyes. "No. I had two Seasons before my mother died."

"I refuse to believe you had no offers."

"I had no offers."

He looked at her, his face suddenly slack, for such a prolonged moment that Evangeline could only laugh. "I have accepted it. It is embarrassing, but seems to be my lot in life. I am actually considering something . . ." She trailed off, uncertain whether she wanted to confide in anyone about an idea that had begun forming the moment she left London. Even her handsome confidante whom she would never see again.

His fingers tightened fractionally on hers, and his expression darkened almost imperceptibly. "You think to find a protector here, someone to set you up as his mistress? Where were you hoping to look? At the ball?"

Evangeline gasped and tugged on her hand, which he still held firmly. "Certainly not! I was thinking of advertising as an art tutor!"

Matteo closed his eyes. "Eva." He paused. "You must promise me that you will not 'advertise' for anything. There are men who would gladly hire you as an art tutor for their children and then expect additional favors for themselves. You cannot trust just anyone."

Evangeline drew her brows together and narrowed her eyes. "And who are you to lecture me on what I may or may not do with my life? You implied you've had mistresses in the past! I believe it is grossly unfair that what is considered reprehensible for a respectable woman is politely ignored in a man. It ought to be equally condemned."

A muscle twitched in his jaw, but he seemed to have the sense to remain silent on the point.

She sniffed. "Besides which, if I want to be some man's mistress, I will be." If she could only stop blushing.

He muttered something rapidly in Italian, and Evangeline was fairly certain she should be grateful she didn't speak the language. His eyes sparked, and he fell silent, watching her with what she could only assume was anger.

What was wrong with him? Weren't Italian men lusty and demonstrative? She would have thought he might have a few friends in mind for her if she were to seriously consider the life of a courtesan. His puritan attitude was baffling after their flirtatious exchange.

He tipped his head to one side suddenly and squinted at her.

"You say your father left behind an estate?"

What on *earth*?

"You have a dowry yet received no offers?"

Evangeline pulled her hand fully from his grasp and threw her arms up in frustration. "No offers! I already told you that—nobody wanted me!" She shifted to stand, but he pulled her back.

"Impossibile. Assolutamente impossibile. A face and body that would tempt a saint, and money as well? You are telling me that gentlemen never called on you?"

"Of course gentlemen called on me," she said, feeling her frustration rise to new heights. Was the man insane? Why was he fixated on her lack of marital offers? "Some several times. But after so many visits, they just . . . stopped coming. I once overheard my stepfather telling my mother there must be something inherently wrong with me, because I scared gentlemen away." Her voice cracked. "You are cruel to belabor the point, and I am leaving. I thank you for showing me the Vincinis."

"*Cara mia*," he said and finally released her when she struggled to stand. "Do you not find it odd that your stepfather told your mother that you had scared the gentlemen away, when he stood to lose your money if you married?"

Flustered, she dropped his mask in his lap and snatched her own from the coffee table where Matteo had laid it and settled it over her face, tying the ribbons firmly into place as she made her way to the door.

"I do not know what you are suggesting, sir, but I find myself in need of some air. In fact, I do believe I will go down to the courtyard and attend the ball."

THREE

The courtyard was awash in the glow of torchlight and echoing with the sounds of laughter, the tinkling of wine glasses and music provided by a small orchestra. Evangeline fumed her way into the midst of it and willed herself not to cry. Odious, handsome Italian! Dredging up humiliating things when he hardly knew her and was in no position to pry.

The petulant voice of her stepsister, Analise, sounded somewhere off to her left. Evangeline gritted her teeth; she would know that voice anywhere.

"The *conte* never attends balls unless he is forced to," she was saying to Daniella. "Charise says her mother spoke to a neighbor who knew the *Conte's* mother, who said that he is Italy's most eligible bachelor! How on earth am I to make an impression if the man won't even show his face?"

"*Nobody* is showing their faces, Analise," Daniella answered. "It's a masquerade ball. And besides, who's to say you would be the one making the impression?"

"Ugh." Evangeline breathed out and twisted through the crowd, seeking to put as much space between herself and the twins as possible. The only thing that could make the evening worse would be if she encountered Robert, as well. She reached the edge of the crush and drew a breath of fresh air next to a cool stone wall.

It was insufferable, really, that she should live her life in the attic of the home she had grown up in, with her stepfather sleeping in her late father's bedroom and those ridiculous girls prancing around as though they owned the place. She had long suspected that Robert Montgomery had married her mother for the money, but her mother had been so lonely that Evangeline had been hard pressed to withhold her support when the engagement had been announced.

Would he have gone so far as to discourage Evangeline's suitors, as Matteo had suggested? Now that Evangeline was away from the Italian's hypnotic gaze and commanding presence, she was clearheaded enough to admit that if such a thing was to come to light, she wouldn't necessarily be surprised. But how to broach the subject?

Her musings only served to solidify what she had come to realize on the voyage to Venice—that she did not want to go back to that house, or to London, even. She would find a way to support herself. All she really needed was a small room and enough money to buy necessities. Better to live in an attic in Italy than be banished to one at home. Despite what Matteo had implied, she was not idiotic. She *would* advertise for a tutoring position. She would be selective and careful. Perhaps at the festival the next night she would make a contact or two.

Feeling infinitely better about her situation, she relaxed and allowed herself to sway to the music. A warm hand on her elbow had her turning to see a man who bowed slightly and asked if she would join him in a dance.

"I would love to," she said and allowed him to guide her

toward the center of the courtyard, where he swung her into a waltz.

He wore a dark green mask with a matching suit coat and cravat. He stood only slightly taller than she was, and Evangeline found herself relaxing in his arms as she matched his easy rhythm. He introduced himself as *Conte* Bellini, one of the younger sons.

"Ah," Evangeline said with a smile. "I overheard some young ladies bemoaning the fact that the most eligible bachelor in all of Italy does not frequent balls. He would be your brother?"

The young *conte* shook his head a bit as he grinned. "My brother, the heir. He has no use for parties."

"I find that younger sons are often much more charming," she said and winked through her mask, finding herself more confident with it on.

Her dance partner laughed as he navigated them around a couple that had clearly already enjoyed a glass or two of wine. At the very least.

"I certainly like to believe I am charming," he said. "And now you must tell me a bit about yourself."

The ensuing conversation was pleasant, and the young *conte* invited her to call him David. They continued talking as the orchestra ended the piece and began with another. He had swept her, laughing, into a third waltz, when a man approached David from behind and tapped him on the shoulder.

Evangeline's heart skipped several beats as she recognized Matteo. With a laugh, David shook his head and bowed slightly, holding his hand out to the other man. "Miss Stuart, my eldest brother, the *Conte* Bellini, Europe's most eligible bachelor."

Her mouth dropped open as she stared first at Matteo and then David, who kissed her knuckles and leaned close. "I will have the rest of this dance later," he said with a grin.

Matteo barked something in Italian at David, who

snorted with laughter and left Evangeline staring at the oldest Bellini son, heir to the fortune and apparently, the most eligible bachelor in Europe. Her humiliation was complete.

This was the man who had questioned her about her courtship failures—and why? Because he believed her stepfather might have sabotaged her future? Matteo, or Count Bellini, rather, was an insensitive clod. She opened her mouth to say so when he placed his hand at her waist and slid it around her back, pulling her close against him as he slowly began turning them to the music.

"You would find yourself ejected from Almacks, I'll have you know," she sputtered as he leaned down.

"Then it is fortuitous indeed that we are here and not at Almacks." His breath was warm and tickled her temple. Her eyes drifted shut, and she inhaled a scent that was uniquely him. "I have wounded your feelings and your pride, *bella*, when I intended to do neither," he murmured, and she felt it down to her toes. "I seek your forgiveness."

"You're a *count*," she spat. "You might have mentioned it."

"Had I, you would not have been nearly so relaxed in my presence. People always react differently when they know I am a Bellini."

Evangeline was begrudgingly mollified; she supposed it was true. She wouldn't have gone anywhere with him had she known he was someone that half of the Western world sought after. She would have felt even more grossly inadequate than she had when she believed him to be merely an Italian gentleman. An incredibly handsome one, yes, and an arrogant one, but not *titled*, for heaven's sake.

"You left before I could apologize, and I've had the very devil of a time trying to find you."

"I was busy," she said and tilted her chin up slightly, doing her best not to look at his face, which was just inches above her own.

"Yes. With my brother," he ground out.

Evangeline smiled. "He's charming."

"Indeed. He's also a scoundrel, and you will most definitely not finish a third waltz with him."

"He's *friendly*. I thought I may appeal to him for help finding a position here."

Matteo's hand pressed against her back. "I thought we agreed you wouldn't seek out a protector," he murmured low in her ear.

"A position as a *tutor*," she said, exasperated. "I am not going to be anyone's mistress. I shall die an old maid, surrounded by oils and canvas and paintbrushes soaking in turpentine." She meant it to sound light, but it felt heavy.

A muscle again worked in his jaw, which she was coming to recognize as his first sign of agitation.

"We are friends now," she added as he turned her toward one side of the courtyard, "so perhaps you may direct me to a family looking for an art tutor, or even a governess."

"Friends," he whispered. He swung her into an alcove along the side and trapped her in the shadows between his arms, her back against the cold stone wall. He pulled her close, tracing his lips along her neck as he murmured Italian words she would have given anything to understand.

Evangeline wound her arms up around his shoulders and ran her fingers into his soft, black curls at the nape of his neck. She closed her eyes as heat pooled low in her abdomen and she realized he was going to kiss her senseless.

A feminine trill of laughter to the side, followed by the low murmur of an answering male, interrupted Matteo's close examination of her neck. His arms tightened around her as he shielded her from sight, should someone come upon them.

With a growl of frustration, he lifted his head, his warm lips inches from hers. "Not here," he murmured against her mouth. "Not like this." He closed his eyes and rested his cheek against her temple. "Where are you staying?"

Evangeline felt as though her brain had been scrambled; she had a difficult time reasoning through his question. "Hotel Morosini," she finally answered.

"We will dance, and you will return to your hotel with those people who call themselves your family, and I will call on you in the morning for breakfast, followed by an intimate day of sightseeing."

"Yes," she whispered.

"And you will be my guest at the Biennales banquet tomorrow evening."

"You're rather presumptuous, aren't you? A gentleman would ask if I am otherwise engaged."

He lifted his head and looked at her. "*Cara mia*, I will personally cancel anything that would have you 'otherwise engaged.'"

She looked at his face—handsome even with the mask, and the eyes behind it, which studied her with concern and something that smoldered just beneath the surface. "Matteo, will you help me?" she asked, tears suddenly clogging her throat. "I do not ask that you find a tutoring position for me, perhaps just an introduction . . . I cannot go back."

"Shhh. No fears, *bella*," he said and loosened his hold on her body, trailing his hands up to gently cup either side of her face. "You are not going back." He kissed the top of her head where her hair met the edge of her mask.

Four

The following morning, her heart beating in anticipation, Evangeline left her bedroom. If one could call it a bedroom; it was more frequently used as a closet, but Robert had convinced the staff that Evangeline preferred small spaces. The twins refused to share a room with her, of course, and truthfully, Evangeline preferred the closet to their company. When faced with that alternative, she didn't mind so much that the foot of the bed was only a meter from the door.

She entered the sitting room of the family's suite, doing her best to ignore the scowls of the twins, who sat at the breakfast table in their dressing robes.

"She thinks she's going somewhere, Papa," Analise pouted to her father, who glanced up from his newspaper and looked at Evangeline.

"What business is it of yours?" Evangeline said as she straightened the bow at the back of her dress.

"That was unkind, Evangeline," Robert said, the mild tone masking a cold intent Evangeline knew all too well. He never screamed or physically harmed her; he simply took things away. "I am surprised at you."

"Where are you going, then?" Daniella asked as she gouged a large piece of grapefruit.

"Out with a new friend," she said, fighting the urge to hold her breath. She had to get out the door, and then Robert wouldn't be able to keep her from leaving.

"I don't believe that is on our itinerary," Robert said and folded his paper. As he stood, a knock sounded, and Evangeline clenched her fists, torn between fury and fear that he would keep her from a day with Matteo.

The twins' harried maid, Marta, answered the sitting room door and opened it wider to reveal *Conte* Bellini in the hallway. He caught her eye and smiled, and she felt a relief so profound, her knees nearly buckled. Robert could not prevent her from leaving with Matteo. It would never do to make a scene.

She moved to the door as Matteo entered, and she made introductions to the twins, who stared at him, mouths agape. Her stepfather looked from her, to Matteo, and back again. Putting on his public smile, Robert extended a hand and expressed his gratitude that the *conte* would entertain his sweet daughter Evangeline.

Matteo shook Robert's hand and then reached for Evangeline, pulling her arm through the crook of his. "It is I who am grateful," he said with a warm smile at Evangeline. "It is as though a breath of fresh air has swept through all of Venice."

Evangeline did her best not to laugh, grateful that Matteo would think to compliment her so grandly before those who sought nothing but her money and her misery. As they made their goodbyes and closed the door behind them, the twins' screeching began in earnest, and Matteo winced.

"Are they always so—"

"Always." She smiled at him, suddenly feeling shy. It was broad daylight, he was handsome as sin, and she wasn't wearing her masquerade mask and gown. She was only herself, without any defenses—Evangeline, the girl who had had two Seasons but no proposals, whose parents were dead, and who had no hope of independence from spiteful "family" unless she could depend upon the kindness of strangers as she sought employment.

"You are even lovelier in the daylight, and I wouldn't have thought it possible," Matteo murmured and brought her fingers to his lips. "I dreamed of you all night."

Evangeline shook her head with a laugh. He was being ridiculous, of course, but she appreciated the sentiment all the same. She would do well to remember that he was likely just a charmer with no interest in forming any real attachments.

"You do not believe me?" he said as they descended the stone steps that led to the canal, where a gondola awaited.

"I believe that you are experienced, and I am not. I also believe that I should guard my heart." She grinned at him and kept her tone light. The sky outside was brilliant blue, and the autumn breeze was pleasant. It was a perfect day, and she wanted to commit every detail to memory.

He handed her carefully into the gondola and settled next to her on the cushioned seat. He placed an arm around her waist and regarded her with dark, intense eyes. "I will guard your heart, *cara mia*," he said softly.

She wanted to believe it, but it was nothing but a fairytale. She was too old to believe in those; she had to be practical. Smiling, she traced a finger down his nose and tapped the tip of it. "Excellent," she said. "You are a good friend. And while you are guarding my heart, I will find employment." She was at ease with him, she realized, and comfortable. His close, intimate manner was softening some of the shell she'd erected around herself, and she had hope, for the first time in a long time, that she might have found a true friend.

He studied her eyes for a moment and captured her hand, lightly nipping her fingertips. When her breath quickened, he slowly smiled. "Mmm hmm," he said. "Friends."

Evangeline was grateful when he turned his attention to sights along the canal and he pulled her close under his arm as he drew her focus to lavish *palazzi* along the way. They were hundreds of years old—grand homes housing grand families—imbued with ancient frescoes and terrazzo or marble floors. Scents of baking bread and pastries wafted along the breeze from shops alongside the canal as the gondolier made his way steadily to St. Mark's Square, where Matteo said they would dine *al fresco*.

"A meal at San Marco is something every visitor to Venice must sample," he said, helping her step from the gondola. He wrapped his arm around her shoulders and led her to the center of the famous square, where the *campanile* began chiming the hour. Pigeons pecking along the square and dining on tourists' crumbs scattered as Evangeline and Matteo crossed the square to a café much beloved by Napoleon's troops.

And with good reason, Evangeline decided as she had her own taste of the food. The thick slices of ciabatta topped with ricotta cheese were divine, and she didn't have to wonder why Napoleon and his men had wanted to stay.

Determined to keep to her Heart-Guarding Resolve, Evangeline conversed with Matteo as one would when getting to know a new friend. He was charming and funny, and he regaled her with tales of his childhood, which had been, for all intents and purposes, peaceful. She gathered that his mother was a bit of a scatterbrain, but he had great affection for her and admired his father greatly. He explained that in Italy, a count's sons were all given the title *conte*, which was why, although Matteo was his father's first heir, his younger brothers were also addressed preferentially.

"But we have spoken of me for much too long," Matteo said as he signaled the server for coffee. "Tell me about your father. Your true father."

Evangeline smiled. "He was also an artist. He taught me all he knew then turned me over to others who could instruct me in different methods. We were very close. When he died . . . I suppose I wanted to die with him. But I had my mother, and she needed me. I believe my art was what saved me."

The breeze ruffled his hair, and she smiled. "You must have been an adorable child," she said. "I can only imagine that hair on a little boy."

He muttered something in Italian, and she laughed. "It has been the very bane of my existence," he told her. "I was grateful when I reached the day where my mother no longer had control of its length. I do believe that if she had had her way, my brothers and I would all have been styled as girls."

"And who could blame her? I must say, it's very unfair when boys are gifted with curls, and girls must burn curls into their hair with hot irons."

"But you do not," he said.

"I suppose I've also been lucky."

"Your hair is the color of deep gold. It matches your eyes." His gaze roamed slowly over her face until she felt an unaccountable need to squirm. Wishing she were sophisticated and urbane, she forced herself to remember that they were friends. He was her good friend.

"Draw something for me," he said and spread a linen napkin on the surface of the table. He pulled a fountain pen from his pocket and handed it to her. "I filled it with ink this morning."

"What would you like?" she asked, taking the pen and blushing when he looked at her with brows raised.

"Again, you ask me this question, and again, I say, I should hate to shock you."

"What would you like me to draw?" she amended with a rueful smile. What a silly friend.

He looked around the square for a moment before pointing to the clock tower. "The *campanile*."

Evangeline shielded her eyes from the sun for a moment before turning her attention to the fabric and began drawing on it, flattening it when it wrinkled. She scowled as she worked, finally finishing the tower with a certain amount of dissatisfaction.

"It's not the best of canvases," she said, sitting back in her seat. Matteo looked at it, studied it, really. What was he thinking? She leaned forward again and added a portion of the Basilica, with its lavish ornamentation and design.

"What colors would you use if this were oil?" he asked.

Evangeline looked at the scene she'd sketched for a moment before examining the drawing. "This time of day, the lighting is different than it would be at sunset, of course." She described the mixtures of differing hues, feeling the familiar shrinking of the noise around her as she contemplated bringing the scene to life on canvas, doing justice to the reality. She traced her paint-stained finger along the napkin, tapping spots on the image where certain angles would require shading effects.

"Did you bring any of your work with you, Eva?"

"I'm sorry?"

She looked up from the drawing, and he chuckled. She smiled sheepishly as he repeated his question.

"I brought a few things," she said with a nod. "Mostly my portfolio, which contains sketches of my original oils and some of my watercolors." She ducked her head, wondering if he would find her habits odd. "I always carry some supplies, even if we're going to the country estate, where I also keep a stash of paints and paper. I just . . ." She paused. "I am unsettled if I am too far from something I can draw on."

"That sounds perfectly reasonable to me. Although I

must say, it is a good thing I carry a pen with me—you are here without even a small purse."

Evangeline cleared her throat. "I left my reticule in my room at the hotel. You were a few minutes early, and I decided it was better to get out the door than go back for it."

Matteo's face hardened. "Does Robert mistreat you?"

Evangeline looked away. "That would depend, I suppose, on the way we define the word mistreat." She looked back at him with a forced smile. "But let us speak of other things. The exhibition will be over this evening, and you'll return to Florence. I would like very much to enjoy your company without thinking about Robert Montgomery."

"Do you truly believe I will leave you and simply return to Florence?"

"I am naïve, Matteo, but not stupid." She laid her hand across his and tipped her head to the side with a genuine smile. "You are proving to be a wonderful friend, but I certainly do not expect you to inconvenience yourself for my sake. I would appreciate a referral or two, perhaps, but that is all."

Evangeline patted his hand, thinking to put an end to the discussion, because her heart was constricting. For all of her brave words, she knew that when he left, the void would be painful.

When she moved to put her hand back in her lap, he turned his and gripped it. "Last evening," he said in an undertone, leaning closer to her, "you were very clear in your plea for my help. You were desperate. Afraid."

She opened her mouth, searching for something to say. "I suppose in the light of day, my situation doesn't seem quite so dire. I feel that I am gaining a sense of your character, Matteo, and I believe you to be a very kind man. For all of your manly exterior, I suspect a kitten resides within."

He scowled.

"What I am trying to say is that I want your friendship,

not your pity. I couldn't bear it . . ." Her eyes burned for a moment with tears, which popped up out of nowhere. "I couldn't bear your pity."

Matteo lifted her chin with his finger when she looked down at their hands, which he still held very much entwined.

"Believe me, *cara mia*, I feel a great many things for you, and pity is not one of them."

She met his gaze, her heart thumping once, hard. He was making it incredibly difficult for her to think of him as her special friend. Her heart would never recover if she fell in love with a man well versed in the art of passion but not necessarily the kind that required commitment.

Evangeline smiled and pulled back. She tucked an errant curl into one of the many pins in her hair and decided to turn the conversation to lighter things.

"Now then," she said briskly. "I have Count Bellini at my disposal to act as my tour guide for the whole day. Where shall we go? I don't suppose you can arrange an advance showing of the exhibition?"

He looked at her for a long moment, his expression unreadable, and she knew he saw through her efforts to change the tide. His mouth finally quirked up in his familiar smile, and he signaled the server for the check.

"*Evangelina*," he said, leaning closer to her as a soft breeze blew across the square. "You may succeed in fooling yourself, but you will not fool me."

FIVE

Unfortunately, Matteo refused to give her an advance showing at the festival; Evangeline had to forgive him, however, when he spent the whole day showing her the sights and sounds of Venice. They had lunch at a small café off the beaten path, and Matteo walked her through streets and side alleys she would never have been able to navigate on her own. Each landmark he showed her was of historical significance, and the frescoes on *palazzo* walls and courtyards had her itching for her paints.

He spoke of his life and asked questions about hers. He taught her several key phrases in Italian and had the grace to not laugh at her attempts. As the day wore on, Evangeline found herself laughing more and more, recapturing the joy she had been certain would never return. He held her close to his side and entwined their fingers as they strolled along the narrow streets. On more than one occasion, he tried to sneak her into a dark alcove, but she laughingly refused his advances. She knew that if he kissed her, she would never be the same.

The sun had begun its western descent by the time Matteo returned Evangeline to the hotel. He handed her out of the gondola and followed her up the steps to the front doors, where she turned to him with a smile.

"I cannot thank you enough for the delightful day, Matteo. It was lovely in every sense of the word."

"I do not wish for you to return to your stepfamily," he said, brows drawn together. "Perhaps I should take you with me to my *palazzo*. It would be entirely appropriate—my whole family is in residence, and you could be my mother's guest, officially. We can send for your trunk. You needn't spend another moment with Robert and his daughters. You would then go to the Biennales with me rather than meeting me there."

Evangeline shook her head and patted his arm. "I need to do this—to cut my ties with Robert myself. I shall tell him tonight that I will not be returning to London."

"And you suppose he will merely let you go with a fond farewell?"

"I do not see how he can fail to benefit from my departure. He has my money and the estates in England. One would think he would be overjoyed to be rid of me."

Matteo's brows drew together. "I do not think it will be so simple, *bella*."

"I must face him by myself." Evangeline stood on tiptoe and kissed Matteo's cheek. "Thank you again for such a splendid day. I'm hard pressed to remember a time more enjoyable."

"Eva." He gripped both of her hands in his and paused for a long moment. "If you do not arrive at the festival by the dinner hour, I will come find you."

"Dinner hour. I shall be there. Robert and the twins plan to attend. I shall arrive with them."

"Very well. I have some details regarding the opening of the exhibition I must arrange."

"I will see you in a matter of two hours then." She gave his hands a small squeeze and turned to enter the hotel.

"Not one minute late, *Evangelina*."

She smiled and gave him a little wave before entering and closing the door behind her. Releasing an unsteady sigh, she made her way toward the staircase that led to the Montgomery suite. Her legs were wobbly, her heart had melted, and she was forced to admit that she was falling in love with the count. He listened to her. He asked for her opinions on everything from political intrigue to her habits as an artist. He cared, and that was the most dangerous part of all.

She reached the suite and entered it, surprised to find the sitting room empty. The maid, Marta, entered from one of the bedrooms and told Evangeline that the others were still out shopping and would return momentarily to prepare for the dinner and exhibition. Marta fidgeted for a moment and finally moved to leave the room.

"Is something amiss, Marta?" Evangeline asked.

The maid turned back, her face creased with worry. "A message came for Mr. Montgomery just before he left." Reaching a hand into her apron pocket, Martha withdrew a sheet of paper, which she thrust at Evangeline. "He instructed me to retrieve the painting for him, but he didn't tell me where he put it. The girls were in an awful hurry. I suppose in all the confusion, he forgot to tell me where it is."

Baffled, Evangeline stared at the woman then took the paper. It was a request that Mr. Montgomery bring along the companion painting to the piece currently on display at the Biennales.

Evangeline looked up at Marta. "What painting are they speaking of, do you know?"

Marta shook her head. "I've looked everywhere and cannot locate any of Mr. Montgomery's paintings. If he has it somewhere in this suite, it's well hidden. He told me specifically that when they return from shopping, they will have but a little time to ready themselves for the exhibition. I had no idea he brought any of his other pieces with him."

"Marta, it is not your fault that you've been unable to locate it. Perhaps it's downstairs in one of the lock boxes." Evangeline frowned. "I wonder . . ." She thought of her trunk and slowly made her way to Robert's bedroom door. "Have you looked in his trunk?" she asked the maid, who was clearly beside herself at the thought of being unprepared when her employer returned.

"No," Marta said.

"Carefully remove everything and lift the bottom panel. It may actually be a false bottom."

A few minutes more had Marta looking for a release mechanism at the bottom of Robert's trunk. "There," Evangeline told her and pointed to the corner. "It lifts up in that spot."

Marta worked with the bottom wooden layer and eventually lifted it out of the way to reveal a beautiful piece of art.

One Evangeline had created.

Six

A fury Evangeline had never known settled around her like a cloak as she paced the sitting room with her painting in hand. By the time the door finally opened to reveal the Montgomerys, Evangeline's temper had risen several notches. As Robert looked from the painting in Evangeline's hand to her face, comprehension dawned on his features. The look was fleeting, however, and he crossed the room in a few angry strides.

"You have gone through my personal belongings?" he said, his lips thinned, eyes flashing.

"Your personal belongings?" Evangeline spat at him. "This is *my* painting! I suppose the others you sent to the Biennales committee are my pieces as well?"

Snatching the painting roughly from her hand, he backhanded Evangeline with enough force to send her sprawling onto the floor. She stared up at him in shock before regaining her equilibrium and pushing herself upright. She stood on shaky legs and blinked to keep angry tears from falling.

To their credit, the twins did not encourage Robert, but rather stood watching the scene with mouths open. "Girls," he said, breathing heavily and red in the face, "go into your rooms and change for dinner. We leave in thirty minutes."

"Yes, Papa," they murmured as if on cue and stumbled to their room with a backward glance at Evangeline.

The poor darlings must be shocked, Evangeline thought. To her knowledge, it was the first time Robert had struck anyone.

"You will not attend the festivities this evening," Robert said, a sickening calm settling into place.

Evangeline fought the urge to cradle her hand to her face, refusing to give him the satisfaction of knowing it still burned like mad. Her neck hurt from snapping to the side, and even her rump was in pain from landing on the hard floor.

"I can certainly see why you would not want me anywhere near the exhibition," Evangeline said, meeting his gaze without flinching, even as her heart beat nearly out of her chest. "Tell me, how were you going to keep me from seeing my own art at Biennales?"

"You were never going to go." Robert straightened his jacket before looking at the painting he still held. He smiled, then, and it was sickening. "Besides, you can clearly see that the signature is mine, not yours."

He pointed to the signature, which had been carefully painted over her own in the lower right-hand corner. Evangeline's eyes widened and she fought the urge to claw his eyes out.

"You have been crooked from the very beginning!"

Matteo's suspicions echoed in her mind, and she saw the past through fresh eyes. "You married my mother for her money, and you have sabotaged any hope I had for a marriage of my own!" She stood her ground as his face grew ever darker with rage. "This is the very last straw. It is unconscionable, inexcusable! I will expose you as a fraud!"

He moved then, more quickly than she would have thought possible, tossing the painting on a sofa and grabbing Evangeline, spinning her so he had her arms painfully pinned behind her back.

Evangeline screamed for help as she saw him, from the corner of her eye, retrieve a heavy vase and bring it crashing down on her head. The world dimmed, and she felt her knees buckle as everything went dark. Her last thought was that Matteo would never find her.

Seven

It was dark when Evangeline awoke, gagged and bound. Her first conscious thought was that she wished she could return to oblivion. Her head ached abominably, and Robert had tied her arms behind her back. She moved and tried to sit up, but winced—her shoulder must have hit the floor first when he tossed her into the bedroom. At least he'd put her in her own room rather than dumping her into the canal, although he seemed to have gone to pains to leave her on the floor when he could have easily dropped her on the bed.

Reprobate!

She coughed, her throat feeling impossibly dry. Her mouth was full of what she figured must be a handkerchief, which had been secured into place with something tied so tightly at the back of her head that her entire face hurt. She finally squirmed her way into a sitting position and was grateful to note that Robert hadn't tied her ankles. Of course, he'd been pushed for time—that would probably explain why she was alive. If she were still in her closet bedroom by the time he returned from the festival, she may indeed get her wish to never leave Venice. Alive, at least.

Anger and frustration flooded over her as she remembered the whole of the confrontation. He had submitted her work as his own and was likely even now showing it off to the art community. Perhaps her life wasn't entirely doomed, she reasoned as she struggled to pass her arms underneath her rear end to have use of her hands. If she were dead and no longer painting, Robert would have no more art to offer the world.

Unless...

Evangeline had dozens of paintings in the attic of the London townhome. He could release a few at a time for the rest of his life, if he was careful. Closing her eyes and crying out in pain as she finally wrangled her arms from behind her back, she stiffened her resolve to escape and be long gone by the time Robert returned.

After untying the strip of fabric holding her wrists bound, she divested herself of the gag and dropped it to the floor. She felt her way to the end table near her bed and fumbled for a bit before finally getting the small lantern lit. Pushing herself up on legs that ached, she clutched her head when the movement sent a stabbing sensation through her. Reaching up, she found the enormous bump Robert had left when he had hit her with the vase.

The door was locked. He might have been in a hurry, but there were certain things she was sure Robert wouldn't leave to chance. Of course the odious man had locked her into her room. He'd likely taken the painting and the twins to the Biennales, showing off "his" talent and garnering critical acclaim.

The world outside her small window showed a bright moon hanging over the canal, where gondolas carried tourists. The window wouldn't open; she knew because she'd tried it on the night of their arrival. It had been painted shut during the inn's last redesign. She supposed she could break the glass and scream for help, but perhaps she could rouse someone in the hotel itself, first.

She pulled her pocket watch from her skirt pocket and noted the time—nearly an hour past dinner. She hoped desperately that Matteo would be as good as his word and come to her rescue, much like Prince Charming in her favorite fairytales as a youth. Truly, he ought to have arrived by now.

She tried the door, all the while knowing it was locked tight, and as luck would have it, the hinges were on the outside of the door. She smacked her fist against it, hard, wondering if there was some way to break it down. Sinking to the floor, she drew up her knees and held her head in her hands. It throbbed with every little movement, and she wasn't certain she was thinking clearly.

After what seemed an eternity, she finally lifted her head and looked at the doorknob. If she had a hammer and chisel, she could weaken the wood and kick it free, but the only thing she had at her disposal was her paints.

Can't very well cut myself out of a room using a paintbrush.

Her heart sank.

But maybe . . . maybe my paint scraper . . .

Evangeline scrambled across the floor to the other side of the bed, ignoring the pain the movement created. Fumbling through her box of paintbrushes and supplies, she found her scraper, which boasted a newly sharpened blade. She made her way to the locked door and examined the knob before the wood.

The process dragged on for so long, Evangeline was afraid she wouldn't escape before the others returned, and her sense of urgency had her pulse racing. Finally, she achieved her objective enough to see the bolt driven into the door frame. With a deep, shuddering breath, she sat at the end of the bed and kicked the bolt with her heel. She was in pain, desperate and exhausted, and she began to wonder if something untoward had happened to Matteo. She thought she knew him well enough to know that he was a man of his word.

When her leg felt ready to collapse and she was very near admitting defeat, she heard a slight crack in the wood. With renewed energy, she kept at it until the door finally swung outward with a bang. Slightly disoriented, and unable to believe she had been successful, she stared into the darkened sitting room with wide eyes.

She moved from the bed, her leg muscles and heel now in as much pain as the rest of her bruised body, and went to her trunk. She tossed out the clothing, reaching for the mechanism that housed a secret compartment like the one in Robert's trunk. Lifting it out of the way, she then retrieved her portfolio, which was thick with the proof she needed to show to the Biennales committee that Robert had stolen her art and entered it as his own.

Evangeline made her way into the sitting room, pausing as she noted the other two bedroom doors wide open. Slowly peering inside Robert's room first, she caught her breath. It was entirely empty. He had packed up and removed all of his things. A quick examination of the twins' room proved the same.

The ramifications of his behavior stung, even though she had been prepared to tell him she was remaining in Italy and to sneak away, if necessary. He had *left* her there, not knowing how badly she was injured and with no guarantee she would be found days, depending on the hotel staff cleaning schedule.

She rubbed her forehead and closed her eyes for a moment, feeling the pain of Robert's final betrayal. Why did he hate her so much? She had been a good child—he couldn't have asked for a nicer wife or stepdaughter.

She was preparing to gather her cloak from her

bedroom when the suite door rattled with a ferocious beating.

"Evangeline!"

Her heart tripped. It was Matteo. She ran to the door and unlocked it, nearly faint with relief that she wasn't alone, that someone cared whether she lived or died.

He crossed the threshold and held her tightly to him before she could even breathe a word. Her eyes filled with tears that began falling in earnest, clouding her vision when he pulled back and held her by the shoulders at arm's length.

"What has the *bastarde* done to you?"

"Matteo," she said through her tears, "he stole my artwork."

He groaned and pulled her again into his arms for a moment before retrieving a handkerchief from his pocket and gently wiping her face. "I know he did, *bella*. I was preparing to force him to admit it when you arrived for dinner. But you never arrived, and when I questioned Robert, he told me you had gone to Rialto, that someone there had offered you work as a governess."

"How did he even know I was thinking of doing that?"

"I assume he was fabricating the tale. And as we had spoken of finding employment for you, his lie held enough ring of truth that I believed him. But I stopped here to check at the reception desk. They told me the entire Montgomery family had checked out and left." He shook his head again and muttered what she assumed was a curse. "I did not think to insist that I be allowed to examine the suite. So I went to Rialto."

Evangeline looked at him through tear-spiked eyelashes. "What brought you back?"

"I looked for nearly three hours but could find no evidence of you being anywhere near Rialto. When it became clear that you hadn't been there, I returned here. Hoping. The staff confirmed that only two young women had left with Mr. Montgomery."

What Happens in Venice

The tears fell again, and she closed her eyes tightly when he gathered her into his arms and led her to the sofa. "*Cara mia*," he said, "I will never again leave your side."

She laughed and wiped at her eyes again, still holding her thick portfolio. "You would tire of me quickly, Matteo. I am quite obnoxious—I have opinions on nearly everything."

"I would not have it any other way," he said. "*Evangelina*, you have come into my life when I despaired of ever finding an equal partner to love. And I do love you. If you do not say you will marry me, I will darken your doorstep every day of my life until you agree."

She looked up at him, hardly daring to believe what he said. "A fairytale," she murmured.

"A true fairytale," he said. "Tell me, *bella*. Am I destined to camp on your front steps every day for the rest of my life? Will you marry me?"

She laughed again, feeling a spark of hope she never thought she'd possess. "Yes, Matteo. I love you, and I will marry you."

He traced his fingertip along her cheek and captured a stray tear. A dark curl fell onto his forehead, and she brushed it out of the way. Catching her hand, he brought her fingertips to his lips and kissed them, his eyes locked with hers. She exhaled quietly, feeling blood thrumming through her veins. Infinitely slowly, he leaned his head toward hers and captured her lips, the sweetest of caresses, which deepened in intensity until he finally released her, the sides of her face held gently between his hands. "*Ti amo, cara mia.*"

"*Ti amo*, Matteo," she whispered.

He continued with his assault on her senses until the pain in her head was hardly noticeable. When he finally let her up for air, he glanced at the portfolio, now firmly smashed between them.

"Oh!" Fighting a blush, she said, "You've quite

distracted me, *Conte* Bellini. I was on a mission when you entered."

His mouth quirked in a smile. "What sort of mission?"

"I was going to the festival to claim what is mine."

"Well, you have me. Your mission is accomplished."

She laughed and pushed gently on his chest. "I want my name restored, Matteo," she said, sobering. "Robert has stolen my art and submitted it as his own."

"I told you when I first arrived. I know, Eva."

She blinked. "You do?"

"I have known from the first sketch you drew for me at the palace. I've done some investigating. I hired a conservationist to examine the paintings. He was able to lift Robert's signature to reveal yours beneath it."

Evangeline's breath caught in her throat. "So everyone knows?"

He nodded. "I apologize for not telling you immediately about my suspicions. I had to be certain. I had planned to tell you tonight when you arrived. How did you discover it?"

"There was a note saying that he was to bring an additional painting with him to the exhibition. I found it and realized what he had done." She felt her eyes burn again, but she told herself that she would not shed another tear over Robert Montgomery.

"And he attacked you."

She nodded. "And locked me in my room."

He looked closely at her wrists, where angry red marks from her bindings were visible by the light of the moon flooding the sitting room. He cursed fluidly; at least, she assumed it was cursing. Now that she was to remain in Italy, she would have to make a point of learning the language.

Gently, and with infinite care, he kissed the inside of each wrist, shaking his head with the tell-tale clenching of his jaw. "How I would love to kill the man myself. But we will allow the justice system to deal with him."

She frowned. "But surely he's left the country by now."

"I called the authorities late this afternoon as soon as I saw your signature on his entries, and they were waiting for him when he arrived at the exhibition with yet another of your pieces. The rest is as I've told you; I went to Rialto to find you, and when I decided to return here, I instructed the police to meet me so that we could begin a thorough search. They will arrive soon, and if you feel you can manage it, I would like you to dictate a statement regarding your imprisonment and Robert's abuse." Matteo frowned as he traced his finger lightly down her bruised cheek.

Evangeline took a deep breath and lifted her chin. "Of course I can manage a statement for the police. I just kicked my way out of a locked room."

Matteo laughed with a groan and touched his forehead to hers. "I knew I ought to have kept you with me. I should never have sent you back into his lair. My only consolation is that he will be facing multiple charges. We do not take kindly to the abuse of women in this country."

Evangeline placed her palm on his cheek. "All is well in the end," she said. "And I am so glad you came for me. I knew you were a good friend."

He gave her a flat look, which had her laughing again, and he kissed her soundly until she was quite breathless. "Friends do not do that," he told her, and she was gratified to see he was rather breathless himself.

"Well, *we* do."

He shook his head and moved her portfolio to the coffee table, tucking her carefully under his arm and pulling her close as they sat back against the sofa in the darkened room looking over the Grand Canal. "I was ready to throttle you for referring to me all day long as your 'friend.' Your 'dear friend,' 'considerate friend,' 'darling friend.' And I do believe I tried to show you on more than one occasion that I felt much more for you than friendship."

She chuckled and winced a bit as she shifted, favoring her injured shoulder. "And I knew that if I let you kiss me, I would be hopelessly lost. I was afraid of falling in love with you if all you cared for was, well, friendship."

"And I had fallen in love with you already."

She looked up at his handsome profile. "When?"

"When you stood on the *loggia*, resplendent in your masquerade gown, put your nose in the air, and told me you knew good art." He grinned and kissed her temple. He sobered a bit, his brow creasing.

"What is it?"

"My home is in Florence—I do have a home here in Venice, but we will spend a fair amount of the year away. I know how you have come to love this city—you will still be happy?"

"Of course I will be happy. I was secretly hoping you had a cousin with children who needed an art tutor, just so I could be close to you. I want to be wherever you are, but I will always hold dear what happened for me in Venice."

About Nancy Campbell Allen

Nancy Campbell Allen has over 10 published novels to her credit. She writes both contemporary romantic adventures and historical fiction, including the Best of State award winning Civil War series, Faith of our Fathers. Nancy has been an avid reader since childhood and wrote her first story in 4th grade.

Nancy's blog: http://ncallen.blogspot.com
Twitter: @necallen

More Timeless Romance Anthologies

For more information about our anthologies, visit our blog: TimelessRomanceAnthologies.blogspot.com

www.ingramcontent.com/pod-product-compliance
Lightning Source LLC
LaVergne TN
LVHW021758060526
838201LV00058B/3146

Lisolo na kolanda Makamwisi matali "Bisomoko"

Molimo, Molema, mpe Nzoto: Volume 1

Dr. Jaerock Lee

Molimo, Molema, Mpe Nzoto: Volume 1 na Dr. Jaerock Lee
Ebimisami na ba Buku Urim (Na Mokambi: Johnny. H. Kim)
235-3, Guro-gu, Seoul, Korea
www.urimbooks.com

Na ba droit d'auteur. Buku oyo to eteni na yango esengeli soko te kobongolama, katiama kati na masini, to kopesama na lolenge moko boye, na electronique, na mechanique, to na photocopie, na enregistreur to lolenge nini, soki nzela epesami ten a mobimisi na yango.

Soko lolenge nini, makomi nioso makamatami na Biblia, NEW AMERICAN STANDARD BIBLE, ®, Copyright © 1960, 1962, 1963, 1968, 1971, 1972, 1973, 1975, 1977, 1995 na Fondation Lockman. Yakosalelama soki nzela epesami.

Copyright © 2012 by Dr. Jaerock Lee
ISBN: 979-11-263-1242-9 03230
Copyright na Traduction © 2012 na Dr. Esther K. Chung. Yakosalelama soki nzela epesami.

Na liboso ebisamaka na Ki Koreen na Ba buku Urim na 2009

Kobimisama na Liboso na Juillet 2012

Ebimisami na Dr. Geumsun Vin
Ibongisama na Ndako na Edition na ba Buku Urim
Mpona koyeba mingi kutana na; urimbook@hotmail.com

Foreword

Na momesano bato balingaka kozala ba success mpe na kobika malamu mpe na esengo. Kasi ata soki bazali na misolo, mpifo, mpe koyebana, moko te akoki kokima kufa. Shir Huangdi, Empereur wa Yambo na China na kala, alukaka nzete na kobika seko, kasi akokaka te kokima kufa na ye. Kasi, kati na Biblia, Nzambe Atalisa biso nzela na kozwa bomoi na seko. Bomoi oyo itiolaka na nzela na Yesu Christu.

Wuta tango nandimelaka Yesu Christu mpe nabandaka kotanga Biblia, Nabandaka kobondela mpona kososola na mozindo motema na Nzambe. Nzambe Ayanolaka ngai sima na ba mbula sambo na mabondeli ebele mpe na kokila bilei. Sima na ngai kofungola egelesia, Nzambe Alimbolelaki ngai makomi mingi kati na Biblia.

Na tango nateyaka mateya mana likolo na molimo, molema, na nzoto, ezalaka na matatoli mingi mpe biyano kati na Koree mpe na bikolo na bapaya. Mingi balobaki ete bamisosolaki bango mpenza, basosolaki baton a lolenge nini bazalaki, mpe bazwaka

v

biyano na makomi mingi na pasi kati na Biblia mpe lokola lokola bososoli lolenge na kozwa bomoi na solo. Basusu kati na bato wana bazali sik'awa na posa na kokoma baton a molimo mpe bakota kati na bo Nzambe na Nzambe mpe bazali kobunda na bokokisi na yango lolenge ikomama kati na 2 Petelo 1:4, oyo itangi ete, "Na yango mpe Asili kotila biso bilaka minene mpe na motuya mingi na ntina ete na bilaka yango bozua likabo na bino kati na lolenge na Nzambe mpe bokima libebi lizali kati na mokili mpona mposa mabe."

Sun tzu Malakisi na Etumba elobi ete soki omiyebi yo mpenza mpe moyini nay o, bokokweya soko te kati na etumba. Mateya na "Molimo, Molema, mpe Nzoto" engengisa pole kati mozindo na biso mpenza mpe mikolakisa biso likolo na bobandi na moto. Soki toyekoli mpe tososoli moto na moto. Tokoyekola mpe ba nzela na kokweyisa mapinga na molili, miye mizalaka konyokola biso, mpo ete tokoka na kobika Bokristo kati na elonga.

Napesi matondi na Geumsun Vin, directrice na Ndako na Edition mpe basali ba oyo bamipesaki bango mpenza mpona

Foreword

bobimi na buku oyo. Nakolikya ete bokofuluka na makambo nioso mpe bokozala nzoto makasi na lolenge molema ikofuluka, mpe lisusu, bokota kati na bo nzambe na NZambe.

Juin 2009,
Jaerock Lee

Kobanda na mobembo kati na Molimo, Molema, mpe Nzoto

"Tika ete Nzambe na Kimya, Ye moko Abulisa bino mpenza; Tika mpe ete bobatelama kati na molimo mpe molema na nzoto na bino na kokabwana te mpe na ekweli te kino ekomonanna Nkolo na biso Yesu Kristu" (1 Batesaloniki 5:23).

Baton a Theologie babanda kolobela likolo na biloko misalaka moto, theory na dikotomie ilobaka ete moto azali biteni mibale: molimo mpe nzoto wana trikotomie elobi ete ezali na biteni misato: molimo, molema, mpe nzoto. Buku oyo efandi likolo na theory na trichotomie.

Na momesano, boyebi ekoki kokabolama kati na boyebi likolo na Nzambe, kobika bomoi na biso kati na mokili oyo. Toki kobika bomoi na elonga mpe tozwa bomoi na seko tango tososoli motema na Nzambe mpe tolanda mokano na Ye.

Bato bakelamaka na elilingi na Nzambe, mpe libanda na Nzambe, bakoki te na kobika. Soki Nzambe Azali te. Soki mpe Nzambe te bato bakoka te kososola ebandeli na bango mpe te. Tokoki koizwa eyano mpona ebandeli na bato kaka soki nani Nzambe Azali.

Molimo, molema, mpe nzoto izali kati kati na ekeke iye tokoki ten a kososola kaka na mayele na moto, bwanya, mpe nguya.. Ezali ekeke iye ikoki kaka kolimbolelama biso epai na

Nzambe ye mei, Ye oyo Asosolaka ebandeli na bato. Yango ezali likanisi na lolenge moko. Yango ezali likanisi moko na oyo asali ordinateur azali na mayele ekoka mpona kolimbola lolenge mpe makambo natali yango, nde ezali mosali nde akoki kosilisa yiki yiki nioso itali kosala na ordinateur. Buku oyo itondisami na mayebi na molimo na dimension na minei iye ikopesa na biso biyano malamu na mituna likolo na molimo, molema, mpe nzoto.

Makambo motangi akoki koyekola na kati na buku oyo isangisi oyo:

1. O nzela na bososoli na molimo ya molimo, molema, mpe nzoto, miye misalaka moto, batangi bakoki kotala kati na bango mpe bazwa mayebi na bomoi yango moko mpenza.

2. Bakoka kokota kati na bososoli na bango mpenza na ba nani bango mpenza bazali mpe eloko nini isala bango. Buku oyo ezali kolakisa nzela mpona batangi bamisosola bango mpenza lolenge ntoma polo Alobi na 1 Bakolinti 15:31, "Nazali kokufa mokolo na mokolo" Mpe bakokisa kosantisama mpe bakoma baton a molimo oyo Nzambe Alikyaka.

3. Tokoka kokima na kokangama na moyini zabolo mpe Satana, mpe tozwa nguya na kobebisa molili kaka tango tokososola likolo nabiso mpenza. Lolenge Yesu Aloba, "Soko Abengi bango banzambe ba oyo Liloba na Nzambe eyeli bango(mpe Likomi ekoki koboyama te)" (Yoane 10:350, buku oyo izali kotalisa nzela mokuse mpona batangi bakota kati na bo nzambe na Nzambe mpe bazwa mapamboli nioso miye Nzambe Alaka.

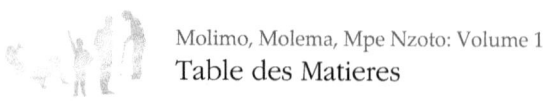

Molimo, Molema, Mpe Nzoto: Volume 1

Table des Matieres

Liloba na Liboso

Kobanda Mobembo kati na Molimo, Molema, mpe Nzoto

Eteni 1 Kosalelama na Nzoto

Chapitre 1 Concepte na Nzoto — 2
Chapitre 2 Kokela — 12
   1. Mystere na Bokabwani na Ba Espace
   2. Espace na Mosuni mpe Espace na Molimo
   3. Moto na Molimo, Molema, mpe Nzoto

Chapitre 3 Moto kati na espace na mosuni — 36
   1. Nkona na Bomoi
   2. Lolenge nini moto abanda
   3. Motema
   4. Misala na mosuni
   5. Kokola

Eteni 2 Kolelama na Molema
(Mosala na molema kati na espace na Mosuni)

Chapitre 1 Kosalema na Molema — 84
   1. Definition na Molema
   2. Misala kili kili na Molema kati na Espace na Nzoto
   3. Molili

Chapitre 2 Mei — 124
Chapitre 3 Makambo na mosuni — 140
Chapitre 4 Likolo na etape na Molimo na Bomoi — 158

Eteni 3 Bozongeli na Molimo

Chapitre 1 Molimo mpe Molimo Ekoka   172
Chapitre 2 Mokano na Nzambe na Ebandeli   196
Chapitre 3 Bato na SoloSolo   206
Chapitre 4 Mokili na Molimo   222

Molimo, Molema, mpe Nzoto: Volume 2

Partie1 Espace Monene na Mokili na Molimo

Chapitre 1 Molili mpe Pole
Chapitre 2 Makoki mpona kokota kati na espace na Pole

Partie 2 Molimo, Molema, mpe Nzoto kati na Espace na Molimo

Chapitre 1 Bisika na bisika na kozala
Chapitre 2 Molimo, Molema, mpe Nzoto kati na Mokili na Molimo

Partie 3 Kotombwama likolo na bosuki na bato

Chapitre 1 Espace na Nzambe
Chapitre 2 Elilingi na Nzambe

 Molimo, Molema, Mpe Nzoto: Volume 1

Partie
1

Kosalema na Nzoto

Nini ezali ebandeli na Moto?
Towuta wapi mpe tozali kokende Wapi?

Yo Osalaki bilembo na katikati na ngai;
Otongaki ngai kati na libumu na mama na ngai.
Nakotonda yo mpo été nasalami na motindo
na kokamwa mingi. ; misala na yo mizali
na kokamwa mpe molim na ngai eyebi yango
malamu..
Nzoto na ngai ebombamaki na Yo te na ntango wana
Esalemaki ngai na ebombelo mpe wana ebongisamaki
Ngai na nse mingi na mokili.
Miso na Yo Imonaki ngai naino esalemaki ngai te;
Mikolo na ngai ikomamaki nioso na mokanda na Yo.
Yango iponamaki mpona ngai, naino ekomaki moko
Na yango te. Nzembo 139:13-16

Chapitre 1

Concepte na Mosuni

Nzoto na moto iye ikozongaka na liboke na mputulu na koleka na tango; bilei nioso moto aliaka; makambo nioso moto amonaka, ayokaka, mpe asepelaka; mpe makambo nioso basalaka- mana nioso mizali ndakisa na 'nzoto'.

Nini Nzoto ezali?

Moto akoki te, na talo moko te, soki bakotikala na mosuni

Makambo nioso kati na univer mizali na ba Dimension mikesana

Dimension na likolo mikonzaka mpe Mikokambaka likolo na ba Dimension na Nse

Kati na lisituale na bato bato baluka eyano na 'Nani Moto Azali?' Eyano na motuna wana ikopesa biso biyano na mituna misusu lokola, "Mpona tina nini tosengeli na kobika bomoi na biso?" mpe lolenge kani tosengeli na kobika bomoi na biso?" Matangi, koluka, mpe kotala likolo na bozali na moto misalema mpenza mingi na mambi ma philosophie mpe religion, kasi ezali pete te mpona kozwa eyano malamu mpe isengeli.

Ata bongo bato na mbala na mbala bamekaka kozwa biyano na mituna ibakisi ete, "Ekelamo na lolenge kani ezali moto?" mpe "Nani Ngai Nazali?" Mituna na lolenge oyo mitunamaka mpo ete biyano na miango mikoki kokoma ba fungola mpona koyeba ntina na bozali na moto. Matangi na mokili oyo mikoki te kopesa biyano malamu na na mituna iye, kasi Nzambe Akoki. Akelaka Univer mpe biloko na kati na yango mpe Akelaka moto. Eyano na Nzambe ezali eyani malamu. Tokoki omona elembo na mituna eye kati na Biblia, oyo izali Liloba na Nzambe.

Ba Theorist bakabolaka moto na biloko mibale, molimo na ye mpe 'nzoto na ye'. Eteni ezali kosala makanisi na moto etalisami lokola molimo mpe eteni mosusu etalisi 'nzoto'. Kasi, Biblia ekaboli moto na biteni misato : molimo, molema, mpe

3

nzoto.

1 Batesaloniki 5:23 etangi ete, "Tika ete Nzambe na kimya Abulisa bino Ye moko mpenza. Tika mpe ete bobatelama kati na molimo mpe na motema mpe na nzoto na kokabwana te mpe na ekweli te kino ekomonana Nkolo na biso Yesu Christo." Molimo mpe molema mizali makambo moko te. Ezali kaka ba nkombo nde mikesani te, kasi mikesani na kozala na yango. Mpona kososola nini 'moto azali', tosengeli koyekola likolo na nzoto, molema, mpe molimo.mizali nini.

Nini nzoto ezali?

Tina naino totala nini dictionaire elobi likolo na 'nzoto'(mosuni). Dictionaire na nkombo Meriam Webster elobi ete mosuni ezali bisika na pete kati na nzoto na nyama mingi mingi na vertebrée ; mingi mingi : eteni etali mosuni na mokuwa na bokeseni na biloko na kati misusu, mikuwa, mpe integument. » Ekoki mpe kobengama eteni eye emonanaka na miso epai na nyama. Kasi, kososola nini mosuni (nzoto) elakisi kati na Biblia tosengeli na kososola limbola na molimo likolo na limbola na dictionnaire.

Biblia esalelaka mingi nkombo 'nzoto' mpe 'mosuni'. Na makambo mingi mitalisami na molimo. Na lolenge na molimo, nzoto etalisi makambo makokufaka, makombongwanaka, mpe suka suka makolimwaka na koleka na tango. Ezali mpe biloko oyo na salite mpe na mbindo. Ba nzete miye mizali na makasa na langi na mpondu mikokawuka mokolo moko mpe mikokufa mpe mizali na bitape mpe nzete mikokoma mokolo moko moto ya koni.ba nzete, makasa, mpe makambo nioso na mokoli makokufaka, makopola mpe makolimwa na boleki na tango. Mazali nioso nzoto (mosuni).

Nini likolo na moto, nkolo na ekelamo nioso? Lelo tozali na bato na ba milliard 7 kati na mokili. Ata na tango oyo bana bebe bakokobaka na kobotama na bisika kati na mokili oyo, mpe na bisika mosusu bato bakokobaka na kokufa. Tango bakufi, ba nzoto na bango mikozonga na mputulu, mpe bazali mpe mosuni. Lisusu, bilei miye miliami, monoko milobanaki, alphabets mpona kokanga makanisi, mpe ba civilization scientifique mpe technologique miye bato balingaka mizali nioso mosuni. Mikobeba, mikombongwana, mpe mikokufaka na boleki na tango. Bongo, makambo nioso miye mizali na mokili oyo tokomonaka na miso, mpe nioso kati na univer lolenge toyebi yango mizali 'mosuni'.

Bato, oyo balongwa na Nzambe, bazali kaka bikelamo na 'mosuni'. Nini baton a masoni bakolisa mpe bakolukaka? Balandaka kaka ba mposa na mosuni,,baposa na miso, mpe lolendo na bizaleli. Ata ba civilisations bato bakolisi mizali kaka mpon kosepelisa ba sense mitano na bato. Mizali mpona kosepelisa nzoto mpe kokokisa ba mposa na bango na nzoto. Na koleka na tango bato baluka mingi makambo na ekobo mpe na pite. Na lolenge civilization ekokolaka ba mposa mabe na nzoto mpe bato bakobebisama mpe lokola.

Na tango ezali na nzoto ikomonanaka, ezali mpe na oyo emonanaka te. Biblia elobi ete, koyina, koswana, zua, koboma, ekobo, mpe makambo nioso masangani na masumu mazali kaka mosuni. Kaka lolenge solo na fololo, mopepe mpe mopepe makasi mizali kasi mikomonanaka te, ezali na mosisa na masumu iye kati na mitema na bato mpe lokola. Maye nioso wana mazali mpe 'mosuni'. Bongo, mosuni ezali nkombo na makambo nioso kati na univer miye mibebaka mpe mibombongwanaka na koleka na tango, mpe mabe nioso lokola, masumu, mabe, bozangi sembo, mpe bozangi mobeko.

Baloma 8:8 elobi ete, "...Ba oyo bazali kotia motema na bango na makambo na nzoto bayebi kosepelisa Nzambe te." Soki nzoto na makomi oyo etalisi kaka nzoto na moto, elakisi ete moto moko te akoki soko kosepelisa Nzambe. Bongo esengeli kozala na limbola mosusu.

Lisusu, Yesu Alobi na Yoane 3:16 ete, "Oyo ebotami na mosuni ezali mosuni, mpe oyo ebotami na molimo ezali molimo," mpe na Yoane 6:63 ete, Molimo ezali ye oyo Akopesaka bomoi; mosuni ezali na lisungi te. Maloba masili ngai kosololana na bino mazali na Molimo mpe mazali bomoi." 'Mosuni' awa elakisi mpe makambo maye makobebaka mpe makombongwana, mpe yango ezali tina Yesu Alobaki ete ezali na lisungi te.

Bato bazali Mpamba, na talo moko te, soki Bakotikalaka kati na Mosuni

Na bokeseni na ba nyama, moto alukaka makambo misusu kati na emotion mpe makanisi na bango. Kasi mizali seko te, mpe mizali nioso mosuni mpe lokola. Makambo bato bakomonaka na tina lokola bozwi, lokumu, mpe mayebi mizali mpe makambo na ntina te, makambo miye mikokufa. Boni mpona mposa ibiangama 'bolingo'? Tango bato mibale balingani sika, bakoki koloba ete bakoki te kobika soki mosusu azali te. Kasi mingi na bato wana babongwanaka sima na kobalana. Kokozwaka nkanda pamba pamba mpe kozanga esengo mpe ata kokoma bato na bitumba kaka mpo ete bakolingaka eloko moko te. Mbongwana nioso kati na bizaleli mizali mpe mosuni. Soki bato bakotikala kati na mosuni, bakeseni mpenza ten a nyama to na nzete. Na miso na Nzambe makambo nioso mazali kaka mosuni miye makobebaka mpe makolimwa.

1 Petelo 1:24 elobi ete, "Bato nioso bazali kaka lokola matiti, kitoko na bango nioso lokola fololo na matiti; matiti makouki mpe fololo ekwei," mpe Yakobo 4:14 elobi ete, "Boyebi makambo na lobi te. Bomoi na bino ezali nini? Bozali bobele londende, komonana mwa ntango moke sima kolimwa."

Nzoto mpe makanisi nioso na bato mizali nioso mpamba wuta bakenda mosika na Liloba na Nzambe oyo Azali molimo. Mokonzi Salomo asepelaka lokumu na lolenge nioso mpe bozwi moto akioki kosepela na mokili oyo, kasi asosolaka bo mpamba na mosuni mpe alobaki ete, "'Bisalasala na mpamba! Bisalasala na mpamba! Nioso ezali bobele mpamba.' Moto akozwa libonza nini na misala nioso na ye oyo ekosalaka ye nan se na moi?" (Mosakoli 1:2-3)

Biloko nioso kati na Univer Mizali na Ba Dimension Mikesana

Ba dimension na physique to mathematique mikokatama na moko na makambo oyo misato mikataka position na mopepe. Mbuma kati na molongo ezali na coordination moko, mpe ibiangami dimension moko. Eloko likolo na pepo izali na coordination mibale, mpe izali na dimension mibale. Na lolenge moko eloko na espace izali na cordination misato, mpe ibiangami dimension misato.

Bisika biso tozali kobika izali na dimension misato kolandana na mayebi na Physique. Na mozindo na malakisi na physique bakobenga tango dimension na minei. Yango ezali bososoli na dimension kati na scince.

Kasi na kotala na molimo, molema mpe nzoto, dimension mikoki kokabolama kati na dimension na mosuni mpe dimension na molimo. Dimension na mosuni mikabolami lisusu kati na dimension na mosuni ikabolami na 'non dimensionel' te na 'dimension na misato'. Yambo, non dimensionel italisi biloko mizanga bomoi. Mabanga, mabele, mai,mpe mabende mizali na categorie oyo. Makambo nioso na bomoi mizwami kati na dimension na liboso, na mibale, to na misato.

Dimension wa yambo italisi biloko mizali na bomoi mpe mipemaka kasi mikoki te kotambola zinga, yango elakisi ete makoki na kotamboli mizali kati na yango te. Isangisi ba fololo, matti, ba nzete mpe ba ndunda misusu. Mizali na ba nzoto, kasi molema na molimo mizali na yango te.

Dimension na mibale isangisi biloko na bomoi miye mipemaka, mikoki kotambola, mpe mizali na nzoto mpe molema. Mizali ba nyama lokola nkosi, ngolu, mpate; mizali ban deke, ba mbisi, mpe nyama mike. Imbwa ikoki koyeba nkolo na yango to kongangela bapaya pamba te bizali na molema.

Dimension na misato isangisi biloko mikopemaka, mikoningana, mpe mizali na molema mpe molimo miye mizali kati na ba nzoto na bango mikomonanaka na miso. Elakisi bato ba oyo bazali bakonzi na bikelamo nioso. Na bokeseni na ba nyama, moto azali na molimo. Bazali na makoki na kokanisa mpe na koluka Nzambe, mpe bakoki kondimela Nzambe.

Ezali mpe na dimension na minei iye ikomonana ten a miso na biso. Ezali dimension na molimo. Nzambe oyo Azali molimo, mantinga na Lola mpe banje, mpe ba Kerubi bango nioso bazali kati na dimension na molimo.

Dimension na Likolo Ikonzaka mpe Mikambaka Likolo na Dimension na Nse

Bikelamo na dimension na mibale mikoki kokonza mpe kokamba likolo na bikelamo nan a dimension na liboso to dimension nan se koleka. Bikellamo na dimension na misato mikoki kokonza bikelamo na dimension na mibale to mpe nse na yango. Bikelamo na dimension nan se mikoki te kososola bikelamo na dimension likolo na bango. Lolenge na bomoi kati na dimension na liboso, mikoki te kososola dimension na mibale mpe bomoi kati na dimension na mibale ikoki te kososola dimension na misato. Ndakisa, toloba été moto songolo aloni nkona na lolenge moko boye kati na elanga, abwakeli yango mai, mpe akolandela yango. Tango nkona ekobimisa nkasa, ikokola lokola na kokoma nzete, mpe ikobimisa ba mbuma. Nkona wana isosoli te nini moto asalelaki yango. Ata tango misopi banyatamaki na moto mpe bakufaki, bakoyeba mpe ntina te. Dimansion na likolo ikoki kokonza mpe kokamba bikelamo na oyo na nse, kasi na momesano dimension nan se izali na nzela mosusu te, kaka na kokambama na oyo na likolo.

Na lolenge moko, bato bango bazali na dimension na misato bakoki ten a kososola mokili na molimo oyo ezali na mokili na dimension minei. Bongo, moto na mosuni akoki te kosala eloko mpona kolonga na ye moko na kokonzama mpe nan se na ba demona. Kasi soki tolongoli mosuni mpe tokomi baton a molimo, tokoki kokota na mokili na dimension minei. Bongo tokoka kokonza mpe kolonga milimo mabe. Nzambe oyo Azali molimo Alingi bana ba Ye basosola mokili na dimension minei. Na lolenge oyo bakoka kososola mokano na Nzambe. Kotosa Ye, mpe kozwa bomoi. Na Genese chapitre 1, liboso na Adamu kolia mbuma na nzete na boyebi malamu mpe mabe, akonzaki mpe akambaka makambo nioso. Na tango wana Adamu azalaka molimo na bomoi mpe azalaka ya dimension na minei. Kasi sima na ye kosumuka, molimo na ye ekufaki. Kaka Adamu ye mei te, kasi ata bakitani na ye sik'awa bazali kati na dimension na misato. Bongo, tika totala lolenge nini moto, ba oyo bakelamaka na Nzambe, bakweyaka na dimension na misato, mpe lolenge kani bakoki kozonga na mokili na dimension na minei.

Chapitre 2
Kokela

Nzambe Mokeli azalaka na likanisi monene mpona koleka na baton a nse na moi. Akabolaka espace na Nzambe kati na espace na molimo mpe espace na mosuni mpe Akelaka Likolo nan se mpe makambo nioso kati na yango.

1. Nkamwa na Bokaboli na ba Espace

2. Espace na Mosuni mpe Espace na Molimo

3. Bato na Molimo, Molema mpe Nzoto

Wuta ata liboso na bikeke, Nzambe Azalaka Ye moko kati na univer. Azalaka lokola Pole mpe Akonzaka likolo na nioso na kokendeke bisika nioso kati na univer monene. Na Yoane 1:5 ekomama ete Nzambe Azali Pole. Etalisi yambo Pole na molimo, kasi etalisi mpe Nzambe oyo Azala lokola Pole na Ebandeli. Moto moko te abota Nzambe. Azali Ekelamo na Kokoka Azalisama na Ye Moko. Bongo, tosengeli te komeka kososola Ye na mayele mpe nguya na biso misuka. Yoane 1:1 ifandisi sekele na 'ebandeli'. Elobi ete, 'Na ebandeli ezalaki Liloba.'' Yango ezali limbola na makambo matali lolenge na Nzambe na kozala na Liloba kati na Pole na nkamwa mpe na kitoko koleka mpe kokonza ba espace nioso kati na univer.

Awa ebandeli, etalisi tango moko liboso na seko, esika oyo moto akoka kososola te. Yango ezali ata liboso na ebandeli na Genese 1:1, oyo ezali ebandeli na kokela. Bongo malkambo na lolenge nini masalema liboso na kokelama na mokili?

1. Bokabwani na Nkamwa na ba Espaces

Mokili na molimo izalaka mosika mingi te. Izali na Bikuke miye mikutana na mokili na molimo na bisika mingi na mapata oyo na mosuni.

Sima na boleki mingi mpenza na tango, Nzambe Alingaka kozala na moto moko na oyo Akoka kokabola bolingo na Ye mpe makambo misusu. Nzambe Azali na Bomoto mpe BoNzambe na mbala moko mpona yango Alingaka kokabola makambo nioso Azalaki na yango mbele kosepela yango kaka Ye mei. Na kakanisa yango na bongo na Ye, Asalaka likanisi mpona boleki na baton a nse na moi. Ezalaki mokano na kokela moto, kopambola bango mpo ete babota mpe bakoma ebele, azwa milimo ebele ba oyo bakokani na Nzambe, mpe asangisa bango kati na bokonzi na Lola. Ezali kaka lolenge moloni akolisaka masangu, kosangisa yango mpe kotia yango na ndako na ebonbelo.

Nzambe Ayebaka ete esengelaki na espace na molimo bisika wapi Akozala mpe espace na mosuni bisika wapi koleka na baton a nse na moi ekosalema. Akabolaki univer monene kati na mokili na molimo mpe na mokili na mosuni. Koloanda wana Nzambe Akoma na lolenge na Nzambe Misato nakozalaka Nzambe Tata, Nzambe Muana, Nzambe Molimo Mosantu. Ezalaki, mpo na boleki na baton a nse na moi yango esengelaki mpona mikolo ekoya, Mobikisi Yesu mpe Molimo Mosantu Bakozala na bosenga.

Emoniseli 22:13 elobi ete, "Ngai Alifa na Omega, Moto na Liboso na moto na Nsuka, Ebandeli na Nsuka." 'Alifa na Omega' italisi Nzambe Tata oyo Azali ebandeli mpe suka na mayebi nioso mpe ba civilization nioso na bato. 'Moto na Liboso na Moto na Suka' etalisi Nzambe Muana, Yesu, oyo Azali Moto na Liboso na Moto na Suka na koleka na baton a nse na moi.

'Ebandeli mpe Suka' etalisi Molimo Mosantu oyo Azali ebandeli mpe Suka na koleka na baton a nse na moi.

Muana Yesu Asala mosala na Mobikisi. Molimo Mosantu Atatola likolo na Mobikisi lokola Mosungi mpe Asilisi koleka na baton a nse na moi. Biblia etalisi Molimo Mosantu na ba lolenge na lolenge na kokokanisa Ye na Pigeon to moto, mpe Azali mpe kotalisama lokola 'Molimo na Muana na Nzambe'. Bagalatia 4 :6 elobi été, "Mpo ete bino bozali bana, Nzambe Atindi Molimo na Muana na Ye kati na mitema na biso, konganga ete, Aba, Tata! Lisusu, Yoane 15:26 elobi ete, "Wana ekoya mosungi, Ye oyo nakotindela bino longwa na Tata, Ye Molimo na solo oyo Auti na Tata, Ye Akotatoli mpona Ngai."

Nzambe Tata, Mwana, mpe Molimo Mosantu bazwaka lolenge moko boye mpona kokokisa mokano na koleka na bato na nse na moi, mpe Balobelaki mokano na makambo nioso elongo. Etalisami kati na buku na Genese 1 oyo elobeli likolo na kokela.

Tango Genese 1:26 elobi ete, "Bongo Nzambe Alobi ete, 'Tika Tozalisa moto na lolenge na Biso na elilingi na Biso,'" Yango elakisi kaka te ete moto asalema na nzoto lolenge na Nzambe Tata, Mwana, mpe Molimo Mosantu. Elakisi molimo, oyo izali moboko na moto, ipesamaka na Nzambe mpe molimo oyo ekokani na Nzambe Mosantu.

Mokili na Mosuni mpe Mokili na Molimo

Tango Nzambe Azalaka Ye moko, Akokaka ten a kososola kati na mokili na mosuni mpe mokili na molimo. Kasi, mpona boleki na baton a nse na moi ezalaki na bosenga na mokili na mosuni bisika wapi bato bakobika. Mpona ntina oyo Akabolaka mokili na mosuni na mokili na molimo.

Kasi kokabola mokili na mosuni na mokili na molimo elakisi te ete na biteni mibale mpenza mpenza lokola tokataka eloko na biteni mibale. Ndakisa, toloba ete ezali na ba gas mibale kati na ndako moko. Tobakisi produit chimique mpo ete moko na yango imonana lokola langi motane, mpo ete ikesana na mosusu. Ata soki ezali na ba gas mibale kati na ndako, miso na biso mikoki kaka komona gas iye izali komonana motane. Ata siki gas mosusu imonani te, ezali solo mpe wana.

Lolenge moko, Nzambe Akabola espace monene na molimo kati na espace na mosuni mpe espace na molimo. Ya solo, mnmokili na mosuni mpe mokili na molimo ezalaka lolenge ba ba gas oyo te na ndakisa. Mikomonana lokola mikabwana, kasi misangisama. Mpe, lokola mikomonana lolenge na kosangisama, mikabolama mpe lokola.

Lokola elembo ete mokili na mosuni mpe mokili na molimo mikabolama na lolenge na nkamwa, Nzambe Atia bikuke na mokili na molimo na bisika bisika kati na univer. Mokili na molimo izalaka bisika moko te na mosika. Ezali na bikuke na bisika ebele kati na mapata iye imonanaka na miso. Soki Nzambe Afongoli biso miso na molimo, mpona ngonga moko tokoka komona mokili na molimo na nzela na bikuke mana.

Ata Setefano Atondisamaka na Molimo Mosantu mpe Amonaka Yesu kotelema na loboko na mobali na Nzambe, ezalaki mpo ete miso na molimo mpe bikuke na mokili na molimo mifungwamaki (Misala 7:55-56). Eliya akamatamaki na bomoi na Lola. Nkolo na lisekwa Nkolo Yesu akamatamaki na Lola. Mose na Eliya bamonanaki na Ngomba na Kombwongana. Tokoki kososola lolenge kani makambo mina misalema mpenza soki tososoli été ezali na bikuke mpona kokoma na mokili na molimo.

Univer izali mpenza monene mpe izanga suka na volume. Bisika tomonaka longwa na mokili oyo (Univer iye imonanaka) ezali etando monene na 46 milliard na ba annee lumiere. Soki mokili na molimo izalaka na suka na oyo na mosuni, ata na vaiseau spaciale na mbangu koleka ikozwa tango molayi mingi mpona kokoma na mokili na molimo. Lisusu, bokoki kobanza distance banje basengeli na kobembuka mpona kokoma na mokili na mosuni longwa na oyo na molimo? Kasi, mpo ete bikuke oyo na mokili na molimo mizali miye mikoki na kofungwama mpe kokangama, moto akoka kobembuka kati na mokili na molimo mpe na mosuni na bo pete lolenge koleka o nzela na ekuke.

Nzambe Asala Ba Likolo Minei

Sima na Nzambe kokabola univer kati na mokili na molimo mpe na mokili na mosuni, Akabola miango na ba Lola ebele kolandana na bosenga. Biblia elobeli ete ezali kaka na Lola moko te kasi ba likolo misusu mizali. Ezali kolobelela biso ete ezali na ba likolo misusu libanda na oyo tokomonaka na miso na biso.

Dutelenome 10:14 etangi ete, "Tala, Lola, na oyo mileki likolo mpe mokili na biloko nioso kati na yango Izali na Yawe Nzambe na yo." mpe Nzembo 68:33 itangi ete, "Epai na Ye oyo Akotambola likolo na Lola, ee Lola oyo eumeli longwa na kalakala; tala Akobimisaka mingongo na Ye, mongongo makasi mpenza." Mpe Mokonzi Salomo Alobi na 1 Mikonzi 8:27 ete, "Solo Nzambe Akofanda na mokili? Tala Lola mpe likolo na Lola ikoki kozingela Ye te, na koleka ndako oyo ngai natongeli Yo yango ekoki te."

Nzambe Asaleli nkombo 'Lola' mpona kolobela mokili na molimo, mpo ete tokoka na pete ba espace kati na mokili na molimo. Ba 'Lola' na mibimba mikabolama na ba Lola minei. Espace mobimba na mosuni ata mokili na biso, systeme solaire na biso, galaxie na biso, mpe univer mobimba italisama lokola Lola na liboso.

2:15). Kobanda Lola na Mibale kino likolo ezali ba espace na molimo. Elanga na Edeni mpe espace bisika Milimo mabe mizali na Likolo na Mibale. Sima na Nzambe kokela moto, akelaka mpe elanga na Edeni, oyo ezali bisika na pole na likolo na mibale. Nzambe Amema moto kati na Elanga na Edeni mpe Atika ye akonza mpe atambwisa likolo na biloko nioso (Genese 2 :15).

Ngwende na Nzambe izalaka na Likolo na misato. Izali Bokonzi na Lola bisika bana na Nzambe bakoingela, ba oyo bakozwa lobiko na nzela na boleki na baton a nse na moi.

Lola na Minei ezali Lola na ebandeli bisika Nzambe

Ameseneke kozala Ye Mei lokola Pole liboso na Ye kokabola espace. Yango Ezali espace na kokamwisa bisika wapi makambo nioso makokisamaka kaka lolenge Nzambe Alingi na Makanisi na Ye. Ezali mpe espace oyo etombwami likolo na bosuki na tango mpe espace.

2. Espace na Mosuni mpe Espace na Molimo

Nini ezali tina ete mingi na batangi na Biblia baluka komona Elanga na Edeni kasi bakoka te? Ezali mpo ete Elanga na Edeni ezalaka na Lola na mibale, oyo ezali espace na molimo.

Espace oyo Nzambe Akabolaka ikoki kokabolama na biteni mibale espace na mosuni mpe espace na molimo. Mpona bana ba Ye oyo Akozwa sima na koleka na bango na nse na moi, Nzambe Asalaki bokonzi na Lola na Lola na misato, mpe Asalaki mabele na likolo na liboso ezala bisika na bokoli na bato.

Genese chapitre 1 etalisi na mokuse lolenge na kokela na Nzambe o mikolo motoba. Nzambe na ebandeli Asalaka mabele na kokoka te. Atiaka naino moboko na mabele mpe sima mapata o nzela na koningana na croute terestre (mabele) mpe na ba phenomene meteorologique. Nzambe Atiaka makasi ma Ye mingi mpona tango molayi, tango mosusu ata kokitaka na mokili Ye mpenza mpona kotala lolenge nini makambo mazalaki kotambola, pamba tem abele ezalaki bisika akozwa bana ba Ye ba bolingo na solo solo.

Muana kati na zemi akolaka malamukati na main a libumu na mama na ye. Lolenge moko, sima na bokeli na mabele mpe moboko itiamaki, mabele mobimba izipamaki na ebele na mai, mpe mai yango ezalaki mai na Bomoi ewutaka na Lola na misato. Mabele ekomaki sik'awa prete mpona kozala bisika na biloko nioso kobika mpo été mai na bomoi itondisamaki likolo na yango. Bongo, Nzambe Abandaki kokela.

Espace na Mosuni, Bisika mpona Bokoli na Bato

Tango Nzambe Alobaki ete, "Tika Pole Ezala" o mokolo na liboso na kokela, ezalaki na pole na molimo iye ilongwaki na Ngwende na Nzambe mpe ezipaki mokili. Na pole oyo nguya na Nzambe ezanga suka mpe nature divine ikotaki na biloko nioso mpe biloko nioso mikonzamaki na mobeko (loi de la nature).

Nzambe Akabolaka pole na molili mpe abengaka pole 'moi', mpe molili Abengaka yango butu mpe koleka na tango ata liboso na Ye Akela moi mpe sanza.

On the second day, God made the expanse and let it separate the waters that covered the Earth into the waters below the expanse and the waters which were above the expanse. God called this expanse heaven, which is the sky visible to our eyes. Now, the basic environment was made that could support all the living things. The air was made for the living things to breathe; the clouds and sky were made where meteorological phenomena could take place. Na mokolo na mibale, Nzambe Asalaka etando mpe atikaka été yango ekabola mai na nse na etando mpe mai na likolo na etando. Nzambe Abengali etando yango Likolo, yango ezali mapata tomonaka na miso na biso. Sik'awa, mokili oyo isengelaki na kozala na biloko nioso na bomoi isalemaka. Mopepe isalemaka mpona bikelamo na bomoi mipema ; Mapata mpe likolo misalemaka mpo été ba phenomene metereologique ikoka na kosalema. Mai nan se na etando izali mai oyo itikalaki na mabele. Izali moto na ba mai miye mikokoma, ba ocean, mai na lamele, mabeke, mpe bibale (Genese 1 :9-10). Mai likolo na etando mitikalaki mpona Edene na likolo na mibale. Na mokolo na misato, Nzambe asala été mai na nse na etando misangana na bisika moko mpona kokabola ba mai na lamele na mabele. Akelaka mpe matiti mpe ba ndunda.

Na mokolo na minei Nzambe Akelaka moi, sanza, mpe minzoto, mpe Atika miango mikonza moi mpe butu. Na mokolo na mitano Asalaka mpe ba mbisi mpe bandeke. Suka suka, na mokolo na motoba Nzambe Akelaka ban yama nioso mpe moto.

Espace na Molimo Imonanaka Te

Elanga na Edene ezali na mokili na molimo na likolo na mibale, kasi ikeseni na mokili na molimo na likolo na misato. Ezali nioso mokili na molimo te wuta ikoki kosangana na dimension na mosuni. Na koloba na mokuse izali lokola bokatikati na molimo mpe na mosuni. Sima na Nzambe kokela moto lokola molimo na bomoi, Alonaka Elanga na bisika na ebimelo na tango, na Edene, mpe Amemaki moto kati na Elanga (Genese 2 :8).

Awa, ebimelo na tango elakisi bisika na mosuni lokola na mokili oyo te. Ezali na limbola na lolenge mosusu lokola' bisika itondisama na pole.' Na mikolo na lelo batangi mingi na Biblia bakanisa été Elanga na Edeni ezalaka bisika moko pembeni na ebale na euphrate mpe Tigre, mpe bakanisa été basala ba recherche makasi mpe bakamba misala mingi na Archeologie kolandana na koluka na bango batikala komona elembo moko te na Elanga na Edeni. Tina ezali été Elanga bisika molimo na bomoi Adamu Abikaka na tango moko, ezali na likolo na mibale, yango ezali espace na molimo.

Elanga na Edeni ezali espace monene kolekela makanisi na biso. Bana oyo Adamu azwaka liboso na kokweya na ye na lisumu bakoba na kobika kuna, na kokobaka na kobota bana mingi koleka. Elanga na Edene ezali na limite na espace ten de bongo ekotikala na kotonda tea ta na sima na koleka na tango.

Kasi na Genese 3:24, tokoki kotanga ete Nzambe Atelemisaka ba Kerubi mpe mopanga na moto kobalola balola na bisika nioso na esika na kobima na tango na Elanga na Edeni.

Yango esalema bongo mpo ete esika na kobima na tango na Elanga ikutana na esika na molili. Milimo mabe baluka tango nioso kokota kati na Elanga mpona ba tina ebele. Yambo, balingaka komeka Adamu mpe na mibale balingaka kozwa mbuma na nzete na bomoi. Balingaka kozwa bomoi na seko na kolia mbuma mpe batelemela Nzambe mpona libela. Adamu azalaka na mosala na kobatela Elanga na Edeni na mapinga na molili. Kasi wuta Adamu akweisamaka na Satana na kolia na nzete na boyebi na malamu mpe na mabe, mpe abimisamaka na mokili oyo, ba kerubi mpe mopanga mokopelaka moto miyaka kozwa mosala na ye.

Tokoka na koloba ete bisika na pole wapi Elanga na Edeni ezali mpe bisika na molili mpona milimo mabe mikutanaka na likolo na mibale. Lisusu, na bisika na pole na likolo na mibale, ezali na bisika wapi bandimi bakozala na elambo na mbula sambo elongo na Nkolo sima na kozonga na Ye na Mibale. Ezali kitoko koleka Elanga na Edeni. Bato nioso, ba oyo babikisama wuta kokelama na mokili bakozala wana, mpe moto ameka kobanza boni monene bisika mikozala.

Ezali mpe na Lola na misato mpe na minei na mokili na molimo, mpe mozindo likolo na yango ikolimbolama na volume na Mibale na Molimo, Molema, mpe Nzoto. Tina oyo Nzambe Akabola espace na mosuni mpe espace na molimo mpe atia kati na yango bisika mingi, ezali nioso wana mpona biso bato. Isalemaka mpona mokano na koleka na baton a nse na moi mpona kozwa ban aba solosolo. Sik'awa na nini mpe lolenge kani moto azalaka?

3. Moto na Molimo, Molema, mpe Nzoto

Lisituale na moto iye ikomama kati na Biblia ibanda na tango Adamu ebimisamaka na Elanga mpona mokili oyo likolo na lisumu na Ye. Lisituale oyo asangisi te tango Adamu abikaka na Elanga na Edeni

1) Adamu, Molimo na Bomoi

Mpona kososola moto wa yambo, Adamu, ezali ebandeli na bososoli na moboko na moto. Nzambe Akelaka Adamu lokola molimo na bomoi mpona koleka na baton a nse na moi. Genese 2:7 elimboli kokelama na Adamu:"Na ntango yango Yawe Nzambe Asalaki moto na mputulu na mokili, mpe Apemaki kati na zolo na ye mpema na bomoi, mpe moto akomaki molimo na bomoi."

Eloko oyo Nzambe Asalelaka mpona kokela moto ezalaki mputulu na mokili. Ezalaki mpo ete moto akoleka nan se na moi na lolenge na elanga.

Ezali mpe mpo ete mabele, oyo ezali mputulu na mokili, ikombongwana na lolenge na yango kolandana na oyo ebakisami likolo na yango. Nzambe Asalaka kaka nzoto na moto na mputulu na mabele te kasi mpe lisusu biloko na ye na kati na nzoto, mikuwa, misisa minene, mpe mike. Mosali malamu na biluku akosala mbeki na chine kitoko na Lima malamu. Wuta Nzambe Asala moto moto na Elilingi na Ye moko, boni kitoko moto asengelaka kozala !

Adamu asalamaka na mposo pembe mpe petwa na langi na miliki. Azalaki na nzoto na mobali mpe nzoto na ye izalaka yakokoka kobanda moto kino suka na misapi na makolo, mpe biloko na ye nioso na kati mpe lokola. Azalaka kitoko. Tango Nzambe Apemaka mpema na bomoi kati na Adamu, Akomaka ekelamu na bomoi. Yango ezali molimo na bomoi. Procedure ezali lolenge moko na mwida oyo ebongisami malamu iye ikoki ten a kopela (kongala) na yango moko. Ekoki kopela soki kaka courant epesameli yango. Motema na Adamu ebandaka kobeta, makila maye kotambola, mpe ba celulles mpe ba organe na ye nioso mibanda kosala kaka sima na ye kozwa mpema na bomoi kowuta na Nzambe. Bongo na ye ebanda kosala, miso ma ye komona, matoyi maye koyoka,mpe nzoto na ye ibanda koningana lolenge alingaki kaka sima na kozwa mpema na bomoi.

Mpema na bomoi ezali mangaliti na nguya na Nzambe. Ekoki mpe kobengama energie na Nzambe. Ezali moboko na nguya mpona kokoba na bomoi. Sima na Nzambe kopema kati na Adamu mpema na bomoi, Adamu ayaka na kozwa lolenge na molimo oyo yango ezalaki lolenge moko na nzoto na ye. Kaka lokola lolenge Adamu azalaki na lolenge mpona nzoto na ye na mosuni, molimo na ye mpe eyaka na kozwa lolenge oyo ekokanaki mpenza na nzoto na ye. Limbola mingi na mozindo na lolenge na molimo ikolimbolama na volume na mibale na buku oyo.

Nzoto na Adamu, oyo azalaki sik'awa molimo na bomoi, ezalaki na nzoto na mosuni na mikuwa mpe mosuni iye ikufaka te. Nzoto ebombaki molimo iye izalaka kososola na Nzambe mpe molema iye ikosunga molimo. Molema mpe nzoto itosaki molimo, mpe na lolenge oyo Abatelaka Liloba na Nzambe mpe asololaki na Nzambe oyo Azalaka molimo.

Kasi tango Adamu akelamaka na ebandeli, azalaka na nzoto na mokolo asi akola, kasi azalaka na mayebi ata moko te. Kaka lolenge bebe akoki kozala na ezaleli na ye moko mpe asala mosala na motuya na mboka kaka na nzela na education, asengelaki mpe kozala na mayebi masengeli kati na ye. Bongo, sima na komema ye kati na Elanga na Edeni, Nzambe Alakisaka Adamu mayebi na solo mpe mayebi na molimo. Nzambe Alakisaka ye harmony na makambo nioso kati na univer, mibeko na mokili na molimo, Liloba na Solo, mpe mayebi mazanga suka na Nzambe. Yango tina Adamu akokaki na kokonza mokili mpe akamba makambo nioso.

Kobika na Tango Molayi iye Ikoki na Kotangama Te

Adamu, molimo na bomoi, akonzaki likolo na Elanga na Edeni mpe mabele lokola nkolo na bikelamu nioso, na kozala na mayebi mpe bwanya na molimo. Nzambe Akanisaka ete esengelaki te azala ye moko, mpe akelaka mwasi Ewa, na moko na mopanzi na ye. Nzambe asalaka ye lokola mosungi mosengeli mpona yempe atikaka bango bakoma nzoto moko. Sik'awa motuna mozali ete, tango boni bango babikaki kati na Elanga na Edeni?

Biblia epesi tango te kasi babikaka kuna na ebele na tango iye ikoki ten a kobanzama. Kasi tokomona na Genese 3:16 oyo elobi ete, "Alobaki na mwasi ete, Nakobakisa mpasi nay o na kobota; okobota bana na mpasi, nde okozala na mposa na mobali na yo, mpe ye akozala na bokonzi likolo na yo.'"

Lokola lifuti na lisumu Ewa asalaki, aswaki elakeli mabe mpe kati na yango pasi na kobota ibakisamaki makasi. Na lolenge mosusu, liboso na ye alakelama mabe, abotaka kati na Elanga na Edeni, kasi azalaka na pasi moke na kobota. Adamu na ewa bazalaka milimo na bomoi baye bakokaka ten a kokoma mibange.nde babikaka tango molayi, molayi na kokoma ebele.

Bato mingi bakanisaka ete Adamu aliaka na nzete na boyebi na malamu mpe na mabe sima na ye kokelama. Basusu batunaka motuna na lolenge oyo: Wuta lisituale na moto iye ikomama kati na Biblia izali kaka mbula 6,000, lolenge nini tokomonaka ba fossille miye mizali mikama na ba nkoto na ba mbula?
Lisituale na moto lolenge ikomama kati na Biblia ibanda kobanda tango Adamu akitisamaka na mokili oyo sima na ye kosumuka. Esangisi tango oyo ye abikaka kati na Elanga na Edeni te. Na tango Adamu azalaka kobika na Elanga na Edeni, mabele ezalaka koleka kati na makambo ebele lokola koningana na croute terestre mpe ba mbongwana na makambo matali geographie mpe kokola mpe kokufa na biloko mingi na bomoi. Basusu kati na bango bakomaka ba fossille. Mpona tina oyo tokoki komona ba fossille miye mimonana kozala ba million na b ambula.

2) Adamu Asalaki Lisumu

Tango Nzambe Amemaka Adamu na Elanga na Edene, Apekisaka eloko moko. Ayebisaka Adamu Alia na nzete na boyebi malamu na mabe te. Kasi sima na koleka na tango molayi, Adamu na Ewa bayaka kolia ya nzete. Bamisamaka na Elanga na Edene mpe bakitaka na mokili, mpe kobanda wana koleka na bato na nse na moi ebandaka.

Lolenge nini Adamu ayaka na kosumuka? Ezalaki na ekelamo oyo azalaka na sima na mpifo monene oyo Adamu Azwaka epai na Nzambe. Ezalaka Lucifer, mokonzo na milimo nioso na mabe. Lucifer akanisaka ete asengelaki kozwa nguya monene na Adamu mpona kotelemela Nzambe mpe kolonga etumba. Asalaka motambo mpe asalelaki nyoka, oyo azalaka kilikili. Lolenge elobama na Genese 3:1 ete, "Nyoka alekaki nyama nioso na kilikili oyo Yawe Nzambe Asilaki kozalisa. Nyoka asalemaka na mputulu oyo izalaki na kilikili kati na yango.

Bongo ezalaki na likama ete indima mabe na bokilikili koleka ba nyama misusu likolo na yango. Lolenge na yango iningisamaki na milimo mabe mpe nyoka akomaki esaleli na bango mpona komeka moto.

Milimo Mabe Bamekaka Moto na Tango Nioso

Na tango wana Adamu azalaka na mpifo monene mingi ete akonzaka Elanga na Edeni mpe mokili oyo, nde ezalaka pete te mpona nyoka komeka Adamu mbala moko. Yango tina iponaki komeka Ewan a yambo. Nyoka atunaka ye na mayele mabe, "Alobaki na mwasi ete, Nzambe Alobaki na bino ete boki kolia mbuma nioso na Elanga te'? (et. 1) Nzambe Atikala kopesa mobeko moko te na Ewa. Eyano na Ewa ekomami ete, "Mwasi azongiselaki nyoka ete, 'Tokoki kolia mbuma na nzete na Elanga. Kasi mpona mbuma na nzete yango na katikati na Elanga Nzambe Alobi ete, Bino bokolia yango te, mpe bokomama yango te noki bokufa te.'" (Genese 3:2-3).

Nzambe Alobaki ete, "Zambi mokolo okolia yango okokufa solo" (Genese 2:17). Kasi Ewa alobaki ete, "bokoki kokufa," Bokoki kokanisa ete ezali kaka na bokeseni moke, kasi elakisi ete abatelaki Liloba na Nzambe na bongo na ye malamu te. Ezali mpe kotalisa ete andimelaki mpenza liloba na Nzambe kati na ye te. Lolenge nyoka amonaki Ewa kobongola Liloba na Nzambe, ibandaki na komeka ye makasi koleka.

Genese 3:4-5 elobi ete, "Nyoka alobaki na mwasi ete, bino bokokufa solo te! Mpo ete Nzambe Ayebi ete na mokolo bokolia yango, miso na bino makofungwama, mpe bino bokozala na lolenge moko na Nzambe, koyeba malamu mpe mabe."

Lokola Satana akotelaki nyoka mpona kotia mposa kati na makanisi na mwasi, nzete na boyebi malamu mpe mabe imonanaki na kokesana mpo ete ikomami ete, "...Emonaki mwasi ete nzete ezalaki malamu na kolia, mpe kitoko na miso, mpe nzete yango izalaki malamu mpona kozipola bososoli na moto" (et. 6).

Ewa atikala na kozala na likanisi na kotelemela Liloba na Nzambe te, kasi lokola mposa ibotaki, aliaki sukasuka na nzete. Apesaki yango na mobali na ye Adamu, mpe aliaki mpe lokola.

Komilongisa na Adamu na Ewa

Na Genese 3:11, Nzambe Atunaka na Adamu ete, "Olei mbuma na nzete yango epekisaki Ngai yo ete olia yango te?"

Nzambe Ayebaki likambo nioso, kasi Alingaka Adamu andima mabe na ye mpe atubela. Kasi Adamu azongisaki ete, "mwasi oyo Opesaki ete azali na ngai, apesi ngai mbuma na nzete yango. Ngai mpe nalei." (et.12) Adamu alingaki koloba ete soki Nzambe Apesaka ye mwasi te, ye alingaki kosala limbo oyo te. Bisika na kondima mabe na ye, alingaki kaka kokima likambo na ye. Ya solo Ewa azalaki oyo apesaki mbuma epai na Adamu alia. Kasi, Adamu azalaka mokonzi na mwasi nde asengelaki kozwa faute na likambo isalamaki.

Sik'awa, Nzambe Atunaka Mwasi na Genese 3:13, "Osali bongo mpona nini? Ata soki Adamu asengelaki kozwa faute, Ewa akokaki te kolongolama na lisumu asalaki. Kasi atiaki mpe faute epai na nyoka nakolobaka ete, "Nyoka akosi ngai, mpe Nalei." Mpe nini ekomelaka Adamu na Ewa ba oyo basalaka masumu mana?

Molimo na Adamu Ikufaka

Genese 2:17 elobi "...Nde mbuma na koyeba mabe na malamu yo okoki kolia yango te. Zambi mokolo okolia yango okokufa solo."

Awa kufa oyo etalisamaki ezali kufa na mosuni te, kasi kufa na molimo. Molimo na moto kokufa elakisi te ete molimo molimwe. Elakisi ete communication na Nzambe ekatani mpe ekoki lisusu kosala te. Molimo ezali, kasi ikoki lisusu te kozwa makambo na molimo kowuta na Nzambe. Likambo oyo ikabwani ten a kokufa.

wuta molimo na Adamu na Ewa mikufaka, Nzambe Akokaki lisusu te kotika bango kati na Elanga na Edeni, oyo ezali na mokili na molimo. Genese 3:22-23 elobi ete "Bongo YaweNzambe Alobaki ete, Awa moto akomi pelamoko na moko na biso, mpona koyeba mabe mpe malamu; bongo na ntina ete atia loboko te mpona kokwa mbuma na nzete na bomoi kolia yango mpe koumela na bomoi na seko na seko'—yango wana Yawe Nzambe Abimisaka ye na Elanga na Edeni, mpona kotimola mabele wana ekamatamaki ye."

Nzambe Alobaki, "Moto akomi lokola moko kati na Biso" mpe elingi te koloba ete Adamu solo akomaki lokola Nzambe. Elakisi ete Adamu ameseneke na koyeba kaka solo, kasi kaka lokola Nzambe ayebi solo na lokuta, Adamu mpe ayaka koyeba likolo na solo te. Na bongo, Adamu oyo azalaka molimo na bomoi, azongaka sasaipi na mosuni. Asengelaka na kokutana na kufa. Asengelaki kozonga na mokili oyo bisika akelamaka na Nzambe. Moto na mosuni akoki te kobika na mokili na molimo. Lisusu, soki Adamu aliaka na nzete na bomooi akokaki kobika seko. Na bongo Nzambe Akokaki lisusu kotika ye kofanda kati na Elanga na Edeni te.

3) Bozongi na Espace na Mosuni

Sima na Adamu kozanga kotosa Nzambe mpe kolia mbuma na nzete na boyebi malamu mpe mabe, makambo nioso mambongwanaki. Akitisamaki na mokili oyo, espace na mosuni, mpe akokaki kobuka mbuma kaka na sima sima na kotoka makasi mpe motoki na mbunzu na ye. Biloko nioso mpe mizalaki nan se na elakeli mabe, mpe mokili kitoko na tango na kokelama na Nzambe ezalaki lisusu te.

Genese 3:17 etangi ete, "Alobaka na Adamu ete, mpo ete oyoki monoko na mwasi nay o, mpe ete osili kolia mbuma na nzete epekisaki ngai yo ete, Okolia yango te, mokili elakami mabe na ntina na yo.Okolia na yango na mpasi na motoki mikolo nioso na bomoi na yo'"

Na makomi oyo, tokoki komona ete, likolo na lisumu na Adamu, kaka Adamu ye moko te kasi biloko nioso na mokili oyo, mingi mingi mobimba na likolo na liboso izwaki elakeli mabe. Makambo nioso na mokili oyo mizalaki na harmony kitoko kasi molongo mosusu na mobeko na mosuni isalemaka. Likolo na elakeli mabe, eyaki na kozala na ba germe mpe ba viruses, mpe ba nyama na ba nzete mibandaki kombongwana.

Na Genese 3:18 Nzambe Akobaki koloba na Adamu ete, "ekobimisela yo nzete mpe nkamba na nzube." Masangu ekoka kokola malamu te likolo na nzube mpe nzete na yango, nde Adamu akokaki kolia kobuka na elanga na mabele kaka na nzela na motoki na pasi. Lokola mabele elakelamaki mabe, ba nzete na pamba pamba mpe ba ndunda miyaki na kozala. Ba nyama mabe mpe bayaka na bozali. Asengelaki sik'awa kolongola biloko mana na mpamba mpona kobalola mabele na elanga mpe kokomisa yango malamu.

Bosenga na Kobalola elanga na Motema

Lokola Adamu asengelaka kobalola mabele, likambo na lolenge moko esalemaka mpona moto oyo sasaipi asengelaki kobongolama na nzela na koleka nan se na moi. Liboso na moto kosumuka, azalaka kaka na motema petwa iye izanga mbeba oyo izalaki kaka na boyebi na molimo. Genese 3:23 elobi ete, "...yango wana Yawe Nzambe abimisaki ye na Elanga na Edeni, mpona kotimola mabele wana ekamatamaki ye." Eteni oyo ekokisi Adamu, oyo asalamaka na mputulu na mokili, na mabele wapi ye akamatamaka. Elakisi ete asengelaki sasaipi kobalola mabele na motema na ye. Liboso na masumu naye, abalolaka elanga na motema na ye te, mpo ete azalaka na mabe moko te kati na motema na ye.

Kasi sima na koboya kotosa na ye, moyini zabolo mpe Satana babandaki kokonza moto. Bakobaki na kokola ebele mpe ebele na makambo na mosuni kati na motema na moto. Moto akobaki na kotondisama na mosuni.

Kotimola mabele bisika wapi moto azwamaki elakisi ete toosengeli kondimela Yesu Christu; tosengeli kosalela Liloba na Nzambe mpona kolongola iye ilonamaki kati na mitema na biso; mpe tosengeli kozongela lolenge na molimo. Soko te, elakisi ete tozali na molimo ekufa mpe tokoki te mpe tokokoka te kosepela bomoi na seko na molimo ekufa. Tina oyo moto akolisami nan se na moi ezali mpona kobongola motema na bison a mosumi mpona kozongela motema petwa na molimo. Motema oyo ezali lolenge moko na motema na Adamu liboso na bokwei.

Mpona Adamu kobimisama libanda na Elanga na Edeni mpe kobika na mokili oyo ezalaki mbongwana makasi mpenza. Ezali pasi makasi mpe emotion oyo mokonzi na ekolo monene akonyokwama soki na mbala moko akomi mosali bilanga. Ewa mpe sik'awa asengelaki konyokwama pasi monene na kobota.

Na tango bazalaka kobika na Elanga na Edeni, ezalaka na kufa te. Kasi sik'awa basengelaki na kokutana na kufa na kobikaka na mokili oyo na mosuni iye ikokufa mpe kobeba. Genese 3:19 elobi ete, "Na motoki na elongi nay o okolia lipa, kino tango ekozonga yo kati na mabele mpo ete okamatamaki na yango; mpo ete ozali mputulu mpe okozonga na mputulu." Lolenge ikomama, sik'awa basengelaki kokufa.

Ya solo molimo na Adamu ewutaka na Nzambe mpe ekokaki ten a kolimwa. Genese 2:7 elobi ete, "Na ntango yango Yawe Nzambe Asalaki motona mputulu na mokili mpe Apemaki kati na zolo na ye mpema nan a bomoi, mpe moto akomaki molimo na bomoi." Mpema na bomoi ezali na seko na Nzambe kati na yango.

Kasi molimo na Adamu izalaki lisusu na mosala te. Bongo, molema ezwaki mosala na mokonzi na moto mpe azwaki bokonzi likolo na nzoto. Wuta tango wana, Adamu asengelaki kokoma mobange mpe sukasuka kokufa kolandana na molongo na mokili na mosuni. Asengelaki kozonga na mabele.

Na tango wana ata soki mokili elakelamaki mabe, masumu mpe mabe elutaka te lokola na mikolo na lelo, bongo Adamu abikaka na mbuka 930 (Genese 5:5).

Kasi na koleka na tango bato bakobaki na kokoma mabe. Lokola libonza na yango molai na bomoi na bango ikitaki. Sima na bango kokita na mokili oyo wuta na Elanga na Edeni, Adamu na Ewa basengelaki na komesana na mokili na sika. Likolo na nioso, basengelaki kobika lokola baton a mosuni, te lokola milimo na boomoi. Bakomaki kolemba na sima na mosala, bongo basengelaki na kopema. Bakomaki na kozwa bokono mpe kobela. Systeme digestive na bango embongwanaki lokola bilei na bango mpe lokola. Basengelaki na kosumba na sima na bango kolia. Makambo nioso mambongwanaki. Koboya na kotosa na Adamu ezalaki ezalaki eloko soko moke te. Elakisi ete lisumu iyaki na bato nioso. Adamu na Ewa mpe bakitani na bango nioso na mokili oyo babandaki bomoi na bango na mosuni na milimo na bango mikufa.

Chapitre 3
Moto na Espace na Musuni

Mosuni ezali lolenge oyo esangani na lisumu, nde bongo moto abongama mpona kosala masumu na espace na mosuni.
Kasi, kati na moboko na moto ezali na nkona na bomoi ipesamaka na Nzambe, mpe na nkona oyo na bomoi koleka na moto nan se na moi ekoki kosalema.

1. Nkona na Bomoi

2. Lolenge nini Moto ayaka na Kozala

3. Conscience

4. Misala na mosuni

5. Kobongolama

Adamu na Ewa babotaka bana mingi na mokili oyo. Ata ete milimo na bango mikufaka, Nzambe Asundolaki bango te. Alakisaka bango likolo na makambo mazalaka motuya mpona bomoi na bango na mokili. Adamu alakisaka ban aba ye solo oyo, nde bango mibale Caina na Abel bayebaka malamu lolenge nini basengelaki na kopesa mbeka epai na Nzambe.

Sima na koleka na tango Caina Amemaka mbeka na ba mbuma na mabele epai na Nzambe, kasi Abele apesaka mbeka na makila oye Nzambe Alingaka. Tango Nzambe Andimaka kaka mbeka na Abele, bisika na Caina kososola mbeba na ye mpe atubela, Caina akomaka mpenza na zua na Abele nde abomaki ye.

Na koleka na tango, lisumu elutaki na komata kino na tango na Noa, mokili itondisamaki mpenza na bitumba na bato yango tina Nzambe Apesaka etumbu na mokili mobimba na mai. Kasi Nzambe Andimaka Noa mpe ban aba ye misato babanda baton a sika. Bongo, nini ekomelaki bato ba oyo bayaka kobika na mokili?

1. Nkona na Bomoi

Sima na Adamu kosumuka, lisolo na ye na Nzambe ikatanaki. Energie na Ye na molimo ebandaki kotanga mpe energie na mosuni eyaki kati na ye mpe ezipaki nkona na bomoi na kati na ye. Nzambe Akelaka Adamu na mputulu na mabele. Na Baebele 'Adamah' elakisi mabele to mokili. Nzambe Asala nzoto na moto na mputulu na mokili mpe Apemaka kati na zolo na ye mpema na bomoi. Kati na buku na Yisaya elobami mpe ete moto asalema na lima.

Na Yisaya 64:8 ekomama ete, "Ee, Yawe, Ozali nde Tata na biso, biso tozali lima, yo Ozali moyem; biso nyoso tozali mosala na loboko naYo."

Molayi te sima na ngai kobanda egelesia oyo, Nzambe Atalisaki ngai emoniseli na Ye moko kosala Adamu na lima. Matiere Nzambe Asalelaki ezalaki mabele esangana na mai, oyo ezali lima. Awa, mai elakisi Liloba na Nzambe (Yoane 4 :14). Lokola mabele mpe mai misangana mpe mpema na bomoi ikotaka kati na yango, makila, oyo ezali bomoi ebanda kotambola mpe ikomaki ekolamo na bomoi (Lewitiko 17 :14).

Mpema na bomoi ezali na nguya na Nzambe kati na yango. Wuta ewuta epai na Nzambe, ekoki te na kolimwa. Biblia elobi te kaka été Adamu akomaka moto. Elobi ete akomaka ekelamo na bomoi. Yango ezali na koloba ete azalaki molimo na bomoi.

Akokaka kobika mpona libela na mpema na bomoi ata soki asalemaka na mputulu na mokili. Na oyo tokokoka kososola ntina nan a eteni na Yoane 10:34-35 yango elobi ete, "Yesu azongiseli bango monoko ete, ekomami kati na mibeko na bino te ete, NALOBI BOZALI BANZAMBE'"? Soko Abengi bango banzambe, baoyo Liloba na Nzambe eyeli bango (mpe Likomi ekoki koboyama te)...'"

Lolenge akelamaka na ebandeli moto akokaki kobika mpona seko na komona kufa soko moke te. Ata soki molimo na Adamu ekufaka likolo na kozanga kotosa na ye, na mozindo na yango ezali nkona na bomoi ipesamaka na Nzambe. Ezali seko mpe na yango nani nani akoki kobotama lokola muana na Nzambe.

Nkona na Bomoi Epesama na Moto Nioso

Tango Nzambe Akelaka Adamu, Alonaka nkona na bomoi iye ikufaka te kati na ye. Nkona na bomoi ezali nkona na ebandeli iye Nzambe Alonaka kati na molimo na Adamu, oyo ezali moboko na molimo na ye. Ezali ebandeli na molimo, moto na nguya mpona kotalela Nzambe mpe kobatela mosala na moto.

Na sanza motoba na zemi Nzambe Apesaka nkona na bomoi na molimo na moto kati na embryon. Kati na nkona oyo na bomoi ezali na motema mpe nguya na Nzambe mpo ete moto akoka kosolola na Nzambe. Bato mingi ba oyo bandimaka bozali na Nzambe te bazalaka soko na bobangi to mpe sososoli mabe likolo na bomoi sima na kufa to bakoki mpenza te kowangana

Nzambe nan se na mitema na bango, mpo ete bazali na nkona na bomoi na mozindo na mitema na bango.

Ba Pyramides mpe makambo misusu mibomba makanisi na bato likoo na bomoi na seko mpe elikya na bango mpona bisika na bopemi na libela.Ata moto na makasi koleka abangaka kufa mpo ete nkona na bomoi kati bango ensosolaka bomoi na koya.

Moto nioso azalaka na nkona na bomoi ipesamaka na Nzambe, mpe alukaka Nzambe na lolenge na ye (Mosakili 3:11). Nkona na bomoi esalaka lokola motema na moto, mpe bongo etalisami mbala moko na bomoi na molimo.Makila matambolaka mpona kotondisa nzoto na oxygene mpe vitamins matondi mpona mosala na motema. Na lolenge moko soki nkona na bomoi ezali na mosala kati na moto, molimo na ye ikokoma mpe na energie mpe bongo akoka kosolola na Nzambe. Na loboko mosusu, soki molimo na ye mokufi, nkona na bomoi ikozala na mosala te mpe moto akoki te kosolola na Nzambe.

Nkona na Bomoi Ezali Moboko na Molimo

Adamu atondisamaka na boyebi na solo ilakisamaka na Nzambe. Nkona na bomoi kati na ye ezalaki mpenza kosala. Atondisamaki na energie na molimo. Akomaka mpenza na bwanya ete akokaka na kopesa nkombo na biloko nioso na bomoi kati na yango mpe kobika lokola nkolo na mokili mobimba, mpe kokonza likolo na yango. Kasi sima na ye kosumuka, lisolo na ye na Nzambe ikatanaki

Wuta kokweya na Adamu bato bakoka kokima kufa te. Mpona bango bazwa lisusu bomoi na seko, basengeli kosilisa likambo na lisumu na lisungi na Nzambe oyo Azali Pole. Mingi, basengeli kondimela Yesu Christu mpe bazwa bolimbisi na masumu. Mpona kosekwisa molimo na biso, Yesu Akufaka na ekulusu na kozwaka masumu na bato nioso. Akomaka nzela, solo, mpe bomoi, na nzela na oyo bato nioso bakoki kozwa bomoi na seko. Tango tondimeli Yesu lokola Mobikisi na biso moko, tokoki kolimbisama na masumu mpe kokoma bana ba Nzambe na koyamba Molimo Mosantu.

Molimo Mosantu asekwisaka nkona na bomoi kati na biso. Yango eza;li lisekwa na molimo na kufa kati na biso. Kobanda tango oyo, nkona na bomoi iye ibungisaki pole na yango ikobanda na kongala lisusu. Ya solo, ekoki kongala na mobimba te lolenge na Adamu, kasi makasi na pole ikokoba na komata na lolenge etape kati na kondima na moto ikokolaka mpe molimo na ye ikokola mpe ikokembisama.

Na lolenge nkona na bomoi ikotondisama na Molimo Mosantu, makasi na pole yango ikobimisa, mpe pole na nzoto na molimo ikongenga makasi. Na lolenge moto akomitondisa na boyebi na solo, akoka kozongela elilingi na Nzambe ibungaka mpe kokoma muana na solo na Nzambe.

41

Nkona na Bomoi na Mosuni

Likolo na nkona na bomoi iye izalin lokola moboko na molimo, ezali mpe na nkona na bomoi na mosuni. Yango ezali mai mpe maki na bato. Nzambe abongisa mokano na koleka na baton a nse na moi mpona kozwa bana na solo solo na ba oyo Akoka kokabola bolingo na solo. Mpe mpona kokokisa mokano yango, apesaka na moto nkona na bomoi mpo ete bakoka na kokoma ebele mpe batondisa mokili. Espace na molimo bisika Nzambe Azalaka mizanga suka, mpe ekozala na solitude mpe malamu te soki moto moko te azali zinga zinga. Tala ntina Nzambe Akelaka Adamu lokola molimo na bomoi mpe atikaka ye akoma ebele ekeke na ekeke mpo ete Nzambe Akoka kozwa bana ebele.

Lolenge na bana oyo Nzambe Alingi ezali ba oyo moilimo ekufaka isekwi, ba oyo bazali na makoki na kosolola na Nzambe, mpe ba oyo bakozala na makoki na kokabola bolingo elongo na Ye mpona libela na Bokonzi na Lola. Mpona kozwa bana na lolenge oyo na solo, Nzambe Apesi moto nioso nkona oyo na bomoi mpe Azala kotabwisa koleka na bato na nse na moi wuta na tango na Adamu. Dawidi asosolaka bolingo mpe mokano oyo na Nzambe mpe Alobaki ete, "Nakotonda yo mpo ete nasalemi na motindo na kokamwa mingi; misala mayo izali nakokamwa mpe molimo na ngai eyebi yango malamu" (Nzembo 139:14).

Lolenge Nini Moto Ayaka na Bozalisami

Moto Akoki kozala cloner na moto mosusu te. Ata soki isalemi ete bakoka na kosala libanda na moto, ezali moto te mpo ete ikozala na molimo kati na yango te. Ekelano cloner ikokesana na nyama te. Bomoi na sika ikobanda tango main a mobali mpe ovule na mwasi misangani.. Mpona bokoli na fœtus kino kokoma moto esengeli na yango kotikala sanza libwa na libumu. Tokoki koyoka nguya na Nzambe oyo ekamwisaka tango tokomona lolenge na bokoli na ebandeli na zemi kino suka na yango.

Na sanza nay ambo misisa na moto mikobanda kokola. Mosala makasi mikobanda na kosalema. Mosala na base esalemi mpo ete makila, mikuwa, misisa minene, misisa mike, mpe biloko na kati mikoka kosalema. Na sanza na mibale, motema mokobanda kobeta mpe ikozwa na lolenge na libanda na moto. Na tango wana moto mpe makolo makoka koyebana. Na zanza na misato elongi ikosalema. Ikoka koningisa moto na yango, nzoto, makolo na maboko na yango moko, mpe nzoto (na muasi to mobali) ikokola.

Kobanda sanza minei placenta ikokisami, nde kopesama na bilei ikomata, molayi mpe mozito na foetus ikomata nokinoki.

Sex na muana mobali to na muasi mpe makoki na koyoka mikomaka malamu na sanza mwanbe. Fetoeus ikoki ata koningana na makelele na libanda. Na sanza libwa, suki ikokoma

43

makasi, suki mike mike na nzoto ikolimwa, ba member miye minene. Sima na mobimba na sanza libwa, bebe na molayi zinga zinga nz ba cm 50 na molayi mpe na kilo na nzoto 3.2kg abotami.

Foetus Izali Bomoi Iye Izalaka na Nzambe

Na development scientifique na lelo, bato bazali na interet monene na ko cloner biloko na bomoi. Kasi lolenge etalisamaki likolo, ata science etombwami na lolenge nini, moto akoka ten a kozala cloner. Ata soki ekokisami été bazala cloner na libanda na bo moto na nzoto, ikozala na molimo kati na yango te. Soki molimo izali te ikokesana na nyama te.

Na nzela na bokoli na moto, na kokesana na ba nyama nioso, ezalaka na ngonga moko kati na tango moto azwaka molimo. Na sanza libwa na zemi, foetus azalaka na ba organs ebele, elongi, mpe makolo na maboko. Izali kokoma Mbeki iye ikoki kofandisa molimo kati na yango. Na etape oyo Nzambe Apesaka nkona na bomoi elongo na molimo. Biblia ezali na makomi likolo na yango. Ezali Makomi elobeli koyanola na fœtus na sanza motoma kati na libumu.

Luka 1:41-44 etangi ete, "Wana eyokaki Elisabeta mbote na Malia, mwana na kati na libumu na ye apombwaki, mpe Elisabeta atondisamaki na Molimo Mosantu, mpe angangaki na mongongo makasi ete yo opambolami kati na basi nioso mpe

Muana na libumu nay o Apambolami. Mpo na nini likambo oyo ebimeli ngai ete mama na Nkolo na ngai ayei epai na ngai? Zambi tala, wana eyokaki mongongo na mbote nay o kati na matoi na ngai, mwana na kati na libumu na ngai apombwi na esengo.'"

Yango esalemaki kaka sima na zemi na Yesu kobanda kati na libumu na Moseka Malia mpe akendaka kotala Elisabeta oyo azalaka na zemi na sanza motoba na Yoane Mobatisi. Kati na libumu na mama na ye Yoane Mobatisi apinbwaki na esengo tango Moseka Malia ayaka. Asosolaki Yesu kati na libumu na Malia mpe atondisamaka na Molimo. Foetus ezali kaka bomoi te kasi ezali mpe ekelama na molimo oyo akoki kotondisama na Molimo kobanda sanza motoba na zemi. Moto azali bomoi iye izalaka na Nzambe kobanda na ebandeli na mokumba. Kaka Nzambe nde azalaka na bokonzi likolo na bomoi. Bongo, tosengeli te kolongola zemi na foetus na lolenge esepelisi biso to na mposa na kosalela yango, ata soki yango ezali naino na molimo te.

Tango oyo na sanza. libwa na zemi wapi foetus akokola kati na libumu izalaka motuya mingi. Ikozwaka biloko nioso izali na bosenga na yango mpona bokoli kowuta na mama, bongo mama asengeli kozala na elieli malamu. Makanisi mpe mabanzo mama azali na yango mpe ikoki na kosimba lolenge na ezaleli, bomoto na ye, mpe mayele na foetus, Ezali lolenge moko na molimo. Ba bebe na ba mama oyo basalelaka Bokonzi na Nzambe mpe bakobondelaka mingi na momesano babotamaka na bizaleli na kimia, mpe bakolaka na bwanya mpe na nzoto malamu.

Bokonzi likolo na bomoi ewutaka epai na Nzambe, kasi amikotisaka na makambo na kozwa mokumba te, mbotama, mpe bokoli na moto. Bizaleli na moto ikatamaka na nzela na energie na bomoi izalaka kati na mai mpe ovule na baboti. Bizaleli misusu mipesamaka mpe mikokolisama kolandana na mokili mpe makambu misusu.

Intervention special na Nzambe

Ezali na makambo misusu epai wapi Nzambe akomikotisa na bokumbi zemi mpe na mbotama na moto. Yambo Ezali tango baboti basepelisi Nzambe na kondima mpe bakobondela makasi. Anana mwasi oyo abikaki na tango na Basambisi, abikaka na pasi mpe minyoko mpo ete akokaka kozwa mwana te, mpe ayaka liboso na Nzambe mpe abondelaka makasi. Akataki mpe ndai ete, soki Nzambe Apesi ye muana mobali, akobonzela ye Nzambe.

Nzambe Ayokaki mabondeli na ye mpe Apambolaki ye azwa mokumba na muana mobali. Lolenge, akataki ndai, amemaki muana na ye epai nan ganga Nzambe na tango akataki mabele mpe abonzaki ye lokola mosali na Nzambe. Samuele asololaka na Nzambe wuta bomwana na ye mpe na sima akomaki mosakoli monene na Yisalele. Na lolenge Anana abatelaki ndai na ye,

Nzambe apambolaki ye abota bana misato babali mpe basi mibale (1 Samwele 2:21).

Ya mibale, Nzambe Asalaka na bomoi na ba oyo batiami pembeni na Nzambe Ye moko, mpona kokokisa mokano na Ye. Mpona kososola yango, tosengeli kososola bokeseni kati na koponama mpe kotiama na pembeni. Ezali koponama na Nzambe tango tosi tobongisi eloko mpe tokopona moto nani akoti na bisika wana kolandana na mondelo totiaki. Ndakisa, Nzambe Abongisa mokano na lobiko na kondimelaka Yesu Christu mpe kobika na Liloba na Nzambe babengami 'babiangami'.

Bato misusu basosolaka mabe na kolobaka ete Nzambe Asi Akata likolo na ba oyo bakobikisama na ba oyo bakobikisama te. Balobaka ete soki osi ondimela Nkolo, Nzambe Akosala na lolenge oyo yo okobikisama kaka, ata soki obikaka kolandamna na Liloba na Nzambe te. Kasi likanisi oyo izalaka bosolo te.

Moto nioso oyo, na makoki ma ye na kopona, akoya kati na bondimi mpe na kati na mokano na lobiko akozwa lobiko. Yango ezali, bango nioso bazali baponami na Nzambe. Kasi ba oyo nioso bakoyaka kati na mokano na lobiko te, to ba oyo bayaka na mbala moko kasi balongwaki na yango mpe balingaki mokili mpe na koyeba mpe na kolinga bakosala lisumu na nko, bakoki kobikissama te kaka soki balongwe na ba nzela na bango mabe.

Nini bongo ezali kotiama pembeni? Ezali tango Nzambe, oyo

Ayebi makambo nioso mpe Abongisa makambo nioso wuta ata liboso na bikeke, Aponi moto moko boye mpe Akotambwisa makambo nioso kati na bomoi na Ye. Ndakisa, Abalayama; Yacobo, tata na BaYisalele nioso; mpe Mose, mokambi na Esode, bango nioso batiamaka na pembeni na Nzambe mpona kokokisa mosala na motuya ipesamma na Nzambe kati na mokano na Ye.

Nzambe Ayebi makambo nioso. Na mokano na koleka na baton a nse na moi Ayebi moto na lolenge nini akobotama na ngonga nini kati na tango nini na lisituale na bato. Mpona kokokisa mokano na Ye, Aponaka baton a lolenge moko boye mpe Andimelaka bango bakokisa mosala monene. Mpo na ba oyo batiama pembeni na lolenge oyo, Nzambe Asalaka na ngonga nioso kati na bomoi na bango kobanda na mbotama na bango.

Baloma 1:1 elobi ete, "Polo, Moumbo na Yesu Christu, mobiangami lokola ntoma, motiami pembeni mpona Sango Malamu na Nzambe." Lolenge ilobama, Ntoma Polo atiamaki ppembeni lokola ntoma na bapaya mpona kopanza Sango Malamu. Mpo ete Azalaki na motema makasi mombongwanaka te, atiamaki pembeni mpona koleka na ba pasi malekelaka makanisi. Epesamelaki mpe ye mosala na kokoma mingi na ba buku kati na Boyokani na Sika. Mpo ete akoka na kokokisa mosala iye, NNzambe Atika ye ayekola Liloba na Nzambe na mozindo wuta bomwana na ye nan se na moko na balakisi na likolo na tango na ye, Gamaliele mpe lokola.

Yoane Mobatisi mpe atiamaka mpe pembeni na Nzambe. Nzambe Asalaka na mbotama na ye, mpe Nzambe Atikaka ye abika bomoi na lolenge mosusu wuta mbotama na ye. Abikaka kaka kati na lisobe, na kozala na lisanga moko ten a mokili. Azalaka na elamba na nsuki na kamela mpe loposo na nyama na loketo na ye; mpe bilei na ye izalaki mayoyo mpe mafuta na nzoi. Na lolenge oyo abongisaka koya na Yesu.

Ezalaki lolenge moko na Mose, mpe lokola. Nzambe Asalaka kobanda mbotama na Mose. Abwakamaka kati na ebale kasi kasi bamonaka ye na muasi mokonzi, mpe akomaka muana na mokonzi. Ata bongo akolisamaki na mama na ye moko mpo ete akoka koyekola likolo na Nzambe mpe baton a ye moko. Lokola mokonzi na Ejipito, azwakka mpe mayebi nioso na mokili. Lolenge elimbolama, kotiama pembeni ezali tangoMnzambe na BoNzambe na Ye akotambwisa bomoi na moto moko boye, na koyebaka likolo na moto na lolenge kani akobotama na tango moko na lisituale na bato.

3. Motema

Mpona moto koluka mpe kokutana na Nzambe mokeli, kozongela elilingi na Nzambe, mpe kokoma moto na motuya etali makasi motema na lolenge nini azali na yango.

Mai mpe ovule na baboti mizali na energie na bomoi, oyo epesamaka epai na bana. Ezali lolenge moko na mtema. Motema (conscience) ezali etape na kokata kati na mabe na malamu. Soki baboti babikaka bomoi malamu na kozalaka na elanga malamu kati na motema, ekopesamela mpe muana mbotama na motema malamu(conscience). Bongo, moboko na boponi mpona conscience na bato ezali energie na bomoi na lolenge nini azwaka kowuta na baboti ba ye.

Kasi ata soki babotami na energie kitoko na bomoi kowuta na baboti, soki bakolisami na bisika mabe, na komonaka mpe koyokaka makambo mabe mingi mpe kolona mabe kati na bango, nde, ekosalema ete motema (conscience) na bangoikobebisama na makambo mabe. Na bokeseni, ba oyo bakolisami na bisika malamu, na komonaka mpe na koyokaka makambo malamu, ekosalemela bango ete bazala na motema (conscience) malamu.

Kosalema na Conscience

Mitema (conscience0 misalemaka kolandana na baboti na lolenge nini moto abotami na ye, bisika wapi moto akolisama, makambo na lolenge nini amonaka, ayokaka, mpe makasi na lolenge nini asalaka mpona kosala bolamu. Bongo, ba oyo babotami na baboti malamu mpe bakolissama na bisika malamu, mpe bakomikambaka na momesano balandaka bolamu na kolanda motema (conscience) na bango malamu. Mpona bango eza;I pete na kondima Sango Malamu mpe kombongwana na bolamu.

Na momesano, bato bakoki kokanisa ete motema

(conscience) ezali eteni malamu kati na biso, kasi na miso na Nzambe yango te. Bato misusu bazalaka na motema malamu mpe na bongo mpe motema makasi na kolanda bolamu na tango basusu bazalaka na conscience mabe mpe balandaka lifuti na bango moko bisika na kolanda solo.

Basusu bazalaka na pasi na motema soki bazwaki kaka eloko na moto mosusu, na tango basusu bakanisaka ete ezali moyibi te mpe yango ezali mabe te. Bato bazali na ba standard na kokata kati na malamu na mabe kolandana na bisika nini bakolisamaka mpe nini balobelaka bango.

Bato bakataka kati na malamu na mabe kolandana na motema (conscience) na moto na moto. Kasi bato mitema na bato mikesana. Ezali na ba bokesani ebele kolandana na ba culture mpe bisika, mpe mikoki te kokoma epimelo na kokata kati na malamu mpe mabe. Standard na solo solo ekoki komonana kaka kati na Liloba na Nzambe, oyo ezali yango moko solo.

Bokeseni kati na Motema mpe Molema

Baloma 7:21-24 elobi ete, "Nazali kokuta motindo oyo kati na ngai ete wana elingi ngai kosala malamu, bobele mabe ezali penepene na ngai. Kati na motema na ngai moto, nasepeli na mibeko na Nzambe; Kasi namoni mobeko mosusu kati na bilembo na nzoto na ngai. Mobeko yango monene ezali kobunda etumba na Mibeko milingi ngai na makanisi na ngai, ezali mpe kokanga ngai moumbo na mobeko na masumu mozali kati na

bilembo na ngai.Ngai moto na mawa mingi! Nani akolongola ngai na nzoto oyo na kufa?"
Kobanda eteni oyo tokoki kososola lolenge nini motema na moto isalema. Kati na motema ezali mote,ma na solo, iye ikoki kobengama 'motema pembe' iye imekaka kolanda mongongo na Molimo Mosantu. Kati na moto oyo na kati ezali na nkona na bomoi. Lisusu, 'ezali na mobeko na lisumu'. Iye izali motema pembe iye isalema na solo te. Ezali mpe na 'mobeko na makanisi na ngai'. Yango ezali conscience. Conscience ezali standard na jugement na ba valeur, oyo moto amisaleli na ye moko. Ezali lisanga na motema pembe na motema moindo. Mpona kososola conscience, tosengeli naino kososola motema.

Ezali na ba definitions mingi mpona kombo 'motema' kati na dictionaire. Ezali na emotion to malamu na kososolama na lolenge na bo mayele,' Kasi limbola na molimo na motema ikesana.

Tango nzambe Akelaka moto na yambo Adamu, Apesaka ye nkona na bomoi elongo na molimo na ye. Adamu azalaka mbaku polele, mpe Nzambe Atiaka mayebi na molimo, lokola bolingo, bolamu, mpe bosolo. Mpo ete Adamu alakisamaka kaka na bosolo, nkona na ye na bomoi isalemaka na molimo na ye mpenza elongo na mayebi kati na yango. Mpo ete atondisamaka kaka na solo, ezalaki na tina moko te kokesanisa kati na molimo mpe motema. Mpo ete ezalaki na lokuta te tina na kombo conscience ezalaki na bosenga te.

Kasi sima na ye kosumuka, molimo na ye izalaki lisusu lolenge moko ten a motema na ye. Na lolenge boyokani na ye na Nzambe ibebisamaki, solo, boyebi na molimo iye itondisaki motema na ye ibandaki na kotanga mpe bisika na yango bozangi solo lokola, koyina, zua, lofundu ibandaki kozwa esika kati na motema na ye mpe kozipa nkona na bomoi. Liboso kozanga solo eya kati na Adamu, ezalaki na tina na kosalela kombo 'motema'. Motema na ye izalaki molimo yango moko. Kasi sima na bosolo te koya likolo na masumu, molimo na ye ikufaki, mpe wuta wana tobanda kosalela nkombo 'motema'.

Motema na moto sima na kokweya na Adamu ekomaki na bisika wapi bozangi na solo, bisika na solo, izipaki nkona na bomoi yanngo elakisi ete molema, bisika na molimo, izipaka nkona na bomoi'. Na koloba na mokuse, motema na solo ezali motema na pembe mpe motema na solo te ezali motema moindo. Mpona bakitani nioso na Adamu oyo abotamaka sima na kokweya na ye, mitema na bango misalema na motema na solo, na bosolo te, mpe conscience oyo basalela na kosangisaka solo mpe bosolo te.

Nature Ezali Moboko na Conscience

Lolenge na kozala na motema na moto ebengami lokola 'nature'. Nature na moto ezalaka na mobimba kaka na baboti te. Embongwanaka mpe kolandana na makambo na lolenge nini moto andimaka na bokoli na ye. Kaka lolenge na mabele ikombongwanaka kolandana na nini tobakiseli yango, ezaleli na moto eikoki mpe kombongwana kolandana na nini tokomonaka, koyoka, mpe ikomata na motema.

Bankitani nioso na Adamu oyo babotamaka na mokili oyo bayamba yango o nzela na energie na bomoi na baboti ezaleli oyo, ezali lisanga na solo mpe na solo te. Na loboko moko, ata soki babotama na nature malamu (bizaleli), ekozala mabe soki bandimi makambo mabe na environement na malonga te. Na loboko mosusu, soki balakisama na makambo malamu na bisika malamu, mingi mingi moke na mabe nde ikolonama kati na bango. Nature na moto na moto ikoki kombongwana na kobakisa solo te to solo kati na yango.

Ezali pete na kososola likolo na motema (conscience) soki liboso tososoli nature na moto, mpo ete conscience ezali epimelo na bokata oyo esalemaka likolo na nature. Bokondima boyebi ezwama na solo mpe bosolo te kati na mozindo na nature, mpe ikokoma lolenge na kokatela. Yango ezali conscience. Bongo, kati na conscience na moto, ezali na motema na solo, mabe na nature na moto mpe komilongisa.

Na kokende na mikolo, mokili ekobi na koleka na masumu mpe mabe, mpe conscience na bato ikokobaka na kokokoba kati na mabe. Bazali kokitana na mabe na koleka kowuta na baboti na bango, na likolo na yango, bazali kondima lokuta mingi kati na bomoi na bango. Likambo oyo ikokoba mpe kokoba ekeke na ekeke. Lolenge ba conscience na bango mikokoba na kokoma mabe mpe kokangama na koleka, ekokoma mabe mingi mpona bango bandima Sango Malamu. Kutu, ezali pasi mpona bango bayamba misala na Satana mpe basumuka.

4. Misala na Mosuni

Tango mutu akosala masumu, kuna ekozala solo na lifuti kolandana na mobeko na mokili na molimo. Nzambe Akosembolela ye loboko mpona kopesa ye lisungi na kotubela mpe kolongwa na masumu, kasi soki akoleka mondelo, ekozala na mimekano mpe pasi, to makama na lolenge lolenge.

Moto nioso abotama na nature na masumu, mpo ete nature na lisumu na Adamu moto way ambo epesamaka na bana na nzela na energie na bomoi na baboti. Tokoki ata komona bana bebe mike kotalisa kanda mpe kotungisama na bango, ndakisa, na kolelaka mingi. Tango mosusu, soki tokomema bebe na kanda mpe na kolela te, ekolela mpenza mingi ete ekomonan lokola akoki lisusu kopema te. Sima akoboya na komemana mpo ete azali na nkanda mingi. Ata ba bebe babotami sika balakisaka bizaleli na lolenge oyo mpo ete bakitana na ezaleli na motomoto, koyina, to zua kowuta na baboti na bango. Yango ezali mpo ete bato nioso bazali na nature na masumu kati na mitema na bango, mpe yango ezali masumu na makila.

Lisusu, bato basalaka masumu kati na kokola na bango. Kaka lokola emant ebendaka ebende, ba oyo babikaka na espace na mosuni bakokoba na kondima oyo ezali sembo te mpe bakosala masumu. Masumu oyo bato bakosalaka ikoki kokabolama na biteni mibale masumu kati na motema mpe na misala. Masumu na lolenge na lolenge mikesani na monene, mpe masumu na misala mikosambisama mpenza (2 Bakolinti 5:10). Masumu makosalemaka na misala mibengami 'misala na nzoto'.

Mosuni mpe Misala na Mosuni

Genese 6:3 elobi ete," "Bongo Yawe Alobaki ete Molimo na Ngai Akoumela seko kati na bato te, mpo ete moto azali bobele mosuni, mpe mikolo na ye ekozala mbula mokama na ntuku na mibale." Here, 'flesh' does not simply refer to the physical body. It means man had become a fleshly being who is stained with sins Awa, 'mosuni' elakisi kaka nzoto na mosuni te. Elakisi moto akomi ekelamo na mosuni oyo abebisami na masumu mpe na mabe. Moto na mosuni na lolenge oyo akoki te kobika seko na Nzambe, nde bongo bakoki kobikisama te. Bikeke mingi te sima na Adamu kobengama na Elanga na Edeni mpe abanda bomoi na ye na mokili oyo, bankitani na ye noki noki babandaka kosala misala na mosuni.

Nzambe Azalaki na Noa oyo azalaki moto na semboo na ekeke na ye, abongisa masuwa mpe akebisa bato balongwa na masumu na bango. Kasi moto moko te soko libota na Noa balingaki kokende kati na masuwa. Kolandana na mobeko na molimo iye ilobaka 'lifuti na masumu izali kufa' (Baloma 6:23), moto nioso na ekeke na Noa abebisamaki na Mbonge.

Sik'awa, nini ezali limbola na molimo na 'mosuni'? Elobeli nature na bosolo te kati na motema na moto na kolimbolama na misala moko boye'. Na maloba mosusu, likunia, moto moto, koyina, moyimi, makanisi na bondumba, lolendo, mpe nioso na solo te kati na motema na moto mikotassama na lolenge na bitumba, maloba mabe, bondumba, to koboma. Misala nioso oyo mikobengama na mobimba 'mosuni', mpe moko na moko na misala oyo mizali misala na mosuni.

Kasi masumu mitalisamaka na misala te kasi kaka kosalema na makanisi mpe mabanzo mibengama 'makambo na mosuni'. Makambo na mosuni mikoki mokolo moko kotalisama lokola misala na mosuni, na lolenge mokolongolama te kati na motema. Ba sete mingi likolo na makambo na mosuni mikolobelama na eteni na 2 'Kosalema na molema'.

Tango makabo na mosuni mitalisami lokola misala na mosuni, ezali bozangi na bosembo mpe bozangi na mobeko. Soki tozali na nature na masumu kati na motema, ezali bozangi na bosembo te, kasi soki itiami na misala ekomi bozangi bosembo. Soki tolongoli makambo oyo na mosuni te mpe misala na mosuni te kasi tokokoba na kosala yango, ikotonga efelo na masumu kati na Nzambe mpe biso. Bongo, Satana akofunda biso mpona komemela biso mimekano mpe pasi. Tokoki komonana na likama mpo ete Nzambe Akoka te kobatela biso. Toyebi te nini ekoki kokoma lobi soki tozali na nse na kobatelama na Nzambe te. Mpona ntina oyo tokoka mpe te kozwa biyano na mabondeli na biso.

Misala na Mosuni Mimonanaka

Soki mabe eluti na mokili, moko na masumu mimonanaka mpenza ezali ekobo mpe pete. Sodome na Gomora mitondisamaki na pite, mpe mibebisamaka na moto na sufulu. Soki botali biloko miye mitikalaka na engomba na Pompei, mitalisi biso boni ekobo mpe na makambo na soni bazalaka na yango na mokili na bango.

Baga;atia 5:19-21 mitalisi misala na mosuni mimonani:

Misala na nzoto imonani polele, yango oyo:ekobo, makambo na bosoto,pite,kosambela bikeko, ndoki, nkaka, kowelana, zua, kanda,, kolulela, kokabwana,, koponapona, kobota bato, kolanga masanga, bilambo na lokoso mpe makambo na motindo yango. Nazali kokebisa bino lokola ekebisaki ngai bino liboso ete baoyo bakosalaka makambo yango bakosangola Bokonzi na Nzambe te.

Ata lelo misala eye na mosuni mileki kati na mokili. Tika ngai napesa bino ba ndakisa na misala na yango na mosuni.

Yambo ezali bondumba. Bondumba ekoki kozala na nzoto to na molimo. Na mosuni, elakisi ekobo to kolalana. Ata ba oyo ba balongani na libala balongwe te. Lelo, ba novella, ba filme, to ba serie elakisi ekobo lokola bolingo kitoko, na kokomisa bato motema makasi likolo na masumu mpe bososoli na bango pamba. Eza;li mpe na biloko ebele na pamba miye mikopesaka makasi na ekobo.

Kasi ezali mpe na ekobo na molimo mpona bandimi. Mpona nini bakokendaka epai nan ganga kisi, kozala na kisi to lititi, to koloka, bongo yango ezali ekobo na molimo (1 Bakolinti 10:21).

Soki BaKristu bakotia elikya epai na Nzambe te oyo Akambaka bomoi, kufa, mapamboli, bilakeli mabe, kasi bakolikya na bikeko, ezali kindumba na molimo, oyo ezali lolenge moko na kotiola Nzambe..

Ya mibale, makambo ya bosoto ezali kolanda kolulela mpe makambo mingi mazanga sembo, mpe tango bomoi na moto etondisama na maloba mpe misala miye mitonda ekobo. Ezali eloko elekela etape na moto nioso mpona ekobo, oy ezali na ndakisa, kolala na ba nyama, kolalana lisanga na bato, mpe kolala mibali to basin a basi (Lewitiko 18:22-30). Koleka na masumu, mpe motema libanga bato bakokoba na kozala mpona makambo na bondumba.

Makambo oyo ezali koboya kotosa mpe kotelemela Nzambe (Baloma 1:26-27). Mizali masumu malongolaka na lobiko (1 Bakolinti 6:26-27). Miye mikomatisaka nkanda na Nzambe (Dutelonome 13:18). Kolongola nzoto na muasi to na mobali, to mpona mobali kolata bilamba na basi, to mpona muasi kolata bilamba na mibali mizali nioso nkele liboso na Nzambe (Dutelenome 22:5).

Misato, kongumbamela bikeko izali mpe mabe mingi liboso na Nzambe. Ezali na kongumbamela na mosuni mpe na molimo. Kongumbamela bikeko ezali kosalela mpe kongumbamela bilili miye misalema na nzete, mabanga, mabende, bisika na koluka Nzambe mokeli Mokeli (Esode 20:4-5). Kongumbammela mingi ikomema bilakeli mabe likolo na bakitani na ekeke na misato kino na minei na bana. Soki bokotala mabota mangumbamelaka mingi bikeko, moyini zabolo mpe Satana bakokobaka na komemela bango mimekano mpe minyoko, mpo ete mikakatano mitika te kati na mabota wana. Mingi mingi, ezalaka na ebele na bandeko na mabota wan aba oyo bakangama na milimo mabe, ba oyo bazalaka na likama na moto to milangwa. Ba oyo babotama na mabota na lolenge oyo, ata soki bandimela Nkolo, moyini zabolo mpe Satana bakotungisaka bango, mpe bakomona yango pasi kobika bomoi kati na bondimi.

Kongumbamela bikeko na molimo ezali tango mondimi na Nzambe akolinga eloko koleka Nzambe. Soki bakobuka mokolo na Nkolo, mpona kokende kotala nba filme, ba novella, masano, to biloko misusu na kosepelisa nzoto, to soki bakobkwabisa mosala na bango kati na kondima mpona makango na mobali to mpe ya mwasi, ezali kongimbamela bikeko na molimo. Libanda na oyo, soki bokolinga eloko- libota, bana, bisengo na mokili, biloko na motuya, mpifo, koyebana, moyimi, to boyebi-koleka Nzambe, nde ekozala kongumbamela bikeko.

Minei, kondiki ezali kosalela nguya izwamaka na lisungi to kokambama na milimo mabe mingi mingi mpona soloka. Ezali malamu te kokende epai na ba mbikudi na kolobaka ete bondimela Nzambe. Ata bapagano bamemaka makama minene na kolokaka, mpo été bonganga ikomemaka milimo mabe.

Ndakisa, soki okosalaka bonganga mpona kolongola likambo songolo, makambo manea makokoma pasi koleka bisika misengelaki na kolongwa. Sima na bondoki, milimo mabe mikomonana lokola mizwi kimya mpona ngonga moko bisika misengelaki na kolongwa. Kasi sima na tango bakomema likama makasi koleka mpona kozwa mbeka monene koleka. Tango misusu, bakomonana lokola bakolobaka makambo makoya, mpo ete bakoka na kongumbamelama. Bondoki ikoki mpe kozala eloko mpona kokosa baninga, mpe bongo, tosengeli na kokeba mpe lokola. Soki otiki moto akweya na libulu na kosalela mayele mabe, ezali solo misala na mosuni, mpe lolenge na komema libebi likolo na bino moko.

Motoba, kokangela motema ezali makambo miye mikotalisaka koyina to mokano mabe. Ezali kolinga basusu babebisama mpe komema yango na kokokisama. Ba oyo bazalaka na koyina bayinaka basusu na makanisi mabe kaka mpo ete balingaka moninga te. Soki monene na koyina wana eleki makasi, bakoki kopasuka, mpe komikotisa na kokosela basusu makambo to mpe kokosa.

Motoba, kobunda ezali mabe to mpe tango mosusu kosuana makasi to kokabola. Ezali kobimisa ba groupe kati na lingomba kaka mpo ete basusu bazali na makanisi makesani na biso. Bakolobaka mabe na basusu mpe bakolekaka na kosambisa mpe kokatela mabe. Bongo, lingomba ekokabolama na ba groupe ebele.

Sambo, dissension ezali kokabola na groupe na kolandana na makanisi na bango moko. Ata mabota mazali kokabwana, mpe ekoki na kozala na bokabwani kati na lingomba mpe lokola. Mwana na Dawidi Absalom atiolaki mpe amikabolaki na tata na ye moko mpona koluka mposa na ye moko. Atombekelaki tata na ye mpona kokoma mokonzi. Nzambe Abwakisaki moto na lolenge oyo. Absalom akutanaka na kufa na pasi.

Mwambe, ezali masanga. Tango masanga makoli, mikoki kokoma bopengwi. 2 Petelo 2:1 ilobi ete, "
Kopengwa ezali kowangana Yesu Christu (1 Yone 2:22-23; 4:2-3). Balobaka ete bandimela Nzambe kasi bakowangana Nzambe Misato, to Yesu Christu oyo Asombaka biso na makila ma ye, bongo komema libebi na solo likolo na bango. Biblia elobeli biso solo mopengwi ezali ye oyo azali azali kowangana Yesu Christu, nde tosengeli te kokatela mabe ba oyo bandimeli Nzambe Misato mpe Yesu Christu.

Mwambe, ezali tango zua eluti mpe ekomi misala makasi.

Likunia ezali koyoka malamu te mpe kokabwana na bato to mpe koyina basusu tango basusu bamonani malamu koleka biso moko. Soki likunia oyo ikoli, ekoki kozala na misala mingi mikosalaka bato mabe. Saulo azalaka na zua na moto na ye moko Dawidi mpo ete Dawidi alingamaka koleka lolenge ye azalaka. Azalelaka ata mampinga na ye mpona koboma Dawidi, mpe abomaka bato mpe ban ganga Nzambe na ba engomba ba oyo babombaka Dawidi.

Zomi ezali kolangwa masanga. Noa asalaka mbeba sima na ye komela vigno sima na kobebisama na mokili na mai, mpe ememaka likambo na pasi makasi. Alakelaka mabe muana na ye na mibale Ham oyo atalisaka likambo na ye.

Baefese 5:18 elobi ete, "Basusu balobaka ete tango mosusu kopo moko ezali malamu. Kasi ezala kaka lisumu mpo ete, ezala kopo moko to mibale, bozali komela masanga mpona kolangwa. Lisusu, ba oyo bazali kolangwa basalaka masumu ebele na kokoka te komikamba bango moko.

Biblia elobeli komela vigno mpo ete, na Yisalele mai ezalaka mingi te, bongo bisika na mai, Nzambe Andimelaka bango vigno, oyo ezali mpenza jus oyo ewuti na vigno. To bimeli na makasi iye isalema na ba mbuma oyo ezali na sukali mingi (Dutelenome 14:26). Kasi kutu, Nzambe Andimela bato bamela alcohol te (Lewitiko 10:9; Mituya 6:3; Masese 23:31; Yelemia 35:6; Daniele 1:8; Luka 1:15; Baloma 14:21). Nzambe Andimela kaka kosalela moke na vigno na makambo na lolenge moko boye.

Mpona yango, ata soki bana Yisalele bamelaka vigno na bisika na mai, bamelaki mpona kolangwa to kosepelisa nzoto te.

Suka, bilambo na lokoso ezali kosepela na masanga, basi, kobeta masano na mbongo, mpe makambo misusu na baposa mabe na kosanga komikanga. Baton a lolenge oyo bakoka te kokokisa misala na bango lokola bato. Soki ozangi komikanga ezali mpe lolenge na bilambo na lokoso. Soki ozali kobika bomoi na komitalisa mingi mpenza, to okobika bomoi na kopanza misolo mingi lolenge pokolingaka, ezali mpe bilambo na lokoso. Soki okobika bomoi na lolenge oyo ata sima na kondimela Nkolo, okoka te soko kopesa motema nay o epai na Nzambe to kolongola masumu, nde bongo okoka te kosangola Bokonzi na Nzambe.

Tina na Kozanga Kosangola Bokonzi na Nzambe

Kino awa totali kati na misala na nzoto mimonani polele. Nini bongo, ezali Tina mpona bato kosala misala na lolenge eye na mosuni? Ezali mpo ete balingi te kotia Nzambe mokeli kati na mitema na bango. Italisama kati na Baloma 1:28-32 été, "Balingaki kotosa Nzambe kati na makanisi na bango te. Bongo Ye Atiki bango kati na makanisi na mpemba ete basala makambo na nsoni. Batondi ndenge nioso na bokeseni na mabe, na bilulela na nko; batondi na zua na mposa na koboma bato, na kowelana, na kosilisa bamosusu, na kokana mabe na kopalanganisa sango mabe; na kotukaka, na koyina Nzambe, na lolendo, na ngambo, na maloba mpamba, na koluka ndenge na sika na mabe, na kotiola baboti; bayibi, baboyi kondima, bazangi bolingo, bazangi mawa. Bayebi ekateli na Nzambe ete baoyo bakosalaka makambo ndenge yango babongi kokufa, nde ata bongo, bazali kosalaka yango. Mpe na koleka mpenza, bazali kosanzola baoyo bakosalaka bongo."

Elobi malamu ete bokosangola Bokonzi na Nzambe te soki bokosalaka misala na nzoto mimonani. Yasolo, elakisi te etet bokokoka te kobikisama kaka mpo ete bosali masumu na mbala mibale likolo na kondima na pete.

Ezali ya solo te ete bandimi na sika ba oyo bayebi solo malamu ten a kondima elemba bakozwa lobiko te kaka mpo ete naino balongoli misala na mosuni te. Bato nioso bazalaka na masumu kino tango kondima na bango ikokola, mpe bakoki na kozwa bolimbisi na masumu na bango na komitika na makila na Nkolo. Kasi soko bakokobaka na kosala misala na mosuni na kolongwa na yango te, bakoka te kozwa lobiko.

Masumu Makomemaka na Kufa

1 Yoane 5:16-17 elobi ete, There is a sin leading to death; I do not say that he should make request for this." "Soko moto nani nani amoni ndeko na ye kosala lisumu lizali lisumu na kufa te, abondela mpe Akopesa ye bomoi, na bango bazali kosala lisumu na kufa te. Lisumu na kufa ezali; nalobi te ete abondela mpona tina na yango.' Lolenge ikomama, tokoki komona ete ezali na

masumu makomemaka na kufa mpe oyo mikomemaka na kufa te.

Sik'awa Nini masumu makomemaka na kufa, miye mikolongola makoki na bison a kosangola Bokonzi na Nzambe?

Baebele 10:26-27 elobi ete, "Pamba te, soki tokosalaka masumu na nko sima na kozwa boyebi na solo, mbeka mpona masumu ezali lisusu te. Etikali bobele kotalela esambiseli na nsomo mpe moto na nkanda oyo ekozikisa batelemeli." Soki tokokobaka na kosumuka na koyebaka ete mizali masumu, ezali kotelemela Nzambe. Nzambe Akopesa molimo na tubela na baton na lolenge oyo te.

Baebele 6:4-6 elobi mpe ete, "Pamba te, mpona bango basili kongengelama pole mpe koleta likabo na likolo mpe kosangana na Molimo Mosantu, mpe bayoki elengi na Liloba na Nzambe mpe nguya na ekeke ekoya; nsoko na sima basili kopengwa, nzela na kobongola bango lisusu na motema ezali te mpo bazali kobakisa Mwana na Nzambe na ekulusu bango mpenza, mpe bazali kotiola Ye." Soki bokotelemela Nzambe sima na koyoka solo mpe komonana na misala na Molimo Mosantu, molimo na tubela ikopesama soko te, bongo mpe bokobikisama te.

Soki bokokokatela misala na Molimo Mosantu lokola misala na zabolo to na lipengwi, bokoka mpe te kobikisama, mpo ete ezali mpenza kotiola mpe kotelemela Molimo Mosantu (Matai

12:31-32).

Tosengeli kososola ete ezali na masumu maye makoki na kolimbisama te mpe masengeli soko te kosalema. Lisusu, ata masumu na momesano makoki na komata mpona kokoma masumu minene soki makobombama. Bongo, tosengeli na kobatelama kati na solo na tango nioso.

5. Kokolisama

Kokolisama na bato ilakisi na makambo nioso na kokela na Nzambe moto na mokili oyo mpe kokamba lisituale na bato kino esambiseli mpona Ye kozwa bana na solo.

Kokolisama ezali nzela na moloni bilanga kolona nkona mpe kobuka na nzela na motoki na ye mpona kokolisa masango. Nzambe mpe alonaka nkona way ambo ebengami Adamu na Ewa na mokili oyo mpona kozwa mbuma na bana na solo na nzela na motoki na Ye na kokolisa bango na mokili oyo. JKino lelo Azala na kokamba koleka na baton a nse na moi. Nzambe Asi Ayebaka ete moto akokweya na bozangi botosi mpe Ye Akoyoka pasi. Kasi Akolisaka bato kino suka mpo ete Ayebi ete ekozala na bana na solo solo ba oyo bakolongola mabe na bolingo na bango mpona Nzambe mpe bazali na motema na Nzambe.

Moto Akelama na mputulu na mokili, bongo bazali na lolenge iye ikokani na mabele. Soki boloni nkona kati na elanga, nkona ekobimisa nkasa, ikokola, mpe ikobota ba mbuma.

Tokoki komona ete mabele izali na nguya na kobimis bomoi na sika. Lisusu, lolenge na mabele ikombongwanaka kolandana na nini bokobakisa kati na yango. Ezali lolenge moko na moto. Ba oyo bamesana na kosilika bakokoma na nkanda makasi na koleka. Ba oyo bamesana na lokuta bakozala na lokuta na koleka kati na bango. Sima na Adamu kosumuka, ye na bankitani na ye bakomaka baton a mosuni mpe bakobaki na kobebisama kati na bosolo te noki noki.

Mpona yango moto asengelaki na kobalola mabele na motema na ye mpe kozongela motema na molimo na nzela na 'boleki na baton a nse na moi'. Na nioso, ntina na moto kokolisama na mokili oyo ezali mpona bango kobongisa mitema na bango mpe kozongela motema petwa iye Adamu azalaka na yango liboso na kokweya na ye. Nzambe Apesa na biso lisese iye ikokani na kotimola mabele kati na Biblia mpo ete tokoka na kososola mokano na Ye (Matai 13; Malako 4; Luka 8).

Na Matai 13, Yesu Akokanisi motema na moto na mabele na balabala, na etonda mabanga, na ba njube, mpe mabele kitoko. Tosengeli kotala motema na lolenge nini tozali na yango mpe tobalola yango mpo ete ekoma motema malamu iye Nzambe Alikyaka.

Lolenge Minei na Elanga na Motema

Yambo. Mabele na balabala izali mabele ikomisama makasi na kotambola na bato mpona tango molayi. Solo, ezali ata elanga te, mpe nkona moko te ikobota likolo na yango. Ezali na mosala na bomoi kuna te.

Na molimo mabele na balabala elakisi motema na ba oyo bakondimaka soko te Liloba na Nzambe. Mitema na bango mikomisama mpenza makasi na boyebi na bango mpe lofundu ete nkona na Sango Malamu ikoki ten a kolonama. Na tango na Yesu bakambi na Bayuda bazalaki mito mangongi likolo na makanisi na bango mpe bokoko ete babwakisaka Yesu mpe Sango Malamu. Lelo, ba oyo bazali na mitema na mabele na balabala bazali mpenza na mito makasi nde bafongolaka te makanisi na bango mpe bakobwakisa Sango Malamu ata soki balakisi bango nguya na Nzambe.

Balabala ezali makasi mingi, mpe bankona mikoki te na kotiama na kati na mabele. Bongo, ban deke bakoya mpe bakolia ba nkona. Awa, ban deke elakisi Satana. Satana alongoli Liloba na Nzambe mpo ete bato bakoka ten a kozwa kondima. Bayaka na ndako na Nzambe mpo ete bato bamemaki bango na makasi, kasi balingi te kondimela Lilobba na Nzambe iye iteyami. Bakoluka kutu kokatela mabe basalito mpe mateya likolo na makanisi na bango moko. Ba oyo bazalaka na mitema miyeisama makasi mpe bakofungolaka mitema te bakooki te kozwa lobiko mpon ete nkona na Liloba na Nzambe ikoki te kobota mbuma kati na bango.

Mibale ezali elanga itondi mabanga ezali moke malamu koleka oyo na nzela. Moto lokola balabala azalaka na likanisi moko ten a kondimela Liloba na Nzambe, kasi moto na mabele, lokola elanga itondi mabanga akososola Liloba oyo ayoki. Soki oloni ba nkona Malako 4:5-6 "Nkona mosusu ekwi na esika na mabanga, mpe kuna mabele ezalaki mingi te. Ibimi noki pamba te izangi mabele. Wana ebimi moi, iziki mpe ikaoki mpona kozanga ntina. Nkona mosusu ikwei kati na nzube, mpe nzube ikoli mpe ikibisi yango; bongo iboti mbuma te." Ba oyo bazali na motema na mabele na mabanga basosolaka Liloba na Nzambe kasi bakoki te kondima yango na kondima. Malako 4:17 elobi ete, "...Bazali na ntina kati bango mpenza te, kasi bakoumela moke, na nsima wana ekobima mpasi mpe minyoko, na ntina na Liloba, bakobetaka libaku nokinoki." Awa Liloba elakisi Liloba na Nzambe Oyo Elobelaka biso makambo lokola, "Batela Sabata, pesa moko na zomi ekoka, kongumbamela ba nzambe na bikeko te, salela basusu mpe mikitisa," Tango bakoyoka Liloba na Nzambe bakanisi ete bakobatela Liloba na Ye, kasi bakoki te kobatela ekateli na bango tango bakutani na mikakatano. Bakosepela tango bazwi ngolu na Nzambe, kasi na pasi bakobongola bizaleli na bango. Bayoka mpe bayebi Liloba na Ye, kasi bazali na makasi na kosalela yango te mpo ete Liloba na Ye ikolisamaka kati na motema na bango lokola kondima na solo.

Ya misato, ba oyo bazali na motema elanga na nzube basosolaka Liloba na Nzambe mpe babandaka kosalela yango. Kasi bakoki te kosalela Liloba na Nzambe na mobimba, mpe ezali na mbuma kitoko te. Malako 4:19 elobi ete, "...Kasi bitungisi na makambo na mokili mpe bozimbisi na misolo, mpe mposa na biloko mosusu, ikoti mpe ikibisi Liloba mpe iboti mbuma te."

Ba oyo bazali na motema na lolenge oyo bamonanaka lokola bandimi malamu ba oyo basalelaka Liloba na Nzambe, kasi bazali naino na mimekano mpe bapasi mpe bokoli na bango na molimo izali malembe. Ezali pamba te bazali komonana na misala na Nzambe ten a komikosaka na mitungisi na mokili, mpe kokosama na nkita, mpe baposa na biloko misusu. Ndakisa, toloba ete bakweyi na bombongo na bango mpe bakoki ata kokota na boloko. Awa, soki likambo esali ete bafuta nyongo na bango kaka na moke na oyo bazali na yango, mpe Satana ameki bango na nzela na oyo, bakoki solo komekama. Nzambe akoki kosimba bango kaka soki batamboli na boyengebeni ata pasi na lolenge nini ekozala, kasi bango bakomikweyisa na momekano na Satana.

Ata soki bazali na mposa na kotosa Liloba na Nzambe, bakoki te mpenza kotosa na kondima mpo ete makanisi na bango mitondisama na makanisi na bomoto. Babondelaka ete batiki makambo nioso na moboko na Nzambe, kasi bazali naino kosalela ba experinces na bango mpe makanisi. Bakotiaka mikano na bango liboso, nde makambo makokkendeke mpenza malamu na bango te, ata soki makomonan lokola matamboli malamu. Yakobo 1:8 elobi ete baton a lolenge wana bazali na mitema mibale.

Tango ezali kaka na kobima na ba nzube, ikomona ete mpasi moko te izali. Kasi soki bakokola, likambo ikozala mpenza na bokeseni. Mikosala esobe na nzube mpe mikokanga ba nkona misusu malamu na kokola. Bongo, soki ezali na likambo moko iye ikotelemela bison a kotosa Liloba na Nzambe, tosengeli na kolongola yango mbala moko ata soki ikomonan lokola mabe.

Minei, izali mabele iye izali malamu mpe ibalolami malamu na moloni. Mabele makasi ibalolami, mpe mabanga na ba nzube milongolami. Elakisi été bokotelemela makambo Nzambe Apekisi mpe bozali kolongola makambo Nzambe Ayebisi na biso tolongola. Ezali na mabanga mpe bipekiseli misusu, mpe na tango Liloba na Nzambe Ekwei kati na yango, ikobota mbuma mbala 30. 60, to 100 na nini elonamaki. Bato na lolenge oyo bakozwa biyano na mabondeli na bango.

Mpona kotala boni malamu tokolisi motema na mabele malamu, tokoki kotala boni malamu tokosalelaka Lilona na Nzambe. Mingi na mabele malamu tokozala na yango, Liloba na Nzambe ikozala pete mpona kobika kati na yango.Bato misusu bayebi Liloba na Ye kasi bakoki te kosalela yango mpona bolembu, goigoi, makanisi na bosolo te, mpe ba mposa. Ba oyo bazali na motema na mabele malamu bazalaka na mitungisi oyo te, nde basosolaka mpe bakosalela Liloba na Nzambe kaka na tango bayoki yango. Na tango basosoli ete likambo izali mokkano na Nzambe mpe ikosepelisaka Nzambe, bakosala kaka yango.

Na loolenge bozali kokolisa mitema na bino, bokoya na kolinga ba oyo bomesana na koyina. Bokoki sik'awa kolimbisa ba oyo bokokaka kolimbisa te. Likunia mpe kokanisela mabe mikombongwana na bolingo mpe ngolu. Makanisi na komimmatisa mikombongwana na komikitisa mpe kosalela bato. Mpona kolongola mabe na lolenge oyo kokata ngenga na motema na moto kokomisa yango mabbele malamu. Nde, na lolenge nkona na Liloba na Nzambe ikokweya na motema na mabele malamu, ikobimisa nkasa mpe ikokola nokinoki mpona kobimisa ba mbuma libwa na Molimo Mosantu ebele, mpe ba mbuma na pole.

Na lolenge bokobongola mitema na bino na mabele malamu, bokoki kozwa bondimi na molimo kowuta likolo. Bokoki mpe kobondela makasi mpona kokitisa nguya na Nzambe wuta likolo, koyoka mongongo na Molimo Mosantu malamu mpe kokokisa mokano na Nzambe. Baton a lolenge oyo bazali lolenge na mbuma oyo Nzambe Alikyaka kobuka na nzela na koleka na baton a nse na moi.

Lolenge Na Mbeki: Elanga na Motema

Eloko moko na motuya na kobaloola mabele na motema na biso ezali lolenge nna Mbeki. Lolenge na Mbeki elandani na lolenge na eluku na yango. Ilakisi biso lolenge kani moto ayokaka Liloba na Nzambe, kobatela yango na makanisi, mpe kosalela yango. Biblia ipesi kokokana na Mbeki na wolo, palata, libaya, to eluku (2 Timote 2:20-21).

Bango nioso bayokaka Liloba moko na Nzambe, kasi bayokaka yango na bokeseni. Basusu bandimaka yango na ba 'Amen' tango basusu batikaka yango eleka mosika na bango mpo ete Ekokani na makanisi na bango te. Basusu bayokaka yango na motema na kolikya mingi mpe bakomekaka kosallela yango na tango basusu bayokaka ete bapambolami na mateya kasi sima bakobosana yango.

Ba bokeseni mana miyaka na bokeseni na ba lolenge na ba Mbeki. Soki bokomikanaba na Liloba na Nzambe bozali koyoka, Ekolonama na bokeseni kati na mitema na bino na tango boyoki Liloba na Ye na konimba mpe na makanisi kotambola. Ata sooki boyoki mateya na lolenge moko, lifuti mikozala na bokeseni kati na kobatela yango na mozindo na motema na bino mpe koyoka yango kaka tango moko.

Misala 17:11 elobi ete, "Bango wana balekaki Batesaloniki na malamu mingi, mpo ete bayambaki Liloba na mposa mingi, mpe batangi Makomi mokolo na mokolo, kotala soko makambo yango mazali boye," Mpe Baebele 2:1 elobeli biso ete, "Yango wana, ekoki na biso kotia motema na etingia na koleka na makambo masili biso koyoka ete topengwa na nzela te."

Soki bokoyoka Liloba na Nzambe na molende, kobatela yango na bongo, mpe kosalela yango lolenge Esengi, tokoki koloba ete lolenge na Mbeki na bino izali malamu. Ba oyo na lolenge malamu na Mbeki batosakka Liloba nna Nzambbe, nde bakoki nokinoki kobalola mabbele malamu na motema. Bongo, lolenge bazali na mabele malamu na motema, bakobatela Liloba na Nzambe na momesano nan se na mitema na bango mpe kosalela yango.

Lolenge malamu na Mbeki isungaka kobalola mabele malamu, mpe mabele malamu mpe ikosunga na kobimisa lolenge malamu na Mbeki. Lokola elobama na Luka 2:19 ete, "Nde Malia abombaki makambo oyo nioso, mpe azalaki kobanza banza yango kati na motema na ye." Moseka Malia azalaka na mbeki kitoko mpona kobatela Liloba na Nzambe na makanisi na ye, mpe azwaka lipamboli na kobota Yesu na Molimo Mosantu.

1 Bakolinti 3:9 ilobi ete, " 'Pambba te tozali basalani na Nzambe elongo; bino bozali elanga na Nzambe, bozali ndako na Nzambe." Tozali elanga iye Nzambe azali kobalola. Tokoki kozala na motema petwa mpe malamu lokola mabele malamu mpe Mbeki mmalamu mmpe tosalelama mpona makambo na motuya epai na Nzambe soki tokoyoka mpe tokobatela Liloba na Nzambe kati na bongo mpe kosalela yango.

Lolenge na Motema: Monene na Mbeki

Ezali na likamboo mosusun iye ilandisami na lolenge na Mbeki. Yango ezali likolo na lolenge kani moto akoyeisa moonene mpe akosalela motema na ye. Lolenge na Mbeki etali eloko esaleli Mbeki tango lolenge na motema etali monene na Mbeki. Ikoki kokabolana na ba lolenge minei.

Yambo ezali ba oyo bakosalaka koleka oyo basengelaki na kosala. Yango ezali ezaleli na motema elekii malamu. Ndakisa, baboti basengi bana na bango balokota bosoto na nse. Bongo, bana bakolokota kaka bosoto te kasi mpe lisusu bakosulola ndako. Balekeli bozeli na baboti na bango, mpe bongo bakopesa esengo na baboti na bango. Setefano na Filipi bazalaki kaka ba mpaka kasi bazalaki sembo kaka lolenge na ba ntoma basantu. Bazalaki esengo mingi na miso na Nzambe mpe batalisaka nguya makasi, bilembo, mpe bikamwiseli.

Category na mibale ezali ba oyo bakosalaka kaka oyo esengami na bango kosala. Bato na lolenge oyo bakozwa mokumba na bango moko, kasi bakipaka mpenza te oyo na basusu to mpe na ba oyo zingazinga na bango. Soki baboti bakosenga bango balokota bosoto, bakolokota bosoto. Bakoki kondimama mpona botosi na bango, kasi bakoki te kokoma esengoo monene epai na Nzambe. Bandimi misusu bakweyaka na etuluku oyo ata na kati na ndako na Nzambe; basalaka kaka mosalla na bango mpe bamitungisakka mpenza te likolo na bato misusu. Baton a lolenge eye bakoki mpenza te kokoma esengo monene na miso na Nzambe.

Categorie na misato ezali ba oyo bakosalaka mpo ete ezali mosala na bango. Basalaka mosala na esengo mpe matondi te kasi na koyimayima mpe komilela. Baton a lolenge oyo bazali na negation na makambo nioso mpe bazali na moyimi na komikaba bango moko mpe kosunga basusu. Soki epesameli bango mosala na lolenge moko, bakoki kosala yango na komoona ete ezali mosala epesameli bango, kasi bakopesaka pasi na basusu. Nzambe Atalaka motema na biso. Asepelaka tango tokokokisa mosala na bison a komikanba mpe mpona bolingo na biso mpona Nzambe mbe na koyoka lokola batindiki biso mpe na makanisi na kokokisa kaka mosala.

Categorie na minei ezali ba oyo bakosalaka mabe. Baton a lolenge oyo bazalaka na lolenge na komikaba te to mpe na kosala te. Bango mpe bapesaka kilo na basusu te. Babetisaka sete na makanisi na bango moko mpe na boyebi na bango mpe bakopesa pasi na basusu. Soki baton a lolenge oyo bazali basali na Nzambe to mpe bakambi ba oyo bakotambwisa bandimi, bakoka te kotambwisa bango kati na bolingo nde bakobungisa milimo to kokweisa bango. Bakolakisakka basusu misapi tango lifuti na likambo libimi mabe mpe suka suka bakolongwa na mosala na bango. Bongo, ezali malamu ete epesamela bango mosalal moko ten a ebandeli.

Sik'awa tika totala ezaleli na lolenge nini na motema tozali na yango. Ata soki motema na biso izali monene na kokoka te, tokoki kobongola yango na motema monene. Mpona kosala bongo, tosengeli na momesano kosantisa mitema na biso mpe kozala na Mbeki na lolenge malamu. Tokoki te kaka kozala na lolenge malamu na motema na tango tozali na lolenge mabe na Mbeki. Ezali mpe lolenge na kokolisa ezaleli malamu na motema soki tomikabi mbeka biso mpenza na komipesa mpe na molende na mosala nioso.

Ba oyo na lolenge malamu na motemma bakoki kosala makambo minene liboso na Nzambe mpe kopesa nkembo monene na Nzambe. Ezalaki likambo moko na Yosefe. Yosefe atikisamaka na Ejipito na maboko na bandeko na ye moko, mpe akomaka moumbo na Potifar, mokapitene na mapinga na babateli na Falo. Kasi amilelaka te likolo na bomoi na ye kak mpo ete atekisamaka lokola moumbo. Asalaka mosala ma ye na malamu mingi ete andimamaka na nkolo na ye, mpe atiamaki na bokambi na mambi nyoso matali ndako na ye. Na sima bafundaka ye na likambo asalaka te mpe akotaka boloko. Kasi atikalaka sembo lolenge amesanaka na kozala, mpe suka suka akomaka ministre wa yambo na Ejipito mobimba. Abikisaka ekolo mpe libota na ye na bokawuki makasi mpe atiaka moboko na kobanda ekolo na Yisalele.

Soki azalaka na ezaleli malamu kati na motema te, akokaka kaka kosala nini esengamelaka ye epai na nkolo na ye. Akokaka kosuka na kokufa lokola moumbo na Ejipito to bomoi kati na boloko. Kasi Yosefe asalelamaki makasi na Nzambe mpo ete asalaka oyo ekoki ye na miso na Nzambe ma makambo nioso mpe asalaka na motema monene.

Masango to Matiti mabe?

Nzambe Abanda kokolisa bato mpona tango molayi na mokili oyo na mosuni wuta bokwei na Adama. Tango tango ekokaka, akokabola masango na matiti mabe mpe Akomema masango kati na bokonzi na Lola mpe matiti mabe kati na Lifelo. Matai 3:12 elobi ete, "Azali na epupelo kati na loboko na ye mpe Akopetola etutelo na Ye mpe Akoyanganisa masango na Ye na ebombelo, nde akozikisa matiti na moto mokozimama te." Awa, masango elakisi ba oyo balingaka Nzambe mpe bakosalelaka Liloba na Nzambe mpona kobika kati na solo. Na ngambo mosusu, ba oyo babikaka kati na Liloba te kasi na mabe mpe lolenge na solo te, mpe ba oyo bakondimela Yesu Christu te mpe bakosalaka misalaa na nzoto bazali matiti mabe.

Nzambe Alingi moto nioso akoma masango mpe azwa lobiko (1 Timote 2:4). Ezali kaka lolenge na moloni akolinga kobuka na ba nkona nioso alonaki kati na elanga. Kasi na tango na kobuka ezalaka kaka na matiti mabe, mpe na loolenge moko moto nioso ten a booleki na baton a nse na moi akokoma masango oyo akoki kobikisama.

Soki tokososola likambo oyo na koleka na baton a nse na moi te, moto akoki kotuna motuna eye,: Ilobama ete Nzambe Azali bolingo, mpe mpona ini asengeli na kobikisa basusu mpe kotika basusu bakende na nzela na libebi?" Kasi lobiko na motona moto ezali mpona kokata na Nzambe te. Itali kopona moto na moto. Moto nioso oyo akobikaka kati na espace na mosuni asengeli kopona nzela na Lola to na Lifelo.

Yesu Aloba na Matai 7:21, "Moto nioso te akoloba na Ngai Nkolo Nkolo nde akoingela na Bookonzi na likolo, kasi ye oyo

akosala mokano na Tata nna Ngai na Lola nde akoiingela."
"Ekozala boye na suka na ekeke; banje bakobima mpe bakoolongola mabe kati na malamu, mpe bakobwakka bango kati na litumbu na moto. Bileli ikozala wana mpe kokatakata n amino."

Awa bayengebeni elakisi bandimi. Elakisi ete Nzambe Akokabola matiti mabe na masango kati na bandimi. Ata soki bandimeli Yesu Christu mpe bakoya na nadako na Nzambe, bazali mabe soki bakolandaka mokano na Nzambe te. Bazali kaka matiti mabe baye basengeli kobwakama kati na moto na Lifelo.

Nzambe Azali kolakisa biso likolo na motema na Nzambe Mokeli, mokano na koleka na baton a nse na moi mpe tina mpenza na bomoi o nzela na Biblia. Alingi biso tobimisa bizaleli malamu na ba Mbeki na biso mpe na mitema, mpe tobima lokola bana ba solo ba Nzambe--- masango na bokonzi na Lola. Kasi bato boni bazali kolanda makambo na mpamba mpamba na mokili oyo iye itondisami na masumu mpe bozangi na mibeko? Ezali mpo ete bakambami na milema na bango.

Molimo, Molema, Mpe Nzoto: Volume 1

Eteni
2

Kosalema na Molema
(Mosala na Molema Kati na Espace na Mosuni)

Makanisi na bato mawutaka wapi?
Ezali Molema na ngai kofuluka?

"Tozali kokeisa maloba mpe bisika milai nyoso bizali kotelemela boyebi na Nzambe. Tozali kokanga makanisi nioso na nkanga ete matosa Klisto. Toseligwi ete topesa nkanza nioso etumbu wana bino bosili kotosa."
(2 Bakolinti 10:5-6)

Chapitre 1
Kosalema na Molema

Kobanda tango molimo na moto ekufaki, molema nna ye izwaki bisika na mokonzi na moto na tango azali kobika na espace na mosuni oyo. Molema ekomaka nan se na kokonzama na Satana, mpe moto ayakka na kozwa misala na lolenge na lolenge na molema.

1. Molema ezali nini

2. Misala na Lolenge na lolenge na molema kati na Espace na Mosuni

3. Molili

Tomoni bikamwa na kokela na Nzambe tango tokomonaka bikelamo lokola ba ngembo ba oyo bazwaka bilei na bango na systeme na mongongo; tango tomoni basaumon mpe bandeke na lolenge na lolenge bakobembukaka ba nkoto naba kilometer mpona kozonga na bisika babotamaka mpe kobota, mpe bandeke batobolaka ba nzete na ba mbla koleka monkoto na minute moko.

Ezali mpo ete bazali na molimo mpe nguya na kokanisa ya likolo kati na bongo na bango. Moto azali na mayele mpe bakoki kokolisa mayele mpe civilization mpona kokonza makambo nioso. Yango ezali eteni na kokanisa na moto iye ezwami kati na molema.

1. Molema Ezali Nini

Eloko na kokanisa kati na bongo, mayebi mazwami kati na mabanzo, mpe makanisi masalemaka na kozongisa mayele yango nioso mabiangami 'molema'.

Tina tosengeli na kososola malamu boyokani nakati na molimo, molema, na nzoto ezali ete tokoki kososola malamu misala na molema. Na kosalaka bongo, tokoki kozongela mosala na molema iye Nzambe Alingaka. Mpona molema na biso kolongwa na nse na kokonzama na Satana, molimo na biso esengeli kozala nkolo mpe kokonza molema na biso.

Dictionaire na Meriam-Webster Etalisi molema lokola eloko ezanga komonana, kotambwisaka moto, to tina na kozongisa na mokolo bomoi na moto; mambi matali molimo kati na moto, matali bato na molimo, to univer. Kasi limbola kati na Biblia mpona molema ikesani na oyo.

Nzambe atia kati na bongo na bato eloko izongisaka makanisi. Na lolenge oyo moto akoki kotia mayebi na kati na systeme oyo na kobomba mpe kobimisa yango. Tango eloko kati na yango ebimisami, ibiangami 'makanisi'. Mingi mingi, makanisi ezali kozongisa mpe kobanza makambo maye matiamaki kati na eloko na kobanza. Eloko yango na memoire, mayebi kati na yango, mpe kobimisa na mayebi tango mazwami lokola mobimba mitalisami lokola 'molema'.

Molema na moto ekoki kokokanisama na data ebombaka makambo, ekoluka mango, mpe ikosalela yango kati na ordinateur. Bato bazali na molema bongo bakoki kobanza mpe kokanisa, nde bongo molema izali na motuya lolenge motema izali mpona moto. Kolandana na data na lolenge nini moto amona, ayoka, mpe abomba, mpe lolenge kani akokanisa mpe akosalela data yango ezali na forme nini ya nguya na kokanisa makambo iye ikesana na basusu. Mayele na mokolo na mokolo to IQ na englais ikatanaka mingi na makila (baboti), kasi ikoki mpe na kombongwana na makambo moto abakisi lokola kotanga mpe makambo moto akutani na yango. Ata soki bato mibale babotami na niveau moko na IQ, yango ekoki kokesana kolandana na lolenge kani bazali komeka.

Motuya na Mosala na Molema

Mosala na molema mikokesanaka kolandana na makambo na lolenge nini tokotia na kati na eloko na makanisi na biso. Bato bamonaka, bayokaka mpe bayokakak na motema, makambo mpe bakokanisaka mingi na makambo mana mpona kobongisa lobi to mpe banza mpe kososola kati na malamu mpe mabe. Nzoto ezali lokola Mbeki iye ifandisi molimo mpe molema. Molema ikosala mosala na motuya mingi mpona mambi matali ezaleli(character) na moto, lolenge na kozala, mpe standard na kokata makambo na ye na nzela na mosala na 'kokanisa'. Kolonga na moto to kozwa te efandisama mingi kati na misala na molema.

Oyo ezali likambo isalemaka na mua mboka moke ibengami Kodamuri, izali 110km sudouest na Calcuta, na Inde, na mbula 1920. Pasteur Singh mpe muasi na ye bazalaka ba missionaires kuna, mpe bayokaka epai na baton a mboka likolo na elima oyo azalaka lokola moto, kobikaka na ba imbwa na zamba kati na grotte. Tango Pasteur Singh akangaka elima, bazalaka bana bilenge basi mibale.

Kolandana na lokasa na ba sango iye Pasteur Singh abombaka, bana basi bazalaka bato kaka na elongi. Bizaleli na bango nioso mizalaka na ba imbwa na zamba. Moko na bango akufaka na kala te, mpe mosusu oyo nkombo na ye izalaka Gamara abikaka na ba Singh mpona mbula libwa mpe akufaka na lolenge na poison na makila ebengama uremia.

Na moi Gamara akokota kati na ndako mpe kotala mur kati na molili, na koniganaka te, akonimba. Kasi nab utu, akonguluma zinga na zinga na ndako mpe akonganga lokola imbwa ya zamba mpe bakoyoka mongongo na ye kowuta na mosika. Akolembola bilei na kosalela maboko te. Akobanda kokima na maboko mpe makolo maye nioso na mabele lokola imbwa na zamba. Soki bana misusu bakopusana penepene na ye, akolakisa mino ma ye mpe akokima na mosika.

Ba Singh bamekaka kokomisa muana muasi imbwa na zamba moto na solo, kasi ezalaka pete te. Kaka na sima na mbula misato nde abandaka kolia na maboko, mpe sima na mbula mitano abandaka kotalisa lolenge na elongo nna mawa to esengo. Ba emotion na Gamara iye akokaka kotalisa na tango na kufa na ye mizalaki lokola na imbwa ba oyo baningisaka mokila na esengo tango bakutani na nkolo na bango.

Lisolo oyo elobeli biso ete molema na moto izali na boyokani na kosala ete bato bazala bato. Gamara akolaka na komona bizaleli na ba imbwa na zamba. Pamba te akokaka kotia mayebi masengela mpona bato, molema ma ye ikokaka kokola te. Lokola akolisamaka na ba imbwa na zamba, akokaka kaka kozala na bizaleli na bango.

Bokeseni Kati na Moto na Ba Nyama

Moto asalema na molimo, molema, mpe nzoto. Motuya koleka na oyo misato izali molimo. Moolimo na moto ipesamakka na Nzambe oyo Azali Molimo, mpe ikoki te kozanga kozala. Nzoto ikufaka mpe ikozoongakka na liboke na mpuutulu, kasi molimo na molema mikokendaka soko na Lola to na lifelo.

Tango Nzambe Asalaka ba nyama, Apemaka mpema na bomoi kati bango te lolenge na Bato, nde ba nyama bazalaka kaka nzoto na molema. Ba nyama bazali mpe na eloko na memoire kati na bongo na bango. Bakoki kobanza makambo bamonaka mpe bayokaka kati na mikolo na bomoi na bango. Kasi mpo ete bazzali na molimo te, bazali na motema na molimo te. Nini bakomonaka mpe bakoyoka izwami kaka kati système na kobomba na mémoire na bango kati na bongo.

Mosakoli 3:21 elobi ete, "Nani ayebi soko mpema na moto ekokenda likolo mpe mpema na nyama ikokitaka nan se?" Makomi oyo elobi ete 'mpema na moto.' Liloba 'mpema', oyo ekotalisa molema na moto, esalellami mpo ete, na tango na Boyokani na Kala liboso na koya na Yesuu na mokili oyo, molimo oyo itikalaka kati na moto izalaka 'kufa'. Bongo, ezala ete babikisamaka to te, na tango bazalaka kokufa ezalaki kolobama ete mpema na bango to 'molema' itikaki bango. Molema na moto 'kokende likolo' ilakisi ete molema na bangoikolimwaka te kasi ikokenda soko na Lola to mpe na lifelo. Na loboko mosusu, molema na nyama ikokitaka nan se na mabbele, yango ilakisi ete ikotika kozala. Bongo na bango ikokufaka na tango nyama akufi mpe biloko kati na yango mpe mikotika na kozala. Bakozala lisusu na mosala na molema moko te. Na masapo to masolo misusu, nyau moindo to nyoka bakotelemelaka bato, kkasi masapo mana masengeli te kondimama solo.

Ba nyama bazalaka na mosala na molema, kasi yango isuka mpenza yango izali motuya mpona kobika na bango. Ezali oyo tobengi instinct. Na momesano na yango bakobangaka kufa. Bakoki kozwa makasi to kotalisa soki babangisi bango kasi bakoki te na koluka kozongisa. Ba nyama bazalaka na molimo te, nde bongo bakoki ten a koluka Nzambe. Bongo mbisi akkoki na kobbanza lolenge kani ikutana na Nzambe lokola azali kotiola? Kasi moto, azali na dimension iye ikesana mpenza kati na mosala na molema, iye itobwama mpenza likolo na ba nyama. Moto azali na makoki na kokanisa likolo na makambo miye mizali kaka na instinct te mpona kobika. Bakoki kodeveloper civilization, kokanisa likolo na ntina na bomoi, to kokolisa makanisi na philosophie to mpe na banzmbe.

Moto azali na mosala na molema itombwama na dimension na liboso mpo ete, na likolo na ba nzoto na bango mpe molema, epesamela bango mpe molimo. Ata bato wan aba oyo bandimelaka Nzambe te bazali na molimo. Yango ekoki kotalisa na moke lolenge nini bakoki koyoka mokili na molimo mpe bazali na bobangi na bomoi sima na kufa. Na molimo oyo oyo ezali lolenge moko na kufa bakambami mpenza na molema na bango. Bakambami na molema, basalaka masumu mpe suka suka bakokenda lifelo lokola lifuta.

lMoto na Molema

Tango Adamu Akelamaka, azalaka moto na molimo oyo

azalaka kosolola na Nzambe. Mingi mingi, molimo na ye ezalaka mokonzi na ye mpe molema ezalaka lokola mosaleli na ye iye izalaka kotosa molimo na ye. Ya solo, ata wana molema ezalaka na mosala na kokanisa mpe kobanza, kasi mpo ete ezalaki na bozangi na solo te to makanisi mabe, molema ilandaka kaka mitindo na molimo iye izalaka kotosa Liloba na Nzambe.

Kasi sima na Adamu kolia na nzete na boyebi malamu mpe mabe mpe molimo na ye ikufaka, akomaka moto na molema iye ikambamaka na Satana. Abandaka kotia makanisi mpe misala na lokuta. Bongo bato babandaki kokende mosika na solo, mpo ete Satana akonzaka milema na bango mpe akambaka bango na nzela na libebi. Bongo, moto na molema ezali ba oyo molimo na bango ikufaka mpe bakoki kozwa mayebi moko ten a molimo kowuta na Nzambe.

Moto na molema oyo molimo na ye ikufa akoki te kozwa lobiko. Ezalaki lolenge moko kati na Ananias na Safila na egelesia na ebandeli. Bandimelaka Nzambe, kasi bazalaka na kondima na solo te. Baningisamaki na Satana mpona kokosa Molimo Mosantu mpe Nzambe. Nini ekomelaki bango?

Misala 5:4-5 etango ete, "Obuki lokuta na bato te, kasi obuki lokuta na Nzambe.' Eyoki anania maloba oyo, akwei nan se mpe akufi; nsomo monene ekangi bango nioso bayoki bongo."

Mpo ete elobi ete apemaki mpema na suka, tokoki komona ete abikisamaki te. Na loboko mosusu, Setefano azalaka moto na molimo oyo atosaka mokano na Nzambe. Azalaka na bolingo monene mpona kobondela ata mpona ba oyo bazalaki kobeta ye mabanga. Atikaki molimo na ye na maboko na Nkolo na tango azalaka kobomama.

Misala 7:59 ilobi ete, "Bongo baboli Setefano na mabanga wana ebondelaki ye ete, 'Nkolo Yesu yamba molimo na ngai!'". Ayambaka Molimo Mosantu na kondimela Yesu Christu mpe Molimo na ye ezongelaki bomoi, nde bongo abondelaki ete "... Yamba molimo na ngai!" Elakisi ete abikisamaki. Ezali na likomi iye ilobeli kaka bomoi bisika na 'molema' to 'molimo'. Tango Eliya azongisaka muana na muasi akufela mobali na zarepta, elobi ete bomoi na muana ezongaka. "Yawe Ayokaki mongongo na Eliya mpe bomoi na muana ezongelaki ye mpe azongelaki bomoi" (1 Bakonzi 17:22).

Lolenge italisami, na tango na Boyokani na Kala, bato bayambaka Molimo Mosantu te, mpe Milimo na bango ikokaka te kozongela bomoi, Bongo, Biblia elobeli molimo tea ta soki muana abikisamaki.

Pona Nini Nzambe Apesaka Motindo na Kobebisa bato na Amaleke nioso?

Tango bana Yisalele babimaka na Ejipito mpe bazalaka kosotambola na nzela na Canana, mapinga ba Amaleke batelemelaki bango. Babangaki Nzambe oyo Azalaka na bana Yisalele teata na sima na koyoka liklo na misala minene na Nzambe misalemaka na Ejipito. Babundisaka bana Yisalele kati na babundi nioso na sima na bango mpe na tango bango bazalaka makasi te mpe na kobanga (Dutelenome 25:17-18).
Nzambe Apesaka Mokonzi Saulo mitindo ete abebisa Amaleke mpona yango (1 Samuele chapitre 15). Nzambe Apesaka ye mitindo na koboma mibali nioso, basi nioso mpe

bana, mike mpe mikolo, mpe at aba nyama na bango. Soki tozali na bososoli na molimo te, tokoka te kososola motindo na lolenge oyo. Moto akoki na komituna, "Nzambe Azali malamu mpe bolingo. Pona nini Akoki kopesa motindo eye mpona koboma mpenza bato lokola bazalaki ban yama?"

Kasi soki bokososola tina na molimo na likambo oyo, nde bokoka kososola tina nini Nzambe Apesaka motindo oyo. Ba nyama mpe bazalaka na nguya na makanisi, nde tango bazali kobokolama bakoki mpe na kokanga mpe bakotosa bakolo na bango. Kasi mpo ete bazali na molimo te, bakozonga kaka na ndambo na mputulu. Bazali na ntina moko ten a miso na Nzambe. Na lolenge oyo, ba oyo molimo na bango ikufa mpe bakoki kobikisama te bakokweya kati na Lifelo, mpe lokola ba nyama na molimo, bazali na talo moko te na miso na Nzambe.

Mingi mingi bato na Amaleke bazalaka kilikili mpe na maw ate. Ata tango na lolenge kani epesamelaka bango, bazalaka na libaku moko te na kolongwa mpe na kotubela mbe na ebandeli. Soki ezalaka na moto oyo azalaka sembo to moto nani oyo alingaka kotubela to kolongwa na banzela na bango, Nzambe Alingaka komeka kobikisa ye na lolenge nioso. Bokanisa elaka na Nzambe ete akobebisa mboka etondisama masumu, Sodome na Gomora ata soki bayengebene zomi bazalaka.

Nzambe Atondisama na mawa mpe Azali malembe na nkanda. Kasi mpona bato wana na Amaleke, bazalaka na libaku moko te mpona kozwa lobiko at aba tango boni ipesamelaki bango. Bazalaka masango te kasi matiti mabe iye ikokweya kati na libebi. Yango tina Nzambe apesaka motindo na kobebisa bato nioso na Amaleke ba oyo batelemelaka Nzambe.

Mosakoli 3:18 itangi ete, "Nalobaki na motema na ngai mpona bana na bato ete, Nzambe Azali komeka bango mpo ete Amonisa bango ete bazali bobele nyama Tango Nzambe amekaka bango, bakeseneke te na ba nyama. Ba oyo molimo na bango ikufa basalaka kaka na molema na nzoto. Bongo bazali kaka lolenge na nyama. Ya solo, na mokili oyo itondisama na masumu, ezali na bato mingi bazali ata mabe koleka nyama. Bango solo bakoka kobokisama te. Na loboko moko, ba nyama bakokufaka mpe babebaka. Mpe na ngambo mosiusu, soki babikisami te, bato basengeli na kokende na Lifelo. Na suka, bazali mosika mabe koleka ba nyama.

2. Misala Kilikili na Molema Kati na Espace na Mosuni

Kati na moto na ebandeli, molimo ezalaki mokonzi na moto, kasi likolo na lisumu na Adamu, molimo na ye ekufaki. Energie na molimo ebandaki kobima, mpe energie na mosuni izwaka bisika. Wuta wana mosala na molema iye ifandisama kati na bosolo te ibanda.

Ezali na operation mibale na molema. Moko ezali kati na mosuni mpe mosusu ezali kati na molimo. Na tango Adamu azalaka molimo na bomoi, apesamelaka ye kaka solo eoutaka na Nzambe. Na lolenge oyo. Na lolenge oyo azalaka kaka na mosala na molema efanda kati na molimo. Mingi mingi, yango izalaka kati na solo. Kasi tango molimo na ye ikufaka, mosala na molema kati na lokuta ibandaka.

Luka 4:6 itangi ete, "Satana Alobaki na ye ete, nakopesa yo bokonzi oyo nioso, mpe nkembo na yango, mpo ete esili kopesama na ngai, mpe soko nandimi kopesa nani yango nakopesa yango na ye.'" Oyo ezali likambo bisika wapi zabolo azali komeka Yesu. Zabolo alobi ete bokonzi esili kopesamela ye, mpe te ete azalaki na yango wuta ebandeli. Adamu akelamaka lokola nkolo na bikelamo nioso, kasi akomaka moumbo na zabolo mpo ete atosaka masumu. Mpo tina yango bokonzi na Adamu epesamelaka na zabolo mpe Satana. Kobanda wana molema ikomaka mokonzi na moto mpe bato nioso bakweyaka nan se na bokonzi na moyini zabolo mpe Satana.

Satana akoki te kokonza likolo na molimo to motema solo na moto. Ikokonza molema na moto mpona kolongola molimo na ye. Satana akotia lokuta na lolenge na lolenge kati na makanisi na bato, akoki kokonza motema na moto mpe lokola.

Tango Adamu azalaka molimo na bomoi, azalaka kaka na boyebi na solo, nde bongo motema na ye kaka ezalaka molimo na ye. Kasi wuta lisolo na Nzambe ikatanaka, akokaki lisusu te kopesamela boyebi na solo to mpe lisusu energie na molimo te. Kutu, ayaka kondima boyebi na solo te iye ipesamaka na Satana na nzela na molema. Mayebi oyo na solo te ewutaka na motema na solo te kati na motema na moto.

KObebisa Mosala na Molema Ifandisama Kati na Mosuni

. Bosi boloba maloba moko to mpe bosala eloko oyo botikala kokanisa te ete bokosala to bokoloba? Yango ezali mpo ete moto akambama na molema. Mpo ete molema ezali kozipa molimo, molimo na biso ikoki kosala kaka tango tokweisi mosala na molema iye izwami kati na mosuni. Bongo, lolenge nini tokoki na kokweisa misala na molema mifanda kati na mosuni? Eloko ya motuya koleka ezali ete tosengeli kondima ete boyebi mpe makanisi na biso mizali malamu te. Kaka bongo tokoki kobongama mpona kondima Liloba na solo, oyo ekesana na makanisi na biso.

Yesu Asalelaka masese mpona kokweisa makanisi na sembo ten a bato (Matai 13:34). Bakokaka te kosososla makambo na molimo mpo ete ba nkona na bango na bomoi mikibisamaki na molema, bongo Yesu amekaka kotika bango basosola na nzela na maseses na kosalelaka biloko na mokili oyo. Kasi ezala Bafalisai to mpe bayekoli ba Ye basosolaka Ye. Basosolaki makambo nioso na lolenge na mabanzo mpe na makanisi na bango mpe makanisi na mosuni na bosolo te, nde bongo bakokaki kososola eloko moko na molimo te.

Bato na Mobeko na tango wana bakatelaka Yesu mpo ete Abikisaka mobeli na mokolo na Sabata. Soki bokokanisa na makanisi na bato nioso, bokoka komona ete Yesu azali moto oyo andimama mpe alingama na Nzambe mpo ete Atalisa nguya oyo kakaNzambe Akokaki kotalisa. Kasi bato wana na mibeko bakokaka te kososola motenma na Nzambe mpona bokoko na bakolo na bango mpe boyebi mingi kati na makanisi na bango. Yesu Atikaka bango basosola makanisi na bango mabe mpe oyo bamisalela na makanisi.

Luka 13:15-16 elobi ete, "Kasi Nkolo Azongiseli bango ete, Bakosi! Moko na moko na bino akokangola ngombe na ye soko mpunda na ye na ndako, kokenda komelisa yango na sabata te? Mwasi oyo azali mwana na Abalayama oyo Satana akangaki mbula zomi na mwambe, ebongaki akangolama na kamba na ye oyo na mokolo na sabata te?'"

Lolenge Alobaki boye batelemeli na Ye nioso bayokaki soni; mpe etiluku mobimba bazalaki kosepela likolo na makambo nioso na nkembo mazalaki kosalema epai na Ye. Solo, bazalaka na libaku malamu na kososola mabe na makanisi na bango mpe solo na bango mabe. Yesu Amekaka kokweisa makanisi na bato pamba te bakokaki kofungola mitema na bango kaka na tango makanisi na bango makatanaki.

Botika totala kati na Emoniseli 3:20, oyo itangi ete:

Yoka natelemi na ekuke, mpe nazali kobeta; soki nani akoyoka mongongo na ngai mpe akozipola monoko na ndako, nakokota epai na ye mpe tokolia elambo elongo, ye na Ngai.

Kati na eteni oyo, 'ekuke' etalisi ekuke na makanisi, mingi mingi 'Molema'. Nkolo Azali kobeta na ekuke na makanisi na bison a Liloba na solo. Na tango oyo soki tofungoli ekuke na makanisi na bis, mingi soki tokweisi molema na biso mpe tondimeli Liloba na Nkolo, ekuke na motema na biso ikofungwama. Lolenge oyo, tango liloba na Ye eyei kati na mitema na biso, tobandi kosalela Liloba na Nzambe. Yango ezali 'kolia' na Nkolo. Soki tondimi kaka Liloba na Ye na 'Amen', ata soki Liloba na Ye ikokani te na makanisi na biso to makambo toyeba, nde, tokokoka kokweisa misala na lokuta na molema.

Lolenge elimbolelami, tosengeli naino kofungola ekuke na makanisi na biso mpe ekuke na motema na biso, mpo ete Sango Malamu ekoka kokoma na nkona na bomoi, oyo izingama na molema na moto. Ezali mingi lokola mopaya akei kotala na ndako mosusu. Mpona mopaya oyo azali libanda na ndako kokutana na nkolo ndako, asengeli kofungola ekuke monene, akenda kati na ndako, mpe kofungola ekuke mosusu na kati na ndako na kolia bilei mpona kokota kuna.

Ezali na ba lolenge mingi na kokweisa misala na molema miye mifandisama kati na mosuni. Mpona kotika bato afongola ekuke na makanisi na bango mpe motema na kondima Sanngo Malamu, mpona bato misusu ezali malamu kotalisa bbango nguya na Nzambe to mpe kopesa bango masese malamu to mpe masapo. Lisusu, tosengeli na tango iso kokweisa lokuta na mosala na molema kati na bokoli na kondima na biso mpona ba oyo basi bandimela Sango Malamu. Ezali na bandimi ebele ba oyo bakobaka ten a kokolisa kondima na bango mpe molimo. Yango ezali mpo ete bazali na bososoli iye ikokobaka te likolo na operation na molema efandisama kati na mosuni.

Kosalelama na Mabanzo

Mpona biso kozala na mosala na molema iye ilingama, tosengeli koyeba lolenge kani mayebi itiama kati na biso mikotikalaka lokola mabanzo. Tango mosusu tokomona to tokoyoka likambo, kasi na sima tokokanisa yango malamu te. Na loboko mosusu, tokokanisa eloko moko malamu mpenza nde tokobosanaka yango soko tea ta sima na tango molayi. Bokeseni iyaka na lolenge kani tosalelaki mpona kotia makambo kati na memoire na biso.

Lolenge na yambo na kotia makambo kati na bongo na biso ezali kaka kososola yango na komonaka yango mbala na mbala. Toyoki mpe tomoni likambo, kasi tokolanda yango soko te. Toloba ete ete bozali kozonga na mboka na bino na train. Bokomona bilanga na masango mpe biloko misusu. Kasi soki bozali na makanisi misusu, na sima na bino kokoma na mboka na bino bokoka mpe mpenza kokanisa nini bomonaki na tango bozalaki na train. Lisusu, soki motangi bazali kolota kati na kelasi na moi, bakoki te kokanisa nini batangisaki na kelasi.

Ya mibale, ezali na memoire na tango moko boye. Tango bomoni elanga na masango libanda na fenetre na train, bokoki kobeta lisolo na yango elongo na baboti na bino. Bokokanisa tata na bino oyo azali mosali bilanga tango bomoni bilanga, mpe na sima bokoki kokanisa kaka moke nini bomonaka. Lisusu, kati na kelasi, batangi bakoki kaka kokanisa nini molakisi azali koloba. Bakoki kobanza nini bayokaka kaka sima na kelasi, kasi bakobosana yango na sima na mua mikolo.

Misato, ezali kolona mabanzo. Soki bozali basali bilanga, tango bomoni bilanga na masango mpe biloko misusu, bokotia miso na nini bozali komona. Bokomona mpenza lolenge nini elanga izali kokambama, lolenge nini ndako na ebombelo itongami, mpe bokoluka kosala lolenge moko na elanga na bino. Bokotala yango malamu mpe bokolona yango kati na bongo na bino, mpo ete bokoka kososola ba detail ata na sima na kokoma na mboka na bino. Lisusu, kati na kelasi, toloba ete molakisi alobi ete, tokokende na kozala na examen sima na kelasi oyo. Bokolongolama ba point mitano

Minei ezali kolona kati na bongo mpe na motema. Toloba ete bozali kotala filme na mawa. Bokosepeli na acteur mpe bomokotisi kati na yango makasi mpenza ete bokolela mingi mpenza. Na likambo oyo, lisolo ekolonama kaka na memoire na yo te kasi mpe na motema. Mingi mingi, ikolonama na sentiment na motema mpe kati na mabanzo na ba cellule na bongo. Makambo na lolenge iye mitiamaka makasi kati na mabanzo mpe motema nde ikolongwa kaka soki bongo izwi likama. Lisusu, ata soki bongo iningani, oyo ezali kati na motema ikotikala.

Soki muana moke amoni lolenge kani mama na ye akufaki na likama na mituka, boni shock akozala na yango! Na likambo oyo, elilingi na likambo isalemaka mpe pasi na yango ikolonama kati na motema na ye. Ikolonama kati na memoire mpe na motema na ye nde ekozala pasi mpona ye kobosana yango. Totali likolo na ba lolenge minei na kokanga makambo. Soki tososoli yango malamu, ekosunga bison a kokamba misala na molema.

Makambo Bolingi Kobosana, Kasi Mizali Tango Nioso Kobanzama

Tango misusu, tozongisamaka tango nioso na makambo iye tolingaki kokanisa te. Nini ezali tina? Yango ezali mpo ete elonama kati na bongo mpe na motema elongo na emotion.

Toloba ete boyinaka moto. Tango nioso bokokanisa likolo na ye, bokonyokwama likolo na koyina bozali na yango. Na likambo na lolenge iye, bosengeli naino kokanisa likolo na Liloba na Nzambe. Nzambe Alobeli biso ete tosengeli kkolinga ata bayini na biso, mpe Yesu Abondelaka mpona ba oyo babakaki Ye na ekulusu balimbisama. Lolenge na motema oyo Nzambe Alingaka ezali bolamu mpe bolingo, nde tosengeli na kolongola motema na solo te ipesamaka na moyini zabolo mpe Satana.

Na makambo mingi soki tokotala mama na tina, tokomona ete toyinaka baniinga mpona makambo mike. Tokoki kososola ete tozali kotosa kolandana na Liloba na Nzambe te soki tokomitala kolandana na 1 Bakolinti chapitre 13 iye elobi été tosengeli koluka lifuti na basusu, tozala na bopole mpe na bososoli na basusu. Na lolenge tokososola ete tozali kobika na sembo te, koyina kati na mitema na biso ikobanda kosopana libanda. Soki totondisi mpe totie bolamu na liboso, tokonyokwama na makanisi mabe te. Ata soki basusu bakosala likambo bokolingaka te, bokozala na koyini likolo na bango te kolandana na lolenge bokotia sentiment na bolamu na kokanisaka été, 'Basengeli kozala na tina."

Tosengeli Koyeba Nini Ezali Ete Isanganaka na Solo Te

Sik'awa nini tosengeli kosala likolo na bosolo te oyo tosili kotia elongo na ba sentiment na solo te?

Soki eloko ilonami na mozindo na motema na bino, bokobanda kokanisa yango ata soki bozalaki na bosenga na kokanisa yango te. Na likambo na lolenge oyo, tosengeli na kobongola sentiment na makambo matali yango. Bisika na koboya kokanisa yango, tobongola makanisi. Ndakisa, bokoki kobongola makanisi na bino likolo na moto boyinaka. Bokoki kobanda kokanisa na lolenge na ye mpe bososola ete akokaki kosala lolenge asalaki na position na ye.

Lisusu, bokoki kokanisa likolo na makambo malamu maye mpe kobondela mpona ye, mpe lokola. Na lolenge bokomeka kolobana na ye na maloba na kopesa makasi, kopesa ye mu aba cadeau moke, mpe kolakisa misala na bolingo, ba sentiment na koyina makokoma oyo na bolingo. Bongo, bokonyokwama lisusu te tango bokokanisa likolo na ye.

Liboso na ngai nayamba Nkolo, na tango nazalaka na mbeto na mobeli mpona ba mbula sambo, nayinaka bato mingi. Nazalaka na libiki te mpe nazalaka na elikya moko ten a kobika. Ba nyongo mizalaki kaka komata mpe libota na ngai ekomaki penepene na kokweya. Muasi na ngai asengalaki na kozwa bomoi mpe ba ndeko na ngai bayambaki libota na ngai te mpo ete tozalaka mokumba mpona bango.

Boyokani malamu kati na bandeko na ngai mibali ikweyaki, mpe lokola. Na tango wana nakanisaka kaka likolo na pasi na ngai, mpe nayokaki bango mabe mpona kobwaka ngai. Nazalaka na nkanda na muasi na ngai oyo mbala na mbala akokanga bisaka mpe kokenda, mpe bandeko na ye ba oyo bayokisaka ngai pasi na maloba makasi. Tango nioso nazalaka komona bango kotala ngai na miso na komituna, koyina na ngai mpe motema pasi imataki. Kasi mokolo moko ba nkanda wana mpe kokangela motema milimwaka.

Na lolenge nandimelaka Nkolo mpe nayokaka Liloba na Nzambe, nasosolaka mbeba na ngai. Nzambe Alobeli biso ete tolinga ata bayini na biso mpe Apesaka Muana na Ye se moko na likinda lokola mbeka mpona biso. Bongo moto na lolenge nini nazalaka mpo ete nakoka kokangela motema! Nayakka kobanda kokanisa na bisika na bango. Toloba ete nazalaka na ndeko muasi mpe akutanaka na mobali goigoi. Asengelaki kosala makasi mingi mpona komema misolo. Bongo, nini nasengelaki kokanisa mpona likambo wana? Tango nayaka komitia na bisika na bango, nakokaka kososola bango, mpe nasososlaka ete mbeba nioso ezalaka na ngambo na ngai.

Na lolenge nabongolaka makanisi na ngai, nazalaka kutu kopesa matondi na libota na muasi na ngai. Tango misusu basungaka biso na mua loso to makambo misusu na bosenga, mpe nazalaka kopesa matondi mpona yango. Lisusu, na tango na ba kokoso wana, Nayaka kondimela Nkolo mpe koyeba likolo na Lola, nde nazalaka kopesa matondi mpona wana mpe lokola. Na lolenge nabongolaka makanisi na ngai, nazalaka na matondi ete nakomaka moto na bokono mpe nakutanakkaa na muasi na ngai. Koyina na ngai nioso ibmbongwanaki na bolingo.

103

Misala na molema Mizalaka kati na Bosolo te

Soki bozali na misala na molema mizwamaka kati na solo te, bokomiyokisa kaka pasi te kasi at aba oyo zinga zinga na bino. Bongo, sik'awa botika totala misala na molema miye mizwama kati na bosolo te, oyo tokoki komona kati na bomoi na biso na mokolo na mokolo.

Yambo, ezali kozanga kososola basusu mpe kokoka te kososola mpe kondima basusu.

Bato bakolisaka ba pasa na lolenge na lolenge, ba valeurs, mpe lolenge na komona likambo malamu. Bato misusu balingaka kongala, mpe lolenge na bango moko na kambo matali bilamba na bango tango basusu balingaka simple mpe petwa. Ata mpona filme moko bato misusu bakomona yango malamu na tango basusu bakomona yango kolalisa.

Likolo na bokeseni oyo, toyaka na kozala na koyoka mabe likolo na basusu ba oyo bazali na bokeseni na bison a kozanga na kobetisa yango sete. Moto moko azali na ezaleli na kobimisa makambo mpe na kotalisa polele, mpe alobelaka makambo esepelisaka ye te. Mosusu atalisaka sentiment na ye malamu mingi te, mpe azwaka tango molayi mpona kokata likambo mpo ete akanisaka likolo na ba nzela nioso. Na loboko mosusu, epai na moto na suka moto na liboso akomona ye malili to na makoki ekoka te. Na loboko mosusu, oyo ya suka akomona ya liboso motomoto mpe na bizaleli ya mua mobundi mpe akoluka kokima ye.

Lolenge na lisese, ezali mosala na molema na bosolo te soki

okoki te kondima mpe kososola basusu. Soki tokolinga kaka oyo tolingaka, mpe soki tokokanisaka kaka nini tomoni lokola malamu na miso na biso bongo tokoka mpe kondima mpe kososola basusu.

Ya mibale, ezali kokatela bato

Kokatela ezali kozwa conclusion likolo na moto to eloko kolandana na lolenge na bison a kokanisa to lolenge toyoki kati na biso. Na ba mboka misusu ezalaka bizaleli mabe kolelisa zolo nay o na tango ofandi na mesa na kolia bilei. Na ba mboka misusu, ezali mabe te. Na ba mboka misusu bamonaka yango mabe kobwaka bilei tango na ba mboka misusu kotika bilei ezali ezaleli na bolamu indimamaka.

Moto moko komonaka mosusu kolia na maboko ma ye atunaka ye soki ezali bosoto ten a kolia na maboko. Ye ayanolaki ete, "Nasukolaki maboko nde namoni ete ezali petwa. Kasi nayebi te soki kanya oyo to mbeli oyo izali petwa na lolenge nini. Kolandana na bisika nini tokolisami mpe makambo na lolenge nini toyekoli, sentiment mpe makanisi mikokesana ata mpona likambo moko. Bongo, tosengeli te kokatela na mabe to malamu mpona likambo na epimeli na bato, oyo yango ezali solo te.

Basusu bakosambisaka na kokanisa ete bato bakolanda bango. Ba oyo balobaka lokuta bakanisaka ete bato bakolanda bango. ba oyo bamesana na kotonga bakanisaka basusu bakosalaka lolenge moko.

Toloba ete mobali mpe mwasi boyebi malamu batelemi bisika

moko na hotel. Bokoki bongo kokatela bango na kokaniisaka ete, "Basengelaki kozala elongo kati na hotel. Nakanisi ete bazalaki kotalana na lolenge na special."

Kasi ezali na nzela ten a koyeba soki soki mobali na mwasi bazalaki kosolola kati na ndako na café na hotel to bakutanaki na bango kaka na nzela. Soki bokokatela to kosambisa bango kaka mpe bokopanza sango na lolenge oyo epai na basusu, bato oyo bakoki konyokwama injustice makasi, desavantage to kobungisa likolo na lisolo na lokuta.

Biyano isengela te mpe miwutaka na kokanisela. Soki botuni moto oyo amesana koya na retard na mosala, "Tango nini oyaki lelo?" ye akoki koyanola ete, "Nazalaki na retard te lelo." Bokoki kotuna ye tango nini ayaki, kasi ye asi akanisi ete bokaniseli ye mabe mpe akoyanola na eyano oyo isengelaki soko moke te.

1 Bakolinti 4:5 itangi ete, " Boye bokata likambo liboso nan tango te, naino Nkolo ayei te. Ye Akokomisa makambo mabombami na molili epai na pole, mpe akozipola mikano kati na mitema. ;boye na tango na yango moto na moto akozua lisanjoli na ye epai na Nzambe."

Ezali na ba lolenge mingi na kokatela mpe kokanisela kati na mokili, kaka te kati na moto na moto kasi mpe na mabota, na mokili, na politique, mpe ata na ba mboka. Maben a lolenge oyo imemaka kaka kowelana mpe ikomemaka kaka bozangi na esengo. Bato babikaka na kokatelaka mingi kasi bango basosolaka ata yango te. Ya solo, tango misusu kokatela na bango ikoki kozala solo, kokatela yango moko izali mabe mpe Nzambe Apekisa yango, nde bongo tosengeli ten a kokatela.

Ya Misato, Ezali Kokatela mabe.

Bato basambisaka kaka basusu na makanisi na bango moko kasi mpe lisusu bakokatelaka bango. Basusu banyokwamaka likolo na pasi monene na bongo likolo na kolobelaka bango mabe na internet. Kolekisaka kosambisa mpe kokatelaka mabe imesana mingi kosalema kati na bomoi na bison a mokolo na mokolo. Soki moto aleki kaka na kopesaka yo mbote te, bokoki kokatela ye na kolobaka ete abeti yo kara na nko. Tango mosusu ezalaki ete amonaki yo te to mpe azalaki kokanisa makambo misusu, kasi yo okobi kaka na kokatela ye kolandana na makanisi na yo moko.

Tala ntina Yakobo 4:11-12 ikebisi biso ete:

"Ba ndeko botonganaka te, ye oyo akotonga ndeko na ye, soko akosambisa ndeko na ye, azali kotonga Mibeko soko kosambisa Mibeko. Soko ozali kosambisa Mibeko, ozali motosi na mibeko te, kasi mosambisi. Mopesi na Mibeko mpe Mosambisi Azali bobele moko; ye wana na nguya na kobikisa mpe kobebisa. Yon de nani kosambisa mozalani na yo?"

Kosambisa mpe kokatela basusu ezali lolendo na kosala lokola Nzambe. Baton a lolenge oyo basi bakatelami bango moko. Ezali ata likambo na makasi koleka kosambisa mpe kokatela misala na nguya na Nzambe to mpe mokano na Nzambe na makanisi na bango malamu te mpe boyebi.

Soki moto akolobaka ete, "Nabikisamaki na bokono izanga suka na nzela na mabondeli!" bongo ba oyo bazali na motema malamu bakondimela yango. Kasi basusu bakosambisa maye malobamaki na kokanisaka ete, "Lolenge kani bokono ibikisama kaka na libondeli? Diagnostique na yango isalemaka malamu te to mpe akanisi kaka ete akomi malamu." Basusu bakoki kutu kokatela ye mabe nakolobaka été alobi lokuta. Bazali kosambisa mpe kokatela mabe ata na makambo makomami kati na Biblia likolo na mai monana kokabwana, moi mpe sanza kotelema, mpe mai bololo kombongwana na mai kitoko, na kolobaka été mazali kaka masapo.

Bato misusu balobaka ete bandimela Nzambe kasi bakosambisa mpe kokatela misala na Molimo Mosantu. Soki moto Alobi ete miso ma ye na molimo mifungwamaki mpo ete akoka komona mokili na molimo, to ete azali kosolola na Nzambe, bakolobaka ete alobi solo te mpe azali moto na soloka. Misala oyo mikomama solo kati na Biblia, kasi bazali kokatela mabe makambo oyo kati na makanisi na bondimi na bango moko mpenza.

Ezalaki na bato mingi lolenge oyo na tango na ba Yesu. Tango Yesu Abikisaka babeli na mokolo na Sabata, basengelaka na kotala ete nguya na Nzambe italisami na nzela na Yesu. Soki ekokanaka na mokano na Nzambe te, misala iye mikokaka kosalema ten a nzela na Yesu. Kasi Bafalisai basambisaka mpe bakatelaka mabe Yesu, Muana na Nzambe, kati na makanisi na bango moko mpe oyo bango bamonaki lokola sembo. Soki bokosambisa mpe kokatela misala na Nzambe, ata mpo ete boyebi bosolo malamu te, ezali kaka lisumu monene. Bosengeli kokeba makasi mpo ete bokozala na libaku malamu ten a kotubela soki bokotelemela to mpe bokoloba mabe, to kotuka Molimo Mosantu.

Mosala na misato na molema ifandisama na solo te ezali kopesa sango na lokuta to na sembo te.

Tango tokopesa sango, tokendaka na kotia makanisi na biso moko mpe sentiment mpe na bongo sango ekobeba. Ata soki topesi sango lolenge epesamaki, limbola na yango na ebandeli ikoki kombongwana kolandana na mongongo to mpe lolenge na elongi. Ndakisa, ata soki tobengi moto moko na lolenge na mongongo moko lokola "Eh!", kobenga ye na mongongo na kokita mpe na bondeko, to kobenga ye na mongongo na konganga to mabe ikomema likambo na kokesana. Lisusu, soki tokoki te kopesa maloba na lolenge moko mpenza kasi tobongoli yango na maloba na biso moko, lolenge na yango na ebandeli ikoki mpe kobebisama.

Tokoki komona ba ndakisa oyo na bomoi na bison a mokolo na mokolo mpe lisusu kobakisama to kokomisama mokuse nna oyo tolobaki. Tango mosusu context ikoki kobongolama. : "Yango ezali solo te?" ikokoma 'ezali solo", bongo te "mpe tozali kobongisa ko..." to 'Tokoki..' ikokoma 'Imonani lokola tokokende na...'

Kasi soki tozali na motema na solo, tokobebisa makambo ten a lolenge na bison a kokanisa. Tokokoka kolekisa basango malamu mpe lolenge mizali kaka soki tolongoli mabe kati na motema mpe bizaleli lokola koluka kaka lifuti na biso moko, na koluka na kozala na kopesa na bosembo te, na kosambisaka noki

109

noki, mpe kolobaka mabe mpona bato misusu. Kobanda na Yoane 21:18 ezali Liloba na Nkolo Yesu likolo na kobomama na Petelo Elobi ete, "Solo solo nnazali koloba nay o ete, ezalaki yo elenge, omikangaki loketo mpe otambolaki epai ezalaki nay o mposa. Nde ekozala yo mobange, okosembola maboko nay o mpe mosusu akokanga yo loketo mpe akomema yo esika ezali yon a mposa te."

Bongo Pettelo akomki kolinga koyeba likolo na Yoanne atunaka motuna ete, "Nkolo, boni mpona moto oyo?" (et.22) ,Bongo Yesu Azongisi ete, "Soko nalingi ete aumela nkino ekoya ngai, ezali likambo na yo? Yo bila Ngai! Lolenge kani bokanisi ete sango oyo epesamaki na bayekoli misusu? Biblia elobi ete balobaki ete moyekoli oyo akokufa te. Yesu Alingaki koloba ete ezali likambo na Petelo te koluka koyeba likolo na Yoane ata soki esengelaki na ye kobika kino bozongi na Nkolo. Kasi bayekoli bapesaka sango malamu ten a kobakisa makanisi na bango moko.

Mitano ezali sentiment mabe to koyoka mabe

Mpo ete tozali na sentiment na mosuni lokola kolemba na likambo, koswama kati na motema, koyoka zua, kozua kanda, mpe kozala na kolinga basusu te, tozali na misala na solo ten a molema kowuta na bango. Ata mpona lilob amoko toyoki, kozongisa na biso ikomaka na bokeseni kolandana na sentiment na biso.

Toloba ete mokonzi na companie alobeli mosali na ye ete, "Bongo yo okoki kosala mosala malamu te?" na kotalisaka mbeba. Na likambo oyo, bato misusu bakoyamba yango na komikitisa mpe na koseka mpe koloba kaka, "Iye, nakomeka kosala malamu mbala ekoya." Kasi ba oyo bazalaki na komitungisa likolo na mokonzi bakoki kozala na motema pasi to koyoka malamu te mpona liloba yango. Bakoki kokanisa ete, 'Bongo esengelaki ye koloba na lolenge wana mabe? To 'Boni boni mpona ye moko?' Asalaka ata mosala na ye malamu te.'

To mokonzi apesi bino toil nakolobaka ete, "Nakanisi ete ekozala malamu soki obongisi bisika oyo na lolenge oyo." Bongo, basusu kati na bino bakoki kaka kondima yango mpe koloba ete, "Yango ezali mpe likanisi malamu. Matondi mpona toil nay o," mpe kozwa toil wana na motema. Kasi bato misusu na likambo oyo bakoyoka malamu te mpe lolendo na bango ikotutana. Mpona koyoka mabe mana, bakobanda tango mosusu komilela na kokanisaka ete, 'Nasalaki oyo esengelaki ngai kosala mpona mosala malamu, bongo lolenge kani aloba maloba eye? Soki ye akoki, mpona nini te asala yango ye moko?

Kati na Biblia, totangi likolo na Yesu kopamela Petelo (Matai 16:23). Tango ngonga na Yesu komema ekulusu ebelemaki, Atikaki bayekoli bayeba nini ekokoma. Petelo alingaka Mokolo na ye konyokwama te nde alobaki été, 'Nzambe Apekisa yango, Nkolo ! Yango ekosalamela yo te" (v.22).

Na tango oyo Yesu Alingaki kolobela ye na lolenge lokola nayebi nini ozali koyoka. Napesi matondi mpona yango. Kasi nasengeli kokenda." Kasi kutu, Apamelaki ye nakoloba ete, "Mosika na Ngai, Satana! Ozali libaku mpona ngai mpo ete ozali kokanisa lolenge na Nzambe te kasi lolenge na bato" (et.23).

Mpo ete nzela na lobiko ekokaki kofungwamela basumuki kaka soki Yesu Azwaka ekulusu na pasi, kotelemela yango ezalaki lolenge moko na kotelemela mokano na Nzambe. Kasi Petelo ayokaki motema psi to ayimakiyimaki mpona Yesu te mpo ete andimaka ete liloba na Yesu ezalaki na ntina. Na motema malamu boye Petelo akomaki na sima ntoma oyo atalisaka nguya na nkamwa na Nzambe.

Na loboko mosusu, nini ekomelaka Yudasi Iscariot? Na Matai 26, Malian a Betania asopaka malasi na motuya mingi likolo na Yesu, Yudasi akanisaki ete ezalaki kobungisa. Ye alobaki ete, "Zambi ekokaki kotekisa oyo na mosolo mingi mpe kopesa epai na babola. (et.9). Kasi alingaki solo koyiba misolo.

Aya Yesu Apesi lokumu na oyo Malia asalaka kati na mokano na Nzambe yango ezalaka kobongisa Lilita na Ye. Kasi, Yudasi ayokaki lokola komilela epai na Yesu mpo ete Yesu Andimaka maloba ma ye te. Suka suka, asalaka lisumu monene na kobongisa lolenge na kotekisa Yesu.

Lelo bato mingi bbazali na misala na molema iye izali libanda na solo. Kasi ata tango tokosala eloko, tokozala na mosala moko te na molema na lolenge été tozali koyoka likambo moko te likolo na yango. Tango tomoni likambo, tosengeli kaka kotelema na etape na komona. Tosengeli te kosalela makanisi na biso mpona kosambisa mpe kokatela, yango izali lisumu. Komibatela biso mpenza kati na solo, ezali malamu koleka ete tomona te to koyoka te eloko nini ezali solo te. Kasi ata soki tosengeli koya na bokutani na eloko moko na bosolo te, tokokoba na kozala kati na bolamu soki tokokanisa mpe komiyoka kati na bolamu.

3. Molili

Satana azali na nguya moko na molili oyo Lucifer azalaka na yango mpe apusaka bato bazala na makanisi mabe mpe mitema mabe mpe kosala kati na mabe.

Boye ezalaka milimo mabe nde mimemaka biso tozala na misala na molema mifandisama kati na solo te. Mokili na milimo mabe indimamaka na Nzambe mpo ete izala mpona kokokisa mokano na koleka na baton a nse na moi. Bazali na nguya na mopepe na tango na koleka na bato na nse na moi izali kosalema. Baefese 2:2 elobi ete, "...wana etambolaki bino kati na yango kobila nzela na mokili oyo, kobila mokolo na nguya na mopepe. Molimo yango azali sasaipi kosala mosala kati na bana na nkanza."

Nzambe Apesaka bango bokonzi na kokamba makambo na molili kino tango Nzambe Asilisa bokoli na baton a nse na moi.

Milimo mabe mana mizalaka na molili bakweisaka bato mpona kosala masumu mpe kotelemela Nzambe. Bazali mpe na molongo makasi. Mokolo, Lucifer, akonzaka molili, kopesa mitindo mpe kokonza ba sinzili na milimo mabe. Ezali na bikelamo mingi mikosungaka Lucifer. Bazali ba dalagona bango bazali na nguya mpe banje na bango (Emoniseli 12:7). Izali mpe na Satana, zabolo, na ba demona.

Lucifer, Mokonzi Kati na Mokili na Molili

Lucifer azalaka angelu mokolo oyo akumisaka Nzambe na

mongongo kitoko mpe mandanda na misiki. Na lolenge azalaka kosepela ebongo itombwama mpe mpifo mpe na kolingama mingi na Nzambe mpona tango molayi mingi mpenza, ayaka suka suka kokoma na lolendo mpe atelemelaki Nzambe.

Emoniseli 18:7 elobi ete, "Na motindo oyo ekumisaki ye nzoto na ye mpe esepelaki ye mosolo, bopesa ye mpasi mpe mawa bobele bongo. Mpo ete na motema na ye alobi ete, 'Nakofanda mokonzi mwasi, nakufeli mobali te, mpe nakomona mawa soko moke te;'" mpe Emoniseli 19:2 elobi ete, "...mpo ete bikateli na Ye mizali na solo mpe na sembo. Mpo ete Akweisi mwasi na pite yango monene oyo abebisaki mokili na pite na ye; abukanisi ye mpona makila na baombo na Ye."

Na makomi likolo, 'mwasi na pite yango monene' mpe 'mokonzi mwasi' yango mibale ilobeli Lucifer. Lucifer azali na lolenge na mwasi. Elakisi te ete azali na nzoto na kati na mwasi. Azali kaka mwasi na motindo oyo lokola komonana na libanda, emotion, lolenge na kosala, mpe lolenge na koloba.

Basusu bakoki kokanisa ete Lucifer Azali azali lokola mobali mpo ete Yisaya 14:12. Yango ilobi ete, "Osili kokweya longwa na Lola boni? E monzoto na ntongotongo, mwana na kobima na moi! Osili kokatama kino mabele boni! yo oyo obukaki mabota!" Awa awa muana mobali elakisi te ete Lucifer azali mobali. Nzambe Atikala kobenga angelu muana te (Baebele 1:5). Ata soki tobotaki moto te, soki moto wana azali kosalela bison a bomipesa mingi, akolinga mpe akosala na bosembo, tokoki kozwa moto wana lokola muana na biso moko. Nzambe kobengaka Lucifer muana ezali na limbola iye.

Lelo, na kozanga kososola yango, bato bazali kokokana na lolenge na Lucifer na lolenge na kosala basuki na bango mpe na maquillage. Na nzela na mode mpe milato na mokili, Lucifer azali kokonza makanisi na mabanzo na bato lolenge elingi ye. Mingi mingi, Lucifer Atiaka influence monene kati na miziki na mokili.

Atindikaka mpe bato kati na kosumuka mpe na makambo mpamba mpamba na nzela na makambo na mikolo oyo lokola ordinateur. Akweisaka bakonzi mabe mpo ete batelemela Nzambe. Ba mboka misusu banyokolaka BaKristu na momesano. Nyoso wana isalemaka na kotindika mpe mayele na Lucifer.

Lisusu, Lucifer amekaka bato na ba lolenge mingi na bondoki mpe magie, mpe amemaka ba n ganga na bato na soloka ete bangumbamelaka ye. Amekaka na makoki na ye nioso komema ata molimo moko na Lifelo mpe amemaka bato batelemela Nzambe.

Ba Dalagona mpe Banje na Bango

Ba dalagona basalaka lokola mikonzi na milimo mabe nan se na Lucifer. Bato bakanisaka été dalagona azalaka nyama na ndoto. Kasi ba dalagona bazalaka na mokili na milimo mabe. Ezali kaka mpo ete bamonanaka te mpo ete bazali bikelamo na molimo. Lolenge italisama na momesano likolo na dalagona, bazalaka na maseke na mboloko, miso na demona, mpe matoyi makokana na ngombe. Bazali na ba ecaille na poso mpe makolo minei. Bazalaka lokola ba reptile minene (miselekete).

Ba dalagona na tango na kokelama na bango, bazalaka na masala milayi, kitoko, mpe bozenga. Bazalaka kozinga Ngwende na Nzambe. Balingamaka epai na Nzambe lokola bibwele mpe babikaka penepene na Nzambe. Bazalaka na nguya monene mpe mpifo mpe bazalaka na ba kerubi ebele koleka nan se na bokonzi na bango. Kasi na tango batelemelaka Nzambe elongo na Lucifer, banje na bango bakweyaka na botomboki mpe batelemelaka Nzambe mpe lokola. Banje bana na ba dalagona bazali mpe na ba lolenge na nsomo na ba nyama. Bazali na nguya na mopepe elongo na ba dalagona mpe bakomemaka baton a kosumuka mpe na mabe.

Ya solo, Lucifer azali na likolo koleka na mokili na milimo mabe, kasi mpona mosala, apesa bokonzi na ba dalagona mpe na banje na bango mpona kobundisa bikelamo na molimo na Nzambe mpe bakonza kati na mopepe. Wuta kala kala, ba dalagona bazala kotindika bato mpo ete basala to bakoma elilingi na ba dalagona mpona komema baton a kongumbamela bango. Lelo, ba religion misusu ba komisaka ba dalagona nzambe mpe bangumbamelaka bango, mpe bato wana bakonzami na ba dalagona.

Emoniseli 12:7-9 elobeli ba dalagona na banje na bango na lolenge eye:
Etumba ebimaki na likolo Mikaele na banje na ye babundi etumba na ba dalagona. Dalogona abundaki na banje na ye, nde

balongaki te, nde esika kati na likolo ezuami mpona bango lisusu te. Dalagona yango monene abwakami, ye nyoka na kalakala, oyo abiangami motelemeli mpe Satana, mozimbisi na baton a mokili mobimba abwakami nan se, banje na ye mpe babwakami na ye elongo.

Dalagona batindikaka bato mabe na nzela na banje na bango. Bato mabe na lolenge oyo bakotika tea ta na kosalaka makambo mabe kolela lokola koboma bato to mpe kotekisa bato. Banje na ba dalagona bazali na ba lolenge na ba nyama miye mitalisama na buku na Lewitiko miye Nzambe ayinaka. Mbe makotalisama na lolenge lolenge kolandana na lolenge na nyama, mpo ete nyama na nyama azali na lolenge na ye moko lokola koboma, mayele mabe, bosoto, to kosangana na bisika moke.

Lucifer asalaka na nzela na dalagona, mpe banje na ba dalagona basalaka kolandana na mitindo mipesamaka na ba dalagona. Na kokokanisa na mboka, Lucifer azali lokola mokonzi (roi), mpe dalagona bazali lokola minister way ambo to general commandant na manpinga oyo azali kosala mosala na kotala ba minister mpe ba soda. Tango ba dalagona bazali kati na mosala, bazwaka mitindo mbala miko ten a Lucifer na tango nioso. Lucifer asi alona makanisi mpe bongo na ye kati na ba dalagona, nde bongo soki dalagona bakosala eloko ikokani mbala moko na ba posa na Lucifer.

Satana azali na Motema mpe Nguya na Lucifer

Milimo mabe bakoki kokonza baton a lolenge mitema na bango mibebisama na molili, kasi ba demona to zabolo batumbolaka baton a ebandeli te. Na liboso, ezali Satana nde asalaka likolo na bato, mpe zabolo alandi, mpe suka ezali ba demona. Na koloba na mokuse, Satana azali motema na Lucifer. Izalaka na lolenge moko te kasi yango ikosalaka mosala kati na makanisi na bato. Satana azali na nguya na molili Lucifer azalaka na yango, mpe amemaka baton a kozala na makanisi mpe na mabanzo mabe mpona kosala misala mabe.

Mpo ete Satana azali ekelamo na molimo (Yobo 1:6-7), isalaka na lolenge ebele kolandana elembo na molili moto azali na yango. Na ba oyo balobaka lokuta, azalaka na molimo na lokuta (1 Bakonzi 22:21-23). Na ba oyo balingaka komema bokabwani na kotutisa ngambo moko na mosusu mito, asalaki na molimo wana (1 Yoane 4:6). Na ba oyo balingaka misala na bosoto, asalaka na molimo na mbindo (Emoniseli 18:2).

Lolenge na limboli, Lucifer, dalagona, mpe Satana bazali na misala mikesana mpe ba longele mikesana, kas bazali na makanisi moko mpe mabanzo mpe nguya na kosala mabe. Sasaipi, tika totala lolenge nini Satana asalaka likolo na bato.

Satanna azali lokola onde radio oyo epanzanaka na mopepe. Ipanzaka makanisi na yango mpe nguya tango nioso na mopepe. Nde, kaka lokola onde na radio ikoki koyambama na nzela na antene itiama mpona koyamba yango na ba oyo bandimi koyamba yango. Antenne awa ezali bosolo te, molili oyo ezali kati na motema na bato.

Ndakisa, lolenge na koyina kati na motema ikoki kosala lokola antenne mpona kondima signal na radio iye ipanzani na mopepe na Satana. Satana atiaka nguya na molili kati na makanisi na bato na lolenge ba onde radio oyo na molili iye isalema na Satana mpe solo te kati na motema na moto ikomi na frequence moko mpe mikutani. Na nzela na oyo, motema na solo te ikozwa makasi mpe ikobanda kosala. Yango izalaka tango tolobaka été 'moto azali koyamba misala na Satana', to azali koyoka mongongo na Satana. Na lolenge bazali koyoka mongongo na Satana na lolenge oyo, bakosumuka na makanisi, mpe na sima bakosala masumu na misala. Tango lolenge na mabe lokola koyina to likunia ikozwa misala na Satana, bakoluka kosala mosusu mabe. Tango yango ikoli lisusu makasi bakoki ata kosala lisumu na koboma.

Satana asalaka na nzela Couloir na Makanisi

Moto azali na motema na solo mpe na solo te. Tango tondimeli Yesu Christu mpe tokomi bana na Nzambe, Molimo Mosantu Akoya kati na mitema na biso mpe akoningisa motema na biso na solo. Elakisi été tozali koyoka mongongo na Molimo Mosantu kati na mitema na biso. Na bokeseni, Satana asalaki na libanda, nde alukaka couloir mpona kokota kati na mitema na bato Nzela (couloir) wana ezali makanisi na bato.

Bato bandimaka nini bamonaka, bayokaka, mpe bayekolaka elongo na sentiment mpe bakobomba miango kasi na makanisi mpe motema. Na tango esengeli to tango ikoki mabanzo mana mikomatisama. Yango izali 'makanisi'. Makanisi makesanaka kolandana na sentiment nini bozalaki na yango tango bobombaki likambo kati na mabanzo na bino. Ata na likambo na lolenge moko, bato misusu bakangaka yango kaka na kolandanna na bosolo, mpe bazali na makanisi na solo, tango ba oyo babombaka

yango na solo te bakozala na makanisi na bosolo te.
Bato mingi balakisanaka na solo te oyo ezali Liloba na Nzambe. Yango tina bazalaka na solo te mingi koleka solo kati na mitema na bango. Satana aningisaka bato na lolenge oyo mpo été bazala na makanisi na lokuta. Yango iyebana lokola 'makanisi na mosuni'. Na lolenge bato bazali koyamba misala na Satana, bakoki te kotosa Mobeko na Nzambe. Bakangami kati na masumu mpe suka suka bakokutana na kufa (Baloma 6 :16, 8 :6-7).

Na Lolenge Nini Satana Azwaka Bokonzi Likolo na Mitema na Bato?

Na momesano, Satana asalaka na libanda na nzela na couloir na makanisi na bato, kasi ezali na ba ndenge mosusu. Ndakisa kati na Biblia elobi ete Satana akotaki kati na Yudasi Iscariot, moko na bayekoli zomi na mibale na Nkolo Yesu. Awa, Satana 'kokota kati na ye' elakisi ete akobaki na koyamba misala na Satana mpe suka suka akabaki motema na ye nioso na Satana. Na lolenge oyo akangamaki mobimba na Satana.

Yudasi Iscariot amonaki nguya na nkamwa na Nzambe mpe na tango azalaka kolanda Yesu alakisamaki kaka na bolamu, kasi wuta alongolaka moyimi na ye te, azalaka koyiba misolo na Nzambe na libenga na misolo (Yoane 12:6).
Azalaki mpe na moyimi na koluka lokumu mingi mpe nguya tango Mesia, Yesu, akozwa Ngwende na mokili oyo. Kasi makambo amonaki mikeseneke na oyo akanisaka, nde moke moke atikaka motema na ye epai na Satana, nde atekisaka

Mokolo na ye mpona makuta ntuku misato na palata. Tolobaka ete Satana akoti kati na moto na tango Satana azwi bokonzi mobimba kati na motema na moto.

Na misala 5:3, Petelo alobaki ete motema na Ananias na Safila mitondisamaki na Satana mpe babombaki ndambo na misolo bazwaki na kotekisa elanga na bango mpe bakosaki Molimo Mosantu.

Petelo alobaki boye mpo ete ezalaki na makambo mingi na lolenge moko. Bongo liloba Satana akoteli to mpe atondi kati na moto elakisi ete bato bazali na Satana ye moko kati na mitema na bango, mpe bango moko bakomi lokola Satana. Na miso na molimo, Satana azali lokola molinga moindo. Energie na molili, oyo izalaka lokola milinga moindo, ezingaka bato oyo bayambaka misala na Satana na monene na yango. Mpona kozwa mosala na Satan ate tosengeli naino kokata makanisi nioso na bosolo te. Lisusu, tosengeli kopikola motema na likuta kati na biso. Yango elingi kolakisa été tosengeli kolongola antenne iye ikoki koyamba misala na Satana.

Zabolo na ba demona

Kati na bikelamo na molilili, bazali na elongi, miso, zolo, matoyi, mpe monoko lokola banje. Bazali na maboko na makolo mpe lokola. Zabolo amemaka baton a kosala masumu mpe amemelaka bango mimekano mpe mikakatano na lolenge lolenge.

Kasi yango elakisi te ete zabolo akotaka kati na bato mpona kosala yango. Na mitindo na Satana, zabolo akambaka bato oyo bapesa mitema na bango na molili mpe amemaka bango na kosala makambo mabe maye mandimanaka te. Kasi ba tango misusu zabolo akonzaka bato misusu mbala moko lokola bisalelo na bango. Ba oyo batekisa milimo na bango na zabolo, lokola bandoki to baton a soloka bakonzamaka na zabolo mpona kosala lokola bisalelo na zabolo. Bamemaka bato misusu na kosala makambo na zabolo mpe lokola. Bongo, Biblia elobi ete ba oyobasalaka masumu bazali ya zabolo (Yoane 8:44; 1 Yoane 3:8).

Yoane 6:70 elobi ete, "Yesu azongiseli bango ete, 'Ngai naponi bino ba zomi na mibale te? Nde moko kati na bino azali zabolo;'" Yesu Azalaki kolobela Yudasi Iscariot oyo akotekisa Yesu. Moto na lolenge oyo akoomaki moumbo na masumu mpe azalaki na likambo moko ten a lobiko azali mwana na zabolo. Na lolenge Satana akotaki kati na Yudasi mpe akonzaki motema na ye, asalaki misala na zabolo, oyo ezalaki kotekisa Yesu. Zabolo azali lokola mokonzi na mibale oyo azwaka mitindo na Satana, mpe na tango azali kokonza ba demona ebele ikomemela bato bokono ebele mpe pasi mpe amema bango bakweya na koleka kati na mabe mingi.

Satana, zabolo, mpe ba demona bazali na molongo. Bakoperaka na pembeni mingi. Yambo, Satana asalaka na makanisi na solo ten a bato mpona kofungola nzela mpona zabolo asala. Elandi, zabolo akobanda kosala na bato mpona komema bango basala misala na mosuni mpe misala misusu na zabolo. Ezali Satana nde asalaka na nzela na makanisi na bato, mpe ezali misala na zabolo komema baton a kotia yango kati na misala.

Biblia etalisaka ete ba demona bazali milimo mabe kasi

bakeseni na banje bakweyaka to mpe na Lucifer (Nzembo 106;28; Yisaya 8:19; Misala 16:16-19; 1 Bakolinti 10:20). Ba demona bameseneke kozala baton a molimo kati na bango, molema, mpe nzoto. Basusu kati na ba oyo babikaka kati na mokili oyo mpe bakufaka na kozanga lobiko bazongaka lisusu na mokili oyo kolandana condition moko, nde bakomaka ba demona. Bato mingi bazalaka na bososoli malamu te likolo na mokili na milimo mabe. Kasi milimo mabe bamekaka komema ata moto moko lisusu na nzela na libebi kino mokolo na suka oyo Nzambe Akanga.

Mpona yango 1 Petelo 5:8 elobi ete, "Bomisenjela, bolala mpongi te,; motelemeli na bino ye mabe, azali kotambola lokola nkosi konguluma, kolukaka soki akolia nani." Mpe Baefese 6;12 elobi ete, "Zambi tozali kobunda na mosuni mpe na makila te, kasi na bakonzi, na ba nguya, mpe na bakonzi na mokili oyo na molili, mpe na ba nguya na milimo mabe na bisika na likolo."

Tosengeli kosenjela mpe kolamuka na molimo na tango nioso mpo ete tokoki te kosunga kasi kaka kokweya na nzela na kufa soki tokobika lokola nguya na molili mikomema biso.

Chapitre 2
Bo yo moko

Bosembo na miso na biso moko isalamaka na tango tolakisami na solo ten a mokili lokola solo. Na lolenge bsembo na miso na biso moko ikembisami koyeba mingi kati na biso ikosalelama. Bongo,

Kino tango bo biso moko isalama

Bosembo na miso na biso moko mpe oyo tomonaka bosolo

Kozala na misala na molema mizalaka kati na solo

Nazali Kokufa Mokolo na Mokolo

Ezalaki na tango libosona ngai nandimela Nkolo. Nazalaka kobundana na malali na ngai mikolo nioso mpe esengo moko nazalaka na yango ezalaka kotanga ba bande desine na masano. Masolo mizalaka mingi kozongisela revenge. Makita yango mikendaka lolenge oyo tango azali bebe konguluma, baboti na elombe babomami epai na moyini. Akokima na libaku malamu kobomama na maboko na muana na mosala kati na ndako. Akutani na mokolo na masano na armes artiaux na kokola na ye. Akomi sik'awa mokolo na masano ye moko mpe akozongisela bayini na

Yesu Atalisi na Matai 5:43-45 "Boyokaki ete bolobaki boye, Olinga mozalani nay o mpe oyina moyini nay o. Nde ngai nazali koloba na bino ete bolinga bayini na bino mpe bobondela mpona banyokoli na bino, Bongo bokozala bana na Tata na bino na Likolo pamba te Akobimisa moi na Ye na bato malamu mpe na bato mabe mpe Akonokisa mbula na Ye na bayengebene mpe na bapengwi."

Bomoi nabikaka ezalaka malamu mpe honenete. Bato mingi bakokaka koloba ete nazalaka moto oyo azalaka na bosenga na 'mobeko' te. Kasi, sima na ngai kondimela Nkolo mpe namitali ngai moko na nzela na Liloba na Nzambe eteyamaka na champagne, nasosolaka ete na lolenge na ngai na kobika ezalaki na makambo mingi na malamu te. Nayokaka mpenza soni nasosolaka ete maloba na ngai, bizaleli na ngai, makanisi, mpe ata motema (conscience) mizalaka nioso mabe. Natubelaka mpenza liboso na Nzambe na kososolaka ete nabikaka bomoi iye izalaka sembo soko moke te.

Wuta mokolo wana na bundaka mpona kososola bosembo na ngai na miso na ngai moko mpe bosolo nakosalela mabe mpe nakweisa yango. Namiboyaki na bosembo namisalelaki mpe namimonaki mpenza pamba. Na kotangaka Biblia na misalelaki sembo kati na solo. Nakilaka mpe nabondelaka na kolemba te mpona kolongola solo te kati na motema na ngai. Lokola lifuti, nakokaki komona ete mabe na ngai elongwaki mpe nabandaka koyoka mongongo mpe kozwa litambwisi na Molimo Mosantu.

Kino Sembo na biso moko Isalema

Lolenge nini bato basalaka mitema na bango mpe bakotiaka ba valeurs na bango? Yambo ezalaka likambo bango basangola. Bana bakokanaka na baboti na bango. Basangolaka lolenge na bango, bizaleli, bomoto, mpe ba lolenge misusu na genetique kowuta na baboti na bango. Na koree balobaka ete 'tozwaka makila na baboti'. Kasi ezalaka mpenza makila te, kasi energie na bomi, to 'chi'. Chi ezali moboko na energie nioso oyo ewutaka na nzoto mobimba. Nayebi libota wapi mwana mobali na bango azalaka na elembo monen na mbotama likolo na mbebo na ye. Mama na ye amesa kozala na eloko moko na bisika moko, kasi alongolaka yango na surirgie, elembo na mbotama ikobaki na kopesama na muana na ye.

Mai na ovaire na moto mizalaka na energie na bomoi. Mizalaka kaka na lolenge na libanda te, kasi mizalaka mpe na personalite, temperament, mayele, mpe bizaleli. Soki chi na tata ezali makasi na tango na kopesa mokumba, muana akokokana mingi na tata. Soki ya mama ezali makasi koleka muan akokokana na mama. Yango ekomisaka motema na muana na muana ikesana.

Lisusu, na lolenge moto azali kokola mpe akomi mokolo makambo mingi makolakisama, mpe makokoma mpe eteni kati na elanga na motema. Kobanda mbula mitano, bato bakobanda na komisalela 'bo ngai' kolandana na makambo bato bakomonaka, bakoyokaka, mpe bayekolaka. Na mbula zomi na mwambe, bo ngai na moto ikozwaka lisusu makasi na koleka. Kasi, likambo ezali ete makambo mingi na solo te tomonaka yango solo, mpe tobanzaka yango lokola solo.

Ezali makambo mingi na lokuta maye toyekolaka na mokili oyo. Ya solo na kelasi toyekolaka makambo mingi mazali kosunga mpe masengeli mpona bomoi na biso, kasi ezali na makambu matalisama maye mazali solo te, lokola evolution na Darwinisme. Na tango baboti batangisaka bana na bango balakisaka bango mpe makambo misusu na solo te lokola mazalaki solo. Toloba ete muana azalaki libanda mpe ebetamaki na muana mosusu to bana. Na nkkanda baboti bakoki koloba likambo lokola, "Oliaka mbala misato na mokolo kaka lokola bana misusu mpe osengeli kozala makasi, bongo pona nini ozali kobetama? Soki babeti yo mbala moko, zongisela bango mbala mibale! Bongo ozalaka na maboko mpe na makolo kaka lolenge na bana nioso? Osengeli koyekola na komitalaka yo moko." Bana bazwamaka na na lolenge na pamba soki babetami epai na baninga na bango. Sasaipi, conscience na lolenge nini bango bakokolisa? Bakomimona ete bazali ba zoba mpe basengeli te kotika basusu babeta bango. Soki basusu bakobeta bango mbala moko bakomona ete bazali na tina na kobeta mbala mibale. Na maloba mosusu, bakotia eloko mabe kati na bango lokola izalaki bolamu.

Lolenge nini baboti oyo ba oyo balandaka solo bayekolisaka bana na bango? Bakotala likambo mpe bakoyekolisa bango na bolamu mpe na solo mpo ete bakoka kozala na kimya na kolobaka likambo lokola ete, Wawa, meka kaka kososola bango? Yo mpe tala soki osalaki bango mabe te. Nzambe Alobeli biso tolonga mabe na bolamu."

Soki bana balakisami kaka na Liloba na Nzambe na makambo nioso, bakokoka kokolisa conscience malamu mpe ekoka na makambo nioso. Kasi na makambo mingi, baboti bayekolisaka bana na bango kati na solo te mpe lokuta. Tango moboti akokosa, muana mpe akokosa. Toloba ete telephone eleli mpe muana azwi. Akozika eyambeli na liboko na ye mpo ete mobengi akoka koyoka te. Akoloba ete, "Tata, nook Tom aluki yo." Tata akolobela muan na ye na muasi, "Yebisa ye nazali na ndako te."

Muana muasi akotala na tata na ye liboso na kopesa ye telephone makambo na lolenge oyo masalema mingi na kala. Bato bayekolisami na maakambo na solo te na tango na bokoli na bango, mpe na libanda na wana bakokolisa makambo na solo te na kosambisaka mpe kokatelaka mabe na sentiment na bango moko. Na lolenge oyo conscience na solo te ikosalema.

Lisusu, bato mingi bamonaka kaka lifuti na bango. Balandaka kaka oyo ezali intert na bango moko mpe bakanisaka bazali sembo. Soki likambo batalisi to likanisi na bato misusu makokani nan a makanisi nabngo moko te, bakokanisa ete basusu bazali na solo te. Kasi bato misusu mpe bakanisaka lolenge moko. Ezali pasi kokoma na boyokani soko basusu bakokanisaka lolenge moko. Makambo mana makosalemaka mpe epai na bato bazali penepene na basusu, lokola kati na mobali na muasi na ye to babiti na bana. Bato mingi basalaka bo ngai na bango na lolenge oyo, mpe bongo moto asengeli te kotelema na bo ye moko nde izali malamu.

Bosembo na miso na moto ye Moko mpe oyo Moto Amonaka Solo

Bato mingi bamisalelaka lolenge na kokatela bato mpe systeme na ba valeur, na nzela na misala na molema mifandisama kati na solo te. Na bongo, bakobika kati na bosembo na bango moko mpe bosolo na bango moko. Lisusu, solo na bango moko isalema na lokuta bandimaka na mokili mpe bamonaka yango lokola solo. Ba oyo bazalaka na bosembo na lolenge oyo na kozala malamu mpona etape bango moko bamitiela, mpe nakati na ezaleli na bango wana bakomema mpe bato bandimela bango na makasi.

Tango bosembo na miso na moto ye moko ikembisami, ikokoma bosolo na ye moko. Na maloba mosusu, bosolo na ye moko oyo izali structure isalema na bosembo na ye moko. Bosolo na ye moko oyo isalemaka kolandana na lolenge na moto ye moko, bizaleli na ye, biloko alingaka, makanisi. Na likambo bisika ba opinion nioso, imonani malamu soki okotelemela kaka na moko na bango, mpe soki lolenge oyo na komona makambu ikembisami ikokoma solo naaa miso nay o moko. Bongo, tendance ikokolisama mpona kozala na malamu mpe kosalelaka ba oyo bazali kosalela prorate moko, makanisi moko, to bazali kolinga yango, kasi ezali mpe na tendance mosusu na kondima mpenza te ba oyo bandimeli yo te. Yango mpo ete ozali na bosolo na miso na yo moko.

Makambo na lolenge oyo makoki kotalisama na ba lolenge lolenge na bomoi na bison a mokolo na mokolo. Babalani na sika bakoki kozala na koswana na makambo mazangi tina. Mobali akokanisa ete azali sembo na kobimisa dentifrice longwa na likolo na tube na tango mwasi akokanisa ete akoki kobimisa yango bisika nioso alingi. Soki moto na moto akotelema na oyo ye amoni malamu to sembo bakoki kobebana. Kowelana ekoki kobanda kolandana na bosolo oyo bango bakosalela mabe kati na bizaleli na bango miye mikesana.

Toloba ete ezali na muana na mosala kati na company oyo asalaka mosala na ye nioso na ye moko na koyambaka lisungi na moto moko te. Basusu kati na bato oyo bazalaka na bizaleli na kosalaka makambo nioso na bango moko mpo ete bakolisamaka na bisika na pasi mpe basengelaka na kosala bango moko. Ezali te mpo ete bazali ba lolendo. Bongo, soki okosambisa moto na lolenge wana lokola moto na lolendo to na koluka lifuti na ye moko, ezali mpe esambiseli isengela te.

Na makambo mingi, na talatala na solo, nioso na bosembo na miso na moto ye moko mpe oyo nioso afandisa lokola solo

Kuumbwa kwa Nafsi

na ye moko mizali na mbeba. Ba mbeba oyo mimataka kati na mitema na solo te iye isalelaka basusu te, ba oyo balukaka lifuti na bango moko. Ata bandimi bazalaka na makambo oyo nioso kasi basosolaka yango te.

themselves with others and think that they are better than others. Ata Bakanisaka ete balandaka Liloba na Nzambe mpe balongola masumu nioso na lolenge mooko boye, mpe bayebi solo. Na mayebi oyo balakisaka boyebi mingi na bango. Bakosambisaka lolenge basusu bazali kobika bomoi na bango kati na kondima. Bamikokamisaka mpe na basusu mpe bakanisaka ete bango baleki basusu. Na tango moko bamonaka kaka makambo malamu epai na bato misusu, kasi na sima bakobanda kombongwana mpe komona kaka mabe na bango. Bazali kaka kotelema na ba opinion na bango, kasi bakolobaka ete basalaki yango mpona Bokonzi na Nzambe'.

Bato misusu balobaka lokola bayebi makambo nioso mpe bazali sembo. Balobelaka tango nioso likolo na mbeba na bato misusu na kosambisaka bango. Elakisi ete bakoki te na komona ba mbeba na bango moko te kasi kaka oyo na basusu.

Liboso na biso tombongwana mpenza kati na bosolo, biso nioso tozalaka na oyo tomonaka lokola bosembo mpe yango ekolisamaka na kokoma bosolo tokosalelaka mabe. Na lolenge tokozala na mabe kati na mitema na biso, tokozala na misala na molema miye mizalaka kati na solo te mpe misala kati na bosolo. Na yango tokolekisa kosambisa bato mpe tokokatela bango likolo na basusu kati na oyo tomonaka lokola bosolo mpe bosembo na miso na biso moko. Mpona biso kokola na molimo, tosengeli kotala makanisi na biso nioso mpe mabanzo lokola mazalaki pamba. Tosengeli kokweyisa bosolo na biso moko mpe bosembo na miso na biso moko. Mpe tozala na misala na molimo mifandisama kati na solo.

Kozala na Misala na Molema mizalaka Kati na Solo

Tokoki kokola na molimo mpe kombongwana lokola bana na Nzambe na solo na tango tobongoli misala na molema na biso mazalaka kati na solo te kati na ba oyo mifandisamaka na solo. Bongo, nini tosengeli kosala mpona kozala na misala na molema mifandisama kati na solo?

Yambo tosengeli kososolaka mpe koyeba makambo nioso na epimelo na solo

. Bato bazalaka na ba conscience na kokesana, mpe lolenge na mokili mpe ekesana kolandana na tango, bisika, mpe lolenge na kobika. Ata sokibosalaki kati na lolenge malamu, ekoki komonana malamu te na basusu oyo bazali na ba valeur ekesana.

Bato basalaka ba valeur na bango mpe bizaleli mindimanaka na bisika bikesana mpe ba cultures, nna bongo tosengeli te kosambisa basusu na ba standard na bio moko. Epimelo moko na oyo tokoki kososola eloko mabe na mallamu ezali Liloba na Nzambe oyo ezali solo mpenza.

Kati na makambo baton a mokili bamonaka malamu mpe makoka, ezali na makambo makokanaka na Biblia, kasi ezali mpe na ebele mizali te. Toloba ete moko na baninga na bino babomaki moto, kasi moto mosusu afundamaki na tin ate. Na likambo oyo, ba mingi kati na bino bakolinga kobatela kimya na koloba kombo na mosali likambo te. Kasi soki bobateli kimya, na koyeba likolo na innocence na moto oyo afundamaki na tin ate, misala mayo mikoka te komonana lokola sembo na miso na Nzambe.

Liboso nandimela Nkolo, tango nasengelaka kokende kotala moto na ndako na ye na tango na koliampe soki atunaki ngai soki nasi naliaki, Namesanaka koyanola ete, "Iyo nasi naliaki." Natikala te kokanisa ete yango ezalakai sembo te, mpo ete nazalaka koloba yango mpona kokitisa motema na mosusu. Kasi na lolenge na molimo, ekoki kozala Pamela na miso na Nzmbe mpo ete ezali mpenza solo te, ata soki ezali mpenza lisumu te, ata soki ezali lisumu te. Sima na kososola yango, nakomaka ksalela maloba mosusu lokola, "Naliaki te, kasi naza na posa sik'oyo te."

Kososola makambo nioso na solo, tosengeli koyoka mpe koyekola Liloba na solo mpe kobatela yango kati na mitema na biso. Tosengeli kotanga Biblia mpe kokabwana na ba lolenge mabe oyo tomisalelaka na solo ten a mokili oyo. Ata bwanya na lolenge nini eloko ezali na yango kati na mokili oyo, soki ezali kotelemela Liloba na Nzambe, tosengeli kobwakisa yango.

Mibale, mpona kozala na misala na molema mifandisama kati na solo ba sentiment na biso mpe emotion misengeli kozala na lolenge na solo.

Lolenge nini tokotisaka makambo kati na biso esalaka mosala makasi tango tomekaka koyoka kolandana na solo. Namonaka mama oyo azalaki komeka kobeta muana na ye nakolobaka ete, "Soki osali boye, Pasteur akopamela yo!" Azali komeka komema muana na ye na kokanisa ete Pasteur azali moto na somo. Muana na lolenge oyo akobanga to kokima Pasteur bisika na kozala penepene na ye na tango na bokoli na ye.

Na kala kala, namonaka likambo na filme. Muana muasi elenge azalaka moninga na nzoko, mpe nzoko ameseneke kolinga zolo na ye na kongo na muana. Mokolo moko muana azalaki kolala mpe nyoka na ngenge ayaka mpe alingaka kingo na ye. Soki ayebaka ete ezalaki nyoka na ngenge, alingai mpenza kobanza mpe koyoka somo. Kasi miso maye mikangamaka na tango na kolala mpe akanisaka kaka ete ezalaki zolo na nzoko. Nde akamwaki soko moke te. Kutu amonaki ete ezalaki moninga. Sentiment ikesanaka kolandana na makanisi.

Sentiment mikesanaka kolandana na lolenge nini tozali kokanisa. Bato oyo bayokaka nkele na komona mpese, misiopi, to mpe ba millepate basepelaka na gout malamu na soso ata ete soso aliaka biloko oyo. Tokoki komona boni sentiment na eloko etalaka kaka makanisi na biso. Ata moto na lolenge nini tomoni to mpe mosala na lolenge nini tokosalaka, tosengeli kaka kokanisela yango na ndenge na malamu.

Likolo na nioso, mpona biso kokanisa mpe koyoka na lolenge malamu kati na makambo nioso, tosengeli tango nioso komona, koyoka, mpe kobomba kaka makambo malamu. Ezali mingi solo na mikolo oyo tango tokoki komona kaka likambo nioso na nzela na mass media to mpe internet. Mabe na koleka, koboma, mobulu, kokosa bato, koluka lifuti, kokanela, mpe kobwakisa miluti penepene na biso lelo koleka tango nioso na lisituale. Mpona biso komibatela kati na solo, epusi malamu te komona, koyoka, to kotia kati na bongo makambo mana na lolenge tokokoka. Kasi, ata soki tosengeli kokutama na makambo mana, na ngonga moko na tango tokotiaka makambo na solo mpe kati na bolamu. Boni? Bokotunaka!

Ndakisa, ba oyo bayoka masolo na kobangisa likolo na ba demona to ba vampire na bolenge na bango bazalaka na sentiment na bobangi likolo na bango, mingimingi soki bafandi bango moko kati na molili sima na kotala filme na somo. Balengaka mpe bakobanga soki bayoki mongongo monene to ba moni elilingi. Soki bazali na bango moko, eloko moko moke ikoki kosalema mpe bakokota kati na bobandi makasi mpona somo na bango. Kasi soki tokobika kati na pole, Nzambe Akobatela biso mpe milimo mabe mikoka te na kosimba biso. Kutu, bakobanga mpe bakolenga kati na pole na molimo, oyo ebimaka kati na biso. Soki tososoli lakambo oyo, tokoka kobongola sentiment na biso. Tokososola na motema ete milimo mabe bazali bikelamo na kobanga te, nde sentiment na biso ikoka mpe kombongwana. Mpo ete tokoki kokonza mokili na molili, ata soki ba demona bakomonana, tokoki kaka kobengana bango mosika na nkombo na Yesu Christu,

Tika totala lisusu likambo na bato moko bisika bato bazali na sentiment isengela te. Nazalaki na pelerinage na bandeko na lingomba na pembeni na ba mbula 20 eleka. Ezalaki na ekeko na mobali bolumbu kati na stade na Grece. Makomi likolo na yango izalaki mpona kopesa makasi mpe masano mpona bato na nzoto malamu yango ezali moboko mpona ekolo malamu. Kuna nakokaki komona bokeseni kati na bapaya na bikolo misusu na Europa mpe bandimi naegelesia na biso.

Basusu kati na bandeko na biso kati na lingomba bakangaki photo liboso na ekeko na motungisi moko te, kasi basusu kati na bango babungisaki kimya. Balukaki kozala mosika na bisika wana lokola bamonaki esika oyo basengelaki na komona te. Tina oyo balukaki kokima mosika na ekkeko ezalaki mpo ete bazalaki na makanisi na bilulela. Bazali koyoka malamu te liboso na bolumbu, mpe bazalaki na sentiment na lolenge wana tango bamonaki ekeko bolumbu na mobali. Baton a lolenge wana bakoki ata kosambisa ba oyo bazali penepene na ekeko mpona kotanga yango. Kasi ba torite na Europa wana bamonanaki soko kozala na kotungisama moko te to sentiment lokola oyo na bango. Bazalaki kotala ekkeko na kosepela mpona mosala kitoko isalemaki likolo na yango.

Na likambo oyo moto moko te asengelaki kokatela ba touriste na Europa wana nakolobaka ete bazanga soni.Soki tokososola bokeseni na bikolo mpe tobongoli ba sentiment na solo te na oyo na solo, tokoka te koyoka soni to mpe malamu te. Adamu ameseneke kobika na bolumbu na ye na tango azalaka na boyebi na mosuni te, mpo ete azalaka na makanisi moko na ekobo te, mpe lolenge wana na kobika izalaka malamu koleka.

Misato mpona kozala na misala na molema mifandisama kati na solo tosengeli te kondima makambo kaka na oyo tokanisaka, kasi mpe kolandana na likanisi na baninga mpe lokola.

Soki bokososola makambo mpe ba situation kaka na lolenge na bino na kososola, ba experience, mpe lolenge na kokanisa, iozala na misala mingi na molema kati na solo te miye mikomata. Bokobakisa solo to mpe kolongola epai na maloba na basusu kolandana na makanisi na bino moko. Bokoki kososola mabe, kosambisa, kokatela, mpe kobandisa ba sentitiment mabe.

Toloba ete moto oyo azoki kati na likama na ye na nzela azali komilelalela mingi mpenza likolo na pasi na ye.ba oyo batikala na kokutana na likama na lolenge wana te to mpe ba oyo na tolerance monene likolo na pasi bakoki kokanisa ete moto yango azali kokomisa pai yango tango izali kaka eloko moke. Soki bokondimela maloba na bato misusu kolandana na makanisi na bino mpe experinces, bokozala na misala na molema mifandisama kati na solo te. Soki bokomeka kososola kolandana na lolenge na bato misusu, bokoka kososola ye mpe monene na pasi azali koyoka.

Soki bokososola likambo moto mosusu mpe bokondima ye, bokozala na kimya na bato nioso. Bokosengela koyina to mpe kozala eloko iye ezali kopesa kimya te. Ata soki bokonyokwama pota to kotelemela likolo na moto mosusu, soki bokokanisa naino likolo na ye, bokoyina ye te kasi bokokoba na kolinga ye mpe koyokela ye mawa. Soki boyebi likolo na bolingo na Yesu Christu oyo abakamaka mpona biso mpe ngolu na Nzambe. Bokokoka kolinga ata bayini na biso. Ezalaki likambo moko na Setefano. Ata na tango bazalaka kobeta ye mabanga na mabe moko te asalaka, ayinaka ba oyo bazalaka kobeta ye mabanga te kasi abondelaka mpona bango.

Kasi tango mosusu tokoki komona ete ezali pete te kozala na misala na molema mitiama kati na solo lolenge tolingi. Bongo, tosengeli tango nioso kozala ekenge likolo na maloba na biso mpe misala mpe komeka kobongola misala na molema na biso mifandisama kati na lokuta na ba oyo kati na solo. Tokoki kozala na misala na molema mifandisama kati na solo na ngolu mpe makasi na Nzambe mpe lisungi na Molimo Mosantu lolenge tokobondela mpe kokoba na komeka.

Nazali Kokufa Mokolo na Mokolo

Ntoma Polo anyokolaka BaKristu mpo ete azalaka na bosembo makasi na miso na ye moko mpe makanisi na solo naye moko. Kasi sima na kokutana na Nkolo, asosolaka ete bosembo na miso na ye moko mpe makanisi amisalela ye moko mizalaki malamu te, mpe amikitisaka na lolenge oyo eteamonaka nioso azalaka na yango lokola bosoto. Na ebande;I, azalaka na kobundabunda kati na motema na ye na kososola ete mabe izalaka kati na ye izalaki kotelemela bolamu oyo alingaki kosala (Baloma 7:24).

Kasi asalaka esakola na kopesa matondi na kondimaka ete mobeko na bomoi mpe Molimo Mosantu kati na Christo Yesu ikangolaki ye na mobeko na masumu mpe kufa. Na Baloma 7:25, alobaki ete, "Bobele Nzambe mpona Yesu Kristo Nkolo na biso! Matondi na Ye. Bongo ngai moto nakotosaka mibeko na Nzambe na ekaniseli na ngai, nde nakotosaka mobeko na masumu na na nzoto na ngai." nde na 1 Bakolinti 15:31, "Mokolo na mokolo nazali kokufa, nalobi boye bandeko mpona lolendo lozali na ngai mpona bino kati na Klisto Yesu Nkolo na biso."

Alobaki ete, "Mokolo na mokolo nazali kokufa" mpe yango elakisi ete azalaka kokata ngenga na motema na ye na mokolo nioso. Mingi mingi kolongola solo te kati na ye lokolalolendo, komikumisa, koyina, kosambisa, kanda, lofundu, mpe moyimi Lolenge atatolaka ete, alongolaka miango na kobetana na miango kino bisika na kotangisa makila. Nzambe Apesaka ye ngolu mpe makasi, mpe na lisungi na Molimo Mosantu ambongwanaka na moto na molimo oyo azalaka kaka na misala na molema mifandisama kati na solo. Akomaka suka suka ntoma na nguya oyo apanzaka sango malamu na tango azalaka kotalisa bilembo mingi mpe bikamwisi.

Chapitre 3
Makambo na Molimo

Bato misusu basalaka masumu na likunia, zua, kosambisa, kokatela, mpe ekobo kati na makanisi na bango. Balakisama na libanda te, kasi masumu na lolenge oyo misalemaka mpo ete bazali na makambo na masumu kati na bango.

Mosuni mpe Misala na Nzoto

Makambo na Mosuni: Masumu Masalemaka kati na Makanisi

Bilulela naNzoto

Bilulela na Miso

Enzombo na Bomoi Oyo

Mpona ba oyo molimo ikufa, milema na bango mikoma mikonzi na bango mpe mikokonzaka likolo na banzoto na bango. Toloba ete ozali na posa na mai, mpe oluki komela eloko moko. Bongo molema ikopesa motindo na liboko izwa kopo mpe imema yango na monoko na yo. Kasi na ngonga oyo, soki moto abandi kofinga yo mpe ozwi kanda okoki koluka kopanza kopo. Mosala na molema na lolenge nini yango ezali ?

Yango isalemaka tango Satana amemaka molema iye izali kati na mosuni. Moto ayambaka misala na moyini zabolo mpe Satana na lolenge oyo bazali na solo te kati na bango. Soki bakondima misala na Satana, bakoya na kozala makanisi na solo te, mpe soki bandimi misala na zabolo, bakolakisa misala na solo te.

Makanisi na kopasola kopo likolo na nkanda ipesamaki na Satana, mpe soki bokobi mpe bapasoli verre, ezali mosala na zabolo. Likanisi ebengami limabo na mosuni mpe mosala ibengami 'mosala na mosuni'. Tina nini tozali na misala na molema mpe misala mifandisama kati na solo te ezali mpona lolenge na masumu ikonama na moyini zabolo mpe Satana wuta bokweyi na Adamu mpe yango isangana na ba nzoto na bato.

Mosuni mpe Misala na Nzoto

Baloma 8:13 elobi ete, "...Soko bozali baton a nzoto bokokufa mpenza; nde soko na nzela na Molimo bokoboma bizaleli na nzoto, bokobika."

Awa 'bo kokufa' elakisi ete bokokutana na kufa na seko, oyo ezali Lifelo. Bongo, 'mosuni' ezali na limbola oyo etalisi kaka nzoto na biso te. Ezali mpe na limbola na molimo.

Elandi, soki na nzela na Molimo tokoboma bizaleli na nzoto, tokobika. Bongo yango elakisi ete tokolongola misala na mosuni lokola kofandaka, komilalisa nan se, kolia mpe bongo na bongo? Ya solo te! Awa, "nzoto' etalisi eloko to ebombamelo bisika wapi boyebi na molimo iye ipesamaka na moto epai na Nzambe izali kotanga. Mpona kososola limbola na molimo na oyo tosengeli koyekola likolo na moto na lolenge nini Adamu azalaka.

Na tango Adamu azalaka molimo na bomoi, nzoto na ye izalaki na motuya mpe iye ikufaka te. Atikalaka kokoma mobange te mpe akokaka kokufa te to kobeba. Azalakana nzoto na kongala, kitoko, mpe na molimo. Bizaleli na ye mpe mizalaka na bokonzi mingi koleka moto aleki na lokumu na mokili oyo. Kasi wuta tango lisumu eyaki kati na ye mpe lokola lifuti na lisumu na ye, nzoto na ye ikomaki nzoto na pamba iye ikesanaka na oyo na ba nyama te.

Tika napesa bino lisese. Tango ezali na kopo na bimeli kati na yango, kopo ikoki kokokanisama na nzoto na biso mpe bimeli, molimo na biso. Kopo moko ikoki na kozala na talo ikesana kolandana na bimeli nini izali kati na yango. Ezalaki lolenge moko na nzoto na Adamu. Lokola molimo na bomoi, Adamu azalaka kaka na boyebi na solo lokola bolingo, bolamu, bosolo, mpe bosembo, mpe pole na Nzambe, iye ipesamaka na Nzambe. Kasi lokola molimo na ye ikufaka, boyebi na solo itangaki libanda na ye, mpe bisika na solo, apesamaki biloko na mosuni epai na moyini zabolo na Satana. Ambongwanaki kolandana na solo te oyo ikomaki eteni na ye. Elobami été, 'na Molimo, misala na nzoto mibomami." Awa misala na nzoto italisi na misala miye miwutaka na nzoto iye isanganaka na solo te.

Ndakisa, ezalaka na bato oyo batombolaka misapi na bango, babambaka ekuke to mpe batalisaka bizaleli misusu na mabe tango bazwi kanda. Basusu basalelaka monoko mabe na liloba niso bakolobaka. Basusu bakotalaka moto na nzoto mosusu na mposa na bilulela mpe basusu balakisaka makambo na pamba.

Misala na nzoto milakisaka kaka misala miminani na masumu te kasi nioso oyo mizalaka sembo ten a miso na Nzambe. Tango basusu bakolobaka na basusu balakisaka misapi na bango epai na bato to na biloko na kososola yango te. Basusu bakotombolaka mingongo na bango na lolenge bazali kososola na basusu na bisika oyo ikomonana lokola bazali koswana. Makambo mana mako monana lokola pamba, kasi mazali misala mikowutaka na nzoto iye isangana na solo te.

143

Kombo nzoto isalelami mbala ebele kati na Biblia. Na eteni oyo na Yoane 1:14, nkombo 'nzoto' isalelami na limbola na yango isengela, "Liloba Akomi mosuni, mpe Abiki kati na biso mpe tomoni nkembo na Ye, nkembo lokola mwana oyo abotami lokola mwana na linkinda longwa na Tata; Atondi na ngolu mpe na solo.." Kasi esalelamaka mingi na limbola na molimo.

Baloma 8:5 elobi ete, "Mpo ete ba oyoba oyo bazali baton a nzoto bakotia motema na makambo na nzoto; mpe ba oyo bazali bato na Molimo bakotia mitema na makambo na Molimo Mpe Baloma 8:8 ilobi ete, "...Bango bazali kotia motema na makambo na nzoto bakoki te koseepelisa Nzambe."

Awa, mosuni basaleli mosuni na lolenge na molimo, na kotalisa lolenge na masumu isangana na nzoto. Ezali kosangana na lolenge na masumu mpe nzoto bisika wapi boyebi na solo izali kotanga libanda. Moyini zabolo mpe Satana alonaka ba lolenge mingi na masumu kati na moto, mpe misanganaka kati na nzoto. Balakisama mbala moko te kati na misala, kasi bizaleli iye mizali kati na moto mpo ete mikoka kobima lokola misala na ngonga nioso. Tango totango moko na moko na ba lolenge na mosuni, tolobaka ete izali 'eloko na mosuni'. Koyina, likunia, zua, bosolo te, mayele mabe, lolendo, kanda, kosambisa bato, kokatela bato, bilulela, mpe moyimi nioso mana mitalisami lokola 'mosuni', mpe moko na moko kati na yango izali 'eloko na mosuni'.

Limbola na 'Nzoto izali Pamba'

Na tango Yesu Azalaka kobondela na Getesemane, bayekoli balalaki mpongi. Yesu alobelaki Petelo ete, "Bosenjelaka mpe bobondelaka ete boingela kati na komekama te; molimo ezali na mposa, nde nzoto ezali na bolembu." Matai 26:41). Kasi yango elakisi te ete nzoto na bayekoli izalaki na kolemba. Petelo azalaki na nzoto makasi mpo ete azalaki molobi mbisi. Bongo, ilakisi nini 'nzoto izali na bolembu'?

Ilakisi ete wuta Petelo naino ayambaki Molimo Mosantu te, azalaki moto na mosuni oyo alongolaki naino masumu na ye nioso te mpe bongo akolisaka nzoto iye izwami kati na molimo te. Tango moto alongoli masumu mpe akoti kati na molimo, mingi mingi tango akomi moto na molimo mpe moto na solo, molema mpe nzoto na ye mikokambama na molimo na ye. Bongo, ata soki nzoto ilembi makasi, soki bolingi mpenza bolingi kolamuka na motema, bokoki kokima na kokweya kati na mpongi.

Kai na tango Petelo akotaki na molimo, nde wana, akokaki kokonza lolenge na nzoto lokola bolembu mpe kolemba na nzoto. Nde, ata soki alingaki kosenzela akokaki te. Ezalaki na limitation na nzoto naye. Na kozala na ba limite na lolenge oyo ilakisi 'nzoto izali na bolembu.

Kasi sima na lisekwa mpe konetwama na Yesu Christu, Petelo ayambaka Molimo Mosantu. Sik'awa azali kaka kokonza lolenge na ye na mosuni te, kasi mpe abikisaki babeli mingi mpe asekwisa ata mokufi. Ateyaka Sango malamu na mpiko nioso mpe

145

kondima ete aponaka kobakama na ekulusu moto na nse makolo likolo.

Mpona likambo etali Yesu, Ateyaka Sango Malamu na Bokonzi na Nzambe mpe Abikisaka bato butu mpe moi, ata soki soki Akokaka kolia mpe kolala malamu. Kasi mpo ete molimo na Ye izalaka Kokonza nzoto na ye, ata na likambo bisika azalaka na bolembu mingi, Akokaki ata kobondela kino tango motoki na Ye ikomaki lokola ba mbuma na makila kokweyaka na mabele. Yesu Azalaka soko na masumu na makila soko

Bandimi misusu basalaka masumu mpe bakopesaka ba raison na kolobaka ete, "Nzoto na ngai ezali na bolembu." Kasi balobaka yango mpo ete bayebi limbola na molimo na liloba oyo te. Tosengeli koyeba ete Yesu kotangisa makila ma Ye na ekulusu Akangoli biso kaka na masumu na biso te lisusu na bolembu na biso. Tokoki kozala nzoto makasi na molimo mpe nzoto mpe kosala makambo mazali likolo na makoki na bato soki tozali na kondima mpe tokotosaka Liloba na Nzambe. Lisusu, tozali na lisungi na Molimo Mosantu, nde tokoka te koloba ete tokoki te kobondela to mpe tozali na choix moko te kasi na kosala kaka masumu mpo ete nzoto na biso izali na bolembu.

Makambo na Mosuni: Masumu Misalemaka Kati na Makanisi

Soki bato bazali na mosuni, mingi soki bazali na lolenge na masumu oyo isangana na ba nzoto na bango, bakosalaka masumu kaka na makanisi na bango te kasi mpe na misala. Soki bazali na lolenge na lokuta bakokosa baninga na likambo oyo bazali na lifuti te. Soki bakosalaka lisumu kati na motema kasi na misala te, ezali likambo na mosuni.

Toloba ete ete omoni bijoux na moninga nay o. Soki okobanza ata kozwa yango to koyiba yango, bongo osi osali lisumu kati na motema nay o. Bato mingi bamonaka yango lokola lisumu te. Kasi Nzambe Atalaka motema, mpe ata moyini zabolo na Satana bayebi motema na lolenge oyo na moto, nde bakoki komema mafundi mpona lisumu eye, yango ezali makambo na mosuni.

Na Matai 5:28 Yesu Alobi ete, "...Nde Ngai nazali koloba na bino ete, ye nani akotala mwasi na mposa mabe na ye, asili kosala na ye ekobo na motema na ye." Mpe na Yoane 3:15 elobi ete, "Moto na moto oyo akoyinaka ndeko na ye azali mobomi na bato; mpe toyebi ete moto na moto oyo akobomaka bato azali na bomoi na seko koumela kati na ye te." Soki bokosala lisumu kati na motema, elakisi ete botie moboko na kosala misala na masumu.

Bokoki kozala na koseka na elongi na bino mpe komonana lokola bolingi moto ata soki boyinaka mpe bokoluka na kobeta moto yango. Soki likambo isalemi mpe okoki lisusu kokanga motema te, kanda na bino ikoki kotalisama mpe bokoki kobanda koswana to kobunda na moto yango, kasi soki bolongoli mosisa na masumu na koyina yango moko, bokotikala na koyina moto

147

yango tea ta soki akopesa bino pasi mingi.

Lolenge ikomama na Baloma 8:13, "...Soko bazali baton a nzoto bokokufa mpenza; Kaka soki bolongoli makambo na mosuni bokosalaka solo misala na mosuni. Kasi makomi ilobi mpe ete, "...nde soko na nzela na molimo bokoboma bizaleli na nzoto, bokobika." Nde, ekoki kosalema ete bozala na misala na bo Nzambe mpe bulee na lolenge bokolongola misala na mosuni moko na moko. Sik'awa, lolenge kani tokoki noki noki kolongola makambo mpe misala na mosuni?

Baloma 13:13-14 elobi ete, "Totambolaka na ezalali ekoki na moi; na bilambo na lokoso te mpe na kolangwa masanga te, na pite mpe na mobulu te, na kowelana soko na zua te. Kasi bolata Nkolo Yesu Kristu lokola elamba mpe bokanisa te mpona kosepelisa mposa na nzoto." Mpe na 1 Yoane 2:15-16 elobi ete, "Bolinga mokili te soko makambo na kati na mokili te. Soko moto nani akolingaka mokili bolingo na Tata ezali kati na ye te. Pamba te makambo nioso kati na mokili na mposa mabe na nzoto mpe mposa mabe na miso mpe nzombo na bizaleli iuti na Tata te kasi iuti na mokil

Nakotala na makomi oyo, tokoki komona ete makambo nioso kati na mokili misalemaka mpona baposa mabe na nzoto, bapos mabe na miso, mpe enzombo na bizaleli. Posa mbe ezali moto na energie iye ikomemaka moto na koluka mpe kondima makambo makokufaka. Ezali ebele na makasi iye imemaka baton a koyoka malamu likolo na mokili mpe kolinga yango.

Tika sik'awa tokende na bisika wapi Ewa amekamaka na nyoka na Genese 3:6: "Emonaki mwasi ete nzete ezalaki malamu mpona kolia mpe kitoko na miso, mpe nzete yango ezalaki malamu mpona kozipola bososoli na moto, akamataki mbula yango mpe aliaki mpe apesaki na mobali na ye, oyo azalaki na ye elongo, ye mpe aliaki."

Nyoka alobaki na Ewa ete akokaki kokoma lokola Nzambe. Na ngonga oyo andimaka liloba, mosisa na masumu iyaki kati na ye mpe ifandisamaki lokola mosuni. Sik'awa, posa na nzoto iyaki mpe mbuma imonanaki kitoko mpona kolia. Posa na miso iyaki mpe mbuma imonanaki elengi na miso. Enzombo na bizaleli iyaki kati na ye mpe mbuma imonanaki na posa na kokomisa moto na bwanya. Lokola Ewa andimaka baposa na lolenge oyo, alingaka kolia mbuma mpe aliaka. Na kala azalaka na likanisi na koboya kotosa Liloba na Nzambe soko te, kasi lokola posa na ye itindikamaki, mbuma imonanaki malamu mpe kitoko. Lokola alukaki kokoma lokola Nzambe, suka suka atosaki Nzambe te.

Posa mabe na nzoto, posa mabe na miso, mpe enzombo na bizaeli etalisaka biso ete masumu na mabe mizalaka malamu mpe kitoko.Nde mikomatisaka makambo na mosuni mpe suka suka misala na mosuni. Bongo, tokolongola makambo na mosuni, tosengeli naino kolongola ba posa misato oyo. Bongo tokobanda kolongola mosuni yango mpenza kati na mitema na biso.

Soki Ewa pasi monene nini ekomema na kolia mbuma, alingaki te koyoka yango malamu mpona kolia mpe kitoko na miso. Kasi kutu alingaka ata kosimba to komona yango koloba kutu kolia yango te. Na bongo, soki tososoli pasi na lolenge nini ikomemelaka bison a kolinga mokili mpe yango ikomema bison a kokweya kati na etumbu na lifelo, tokolinga soko moke te mokili. Soki tososoli boni pamba masumu nioso mpe makambo na mokili mizali, tokoki na pete kolongola ba posa na biso mpona mosuni. Tinga ngai natalisa yango.

Posa Mabe na Mosuni

Posa mabe na mosuni ezali lolenge na kolanda mosuni mpe kosala masumu. Tango tozali na makambo lokola koyina, kanda, ba posa na moyimi, ba posa na pite, likunia, mpe lolendo, nde wana ba posa mabe na mosuni makoki kotalisama. Tango tokutani na likambo bisika wapi lolenge na masumu maningisami nde posa na yango mpe kilikili ikomatisama. Yango ikomema biso na kobanza été masumu mazali malamu mpe kitoko. Na bisika oyo, makambo na mosuni makomonana mpe makotalisama lokola misala na mosuni.

Ndakisa, toloba ete mondimi na sika azwi ekateli na kotika komela masanga, kasi azali naino na posa na komela masanga, oyo yango ezali eloko na mosuni. Nde soki akei na bar to na bisika wapi bato bazali komela masanga, ba posa na ye mabe na komela masanga mikoningisama. Yango nde ikoningisa posa na ye na komela masanga mpe na kolangwa.

Tika ngai napesa bino ndakisa mosusu. Soki tozali na bizaleli na kosambisaka mpe kokatela bato. Tokoki komona yango lokola esengo na koyoka mpe kopanza bato sango mpe kolobela bato misusu. Soki tozali na kanda kati na biso mpe ezali na likambo ikokanaka na makanisi na biso te, tokoyeisama sika mpe tokoyoka malamu tango tozwi kanda pona moto to eloko, likolo na yango. Soki tokomeka na kominga mpona kolanda bizaleli na mosuni te mpona kozwa kanda, tokomona yango pasi koleka mpe na kokoka te. Soki tozali na ezaleli na lolendo, bongo kati na lolendo na biso tokoki kozala na likambo na komimatisa biso moko. Lisusu kati na lolendo na biso tokoki mpe koluka ete basusu basalela bison a kolandaka bizaleli wana kati na biso. Soki tozali na posa na kokoma bazwi, tokoluka kokoma bazwi ata soki basusu bakoyoka pasi mpe bakonyokwama. Ba posa mabe oyo na mosuni mikomata na lolenge tokosumuka.

Kasi ata soki moto azali mondimi na sika mpe azali na kondima elemba, soki akobondela makasi, azwi ngolu na koyangana na baninga, mpe atondisami na Molimo Mosantu, ba posa mabe na ye na mosuni mikotalisama na pete te. Ata soki baposa na mosuni mikotalisama bisika moko na makanisi na ye, akoka na mbala moko kobengana yango na bosolo. Kasi soki akotika kobondela mpe abungisi kotondisama na Molimo Mosantu, akopesa nzela mpona moyini zabolo mpe Satana aningisa lisusu ba posa mabe na mosuni.

Bongo nini ezali motuya na kolongola baposa mabe na mosuni? Ezali kobatela kotondisama na Molimo Mosantu mpo ete mposa na bino na kolikya molimo itikala makasi koleka posa na bino na koluka mosuni. Tosengeli tango nioso kosenjela na

molimo lolenge ilobama na 1 Petelo 5:8, " "Bosenjela, bolala mpongi te. Motelemeli na bino ye zabolo, azali konguluma lokola nkosi, na kolukaka nani akolia."
Mpona kosala yango, tosengeli te kotika kobondela makasi. Ata soki tokoki kozala na misala ebele na Nzambe, tokobungisa kotondisama na MolimoMosantu soki totiki kobondela. Bongo nzela ikofungwama mpona baposa mabe na mosuni italisama. Na lolenge oyo, tokoka kosumuka na makanisi mpe sima na misala. Yango tina ete ata Yesu, Muana na Nzambe, atalisaka ndakisa malamu na kobondelaka na kotika te kati na bomoi na Ye na mokili oyo. Atikala te kotika kobondela na kokata lisolo Tata mpe Akokisa mokano na Ye.

Ya solo, soki bolongoli masumu mpe bokomi na kobulisama, ekozala na posa moko mabe ten a mosuni komata, mpe na bongo bokokweisama na mosuni te mpona kosumuka. Nde, ba oyo basantisami bakobondela mpona kolongola ba posa mbe na mosuni te, kasi kozwa kotondisama monene na Molimo Mosantu mpe kokokisa bokonzi na Nzambe na koleka.

Nini soki tozali na salite na baton a bilamba na biso? Tokolongola yango kaka te, kasi tokosukola yango kaka na sabuni mpona kolongola mpe solo. Soki ezali na mosopi to nini na elamba na biso, ekokamwisa biso mingi mpe tokoluka na mabala moko kolongola yango. Kasi masumu kati na mitema mizali mabe koleka mpe salite mingi likolo na bosoto na bato to mosopi moko. Lolenge ikomama kati na Matai 15 :18 été, "Nde oyo ekobima kati na moto euti na motema yango wana ekoyeisa moto mbindo" mikobebisa moto na kati na mikuwa mpe mafuta kati na yango mpe ikopesaka pasi makasi.

Bongo nini soki muasi akangi mobali na ye na makango? Boni pasi yango ikozala mpona ye! Ezali lolenge moko na loboko mosusu. Ikomema koswana na kobebisa kimya kati na libota, to ata kozala bokabwani kati na libota. Bongo tosengeli nokinoki kolongola ba pos mabe na mosuni pamba te ibotisaka masumu mpe ba consequeces na malonga te.

Ba Posa Maben a Miso

Ba posa mabe na miso itindikaka motema na koyokaka mpe na komonaka mpe ikomemaka moto na koluka makambo na mosini. Na oyo ibengami ba posa mabe na miso,' ba posa mabe na miso miyaka na komonaka, koyokaka, mpe koyokaka na kati na lolenge mizali kokola. Mingi, nini bazali komona mpe koyoka mikoningisa mitema na bango mpona kopesa bango mposa, mpe na nzela na yango bakozwa mposa mabe na miso.'

Tango bomoi eloko, soki bondimi yango elongo na sentiment, bokozala na sentiment moko tango bokomona lisusu eloko ikokani na yango. Ata soko na komona yango te, soki bokoyoka kaka likolo na likambo yango, bokokanisama na makambo maleka kala nde wan aba posa na bino mabe na miso ikoki koningisama. Soki bokokoba na koyamba ba posa mabe na miso, ikoningisa ba posa na bino mabe na mosuni, mpe na suka bokosuka na kosumuka.

Nini esalemaka tango Dawidi amonaka Bataseba, muasi na Uliya kosukola nzoto? Alongolaka te baposa mabe na miso kasi andimaka yango, bongo na komatisa baposa mabe na mosuni oyo ipesaka ye mposa na kozwa muasi. Suka suka azwaka muasi mpe asalaka kutu lisumu na kotinda mobali na ye Uliya na molongo na liboso na etumba mpona koboma ye. Na kosalaka bongo Dawidi amemaki momekano monene mongi epai na ye.

Soki tolongoli ba posa mabe ten a miso, ikokoba na koningisa mosisa na masumu kati na biso. Ndakisa, soki tokotala bilili na ekobo, ba posa mabe na miso mikoyeila biso, mpe Satana akomema mpe makanisi na bison a nzela na solo te.

Ba oyo bandimela Nzambe te basengeli kondimela te ba posa mabe na miso. Bosengeli te komona to koyoka oyo izali kati na bosolo te, mpe bosengeli ata te kokende na bisika wapi bokoki kozala na bokutani na makambo na solo te. Ata bokobondela mbala boni, bokokila, mpe bokobondelaka butu mobimba mpona kolongola mosuni na bino, soki bokolongola baposa na bino mabe te na miso, baposa na bino mabe na nzoto mikozwa makasi mpe mikoningisama ata mingi koleka. Lokola lifuti, bokoka te kolongola mosuni na makasi mpe bokoyoka été izali pasi mingi mpona kobunda na masumu.

Ndakisa kati na bitumba, soki ba soda likolo na efelo na engomba bazwi lisungi na libanda bakozwa makasi na kokoba kati na bitumba. Ikozala pete te na kobebisa makasi na bayina na efelo. Na bongo npona kolonga engomba tosengeli naino kozinga yango mpe kokata lisungi mikowutaka na kati mpo ete bayini bakoka kozwa bilei to mpe manduki te. Soki tokokoba na kobunda na kobatelaka likambo oyo, manpinga na bayini bakolongama na suka.

Na kosalelaka ba ndakisa, soki mapinga na moyini kati na engomba azali solo te, mingimingi mosuni kati na biso, bongo lisungi na ye kowuta na libanda ikozala ba posa mabe na miso. Soki tolongoli baposa mabe na miso na biso te, tokokoka mpe te kolongola masumu ata sima na kokila mpe mabondeli, mpo ete mosisa na masumu ikokoba na kozwa makasi. Bongo, tosengeli naino kolongola ba posa mabe na miso mpe kobondela mpe kokila mpona komilongola na mosisa na masumu. Nde wana tokokoka kolongola miango na ngolu mpe makasi na Nzambe mpe kotondisama na Molimo Mosantu.

Tika napesa bino ata ndakisa na pete koleka. Soki tokokoba na kotia mai na petwa kati na mbeki na mai na bosoto, mai na bosoto suka suka ikokoma mai na petwa. Kasi nini soki tokotia mai na petwa na tango moko na mai na bosoto? Mai na bosoto kati na mbeki ikokoma mai na petwa te ata tango molayi nini tokosalaka bongo, soki nioso mibale mizali mai na petwa te. Na lolenge moko tosengeli te na kondima lisusu bosolo te, kasi kaka solo mpona biso kolongola mosuni mpe kokolisa motema na molimo.

Enzombo na Bizaleli

Bato bamesana na kozala na mposa na komilakisa. "Enzombo na bizaleli" ezali makambo na pamba mpe enzombo ifandisama katti na bizaleli mpona bisengo na mokili tozali na yango." Ndakisa, balingaka na kotalisa mabota na bango, bana, mobali to muasi, bilamba na talo, bandaku na talo, to ba bijoux. Balukaka kondimama mpona lolenge na bango mpe makoki. Babetaka ata tolo mpona bokamarade na bango na bato bakenda sango to mpe bato minene. Soki bozali na enzombo na bizaleli, talon a bozwi na bino, koyebana, mayebi, makoki, mpe apparence na mokili oyo nde, bokoluka yango mpenza.

Kasi nini tina na kobetaka tolo na makambo eye? Mosakoli 1:2-3 elobi ete makambo nioso nan se na moi mizali pamba. Na lolenge ikomama kati na Nzembo 103:15, "Mpona moto mikolo ma ye mizali pelamoko matiti; akobima lokola fololo na elanga," enzombo na mokili oyo ikoki te kopesa biso valeur ya solo to bomoi. Kasi kutu izali kotelemela Nzambe mpe ikomema biso na kufa. Soki tokolongola mosuni na pamba pamba, tokosikolama na enzombo to posa mabe bongo tokolanda kaka solo.

1 Bakolinti 1:31 elobeli biso ete oyo akosala lofundu asengeli kosala yango kati na Nkolo. Elakisi ete tosengeli ten a komimatisa kasi mpona nkembo na Nzambe. Mingimingi, ezali komimatisa mpona ekulusu mpe Nkolo oyo Abikisa biso mpe likolo na bokonzi na Lola oyo abongisa mpona biso. Lisusu,

tosengeli kobeta tolo likolo na ngolu, mapamboli, nkembo mpe nioso oyo Nzambe Apesa biso. Tango tokobeta tolo kati na Nkolo, Nzambe Akosepela na yango mpe Akozongisela biso na mapamboli na biloko mpe na molimo.

Mosala na moto ezali mpenza kobanga Nzambe, mpe veleur na moto na moto ikokatama kolandana na lolenge akomaki moto na molimo (Mosakoli 12:130.

Tango tolongoli masumu nioso mpe mabe, mingi mingi misala na mosuni mpe makambo na mosuni, mpe tozongeli elilingi ebunga na NZambe, tokoki koleka etape na moto wa yambo Adamu, oyo azalaka molimo na bomoi. Yango elakisi ete tokoki kokoma baton a molimo mpe na molimo ekoka. Bongo, tosengeli te kosala ba provision mpona mosuni mpona baposa na yango, kasi tomilatisa biso moko na Chrsitu.

Chapitre 4

Likolo na Etape na Molimo na Bomoi

Tango tokweisi makanisi na mosuni, misala na molema mifandisama na mosuni mikolimwa, mpe kaka misala na molema mizalaka kati na molimo mikotikala. Molema ikotosa mokonzi molimo mpenzampenza na Amen. Tango mokonzi akosalaka mosala na mokonzi mpe mosali oyo na mosali, tokoloba ete molema na biso mozali kobika malamu.

Bosuki na Motema na Bato

Kokoma Moto na Molimo

Molimo na Bomoi mpe Molimo Mobalolama

Kondima na Molimo Izali Bolingo na Solo

O Nzela na Kobulisama

Ata bana bebe babotami sika bazali bato kasi bakoki kosalela bomoto na bango na mobimba te. Bazali na mayebi moko te. Bakoki ata koyeba baboti na bango te. Bayebi lolenge na komibikisa te. Na lolenge moko Adamu oyo akelamaka lokola molimo na bomoi, akokaka te kosala mosala na ye lokola moto na ebandeli. Akomaka moto na tina mingi kaka sima na ye kozwa boyebi na molimo. Ayaka kobika lokola nkolo na bikelamo nioso na lolenge ayekolaka mayebi na molimo kowuta na Nzambe moko na moko. Na tango wana motema na Adamu ezalaka molimo yango moko, nde ezalaki na tin ate na kosalela liloba 'motema'.

Kasi sima na ye kosumuka molimo na ye ikufaki. Mayebi na molimo mibandaka kotanga kati na ye moke moke, na bisika na yango atondisamaki na mayebi na mosuni kowuta na moyini zabolo na satana. Motema na ye ikokaki te kobengama lisusu molimo, mpe kobanda tango wana ibengamaki 'motema'.

Na ebandeli motema na Adamu ikelamaka na elilingi na Nzambe oyo Azali Molimo. Motema na Adamu ekokaki mpe kokoma monene na lolenge itondisamaki na mayebi na molimo.

Kasi sima na molimo na ye kokufa, boyebi na solo te izingaki molimo, mpe sik'awa monene na motema iyaka na kozwa bosuki. Na nzela na molema iye ikomaka mokonzi na moto, moto abandaka kobakisa boyebi na lolenge na lolenge, mpe babanda kosalela mayebi mana na lolenge mingi. Kolandana na ba mayebi na lolenge na lolenge mpe balolenge mingi na kosalela miango, mitema na bato mibandaka kosalelama na ba lolenge ebele.

Bongo, at aba oyo bazalaka ata na mitema minene bakokite na kokende likolo na makoki mikatelama kolandana na bosolo na miso na moto na moto, bosembo na miso na moto ye moko mpe makambo bango balekela. Kasi tango tosi tondimeli Nkolo Yesu Christo, nde tokokende likolo na ba limite wana na bato. Lisusu, na lolenge tokokolisa mitema na molimo, tokoka koyoka mpe koyekola likolo mokili na molimo izanga suka.

Bosuki na Motema na Moto

Tango bato na molema bakoyoka Liloba na Nzambe, mateya ikotiama liboso kati na ba bongo na bango, nde bongo bakosalela makanisi na moto. Mpona tina oyo bakoka te kondima Liloba na Nzambe na mitema na bango. Na momesano, bakoki te kosalela makambo na molimo to mpe komibongola bango moko na solo. Bakomekaka kososola mokili na molimo na bosuki na mitema na bango, nde bongo bakobanda kosambisa makambo mingi. Bazali mpe na bozangi bososoli mingi mpe bakosambisa ata likolo na ba tata na kondima kati na Biblia.

Tango Nzambe Apesaka mitindo na Abalayama kokabela Ye muana na ye se moko Isaka lokola mbeka, basusu balboa ete esengelaki kozala pasi mingi mpona Abalayama kotosa. Balobaka eloko na lolenge oyo: Nzambe Andimelaki ye abembuka mikolo misato na ngomba Moriya mpona komeka kondima na Abalayama; na nzela, solo Abalayama azalaki na tango na kolekela mitungisi makasi tango akanisaka soko kotosa Nzambe to mpe te. Kasi na suka aponaka kotosa Liloba Nzambe.

Solo Abalayama azalaka na likambo wana? Alongwaka tongotongo ata na kolobela muasi na ye Sara elokomoko te. Atiaka mpenza elikya nea ye nioso na nguya na bolamu naNzambe oyo Akokaka kosekwisa bawa. Mpona tina oyo akokaki kopesa muana na ye Isaka lokola mbeka na kokanisa moko te. Nzambe Amonaki mozindo na motema na ye mpe Andimelaki kondima na ye mpe abengamaka 'moninga na Nzambe'.

Soki moto azosola etape kati na kondima mpe botosi iye ikoki kosepelisa Nzambe, akoki kososola likambo oyo mabe mpo ete azali kokanisa na motema na ye isuka mpe standard na kondima. Tokoki kososola ba oyo balingi Nzambe na etape na likolo koleka mpe kosepelisa Nzambe na lolenge tolongoli masumu na biso mpe tokolisi motema na molimo.

Kokoma Moto na Molimo

Nzambe Azali molimo, mpe Ye Alingi ban aba Ye bakoma

baton a molimo, mpe lokola. Sik'awa nini tosengeli kosala mpona kokoma baton a molimo; ba oyo milimo na bango mikoma mikonzi na milema mpe ba nzoto na bango? Likolo na nioso, tosengeli koongola makanisi na solo te, mingi mingi makanisi na mosuni, mpo ete tokonzama na Satan ate. Kasi tosengeli kutu koyoka mongongo na Molimo Mosantu oyo Aningisaka mitema na biso kati na Liloba na solo. Tosengeli komema milema na bison a kotosaka mpenza mongongo wana. Tango tokoyokaka Liloba na Nzambe, tosengeli kondima yango na ba 'Amen' mpe tobondela makasi mingi kino tango tokososola limbola na molimo na Liloba na Ye.

Na kosalaka bongo, soki tozwi kotondisama na Molimo Mosantu, molimo na biso ikokoma mokonzi, mpe tokoki kokoma na dimension na molimo wapi tokoki kosolola na Nzambe mokolo na mokolo. Lolenge oyo, tango molema izali kotosa mokonzi, molimo, mpenza mpenza mpe ekosala lokola moumbu, nde tokoloba ete 'molema na biso ezali kokende liboso'. Soki molema na biso ezali kokende liboso, tokofuluka na makambo nioso mpe tokozala nzoto malamu.

Soki tososoli malamu mosala na molema mpe tozongeli yango na lolenge Nzambe Alingaka, nde tokozwaka lisusu te mitungisi na Satana. Na lolenge oyo, tokoka kozongela elilingi tobungisa na Nzambe iye Adamu abungisaka likolo na bokwei na ye. Sik'awa molongo kati na molimo, molema, mpe nzoto mikotiama malamu, mpe tokoka kokoma bana na Nzambe na solo. Bongo, tokokoka ata kokende likolo na bisika na molimo na bomoi, iye izalaki etape na Adamu. Tokozwa kaka mpifo mpe nguya na kokonza likolo na makambu nioso kasi lisusu tokosepela sai na seko mpe bisengo na bokonzi na Lola, oyo ezali na etape likolo na Elanga na Edeni. Lokoka ilobama na 2 Bakolinti 5:17, "Bongo, soko moto akomi kati na Klistu akomi na bozalisi na sika; makambo na liboso malimwi, tala makambo na sika mayei. Tokokoma solo bikelamo na sika kati na Nkolo.

Molimo na Bomoi mpe Milimo Mikolisami

Tango totosi mibeko na Nzambe miye miyebisaka biso tosala makambo misusu te, elakisi ete tomitiki na misala na mosuni te mpe tomibateli kati na solo. Na lolenge oyo, tokomata na kkoma baton a molimo. Na lolenge tokoumela lokola bato na mosuni ba oyo bazli kosalela solo te, tokoki kozala na mingi na bakokoso to kozwa ba bokono, kasi wana tokomi bato na molimo, tokokende liboso na makambo nioso mpe tokozala nzoto malamu.

Lisusu, na lolenge tokolongola mabe ndenge Nzambe Asengi na biso kolongola makambo misusu, 'biloko na bison a mosuni' mpe makanisi na mosuni mikokweya, mpo ete tozala na molema itiama kati na solo. Na lolenge tokokanisa kaka kati na solo, tokoyoka mongongo na Molimo Mosantu malamu koleka. Soki solo tokomitika kati na Mibeko na Nzambe oyo Eyebisi bison a kobatela, kosala te, to kolongola makambo misusu, tokoki kondimama lokola baton a molimo mpo ete tokozala na solo te moko kati na biso. Lisusu, soki na mobimba tokokisi mibeko na

Nzambe iye ilobeli biso tosala makambo moko, tokokoma baton a molimo ekoka.

Lisusu, ezali na bokesene monene kati na bato oyo na molimo mpe lolenge Adamu ameseneke na kozala molimo na bomoi. Adamu atikalaka te koyeba likambo moko na mosuni na nzela na koleka na bato na nse na moi, nde akokaka te kotalama lokola ekelamu na molimo na mobimba. Akokaka te kososola eloko moko likolo na mawa, pasi, kufa, to bokabwani oyo esalemaka kati na mosuni. Yango elakisi, akokaki te, na loboko mosusu, kopesa matondi na solo to mpe bolingo. Ata soki Nzambe Alingaka ye mingi, akokaka te kososola malamu nini bolingo yango ezalaki. Azalaki kosepela makambo malamu koleka, kasi akokaka te koyeba ete azalaka kati na bisengo. Akokaka te kozala muana na solo na Nzambe oyo akokaka kokabola motema na ye na Nzambe. Kaka na tango moto aleki na nzela na makambo na mosuni mpe ayebi likolo na yango nde akoki kokoma moto na molimo na solo.

Na tango Adamu azalaka molimo na bomi, akutanaka na eloko moko ten a mosuni. Bongo, azalaka tango nioso na makoki na kondima mosuni mpe kobebisama. Molimo na Adamu ezalaki mobimba mpe na kokoka ten a lolenge esengeli, kasi molimo oyo ekoki kokufa. Yango tina abiangamaka ekelamo na bomoi, oyo elakisi molimo na bomoi. Bongo, lolenge kani molimo na bomoi akoki kondima momekano na Satana. Tika napesa bino lisese.

Toloba ete ezali na bana mibale na botosi mingi kati na libota. Moko na bango azikaka na mai na moto tango mosusu atikala kozika soko te. Mokolo moko, mama atalisi bango mbeki na mai kotoka mpe alobeli bango été basimba yango te. Bamesana kotosa mama na bango malamu mingi, nde bango mibale bakosimba yango te.

Kasi moko na bana asi ayebi ete esengeli kokeba na mai na moto kotoka kati na mbeki, nde akotosa na posa. Akososola mpe motema na mama mpona kolinga bango mpe komeka kobatela bango na kokebisaka bango/ Na bokeseni, muana mosusu oyo atikala kozala na wxperince wan ate akoki kokamua tango amoni Mbeki na mai kati na yango komatisa milinga. Akoka solo kososola posa na mama. Ezali na kaka nzela ete akoka kosimba Mbeki na mayi na moto kati na yango mona koyeba.

Ezalaki lolenge moko na molimo na bomoi Adamu. Ayokaka ete masumu mpe mabe mizali somo, kasi atikala kolekela yango te. Ezalaki na nzela moko te mpona ye kososola malamu nini masumu na mabe mizalaki. Na lolenge akutanaka na bikeseni na makambo te, suka suka andimaka momekano na Satana na boponi na ye moko mpe aliaka mbuma epekisama na kolia.

Na bokeseni na Adamu, Nzambe Alingaka bana ba solo, ba oyo sima na kokutana na mosuni, bazala na motema na molimo mpe ba oyo bakombongwana soko te makanisi na bango na sne na makambo na lolenge nini. Basosoli bokeseni kati na mosuni mpe molimo malamu mpenza. Bakutana na masumu mpe mabe, pasi, mpe mawa na mokili oyo, nde bayebi boni pasi, bosoto, mpe tin ate mosuni ezali. Lisusu, bayebi molimo malumu, oyo ezali bokeseni na mosuni. Bayebi ndenge nini ezali kitoko mpe malamu. Nde na kopona na bango moko, bakotikala lisusu kondima mosuni te. Yango bokeseni kati na molimo n bomoi mpe molimo oyo ekolisama.

Molimo na bomoi akotosa kaka na tango molimo ikolisama akotosa na motema na sima na kokutana na malamu mpe mabe.

Lisusu, bato oyo na molimo ba oyo balongola mabe na lolenge nioso mpe masumu bakozwa lipamboli na kokota na bokonzi na misati na Lola kati na bisika mingi na kobika na Lola mpe moto na molimo ekoka, mboka na Yelusaleme na Sika.

Kondima na Molimo Ezali Bolingo na Solo

Tango tokomi baton a molimo na kotambola na biso kati na kondima, tokokoka kosepela mpe koyoka esengo na dimension oyo ikesana mpenza. Tokozala na kimya na solo kati na motema. Tokosepelaka tango nioso, kobondela na kolemba te, mpe kopesa matondi na makambo nioso lolenge 1 Batesaloniki 5:16-18. Tososoli motema mpe mokano na Nzambe na kopesaka biso esengo na solo, nde tokoka kolinga Nzambe na mitema na solo mpe topesa matondi epai na Ye.

Toyoka ete Nzambe Azali bolingo, kasi yambo tokoma baton a molimo tokoki te mpenza koyeba bolingo wana. Kaka na sima na kososola mokano na Nzambe na nzela na boleki na bato na nse na moi, nde tokokoka kososola na mozindo ete Nzambe Azali mpenza bolingo mpe lolenge nini tosengeli kolinga Ye liboso likolo na nioso.

Na lolenge tokolongolaka mosuni kati na mitema na biso te, bolingo na matondi na biso mizali mpenza solo te. Ata soki tokoloba été tolingi Nzambe mpe tokopesa Ye matondi, tokoka kobongola lolenge na bomoi na biso tango makambo mazali lisusu na lifuti na biso te. Tolobaka été tozali kopesa matondi tango makambo mazali malamu, kasi tokobosana ngolu sima na tango moko tokobosa ngolu. Soki ezali na makambo na pasi liboso na biso, bisika na kokanisa ngolu tozwaka, tokozwa nkaka mpe ata nkanda. Tobosani matondi na biso mpe ngolu tozwaka.

Kasi matondi na baton a molimo miwutaka na mozindo na mitema na bango, bongo mimbongwanaka tea ta na sima na koleka na tango. Basosolaka mokano na Nzambe oyo azali kolekisa baton a nse na moi at aba pasi makasi miwutaka kati na yango, mpe solo bakopesaka matondi na solo kowuta na mitema na bango mibimba. Lisusu, balingaka solo mpe bakopesaka matondi na Nkolo Yesu oyo Amemaka ekulusu mpona biso mpe Molimo Mosantu oyo akambaka biso kati na solo. Bolingo mpe matondi na bango mako mbongwanaka te.

Na Nzela na Kobulisama

Bato babebisamaka na masumu, kasi sima na bango kondimela Yesu Christu mpe bazwi ngolu na lobiko bakoki kombongwana na kondima mpe nguya na Molimo Mosantu. Bakoki bongo nde komata likolo na etape na molimo na bomoi.

Na lolenge oyo solo te izali kobima na bango mpe batondisami na solo, bakoki kokoma baton a molimo na kokokisa kobulisama nkati na bango.

Na mbala mingi, tango bato bamonaka makambo malamu te kati na bango, lokola kokanisa mpe kosala mabe. Na lolenge oyo bakoka na kotalisa bizaleli mabe. Kasi ba oyo babulisama mpe bazali na lokuta moko te kati na bango, mpe na bongo mabe moko te to makanisi mabe moko te makobima kati na bango. Mpona kobanda bamonaka makambo mabe te, kasi ata soki bamoni yango makambo wana mabe mikosanganaka na makanisi to misala mabe te.

Tokoki kondimama lokola babulisami soki tokomisi motema na biso petwa oyo ezali na mbeba moko te to bosoto na kopikolaka mabe oyo itiama nan se na mitema na biso. Ba oyo bazali kaka na makanisi na molimo, ba oyo bamonaka, bayokaka, balobaka, mpe basalaka kaka kati na solo bazali bana na Nzambe na solo ba oyo bakenda na etape likolo na molimo.

Lolenge ikomama na 1 Yoane 5:18 ete,toyebi ete moto na moto oyo abotami na Nzambe akosalaka masumu te mpo ete Ye Akobatela ye mpe ye mabe akotiela ye loboko te," na mokili na molimo, nguya ezali kozanga lisumu. Kozala na lisumu te ezali kobulisama. Mpona yango tokokik kozongela mpifo oyo epesamaka na molimo na bomoi Adamu, mpe kobebisa mpe kokonza moyini zabolo na Satana na lolenge tokolongola masumu na biso.

Tango tokomi baton a molimo, zabolo akoka kutu kosimba

biso te, mpe soki tokomi baton a molimo ekoka mpe totongi bolamu na bolingo, tokokoka kosala misala na nguya na Molimo Mosantu. Tokokoka kokoma baton a molimo mpe na molimo ekoka na kokoma basantisami (1 Batesaloniki 5:23). Soki tokanisi likolo na Nzambe oyo Azali kokolisa bato mpe Akanga motema mpona bango mpona tango molayi mpo ete Azwa bana na solo, nde tokososoola ete likambo na motuya mingi izali kokoma moto na molimo mpe na molimo ekoka.

Molimo, Molema, Mpe Nzoto: Volume 1

Eteni
3

Bosongeli na Molimo

Bongo Ngai Nazali Moto na Mosuni to na Molimo?
Lolenge Nini Molimo mpe Molimo Ekoka Mikesana?

'Yesu azongisi monoko ete,
'solo solo nazali koloba na yo ete soko
moto akobotama na mai mpe na molimo te,
akoka koingela na bokonzi na Nzambe te.
Oyo ebotami na mosuni ezali mosuni,
mpe oyo ebotami na molimo ezali molimo.' "
(1 Yoane 3:5-6)

Chapitre 1
Molimo mpe Molimo Ekoka

Mpo ete milimo na bango mikufa, bato bazali na bosenza na lobiko. Bomoi na biso kati na Christu ezali etape na bokoli na molimo na sima na lisekwa na yango.

Molimo Ezali nini?

Kozongela Molimo

Lolenge na Bokoli na Molimo

Elanga na Mabele Malamu

Bilembo na Mosuni

Bilembo na Kozala na Molimo Ekoka

Mapamboli makopesamaka na Baton a Molimo mpe na Molimo Ekoka

Molimo na moto ikufaka likolo na lisumu na Adamu. Kobanda tango wana molema na bango ikomaka mokonzi. Bakobaki na kondimaka solo te mpe baposa mabe na bango. Na bongo bakoki te kozwa lobiko mpo été bakonzami na molema iye izali na nse na bokonzi na Satana, bakosalaka masumu mpe kokende na Lifelo. Yango tina bato nioso bazali na bosenga na kobika. Nzambe Azali koluka bana na solo ba oyo babikisama na nzela na koleka na bato na nse na moi, mingi, Azali koluka bato na molimo mpe na molimo ekoka.

Lolenge 1 Bakolinti 6:17 elobi ete, "Nde oyo asangani na Nkolo akoma na Ye molimo moko," Bana na Nzambe na solo bazali ba oyo basangana na Yesu Christu na molimo.

Na lolenge tondimeli Yesu Christu, toyei kobika kati na solo na lisungi na Molimo Mosantu. Soki tokobika kati na solo na lolenge na kokoka, elakisi été tokomi bato na molimo ba oyo bazali na motema na Nkolo. Yango ezali tango tozali molimo moko na Nkolo. Ata soki tozali molimo moko, molimo na NZambe mpe oyo na moto mikesana mpenza mpenza. Nzambe Azali molimo yango mpooko na nzoto moko na mosuni te kasi molimo na moto izali kati na nzoto na mosuni. Nzambe Azali na lolenge na molimo iye izali ya bisika na Lola na tango moto azali lolenge na molimo kati na nzoto na mosuni iye ikelama na putulu na mabele. Bongo solo ezali na bokeseni makasi kati na Nzambe Mokeli mpe bato ba oyo bazali bikelamo.

Molimo izali nini?

Bato mingi bakanisaka ete kombo 'molimo' ikokanaka na nkombo na 'molema'. Dictionaire Merriam- Webster elobi ete molimo ezali eloko anime to epusi mpona kopesa bomoi na biloko na mosuni. To eloko na supernatural to essence na yango. Kasi molimo na lolenge na komona na Nzambe ezali eloko oyo ikufaka te, ebebaka te to mpe kombongwana kasi ezali seko. Ezali bomoi mpe solo yango moko.

Soki tokoki komona eloko oyo ezali na lolenge na molimo kati na mokili oyo, ekozala wolo. Kongala embongwanaka te ata sima na koleka na tango, mpe ekufaka to mpe kombongwanaka te. Mpona tina oyo Nzambe akokanisaka kondima na bison a wolo petwa mpe lisusu Akotongaka ba ndako na Lola na wolo mpe mabanga misusu na talo.

Moto way ambo, Adamu, azwaka eteni na lolenge na lolenge original na Nzambe na tango Nzambe Apemaka pema na Ye na bomoi na zolo na ye. Akelamaka lokola molimo non parfait. Yango mpo ete ezalaki na nzela mpona ye kozonga na ekelamo na mosuni na lolenge na mabele. Azalaka kaka molimo ye moko te. Azalaka 'ekelamo na bomoi'.

Pona tina nini Nzambe Akelaka Adamu lokola molimo na bomoi? Ezali mpo ete Alingaka Adamu kokende likolo na dimension na molimo na bomoi na kokutana na mosuni na nzela na bokoli na baton a nse na moi mpe abima lokola moto na molimo ekoka. Yango etiamaka kaka na Adamu te, kasi ezali mpe solo na bakitani na ye nioso. Mpona tina yango Nzambe Abongisa Mobikisi Yesu, mpe Mosungi Molimo Mosantu ata liboso na bikeke.

Kozongela Molimo

Adamu abikaka kati na elanga na Edeni lokola molimo na bomoi mpona tango molayi mingi, kasi na bongo lisolo na ye na Nzambe ebebisamaka likolo na masumu na ye. Na tango wana, Satana abandaka kolona solo te kati na ye na nzela na molema na ye. Na nzela oyo, boyebi na molimo iye ipesamaka na Nzambe ibandaka na kolimwa mpe I remplacamaki na makkambo na mosuni yango ezali ezali solo te oyo epesamaka na Satana.

Na koleka na tango, makambo na mosuni mibutaka na kotondisama kati na moto.lokuta izingaka mpe ikibisaki nkona na bomoi kati na moto. Ezalaki lokola solo te ikangaki mpe ifinaka nkona na bomoi nde wana ikomaka mpenza lisusu na mosala te. Na lolenge nkona na bomoi ikomaki mpenza na mosala te, tokoloba ete molimo 'ikufa.' Na kolobaka ete molimo ikufa elakisi ete mwinda na Nzambe iye ikoki kokomisa nkona na bomoi na mosala ilimwaka. Sik'awa, nini tosengeli kosala mpona kosekwisa molimo ekufa?

Yambo tosengeli kobotama na mai mpe na Molimo.

Na lolenge tozali koyoka Liloba na Nzambe oyo ezali solo mpe tondimeli Yesu Christu lokola Mobikisi na biso moko, Nzambe Akopesa na biso likabo na Molimo Mosantu kati na motema na biso, Yesu Aloba na Yoane 3:5, "Solo solo nazali koloba na yo ete, soko moto akobotama na mai mpe na molimo te, akokoka koingela na bokonzi na Nzambe te." Na oyo tokoki komona ete tokoki kobikisama kaka soki tobotami na mai, yango ezali Liloba na Nzambe, mpe Molimo Mosantu.

Molimo Mosantu ayaka kati na mitema na biso mpe akomema nkona na bison a bomoi kozongela mosala. Yango ezali lisekwa na molimo na bison a kufa. Asungaka biso tolongola mosuni oyo ezali lokuta, kobebisa misala na solo te na molema mpe kopesa biso na boyebi na solo. Soki tokoyamba Molimo Mosantu te, molimo na biso oyo ekufaka ekoka te kosekwa to mpe tokoka te kososola limbola na molimo na Liloba na Nzambe. Liloba oyo tokoki kososola te ikoki te kolonama kati na mitema na biso mpe tokoka te kozwa kondima na molimo. Tokoki kozwa bososoli na molimo mpe kondima na motema kaka na lisungi na Molimo Mosantu. Elongo na oyo, tokoki kozwa makasi na kosalela Liloba na Nzambe mpe kobika na yango na tango tozali kobondela.Soki lisungi na Ye o nzela na mabondeli, ezali na makasi na kosalela Liloba te.

Mibale, tosengeli na kokoba na kobota molimo na nzela na Molimo.

Kurudishwa upya kwa Roho

Tango molimo na biso ekufa esekwi na koyamba Molimo Mosantu, tosengeli kokoba na kotondisaka molimo na bison a boyebi na solo. Yango ezali kobota molimo na nzela na Molimo. Na lolenge tozali kobondela makasi na lisungi na Molimo Mosantu mpona kobunda na masumu, mabe mpe lokuta kati na motema mikolongwa. Lisusu, na lolenge oyo tokondimaka boyebi na solo ikopesamaka na Molimo Mosantu lokola bolingo, bolamu, bosolo, bopolo, mpe limemia, tokokoba na kozwa solo na koleka mpe bolamu na motema. Na maloba mosusu, kondima solo na nzela na Molimo Mosantu ezali kobalusa etape izwamaka na tango bato babisamaka wuta bokwei na Adamu.

Kasi ezali na bato, ba oyo bayambaka Molimo Mosantu kasi babongolaka mitema na bango te. Balandaka posa na Molimo Mosantu te kasi kutu bazali kobika kati na masumu na kolandaka posa na mosuni na bango. Na ebandeli, bakomeka na kolongola masumu, kasi na tango moko boye bakokoma pio te moto te kati na kondima na bango mpe bakotika na kobiunda na masumu. Na tango bakotika kobunda na masumu, bakomipesa na kolinga mokili to bakosala masumu. Mitema na bango miye mikobaka na kopetolama mpe kokomisama pembe mikozonga lisusu na masumu. Ata soki toyambaki Molimo Mosantu, soki mitema na biso mikokobaka kati na solo te, nkona na bomoi kati na biso ikoka te kozwa makasi.

1 Batesaloniki 5:19 ikebisi bison a kolobaka ete, "Bozima Molimo te." Tokoki kokoma na bisika wapi tozali na nkombo ete tozali na bomoi, kasi na lolenge oyo tokobombongwanaka te sima kozwa Molimo Mosantu, tokufa (Emoniseli 3:1). Bongo, ata soki toyambaki Molimo Mosantu, Molimo Mosantu oyo

ikokoba na kozimama soki tokokoba na kobika kati na masumu mpe mabe.

Bongo, tosengeli kokoba na kobongola mitema na biso kino tango ikokoma na mobimba motema na solo. Na 1 Yoane 2:25 elobi ete,Oyo mpe ezali elaka etikelaki Ye bino, ete bomoi na seko." Iyo Nzambe Apesaka biso elaka. Kasi, ezali na condition ekangama na yango. Ezali ete tosengeli kosangana na Nkolo mpe Nzambe na kosalelaka Liloba na Nzambe toyokaka mpona Nzambe Apesa biso bomoi na seko. Tokoki te kozwa lobiko ata soki tolobi ete tondimeli Nkolo kaka soko tokobika kati na Nzambe mpe Nkolo.

Etape na Bokoli na Molimo

Yoane 3;6 elobi ete, "Oyo ebotami na mosuni ezali mosuni, mpe oyo ebotami na molimo ezali molimo." Lolenge ekomama, tokoki te kobota molimo soki tokoumela kati na mosuni.

Bongo, tango toyambi Molimo Mosantu mpe molimo na biso oyo ekufaka isekwisami, molimo esengeli kokoba na kokola. Nini soki bebe azali kokola malamu te to azali lisusu kokola te? Muana akokaka kobika bomoi esengeli te. Ezali lolenge moko na bomoi na molimo. Ban aba Nzambe ba oyo bazwa bomoi basengeli kokolisa kondima na bango mpe kokolisa milimo na bango.

Biblia elobeli biso ete etape kati na kondima na moto na moto ikesana (Baloma 12:3). 1 Yoane 2:12-14, elobeli biso likolo na bitape ebele kati na kondima, na kokabola yango kati na kondima na bana mike, bana, bilenge, mpe batata:

Bana, nazali kokomela bino mpo ete masumu na bino masili kolimbisama epai na bino mpona nkombo na Ye.

Batata nazali kokomela bino mpo ete bosili koyeba ye oyo azali longwa na ebandeli. Bilenge mibali nazali kokomela bino mpo ete bosili kolekela ye mabe.

Bana nasili kokomela bino mpo été bosili koyeba Tata. Batata nasili kokomela bino mpo été bosili koyeba ye oyo azali longwa na ebandeli. Bilenge mibali, nasili kokomela bino mpo été bozali makasi mpe Liloba na Nzambe eumeli kati na bino mpe bosili koleka ye mabe.

Na lolenge tokomibongola mpona kozala na motema na solo, Nzambe Akopesa biso kondima longwa na likolo. Ezali kondima na oyo tokoki kondima na mitema, oyo ezali kobota molimo na nzela na Molimo. Yango ezali oyo Molimo Mosantu esalaka: Molimo Mosantu andimelaka biso tobota molimo mpe Asungaka biso tomatisa kondima na biso. Molimo Mosantu Ayaka kati na mitema na biso mpe Atangisaka biso likolo na masumu, bosembo, mpe esambiseli (Yoane 16:7-8). Asungaka biso tondimela Yesu Christu.

Asungaka mpe biso tososola limbola na molimo ifandisama kati na Liloba na Nzambe mpe tondima yango na mitema na biso. Na nzela oyo, tokoka kozongela elilingi na Nzambe mpe kokoma muana na solo na Nzambe, ba oyo bazali baton a molimo mpe na molimo ekoka.

Mpona molimo na biso kokola, tosengeli naino kobebisa makanisi na bison a mosuni. Makanisi na mosuni masalemaka na tango lokuta kati na motema na biso mikobima na nzela na misala na solo te na molema. Ndakisa, soki bozali na mabe kati na motema mpe boyoki été moko moko atongaki bino, bokozala naino na mosala na solo te na molema. Bokozala na makanisi na mosuni na kokanisaka été moto yango azali na ezaleli mabe, mpe bokoyoka mabe mpe koyoka mabe ikoki na komata.

Na ngonga oyo ezali Satana nde akokambaka molema. Satana azali ye wana nde akotiaka makanisi mabe. Na nzela na misala na molema, solo te kati na motema oyo ezali makambo na mosuni, lokola motomoto, koyina, kokangela motema, mpe lolendo mikoningisama. Bisika na koluka na kososola basusu, bokoluka na kokutana na moto yango mbala moko.

Makambo mana na mosuni mitalisamaka mpe liboso mizali na makanisi na mosuni. Soki bosembo na miso na moto ye moko, makambo oyo amibongisela, to makambo oyo asosola kati na boyebi na ye mibimisami na nzela na misala na molema, mizali mpe makambo na mosuni. Toloba été moto azali na lolenge na ye na makanisi ezali malamu te na kokaba bondimi na ye na makambo mosusu. Bongo akokoba na kokanisa kaka ete makanisi na ye mazali malamu mpe akobuka kondima na basusu ata na situation bisika azali kokanisa ete makanisi ma ye mazali malamu mpe akobuka kimya na basusu na bisika oyo esengelaki na ye kotala etape kati na kondima mpe makambo misusu mpe lokola. Lisusu, toloba ete moto azali na makanisi na ye moko likolo na likambo moko mpe akondima ete ekozala pasi ete akokisa eloko na komonaka realite na likambo. Bongo yango mpe ekomonana mpe kozala makanisi na mosuni.

Ata siima na koyamba Molimo Mosantu na kondimelaka Nkolo Yesu, tokokoba na kozala makanisi na mosuni na lolenge oyo tozali na mosuni oyo naino tolongoli te.. Tozali na makanisi na molimo tango tosaleli boyebi na solo oyo ezali Liloba na Nzambe, kasi tozali na mmakanisi na mosuni tango mayebi na solo te isalelami. Molimo Mosantu Ekoki te kosangisa mayebi mana na solo na lolenge tozali na makanisi mana na mosuni.

Yango tina Baloma 8:5-8 etangi ete, "Pamba te ba oyo bazali bato na nzoto bakotia motema na makambo na nzoto; nde ba oyo bazali kati na molimo bakotia mitema na bango na makambo na Molimo. Kotia motema na makambo na nzooto ekoyeisa bobele kufa nde kotia motema na makambo na molimo Kotia motema na makambo na nzoto ekoyeisa bobele nse kufa, nde kotia motema na makambo na molimo ekoyeisa bomoi mpe kimya. Mpo ete motema motiami epai na nzoto ezali moyini na Nzambe. Pamba te eyebi kotosa mibeko na Nzambe te; ekoki mpe kosalaka boye te. Bango bazali kotia motema na makambo na nzoto bayebi kosepelisa Nzambe te."

Makomi oyo etalisi ete tokoki kokoma na etape na molimo kaka soki tokweisi makanisi na bison a mosuni. Ba oyo baumelaka na mosuni bakoki ten a kosunga na kozala na makanisi na mosuni, mpe lokola lifuti, bazali na makanisi, maloba, mpe bizaleli mizali kotelemela Nzambe.

Moko na ba ndakisa emonana na kotelemela Nzambe likolo na makanisi na bison a mosuni ezali likambo na Mokonzi Saulo na 1 Samuele 15. Nzambe Apesaki ye motindo na kobundisa Amaleki mpena kobebisa makambo nioso kuna. Ezalaki eteni na etumbu iye basengelaki na kozwa mpo ete batelemelaka Nzambe na lolenge makasi na kala.

Kasi Sima na Saulo kolonga etumba, amemaka bam pate malamu na koloba ete alingaka kopesa yango na Nzambe.

Akangaka mpe mokonzi na Amaleki bisika na koboma ye. Alingaka komilakisa na mosala na ye. Aboyaka kotosa mpo ete azalaka na makanisi na mosuni kowuta na moyimi mpe lofundu na ye. Lolenge miso ma ye mizipamaka na moyimi mpe lolendo, akobaka na kosalela makanisi maye na mosuni mpe suka suka akutanaka na kufa na somo.

Mama na likambo na makanisi na mosuni ezali ete tozali na solo te kati na mitema. Soki tozali kaka na mayebi na solo kati na mitema na biso, tokoka te kozala na makanisi na mosuni. Ba oyo bazali na makanisi na mosuni te bakozala sukasuka na makanisi na molimo kaka. Batosoka mongongo mpe kotambwisama na Molimo Mosantu, nde bakoka na kolinga,ma na Nzambe mpe komona misala ma ye.

Nde emonanaka été tosengeli nokinoki kolongola solo te mpe komitondisa na boyebi na solo, yango ezali Liloba na Nzambe. Komitondisa na mayebi na solo elakisi te été toyebi yango kaka na ba bongo na biso, kasi tosengeli kotondisa mpe kobongola mitema na biso na Liloba na Nzambe. Na lolenge moko tosengeli ko remplacer makanisi na biso moko na makanisi na molimo. Tango tokosangana na basusu to tomoni makambo songolo, tosengeli te kosambisa to mpe kokatela na lolenge tomoni, kasi tosengeli komeka komona yango na solo. Tosengeli kotala tango nioso soki tozala kosalela basusu na bolamu, bolingo, mpe bosolo na tango nioso, mpo été tokoka kobongwama. Na lolenge oyo tokoka kokola na molimo.

Kobalola na Mabele Malamu

Masese 4:23 elobi ete, "Batela motema na yo na mpiko nioso mpo ete makambo na bomoi ikoutaka kuna." Elobi ete moto na bomoi iye ekopesaka biso bomoi na seko ewutaka kati na motema. Tokoki kobuka ba mbuma kaka soki toloni nkona kati na elanga mpo ete makoka kobima, kobota fololo, mpe kobimisa mbuma. Mingi na lolenge moko, tokoki ko kobimisa ba mbuma na molimo kaka sima na nkona na Liloba na Nzambe ikweyi kati na elanga na mitema na biso.

Liloba na Nzambe iye ezali moto na bomoi, ezali na lolenge mibale na kosalelama tango ilonami kati na motema. Ipikolaka masumu mpe solo te kati na motema na biso, mpe isungaka biso tobota mbuma. Biblia ezalaka na mingi na Mibeko na Nzambe kasi mibeko mikweyana na mko na misato eye: Sala; Kosala te; Batela; mpe longola makambo misusu. Ndakisa Biblia elobeli biso tolongola moyimi mpe mabe na lolenge nioso. Lisusu, ba ndakisa na 'kosala te' ekoki kozala 'koyina te', to 'kosambisa te'. Lolenge tozali kotosa mibeko oyo, masumu makopikolama na mitema na biso. Elakisi ete Liloba na Nzambe eyaka kati na mitema na biso mpe ikobalola mitema na bison a mabele malamu.

Kasi ikozala na tin ate soki tokotika kak sima na kobalela elanga. Tosengeli kolona nkona na solo mpe bolamu na mabele tobaloli mpo ete tokoka na kobota mbuma libwa na Molimo Mosantu, mpe komema lipamboli na Baton a esengo mpe bolingo na molimo. Kobota mbuma ezali kotosa mibeko miye mizali kolobela bison a kobatela mpe kosala makambo na lolenge moko boye Na lolenge tokobatela mpe kosalela mibeko na Nzambe tokokoka na suka kobota ba mbuma.

Nzela na kokoma baton a molimo, lolenge italisami na eteni na liboso na 'Kokolisama', ezali lolenge moko na kobalola mabele na motema na biso. Tokobalola mabele mabaloma te na elanga na mabele kitoko na kolongolaka mabanga, mpe matiti mabe, na lolenge moko tosengeli kolongola misala nioso na musuni mpa biloko na mosuni na botosi na Liloba na Nzambe oyo elobeli bison a kosala te, mpe kolongola makambo misusu. Moto na moto azali na mabe na lolenge na ye. Bongo, soki tokopikola mosisa na mabe oyo tomoni makasi mingi mpona kolongola, oyo nioso mikangamaki kati na yango mikolongolama na ye elongo. Ndakisa, soki moto azali na etape monene na likunia, ba lolenge misusu na masumu mikangama na yango lokola koyina, kotonga, mpe bosolo te nioso mikopikolama na yango elongo.

Na tango topikolo moko na mosisa na kanda, ba mabe na lolenge misusu lokola koyoka nkaka mpe mabe mikopikolama mpe lokola. Soki tobondeli mpe tomeki na kolongola nkanda, Nzambe Akopesa biso ngolu mpe makasi mpe Molimo Mosantu Akosunga biso mpona kolongola yango. Na lolenge tokokoba na kosalela Liloba na solo kati na bomoi na bison a mokolo naa mokolo, tokotondisama na Molimo Mosantu, mpe makasi na mosuni ikolembisama. Toloba ete moto azwaka nkanda mbala zomi na mokolo, kasi na lolenge frequence ikokita na mbala libwa, sambo, mpe mbala mitano, suka suka ikolimwa. Na kosalaka bongo, soki tobongoli motema na bison a mabele malamu na kolongolaka masumu na makila nioso, motema oyo ekokoma motema na 'molimo'.

Na likolo na wana, tosengeli kolona Liloba na solo oyo elobelaka biso tosala mpe tobatela makambo misusu, lokola bolingo, kolimbisa, kosalela basusu, mpe kozatela mokolo na

Sabata. Awa, tobandi ten a komitondisa na solo kaka na tango tosilisi na kolongola nioso na solo te. Kolongola solo te nioso mpe na bisika kotia solo masengeli kosalema na tango moko. Tango tokomi kaka na solo kati na mitema na biso na nzela oyo, tokoki kondimam été tokomi bato na molimo.

Moko na makambo tosengeli kolongola mpona kokoma baton a molimo ezali mabe oyo izwami kati na lolenge na biso oyo tobotama na yango. Kokokanisa yango na elanga, mabe mana na lolenge na bison a mbotama mizali lokola lolenge na mabele. Mabe mana mipesamaka kowuta na baboti kino na bana na nzela na energie na bomoi tobengi 'chi.' Lisusu, soki tokutani na yango mpe tondimi makambo mabe na tango na bokoli na biso, lolenge na biso ikokoma lisusu mabe na koleka. Mabe kati na bizaleli na biso na mbotama mitalisamaka te na makambo nioso, mpe ezalaka pasi na kososola yango.

Bongo, ata sokintolongoli masumu mpe mabe makoki komonana na miso, kolongola mabe mazali na mozindo kati na biso ezali likambo moko na pete soko te. Mpona kosala yango, tosengeli kobondela makasi mpe kobakisa makasi mpona komona mpe kolongola yango.

Na makambo misusu, tozalaka na botiki kokola kati na bokoli na bison a molimona sima na biso kokoma na bisika moko. Ezali mpona lolenge na mabe kati na biso. Kolongola matiti mabe, tosengeli kopikola mango na mosisa, mpe kaka na makasa to mpe na bitape te. Na lolenge moko, tokoki kozala na motema na molimo kaka sima na biso kososola mpe kolongola mabe kati na bizaleli na biso, mpe lokola. Tango tokomi baton a molimo na lolenge oyo, motema na biso (conscience) ikokoma solo yango mpenza, mpe motema na biso ikotondisama kaka na solo. Yango elakisi ete motema na biso ikomi solo mpenza.

Bilembo na Mosuni

Baton a molimo bazalaka na mabe moko te kati na motema, mpe wuta batondisama na Molimo bazalaka tango nioso na esengo. Kasi yango ezali eloko moko ten a kokoka. Bazali kaka na bilembo na mosuni. Bilembo na mosuni mitalisamaka na bizaleli to mpe na lolenge na mbotama na moto na moto. Ndakisa, basusu bazali solo mpe sembo mpe polele, kasi bzanga bomoto mpe bopole. Basusu bakoki kotondisama na bolingo mpe kosepela na kokabela baninga, kasi bakoki kozala na emotion eleka to maloba na bizaleli na bango mikoki kozala makasi.

Mpo ete bilembo oyo mikotikalaka lokola bilembo na mosuni kati na bomoto na bango, mikobi na koningisa bango ata sima na bango kokota kati na molimo. Ezali lolenge moko na bilamba mizali na bilembo na kala. Langi na ebandeli na elamba ikoki te kozonga ata soki tosukoli yango makasi. Bilembo oyo na mosuni mikoki te kobengama mabe, kasi tosengeli na kolongola yango mpe kotondisama na ba mbuma libwa nioso na Molimo Mosantu, yango ekomema biso kati na molimo ekoka. Tokoki koloba été motema oyo ezali na mabe moko te ezali lokola mabele na elanga ebongisama malamu ezali 'molimo'. Tango nkona elonami kati na elanga na motema oyo ebongisama malamu mpe iboti mbuma kitoko na molimo nde bongo tokoka kobenga motema oyo motema na 'molimo ekoka'.

Tango mokonzi Dawidi akotaka na molimo, Nzambe Andimelaka ye momekano. Mokolo moko Dawidi atindaka Yoaba atanga bato. Elakisi ete batangaka ebele na bato oyo bakokaka kokende na etumba. Yoaba ayebaka ete ezalaka malamu ten a miso na Nzambe mpe amekaki kopekisa Dawidi na kosala yango. Kasi Dawi ayokaka te. Na bongo, nkanda na Nzambe ikitaka, mpe bato mingi bakufaki na likama.

Dawidi ayebakaa malamu mokano nan Nzambe, bongo lolenge kani akokaka kotika likambo na lolenge wana kosalema? Dawidi Abenganamaka na mokonzi Saulo mpona tango molayi mpe abundaka na bitumba ebele na Bikolo bapaya. Balandaka ye na muana na ye moko mpe bomoi na ye izalaka na likama. Kasi sima na tango molayi, lolenge nguya na ye na politiqui ikomaka makasi mpe ngya na ekolo na ye imataka, amilembisaka mpe makanisi na ye mipemisaka. Alingaka sasaipi kobeta tolo likolo na ebele na bato kati na mboka na ye.

Lolenge ikomama na Esode 30:12 ete, "Moto na moto aleki kati na batangi akopesa ndambo na sekele, na lolenge na sekele na esika esanto (sekele moko ekokani na gela ntuku mibale). Akopesa ndambo na sekele lokola makabo na Yawe." Nzambe Apesaka mitindo kosala botangi sima na Esode, kasi ezalaka mpona kobongisa bato wana. Moko na moko na bango asengelaki kopesa ndambo na ye moko epai na Nkolo, mpe ezalaki mpona kososolisa bango ete bomoi na moto nioso ezalaka mpona kobatelama na Yawe mpo ete bamikitisa. Kotanga bato ezalaki lisumu na yango moko te, ekokaki kosalema tango esengeli. Kasi Nzambe Alingaki komikitisa liboso na Yawe na kondimaka likambo ete nguya na kozala na bato ebele ewuta na Nzambe.

Kasi Dawidi atangaka bato ata soki Nzambe Apesaki motindo te. Yangon a kati ezalaki kotalisa motrema na ye oyo imitikaka na Nzambe te kasi na bato, mpona kozala na bato mingi elakisi ete azalaka na mapinga mingi mpe ekolo na ye izalaka makasi. Tango Dawidi asosolaka mbeba na ye, atubelaka mbala moko, kasi asi azalaka na nzela na mimekano makasi. Likama ikitelaka bana na Yisalele ete bato 70,000 bakufaka na mbala moko. Ya solo, bato mingi kokufa isalemaka kaka na lolendo na Dawidi te. Mokonzi akoki kotanga baton a tango nioso, mpe likanisi na ye izalaka kosumuka te. Bongo, na lolenge na bato tokoki te koloba ete asumukaki. Kasi na miso na Nzambe Akoka, Akokaki koloba ete Dawidi amitikaka mobimba na Nzambe te mpe Azalaka na lolendo.

Ezali na makambo maye makoki te komonana mabe na miso na bato, kasi na miso na Nzambe Akoka, ikoki komonana mabe. Yango izali bilembo na mosuni miye mitikalaka tango moto abulisami. Nzambe Andimaka momekano na lolenge oyo na mabele na Yisalele o nzela na Dawidi mpona kokomisa ye na kokoka na koleka, na kolongola bilembo iye na mosuni. Kasi mama na likambo mpona nini likama iyaka na mabele na Yisalele ezali mpo ete masumu na bato imatisaka nkanda na Nzambe. 2 Samuele 24:1 itangi ete, "Nkanda na Yawe epelaki epai na Yisalele mpe Alobisaki Dawidi mpona bango ete, 'kenda kotanga motuya na Yisalele mpe Yuda.'"

Bongo, kati na likama, bato malamu ba oyo bakokaka kobika bazwaka etumbu te. Ba oyo bakufaka bazalaka ba oyo basalaka masumu oyo indimamaka na Nzambe te.

Sima na etumbu, Nzambe atikaka Dawidi apesa mabonza

na masumu na etutelo na Alauna. Dawidi asalaki nini Nzambe alobelaki ye kosala. Azwaki bisika wana mpe abandaka kobongisa kotongama na Tempelo, nde tokoki komona ete azongelaka ngolu na Nzambe. Na nzela na momekano oyo, Dawidi Amikitisaki mingi koleka mpe ezalaki etape mpona ye kokenda na molimo ekoka.

Bilembo na kozala na Molimo Ekoka

Soki tokokisi etape na molimo ekoka, ekozala na bilembo, yango ilakisi ete tokobota mbuma mingi na molimo. Kasi elakisi te ete tokobota mbuma moko te kino tango tokokoma na etape na molimo ekoka. Bato na molimo bazalaka na nzela na kobimisa ba mbuma na bolingo na molimo, ba mbuma na Pole, mbuma libwa na Molimo Mosantu mpe baton a esengo. Wuta bazali na nzela na kobota, naino ba mbuma wana mikoli te. Moto na moto na molimo azali na etape ekesana na kobota mbuma na molimo.

Ndakisa, soki moto atosi mibeko na Nzambe iye ilobeli biso ete 'batela' mpe 'longola' makambo masusu, akokaki ten a kozala na koyina moko to mpe koyoka mabe na likambo nioso. Kasi ekozala na bokeseni na etape na kobimisa mbuma kati na baton a baton a molimo, kolandana na mibeko na Nzambe iye ilobeli biso ete 'tosala' makambo misusu. Ndakisa, Nzambe Ayebisi biso 'tolinga'. Mpe ezali na bisika wapi bozali lisusu koyina basusu te tango ezali na etape mosusu bisika wapi bokoki koningisa mitema na basusu na misala makasi. Lisusu, ezali na etape bisika wapi bokoki ata kopesa bomoi na bino mpona basusu. Tango misala na lolenge oyo mizali lisusu kombongwana mpe ekokisami, tokoka koloba ete bokolisi molimo ekoka.

Ezali na bokeseni kati na moko na moko na etape na kobimisa ba mbuma na Molimo Mosantu. Mpona oyo etali baton a molimo moto akoki kobimisa mbuma na lolenge moko na etape na % 50 na kotondisama na etape mpe mbuma mosusu na 70%. Moto akoki kotondisama na bolingo kasi kozanga komikanga, to kozala na bosembo monene, kasi azangi komikitisa.

Kasi mpona baton a molimo ekoka, bazali na mbuma nioso na Molimo Mosantu na kokoka mpe na etape na kotondisama. Molimo Mosantu aningisaka mpe Atambwisaka mitema na bango na 100%, nde bazali na Harmony na makambo nioso na kozangaka eloko moko te. Bazali na passion na kopela na motema mpona Nkolo na tango bazali na komikanga ekoka mpona kosala malamu na makambo nioso.

Bazalaka na limemia mpe bopolo lokola eteni na coton, kati bongo bazali na bokonzi mpe mpifo lokola kosi. Bazali na bolingo na koluka lifuti na basusu na makambo nioso mpe ata kokaba bomoi na bango mbeka mpona basusu, kasi bazali nan kaka moko te. Batosaka bosembo na Nzambe. Ata tango Nzambe Apesaka bango mitindo mpona kosala likambo ekoki ten a makoki na bato, bakotosaka kaka na 'Iyo' mpe 'Amen'.

Na libanda, misala na kotosa mpona baton a molimo mpe na molimo na kokoka mikoki komonana lokola lolenge moko, kasi na solo, mikesana. Baton a molimo batosaka mpo ete balingaka Nzambe bisika wapi baton a molimo ekoka bakotosaka mpo ete basosola mozindo na motema mpe posa na Nzambe Baton a molimo ekoka bakoma bana na Nzambe na solo ba oyo bazali na motema na Ye, na kokomaka na mobimba na etape na Christu na makambo nioso. Balukaka kobulisama na makambo nioso mpe kimya na moto nioso mpe bazali sembo na ndako mobimba na Nzambe.

Na 1 Batesaloniki 4:3 elobi ete, "Mokano na Nzambe ezali boye ete bobulisama ete botika makambo na pite." Mpe na 1 Batesaloniki 5:23 elobi ete, "Sasaipi tika ete Nzambe na kimya, ye moko Abulisa bino nye. Tika mpe ete bobatelama kati na molimo mpe na motema mpe na nzoto na kokabwana te mpe na ekweli te kino ekomonana Nkolo na biso Yesu Kristu."

Boyei na Nkolo na biso Yesu Christu elakisi ete akoya kozwa bana na ba Ye liboso na ba mbula Sambo na Monyoko Monene. Elakisi ete tosengeli na kokokisa etape na kobulisama ekoka mpe tomibatela mpenza mpona kokutana na Nkolo na biso liboso na yango kosalema. Soki tosi tokokisi molimo na kokoka, molema mpe nzoto na biso mikokoma na molimo mpe, na kozala na mbeba te, tokokoka koyamba Nkolo.

Mapamboli Mapesamaka na Bato na Molimo mpe na Molimo Ekoka

Mpona baton a molimo, milema na bango mikokendaka liboso, nde makambo nioso makokende liboso mpona bango mpe bazali nzoto makasi (3 Yoane 1:2). Balongola ata mabe na mozindo na motema na bango, nde bazali bana bulee na Nzambe na bosolo. Nde, bakoka kosepela mpifo na molimo lokola bana Na Pole.

Yambo bazali nzoto malamu mpe bakozwaka bokono moko te. Tango tokoti kati na molimo, Nzambe Akobatela bison a bokono mpe makama, mpe tokoki kosepela bomoi na nzoto malamu. Ata soki tokomi mibange, tokonuna to mpe kolemba na nzoto te, mpe tokozala lisusu na masusa moko te. Lisusu, soki tokoti na molimo ekoka, ata masusa mikonyolisama. Bakokoma ata bilenge na koleka mpe kozongela makasi na bango.

Tango Abalayama alekaki momekano na kobonza Isaka, akotaka na molimo ekoka; abotaka bana ata sima n ate kokoma na mbula 140. Elakisi ete azongisamaki elenge. Lisusu, Mose azalaka na limemia koleka mpe na bopolo koleka moto nioso nan se na moi, nde bongo asalaka makasi koleka mpona ba mbula 40 sima na ye kozwa kobengama na Nzambe na mbula 80. Ata na tango azalaka na 120, "mpe miso na ye ibebaki te, mpe nguya na nzoto na ye isilaki te." (Dutelenome 34:7).

Mibale, baton a Molimo bazali na mabe kati na motema te, nde moyini zabolo mpe Satana bakoki komema komekama moko te to mimekano likolo na bango.,1 Yoane 5:18 elobi ete, "Toyebi ete moto na moto asili kobotama na Nzambe akosalaka masumu te mpo ete ye oyo abotami na Nzambe Akobatela ye mpe oyo mabe akoyeba kotiela ye maboko te." Moyini zabolo mpe Satana akofunda moto na mosuni mpe akomema momekano mpe pasi epai na bango.

Na ebandeli Yobo azalaka esika wapi nai alongolaki mabe nioso kati na ye, nde tango Satana afundaka ye liboso na Nzambe, Nzambe Andimaka momekano isalema. Yobo asosolaka mabe na ye mpe atubelaka na tango azalaka kokenda na mimekano wana maye mamemanaka na kofunda na Satana. Kasi sima na ye kolongola ata mabe kati na motema na ye mpe akotaki na molimo, Satana akokaki lisusu kofunda Yobo te. Nde, Nzambe Apambolaki ye na mbala mibale na oyo azalka na yango.

Misato, baton a molimo bayokaka malamu mongongo mpe bazwaka kotambwisama na Molimo Mosantu, nde bakotambwisama na nzela na lipamboli na makambo nioso. Mpona bato na molimo, mitema na bango yango moko mimbongwana na bosolo, nde babikaka solo Liloba na Nzambe. Nioso bakosalaka izali na kokokana na solo. Bakozwaka kotindikama malamu na Molimo Mosantu mpe bakotosa yango. Lisusu, soki babondeli mpona likambo kosalema, bakokanga motema na kondima oyo embongwanaka te kino tango libondeli na bango ikoyanolama.

Soki tango nioso tokotosaka boye, Nzambe Akotambwisa biso mpe Akopesa biso bwanya mpe bososoli. Soki mpenza tokotika makambo nioso na maboko na Nzambe, Akobatela biso ata soki na bozangi ekenge tokei bisika oyo ekokanaki na mokano na ye te; ata soki ezali na libulu itiama liboso na biso, Akosala ete tokened kun ate mpe Akosala mpona bolamu na nioso.

Minei, moto na molimo bazwaka noki noki makambo nioso oyo basengaka; bakoki kaka kozwa eyano na likambo oyo bakanisi kati na mitema na bango. 1 Yoane 3:21-22 elobi ete, "Balingami soko mitema na biso mikokweisaka biso te, tozali na molende liboso na Nzambe; mpe soki tokolomba eloko nini, tokozwa yango epai na Ye mpo ete tokokokisa malako na Ye mpe tokosalaka makambo mazali malamu na miso na Ye." Lipamboli oyo ikokitela bango.

Ata ba oyo bazalaka na makoki na lolenge moko te to boyebi bakoki kozwa kaka mapamboli na molimo te kasi mpe mapamboli na biloko ebele kaka soki bakoti kati na molimo, mpo ete Nzambe Akobongisela bango nioso mpe Akotambwisa bango.

Tango toloni mpe tokosenga na kondima, tokozwa mapamboli esili kokakama, mpe koningana mpe kosopana (Luka 6:38), kasi soki tokoti na molimo, tokobuka mbala 30 kolekka, mpe sima na kokota na molimo elekka, tokobuka mbala60 to 100 koleka. Bato wana na molimo mpe molimo ekoka bakoki kozwa eloko nioso kaka na kokanisa kati na mitema.

Lipamboli epesamaka na baton a molimo ekoka ekoki ten a kolimbolama. Basepelaka kati na Nzambe, mpe Nzambe mpe Asepelaka kati na bango, mpe lolenge ikomama na Nzembo 37:4, "Omisepelisa kati na Yawe mpe Ye Akopesa yo mposa nioso na motema nay o," Nzambe na ngambo na Ye Apesaka bango nini nini bakolingaka, ezala misolo, lokumu, mpifo, to nzoto malamu.

Baton a lolenge oyo bakoyoka eloko moko ten a kozanga mpona bango moko, mpe bazali mpenza na eloko moko ten a kobondela mpona bango. Bongo, babondelaka tango nioso mpona bokonzi mpe bosembo na Nzambe mpe mpona Milimo oyo bayebi Nzambe te. Mabondeli na bango mazali kitoko mpe na solo malasi makasi liboso na Nzambe mpo ete mabondeli na bango mazali kitoko mpe mazanga mabe mpe mpona milimo. Bongo, Nzambe Asepelaka na bango mingi.

Na tango ba oyo bakoki na molimo ekoka bakolinga milimo mpe bakotondisa mabondeli makasi, bakoki mpe kotalisa nguya na nkamua lokola na Misala 1:8 elobi ete, "kasi wana ekosila Molimo Mosantu koya na likolo na bino, bokozwa nguya, mpe bokozala batatoli na ngai kati na Yelusaleme, na Yuda mobimba na Samalia kino suka na mokili mobimba." Lolenge ilimbolami, baton a molimo mpe na molimo ekoka balingaka Nzambe koleka nioso mpe basepelisaka Nzambe, mpe bazwaka mapamboli nioso ilakama kati na Biblia.

Chapitre 2

Mokano na Nzambe na Ebandeli

Nzambe Alingaka te Adamu abika seko na koyebaka esengo na solo te, kosepela, matondi, mpe bolingo. Mpona ntina oyo atiaka nzete na boyebi mabe na malamu mpo ete Adamu akoka na kolekela makambo nioso na mosuni.

Tina Nini Nzambe Akelaka Moto lokola Molimo?

Motuya na Makoki na Kopona mpe kobatela na bongo

Tina na Kokelama na Bato

Nzambe Alingi Kozwa Nkembo na Bana na Solo

Kurudishwa upya kwa Roho

Bokoli na baton a nse na moi ezali nzela wapi baton a mosuni bakombongwanaka na baton a molimo. Soki tokososola likambo oyo te mpe tokokende kaka na egelesia, ezali na ntina te kati na yango. Ezali na bato mingi oyo bakendaka na egelesia, ezali na tina moko te kati na yango. Ezali na bato mingi bakokendeke egelesia kasi babotama sika ten a Molimo Mosantu, mpe bongo bazali na assurance moko ten a lobiko. Tina na kobika bomoi kati na bondimi na Christu ezali kaka te kozua lobiko, kasi ezali mpe kozongela elilingi na Nzambe mpe kokabola bolingo na biso elongo na Nzambe mpe kopesa Ye esengo seko lokola ban aba ye ya solo.

Nini ezalaka likanisi na Nzambe nakokela Adamu lokola molimo na bomoi mpe kokamba boleki na baton a nse na mokili oyo? Genese 2:7-8 elobi ete, "Na tango yango Yawe Nzambe Asalaki moto na mputulu na mokili, mpe Apemaki kati na zolo na ye mpema na bomoi, mpe moto akomaki molimo na bomoi. Yawe Nzambe akonaki elanga epai na ebimelo nan tango, kati na Edene, mpe kuna Atiaka moto oyo ye asalaki."

197

Nzambe akelaka ba likolo mpe mokili mingi na Liloba na Ye. Kasi mpona moto, Asalaki ye na maboko na Ye moko. Lisusu, mapinga na Lola mpe banje na Lola bakelamaka bango nioso milimo. Kasi, ata soki eyebanaka mpe ete moto akobika na suka lokola molimo na Lola yango esalamaki mbala moko te. Nini ezali tina na Nzambe kozwa nzela na pasi boye na kokela moto na putulu na mabele? Pona nini Asalaka bango kaka te lokola milimo na ebandeli? Awa efandisami mokano na motuya na Nzambe.

Pona Nini Nzambe Akelaka Bato lokola Milimo?

Soki Nzambe Akelaka baton a mputulu na mokili te kasi lokola milimo, bato balingaka kolekela eleko moko ten a mosuni. Soki bakelamaka kaka lokola milimo, balingaka kotosa Liloba na Nzambe mpe balingaka kolia mbuma na nzete na boyebi malamu mpe mabe soko moke te. Lolenge na mabele ekoki kombongwana kolandana na nini okotia kati na yango. Tina oyo Adamu akokaki kokweya ata soki azalaki kati na espace na molimo, ezali mpo ete akelamaka na mputulu na mokili oyo. Kasi elakisi te ete akweyaka kobanda na ebandeli.

Elanga na Edeni ezali espace na molimo oyo etondisama na energie na Nzambe, mpe yango ekokaki te mpona Satana alona nkona na mosuni kati na motema na Adamu. Kasi mpo ete Nzambe Apesaki na Adamu makoki na kopona, akokaka kondima mosuni soki azalaka na mposa mpe alingaki kosala yango. Ata soki azalaki molimo na bomoi, mosuni ekokotela ye soki andimaka mosuni na posa na ye moko. Sima na koleka na tango molayi, afungolaka motema na ye na mimekano na Satana mpe andimaka mosuni.

Solo, tina oyo Nzambe Apesaka moto makoki na kopona na ebandeli ezalaka mpona koleka na baton a nse na moi. Soki Nzambe Apesaka makoki na kopona epai na Adamu te, Adamu Alingaka kondima eloko moko na mosuni te. Yango mpe elakisi ete koleka na baton a nse na moi elingaka mpe kosalema te. Kati na mokano na Nzambe mpona bato, boleki na bato kati na mokili oyo esengelaka kosalema, lokola kati na boyebi na Ye na nioso, Ye Akelaka Adamu lokola ekelamo na molimo te.

Motuya na Kopona Mpe Kobatela kati na Makanisi

Genese 2:17 etalisi ete, "...nde mbuma na nzete na boyebi na malamu mpe mabe okoki kolia te. Pamba te mokolo okolia yango okokufa solo." Lolenge elimbolama, ezalaki na mozindo kati na mokano na Nzambe kokela Adamu na mputulu na mokili mpe kopesa ye kopona. Ezalaki mpona koleka na moto nan se na moi. Bato bakoki kokoma bana na solo na Nzambe kaka sima na koleka na nzela na mokili oyo.

Moko na likambo oyo lisumu ekotaka kati na Adamu ezalaka mo ete azalaki na makoki na kopona, kasi tina mosusu ezalaki mpo ete abatelaka Liloba na Nzambe kati na bongo na ye te. Mpona kobatela Liloba na Nzambe ezali kokoma yango kati na motema mpe kosalela yango na kombongwana te.

Bato misusu bakobaka na kosalaka mbeba moko na tango basusu basalaka mabe na lolenge wana mbala mibale te. Eyaka na bokeseni na kobatele likambo kati na bongo to kobatela te. Lisumu eyaka kati na Asamu mpo ete ayebaka te motuya na kobatela Liloba na Nzambe kati na bongo na ye. Na loboko mosusu, tokoki kozongela lolenge na molimo na kobatelaka Liloba na Nzambe kati na ba bongo na biso.

Mpona ba oyo milimo na bango mikufaka likolo na lisumu na ebandeli, soki bandimeli Yesu Christu mpe bayambi Molimo Mosantu, milimo na bango iye ikufaka ikosekwa. Kobanda tango wana, na lolenge bakobatelaka Liloba na Nzambe kati na ba bongo na bango mpe bakosalela yango na bomoi na bango, bakobanda kobota molimo na nzela na Molimo. Bakokoka nokinoki kokokisa bokoli na molimo. Bongo, kobatela Liloba na Nzambe mpe kosalela yango na kombongwana te esalaka mosala monene na kozongela molimo.

Tina na Bokeli na Bato

Ezali na bikelamo mingi na molimo kuna na Lola, lokola banje baye batosaka Nzambe tango nioso. Kasi libanda na moke mingi kati na bango, bazalaka na bomoto te. Bazalaka na makoki na kopona ten a oyo bakoka kokabola bolingo na bango. Yango tina Nzambe Akelaka moto nay ambo Adamu, lokola ekelamo na oyo Akoka kokabola bolingo na Ye.

Kaka mpona ngonga moke, kanisa nanu Nzambe kosepela na tango na kosalaka Adamu moto way ambo. Kosalaka bibebu na Adamu, Nzambe Alingaka ye asanjola Nzambe; kosalaka matoyi ma ye, aAlingaka ye ayoka mongongo na Nzambe mpe kotosa yango; kosala miso maye, alingaki ye komona mpe koyoka kitoko na makambo nioso Ye Akelaka mpe apesa nkembo epai na Nzambe. Tina na Nzambe kokela bato ezalaki mpo ete Azwa nkembo na masanjoli kowuta na bango mpe akabola bolingo elongo na bango. Alingaka bana na oyo Akokaka kokabola na bango kitoko na makambo nioso kati na univer mpe na Lola. Alingaka kosepela esengo elongo na bango mpona libela.

Kai na buku na emoniseli, tomoni bana ba Nzambe ba oyo babikisami kosanjola mpe kongumba liboso na Ngwende na Nzambe mpona libela. Tango bakokoma na Lola ekozala mpenza kitoko mpe esengo oyo bango bakoki kosepela te kasi kopesa nkembo epai na Nzambe mpe masanjoli kowuta na mizindo na mitema na bango mpona tina ete mokano na Nzambe izali mpenza mozindo mpe na kokamwisa.

Bato bakelamaka lokola milimo na bomoi na bomoi kasi bakomaka baton a mosuni, kasi soki bakomi lisusu bato na molimo sima na bango kolekela sai, kanda, mpe mawa, bongo bakoki kokoma bana na Nzambe na solo ba oyo bazali kopesa bolingo, matondi, mpe nkembo epai na Nzambe kowuta na mitema na bango mibimba.

Tango Adamu azalaka kobika kati na Elanga na Edeni, akokaki te kondimama lokola muana na solo na Nzambe.

Nzambe Alakisaka ye kaka bolamu mpe solo, nde bongo ayebaka te masumu na mabe mazalaka nini. Azalaka na likanisi te likolo na esengo mpe pasi. Elanga na Edeni ezali espace na molimo, mpe ezali na kobebisama to kufa kun ate. Mpona tina oyo Adamu ayebaka te tina na kufa. Ata soki abikaka na bofuluki mingi mpe ebele, akokaka te koyoka esengo na solo, sai, to kopesa matondi. Mpo ete atikala koyoka mawa to bozangi na esengo moko te, akokaki mpenza koyoka esengo na solo te. Ayyebaka te nini koyina ezalaka, mpe ayebaka te bolingo na solo ezalaka nini. Nzambe Alingaka Adamu abika seko ten a koyebaka likolo na kosepela na solo te, esengo, matondi, mpe bolingo. Yango tina Atiaka nzete na boyebi na malamu mpe mabe kati na Elanga na Edeni, mpo ete Adamu akoka kokutana na mosuni.

Tango ba oyo bakutana na mikili na mosuni bakomi lisusu bana na Nzambe, basosoli malamu boni malamu molimo ezali mpe boni motuya solo ezali. Bakoki sik'oyo kopesa matondi na solo epai na Nzambe mpona kopesa bango likabo na bomoi na seko. Tango tososoli motema oyo na Nzambe, tokoka te kotuna motuna likolo na tina na Nzambe kotia nzete na boyebi malamu mpe mabe mpe kosala ete bato banyokwama likolo na yango. Kasi kutu, tokopesa matondi mpe nkembo epai na Nzambe mpona kopesa Muana na Ye na likinda Yesu mpona kobikisa bato.

Nzambe Alingi Kozwa Nkembo epai na Bana na Solo

Nzambe Azali kokolisa bato kaka mpona kozwa bana na solo te kasi mpe kozwa nkembo na nzela na bango. Yisaya 43:7 elobi ete, "moto na moto oyo abiangami na nkombo na ngai oyo Nasali mpona nkembo na Ngai; ye oyo Natongi ye, ee Nasali ye.." Lisusu, 1 Bakolinti 10:31 elobi ete, "Boye soko bokoliaka, soko bokomelaka, soko bokosala nini, bosala nioso mpona nkembo na nzambe."

Nzambe Azali Nzambe na bolingo mpe bosembo. Abongisa kaka Lola mpe bomoi na seko mpona biso te kasi Apesa Muana na Ye na likinda mpona kobikisa biso. Nzambe Akoki na kozwa nkembo kaka mpona likambo oyo kaka. Kasi oyo Nzambe Alingaki mpenza ezalllaki te kaka kozwa nkembo. Mama na likambo na Nzambe kolinga kozwa nkembo ezali kozongisela bolingo na bato oyo bapesaki nkembo na Nzambe. Yoane 13:32 elobi ete, "Soki Nzambe Akumisami kati na Ye, Nzambe Akokumisa Ye kati na Ye moko, mpe Akokumisa Ye nokinoki."

Tango Nzambe Ayambaka nkembo na nzela na biso, Apesaka biso mapamboli eleka kati na mokili oyo, mpe akopesa biso nkembo na seko na bokonzi na Lola mpe lokola. 1 Bakolinti 15:41 elobi ete, "Nkembo na moi ezali na motindo moko, mpe nkembo na sanza na motindo mosusu, mpe nkembo na minzoto na motindo mosusu; mpo ete monzoto na monzoto na likolo ikeseni na nkembo."

Elobeli biso likolo na bokeseni na bisika na koingela mpe nkembo moko na moko na biso ba oyo tokobikisama tokosepela na bokonzi na Lola. Bisika na koingela na Lola mpe nkembo na kopesama ikokatelama kolandana na lolenge nini tolongoli masumu mpona kozala na mitema petwa mpe bulee mpe lolenge nini tozali kosalela bokonzi na Lola. Soki mapesami, bakoki te kobongolama.

Nzambe Akelaka bato mpona kozwa bana na soloba oyo bazali na molimo. Mokano na Nzambe na ebandeli ezali ete baton a kopona na bango moko bazwa mokano na kolongola mosuni mpe molema oyo efandisama kati na solo te mpe kobongola yango na molimo mpe molimo ekoka. Posa oyo na ebandeli na Nzambe na kokela mpe kolekisa bato na nse na moi ikokokisama na nzela na bato oyo bakomi baton a molimo mpe molimo ekoka.

Bato boni bokanisi ete bazali kobika lelo bomoi oyo ikoki na miso na Nzambe mpona kokela na Ye na Bato? Soki solo tokossossola tina na Nzambe kokela bato, tokokaki solo kozongela elilingi na Nzambe oyo tobungisa likolo na lisumu na Adamu. Tolingaki komona, koyoka, mpe koloba kaka kati na solo. Mpe makanisi na biso nioso mpe misala mikokaki kozala bulee mpe na kokoka. Oyo ezali nzela na kokoma bana na solo na Nzambe ba oyo bazali kopesa esengo na koleka esengo oyo Nzambe Azalaka na yango sima na kokela moto way ambo Adamu. Bana na solo na Nzambe na bakosepela nkembo na Lola oyo ekoki te lolenge oyo a ta komeka kokokana te na nkembo oyo molimo na bomoi Adamu, asepelaka kati na Elanga na Edeni!

Chapitre 3
Bato na Solo na Nzambe

Nzambe Akelaka moto na elilingi na Ye moko. Mokano monene na Nzambe ezali ete tozongela elilingi ebunga na Nzambe mpe tokota kati na boNzambe na Nzambe.

Mosala Nioso na Moto

Nzambe Atambolaki na Enoka

Moninga na Nzambe Abalayama

Mose Alingaka Bato Na ye Koleka Bomoi na Ye Moko.

Ntoma Polo Amonanaka Lokola Nzambe

Abengaki Bango ba nzambe

Soki tokosalela Liloba na Nzambe, tokoki kozongela motema na molimo iye itondisama na boyebi na solo, lokola oyo Adamu azalaka na yango, na kozalaka molimo na bomoi liboso na ye kosumuka. Mosala nioso na bato ezali kozongela elilingi na Nzambe babungisaka tango Adamu asumukaka mpe kokota kati na bo Nzambe na Nzambe. Kati na Biblia, tokoki komona ete ba oyo bayambaki Liloba na Nzambe mpe bandimelaka yango, ba oyo basololaka makambo na sekele na Nzambe, mpe batalisaka nguya na Nzambe mpona kolakisa Nzambe na bomoi, bamonanaka mpenza baton a lokuu ete ata bakonzi bakokaki kongumbamela bango. Ezali mpo ete bazalaka bana na solo na nzambe oyo Aleki Likolo (Nzembo 82:6)

Mokonzi Nabukadanesala na Babele alotaka ndoto mpe ezangisaka ye kimya. Abengaka baton a soloka mpe bakaladi mpona koyebisa ye ndoto na ye mpe kolimbola yango na kolobela bango nini alotaki te. Ekokaki kosalema ten a nguya na moto moko te kasi kaka na Nzambe oy Abikaka na nzoto na bato te.

Sik'awa Daniele oyo Azalaka moto na Nzambe, asengaki na mokonzi apesa ye tango mpona kolimbolela ye ndoto na ye.

Nzambe Atalisaka Daniele makambo na sekele kati nab utu na emoniseli. Daniele akendaka liboso na mokonzi mpe ayebisaki ye ndoto na ye mpe alimbolelaki ye yango. Bongo mokonzi Nabukadanesala akitaki na elongi nan se mpe apesaki lokumu na Daniele, mpe apesaki mitindo na kopesa na ye makabo mpe kotumbela ye malasi, mpe lisusu apesaka nkembo Nzambe.

Mosala Nioso na Moto

Mokonzi Salomo asepelaka nkita koleka mpe koyebana koleka moto nioso. Kolandana na bokonzi na kosangana oyo tata na ye, Dawidi, atiaka, nguya na mboka na ye ikolaka makasi mpe bikolo mingi na zinga zinga na ye mifutaka mpako. Ekolo ezalaki na likolo koleka na nkembo na yango na tango na bokonzi na ye (1 Bakonzi 10).

Kasi na koleka na tango, abosanaki ngolu na Nzambe. Akanisaka ete makambo nioso mazalaki kosalema na makasi na ye moko. Abwakisaki Liloba na Nzambe mpe abukaki motindo na Nzambe mpona kobala basin a bapaya te. Azwaka basi mingi na bapaya na kokende na suma na ba mbula na ye. Lisusu atiaka bisika likolo lokola basin a bapaya balingelaki ye kosala, mpe ye moko angumbamelaka bikeko.

Nzambe Akebisaka ye na mbala mibale ete alanda banzambe na bapaya te kasi salomo Atosaki te. Suka suka, kanda na Nzambe ekitelaki bango na mabota elandi mpe Yisalele ekabolamaka na bokonzi mibale. Akokaki kozwa eloko nioso alingaki kozwa, kasi na mikolo ma ye na suka atatolaki été, 'Bisalasala na mpamba, bisalasala na mpamba, nioso ezali mpamba (Mosakoli 1 :2).

Asosolaka ete makambo nioso na mokili oyo mazali mpamba, mpe asukisaka ete, "Toyoka nsuka na likambo mobimba: Tosa Nzambe mpe batela Mibeko na Ye: yango ezali mosala na bato nioso" (Mosakoli 12:13). Alobi ete mosala nioso na moto ezali kobanga Nzambe mpe kobatela Mibeko na Ye. Yango elakisi nini? Kobanga Nzambe ezali koyina mabe (Mosakoli 8:13). Ba oyo balingaka Nzambe bakolongola mabe mpe bakobatela mibeko ma Ye, mpe na lolenge oyo bakokokisa mosala nioso na bato. Tokoki kobengama baton a kokokisama tango tokomisi mitema na biso lolenge na Nkolo mpenza mpe tozongeli elilingi na Nzambe. Nde, sik'awa tika tozinda kati na ba ndakisa na batata na kondima mpe baton a kondima na solo.

Nzambe Atambolaka na Enoki

Nzambe Atambolaka na Enoki mpona ba mbula nkama misato mpe Akamataka ye na bomoi. Lifuti na masumu izali kufa, mpe likambo ete Enoki akamatamaki na Lola na komona kufa na ye te ezali elembo ete Nzambe Andimaka ye na lisumu te. Akolisaka motema petwa mpe na mbeba te iye ikokanaka na motema na Nzambe. Yango tina Satana akokaka kofunda ye na eloko moko te na tango akamatamaki na bomoi.

Genese 5:21-24 etalisi yango lokola: "Ezalaki Enoka na mbula ntuku motoba na mitano abotaki Metusela. Enoka atambolaki na Nzambe elongo mbula mokama misato na nsima na kobotama na Metusela, mpe abotaki bana babali mpe bana basi. Bongo mikolo nioso na Enoka mizalaki nkama misato na ntuku motoba na mitano. Enoka atambolaki na Nzambe elongo

mpe azalaki te mpo ete Nzambe Akamataki ye."
'Kotambola na Nzambe elakisi ete Nzambe Azalaki na moto yango na tango nioso. Enoki abikaki na mokano na Nzambe mpona mbula mokama na misato. Nzambe Azalaki na ye bisika nioso akendaka.

Nzambe Azali pole, bolamu, mpe bolingo yango mpenza. Kotambola na Nzambe na lolenge wana, tosengeli te kozala na molili moko kati na mitema na biso, mpe tosengeli kotondisama na bolamu mpe bolingo. Enoka abikaka na mokili na masumu, kasi amibatelaka bulee. Asakolaka mpe Liloba na Nzambe na mokili. Yuda 1:14 elobi ete, "Ee, moto na nsambo nsima na Adama, ye Enoka, asalakolaki liboso mpona bango ete, Nkolo Asili koya na bibele na Babulamu na Ye." Lolenge ekomama atikaka na bato bayeba likolo na bozongi na Nkolo mpe Esambiselo.

Biblia elobi eloko moko te likolo na misala minene na Enoka to ete asalaka makambo minene mpona Nzambe. Kasi Nzambe Alingaka Ye mingi mpo ete apesaka lokumu mingi mpe abikaka bomoi esantisama mpe akimaka mabe. Yango tina oyo Nzambe Azwaka ye na mbula moke'. Baton a tango wana babikaka likolo na ba mbula 900 mpe azalaka na mbula 365 na tango akamatamaki. Azalaki elenge mobali na nzoto makasi.

Baebele 11:5 etangi ete, "Mpona kondima Enoka Akamatamaki ete amona kufa, azwamaki te mpo ete Nzambe Atombolaki ye. Mpo ete liboso naino atomwamaki te azwaki litatoli ete asepelisaki Nzambe."

Ata lelo, Nzambe Alingi biso tobika bomoi epetolama mpe na

bonzambe na kozalaka na mitema petwa mpe kitoko na kozalaka na mbindo moko ten a mokili mpo ete Akoka kotambola na biso tango nioso.

Moninga na Nzambe Abalayama

Nzambe Alingaka ete bato bayeba likolo na muana na Nzambe na solo na nzela na Abalayama, 'tata na bandimela'. Moninga ezali moto oyo bokoki kotiela motema mpe kokabola sekele elengo. Y solo , ezalaka na tango na kobingisama kino tango Abalayama akokaki kotiela Nzambe motema na mobimba. Lolenge nini Abalayama andimamaka lokola mining na Nzambe?

Abalayama atosaka kaka na 'Iyo' mpe 'Amen'. Tango azwaka nay ambo kobengama na Nzambe mpona kolongwa mboka na ye, atosaka kaka na koyeba bisika azali kokende te.lisusu, Abalayama alukaka lifuti na basusu mpe alukaka kimya. Azalaka kobika na muana nkasi na ye Lota mpe basengelaki kokabwana, apesaka na muana nkasi na ye apona mabele. Azalaka na makoki na kopona lokola tata leki na ye. Azalaka na makoki na kopona liboso lokola tata leki, kasi amikitisaka.

Abalayama alobaka na Genese 13:9, "Mokili mobimba ezali liboso nay o te? Kabwana na ngai. Soko ookokende na loboko na mwasi, ngai nakokende na loboko na mobali; soko yo okokenda na loboko na mobali ngai nakokenda na loboko na mwasi."

Mpo ete Abalayama azalaka na motema na lolenge oyo, Nzambe Apesaka ye lisusu elaka na lipamboli. Na Genese 13:15-

211

16, Nzambe Alakaka ete, "...Mpo ete mokili oyo ozali komona, nakopesa yango na yo mpe na bana na yo seko.Mpo Nakozalisa mabota nay o lokola mputulu na mokili, boye ete soko boye ete soko moto akoki kotanga mputulu na mokili, nde mabota nay o makotangama."

Mokolo moko, mapinga masangana na bakonzi ebele babundisaki Sodoma na Gomora bisika muana nkasi na Abalayama, Lota, azalaka kobika mpe bazwaka bato lokola lifuti na etumba. Abalayama abimisaki baton a ye na etumba. Ba oyo babotamaki na ndako na ye, nkama misato na zomi na mwambe, mpe alandaka bango mosika koleka Dani. Abotolaki biloko nioso, mpe lisusu amemaka ndeko na ye Lota na biloko na ye, mpe lisusu basi, mpe bato.

Awa , mokonzi na Sodome alingaka kopesa biloko epai na Abalayama mpona kopesa ye matondi, Abalayama azongisaki ete, "Nakokamata eloko ten a oyo ezali nay o, ata ndambo na busi te, soko nsinga na sapato te, na ntina ete yo okoloba te ete, ngai nayeisi Abalayama mozui'" (Genese 14:23). Ezalaki mabe te kozwa eloko epai na mokonzi, kasi aboyaki bosenga na mokonzi mpona kolakisa kaka ete biloko na ye eutaki kaka na Nzambe. Alukaka kaka nkembo na Nzambe na motema na petwa ezaga moyimi, mpe Nzambe Apambolaka ye mingi.

Tango Nzambe Apesaka ye motindo na kobonzela Ye muana na ye Izaka lokola mbeka na kotumba, atosaka mbala moko, mpo ete andimaka Nzambe oyo Akokaki kosekwisa bawa. Na bongo, Nzambe Atiaka ye tata na bandimela, nakolobaka ete, "Nakopambola yo solo mpe nakofulisa yo lokola minzoto na likolo mpe lokola zelo na libongo na mai. Bana ba yo bakobotola bikuke na bayini na bango. Mabota nioso na mokili bakopambolama mpona bana na yo, mpo ete otosi monoko na Ngai" (Genese 22:17-18). Lisusu, Nzambe Alakaki ye ete Muana na Nzambe, Yesu, oyo akobikisa bato, Akobotama na bakoko na ye.

Yoane 15:13 elobi ete, "Moto te azali na bolingo eleki oyo ete moto asopa bomoi na ye mpona baninga na ye." Abalayama alikyaki kobonza muana na ye se moko IZaka, oyo azalaka kutu motuya koleka bomoi na ye moko, bongo kotalisa bolingo na lolenge oyo mpona Nzambe. Nzambe Atiaka Abalayama oyo lokola ndakisa mpona boleki na baton a nse na moi na kobenga yemoninga na Nzambe mpona kondima na ye monene mpe bolingo mpona Nzambe.

Nzambe Azali na nguya nioso nde bongo Akoki kosala eloko nioso mpe Akoki kopesa biso eloko nioso. Kasi Apesaka bana na Ye na lolenge oyo bambongwani kati na kondima na boleki na baton a nse na moi, mpo ete bakoka koyoka bolingo na Nzambe na matondi mpona mapamboli na Ye.

Mose Alingaka Bato Ba Ye Koleka Bomoi na Ye Moko

Tango Mose azalaka muana mokonzi na Ejipito, abomaka moEjipito mpona kosunga moto na ye moko, mpe asengelaki na kokima ndako na mokonzi Falo. Kobanda wana abikaka kati na lisobe lokola mobateli mpate kokamba etonga mpona ba mbule

213

ntuku minei. Mose azalaka na bisika na kokita na kolongolaka suki na bam pate kati na lisobe na Madia, mpe asengelaki kokweisa lolendo na ye nioso mpe bosembo nna miso na ye moko oyo ameseneke kozala na yango lokola muana mokonzi na Ejipito. Nzambe Amonakaka liboso na Mose oyo na komikitisa mpe Apesaka ye mosala na kobimisa bana na Yisalele libanda na Ejipito. Mose asengelaka korisker bomoi na ye mpona kokokisa yango, kasi atosaka mpe akendaka liboso na Falo.

Soki totali bizaleli na bana na Yisalele, tokoki komona motema monene nini Mose azalaka na yango tango andimaka mpe ayambaka bato wana nioso. Tango bato bazalaka na kokoso, bayimakiyimaki liboso na Mose mpe bamekaka ata kobeta ye mabanga.

Tango bazalaka na mai te, bayimakiyimaki ete bazalaka na posa na mai. Tango bazwaki mai, bayimakiyimaki été bazangaki bilei. Tango Nzambe Apesaka bango mana na likolo, bayimakiyimaki été bazangaki misuni. Balobaki ete baliaki bilei malamu na Ejipito, na kokitisa mana na kolobaka ete ezalaka bilei na babola.

Tango Nzambe Ayaka na kobalolelaka bango mokongo, ba nyoka na lisobe bayaka kosua bango. Kasi bakokaka kobikisama mpo ete Nzambe Ayokaki mabondeli na kafukafu na Mose. Bato bamonaka ete Nzambe Azalaka na Mose mpona tango molayi, kasi basalaka nzambe na ekeko mpe bangumbamelaki yango kaka sima na Mose kolongwa na miso na bango. Bakweisamaki mpe na basin a bapaya mpe basalaki ekobo oyo ezalaki mpe

Kurudishwa upya kwa Roho

ekobo na molimo. Atiaki bomoi na ye lokola gage mpona bolimbisi na bango, ata soki bakanisaka te ngolu bazwaka.

Esode 32:31-32Bongo Mose azongaki epai na Yawe mpe alobaki ete, 'Ee bato oyo basali lisumu monene. Nde sasaipi soki olingi kolimbisa lisumu na bango-; kasi soko boye tenabondeli Yo eteOlongola nkombo na ngai na mokanda na yo mokomi Yo."

Awa kolongola nkombo na ye na buku elakisi ete akokaka kobikisama te mpe akonyokwama na moto na selo na Lifelo, oyo ezali kufa na seko. Mose ayebaka likambo oyo malamu mpenza, kasi akolinga bato balimbisama ata na komikaba ye moko lolenge oyo.

Nini bokanisi Nzambe Ayokaka na komonaka Mose oyo? Mose asosolaka na mozindo motema na Nzambe oyo Ayinaka masumu kasi oyo Alingi kobikisa basumuki, mpe Nzambe Asepelaka na ye mpe Alingaki ye mingi mpenza. Nzambe Ayokaka libondeli oyo na Mose na bolingo, mpo ete bana na Yisalele bakoka kokima libebi.

Tolobe ete na ngambo moko ezali na diamant. Ezali na sans tache mpe na monene na lisapi. Mpe na ngambo mosusu ezali na mabanga mikama na monene moko. Bongo, nini wana elozala motuya koleka? Ata mabanga mizali mingi na lolenge nini, moto moko te akozwa yango mpona diamant. Na lolenge moko, valeur na Mose moto moko oyo akokisaka koleka na baton a nse na moi, ezalaka na motuya koleka milio na bato baoyo bakokisaki te

215

(Esode 32:10).

Mituya 12:3 elobeli Mose boye "Moto yango Mose azalaki na bopolo mingi, koleka bato nioso bazalaki na nse na moi", mpe na Mituya 12:7 Nzambe Andimeli ye na koloba ete, "Ezali boye na moombo na ngai Mose te, oyo azali sembo na ndako na Ngai mobimba."

Biblia elobeli bison a bisika mingi na lolenge nini Nzambe Alingaki Mose oyo. Esode 33:11 elobi ete, "Yawe Asololaki na Mose boye elongi na elongi, lokola moto akosololaka na moninga na ye. Lisusu Esode 33, tomoni ete Mose Asengi na Nzambe komilakisa Ye moko mpe Nzambe Ayanoli.

Ntoma Polo Amonanaki Lokola Nzambe

Ntoma Polo asalelaka Nkolo na bomoi na ye nioso mpe ata bongo azalaka tango nioso na motema pasi likolo na kala na ye, mpo ete anyokolaka Nkolo. Nde, ayambaka bakokoso nioso na motema na esengo mpe na kopesa matondi nakolobaka ete, "Pamba te ngai nazali nsima na Bantoma nioso, nabongi kobiangama ntoma te mpo ete naniokolaki lingomba na Nzambe." (1 Bakolinti 15:9).

Akangemaka na boloko, abetama mbala mingi, mingi mingi na danger na kufa. Mbala mitano azwaka fimbo ntuku misato na mwambe epai na Bayuda. Mbala misato abetamaka na nzete, mbala moko abetamaki mabanga, mbala misato masua na ye azindaka, butu mpe moi alekisaka kati na mozindo. AAzalaka na momesano na mibembo, na danger na bibale, danger na miyibi, danger na baton a ekolo na ye, danger na bapaya, danger kati na engomba, danger na lisobe, danger na mai monene, kati na bandeko na lokuta,; azala kati na misala makasi mpe bakokoso, kati na ba butu mingi azanga mpongi, kati na nzala mpe posa na mai, mingi mingi na bilei, kati na malili mpe komonana.

Ba pasi maye mizalaka mpenza minene ete alobaka na 1 Bakolinti 4;9 ete "Mpo ete nabanzi ete Nzambe Abimisi biso bantoma na nsuka na molongo lokola bato bakitisami ete bakufa, ete tozala etaliseli mpona mokili mpe mpona banje mpe mpona bato."

Bongo, tina nini Nzambe Andimelaka ntoma Polo oyo azalaka sembo azwa minyokoli makasi boye mpe ba pasi? Nzambe Alingaka Polo abima moto na motema kitoko oyo ezali petwa lokola mangaliti. Polo azalaka na moto na kotiela motema te kaka Nzambe na situation makasi bisika wapi akokaka kokangama to kobomama na tango nioso, Azwaka bopemi mpe esengo kati na Nzambe. Amiboyaki ye moko mpenza mpe akolisaki motema na Nkolo.

Litatoli elandi na Polo esimbi motema mingi mpo ete abimi lokola moto kitoko na nzela na mimekano. Alingaki te kokima pasi ata moko, ata soki ezalaka pasi mpona moto kondima. Atatolaki bolingo na ye mpona lingomba mpe bandimi na 2 Bakolinti 11:28 ete, "Mpe pembeni na makambo oyo nioso mokolo na mokolo bozito na mikakatano na ngai mpona mangombaekamoli ngai"

Lisusu, na Baloma 9:3, likolo na bato oyo balingaki koboma ye, alobaki ete, "Nabandaki kolikya ete nalakelama mabe ete natangwa longwa na Kristo mpona bandeko na ngai ba oyo bazali libota moko na ngai na nzoto." Awa, bandeko na ngai' elobeli Bayuda mpe Bafalisai ba oyo banyokolaki mpe ba tungisaka Polo makasi mpenza.

Misala 23:12-13 elobi ete, "Wana etanaki ntongo, Bayuda bayangani mwango, mpe bakati ndai ete bakolia te mpe bakomela te kino ekoboma bango Polo. Bango bakataki ndai yango balekaki ntuku minei."

Polo amemaka bango na kozala na nkanda na motema likolo na ye te. Polo atikala kokosa bango sokokosala bango mabe te. Kasi kaka mpo été ateyaka Sango Malamu mpe atalisaka nguya na Nzambe basalaki makita mpe bakataki ndai mpona koboma ye.

Ata bongo, abondelaka ete bato mana bakoka kobika, ata soki elakisaki ete akokaki koboungisa lobiko na ye moko. Yango ezali tina nini Nzambe Apesaka ye nguya na monene boye; akolisaka bolamu monene na oyo akokaka kokaba bomoi na ye moko mpona ba oyo balingaka kosala ye mabe. Nzambe Atikaka ye atalisa misala na nkamwa lokola milimo mabe mpe bokono kolongwa kaka na musuale to bilamba iye isimbaka ye likolo na babeli.

Abengaki bango Banzambe

Yoane 10:35 elobi ete, "Soko Abiangi bango banzambe, baoyo Liloba na Nzambe Eyeli bango (mpe likomi ekoki koboyama te)," Lolenge tokozwa Liloba na Nzambe mpe tokosalela yango, tokokoma baton a solo, minngimingi baton a molimo. Yango ezali nzela na kokokana na Nzambe oyo Azali Molimo; ezali kokoma baton a molimo mpe na sima baton a molimo ekoka. Mpe na lolenge oyo, tokobima lokola bikelamo bazali lokola Nzambe.

Esode 7:1 elobi ete, "Yawe mpe Alobelaki Mose ete, Tala, Nazalisi yo lokola Nzambe na miso na Falo, mpe Alona ndeko na yo akozala mosakoli na yo." Lisusu, Esode 4:16 elobi ete, "Ye akolobela bato mpona yo, mpe ye akozala monoko na yo, yo mpe okozala na ye lokola Nzambe." Lolenge ekomama, Nzambe ekitiselaki Mose nguya na monene boye ete Mose amonanaki lokola Nzambe liboso na bato.

Na Misala 14, na nkombo na Yesu Christu, ntoma Polo atelemisaki mpe atambolisaki moto atikala kotambola ten a bomoi na ye mobimba. NNa lolenge atelemaka mpe atambolaka, bato bakamwaka mingi nde balobaka ete: "Ba nzambe bakomi lokola bato, mpe bakiti nan se epai na biso" (Misala 14:11) Lokola na ndakisa oyo, ba oyo batambolakka na Nzambe bakoki komonana lokola Nzambe mpo ete bazali baton a molimo, ata soki bazali na nzoto na mosuni.

Yango tina etalisami na 2 Petelo 1:4 ete, "Na yango mpe Asili kotiela biso bilaka minene mpe na motuya mingi na ntina ete na bilaka yango bozua likabo na bino kati na lolenge na Nzambe mpe bokima libebi lizali kati na mokili mpona mposa mabe."

Tika biso tososola ete mposa makasi na Nzambe ezali ete bato bakota kati na BoNzambe na Nzambe, mpo ete tokoka kolongola mosuni ikufaka na oyo kaka nguya na molili isepelaka, tobota molimo na nzela na Molimo, mpe solo kokota kati na bo nzambe na Nzambe.

Soki tokomi na etape oyo na molimo ekoka, ekoka elakisi ete tozongeli mpenza molimo. Mpona kozongela mpenza molimo elakisi ete tozongeli elilingi na Nzambe oyo tobungisaka likolo na lisumu na Adamu, mpe bongo elakisi tokoto kati na bo nzambe na Nzambe.

Na tango tokomi na bisika oyo, tokoki kozwa nguya oyo ezalaka na Nzambe. Nguya na Nzambe ezalaka likabo oyo epesamaka epai na bana oyo bakokani na Ye (Nzembo 62:11). Elembo na kozwa nguya na Nzambe ezali bilembo mpe bikamwisi, bikamwisi minene, mpe makambo na kokamwisa, oyo nioso misalemaka na misala na Molimo Mosantu.

Soki tozwi nguya an lolenge oyo, tokoka kotambwisa milimo ebele na nzela na bomoi mpe lobiko. Petelo atalisaki misala mingi minene na nzela na nguya na Molimo Mosantu.

Kaka na koteyaka mbala moko, bato koleka ba nkoto mitano babikisamaki. Nguya na Nzambe ezali elembo ete Nzambe na bomoi Azali na moto wana. Ezali mpe nzela ebongi mpona kolona kondima kati na mitema na bato.

Bato bakondimaka te mpenza kaka soki bamoni bilembo mpe bikamwisi (Yoane 4:48). Bongo, Nzambe Atalisaka nguya na Ye na nzela na baton a molimo ekoka ba oyo bazongela mobimba na molimo mpo ete bato bakoka kondimela Nzambe na bomoi, Mobikisi Yesu Christu, kozali na Lola mpe Lifelo, mpe bosolo kati na Biblia.

Chapitre 4
Mokili na Molimo

Biblia elobelaka biso mingi likolo na mokili na molimo mpe bato bamonaka yango. Ezali mpe mokili na molimo bisika tokokende sima na bomoi oyo na mokili esila.

Ntoma Polo Ayebaka Sekele na Mokili na Molimo

Mokili na Molimo Izanga Suka Ilimbolami Kati na Biblia

Lola mpe Lifelo Mizalaka Solo

Bomoi Sima na Kufa Mpona Milimo Miye Mibikisami Te

Lolenge Moi mpe Sanza Mikesanaka na Nkembo

Lola Ekoki Te Kopimama na Elanga na Edeni

Yelusaleme na Sika, Likabo Malamu Koleka Epesama na Bana na Solo

Tango bato ba oyo bazongeli elilingi na Nzambe bakosilisa bomoi nabango na mokili oyo, bakozonga na mokili na molimo. Na bokeseni na mokili na bison a mosuni, mokili na molimo izali bisika izanga suka. Tokoka te kopima molai na yango, mozindo, to mpe monene.

Mokili monene oyo na molimo ikoki kokabolama kati na espace na Pole iye izali na Nzambe mpe espace na molili oyo ezali na milimo mabe. Na espace na Pole ezali na Bokonzi na Lola iye ibongisama mpona bana na Nzambe ba oyo babikisama na kondima. Baebele 11:1 elobi ete, "Kondima ezali elendiseli na biloko bikolikia biso; ezali mpe elimbweli na biloko mizangi komonana." Lolenge elobama, mokili na molimo ezali mokili oyo ikoki komonana te. Kasi, lokola mopepe na mokili na mosuni ikokaka komonana te kasi mpe koboyama te ete izalaka, na kolikiaka na kondima mpona likambo oyo tokoki kolikya kati na mokili oyo na mosuni, bilembo na bozali na yango mikotalisaka bozali na yango.

Kondima ezali nzela iye ikotisi bison a mokili na molimo. Ezali nzela mpona bis oba oyo tobiki na mokili oyo na mosuni tokutana na Nzambe oyo Azali na mokili na molimo.

Nakondima, tokoki kososola na Nzambe oyo Azali molimo. Tokoki koyoka mpe kososola Liloba na Nzambe na matoyi na biso na molimo mofungwami, mpe na miso na biso na molimo ifungwama, tokoki komona molimi na molimo iye ikoki te komonana na miso na biso. Na lolenge kondima na biso izali komata, tokozala na elikya makasi mpona bokonzi na Lola mpe tososola motema na Nzambe na mozindo. Na lolenge tokososola mpe koyoka bolingo na Ye, tokoka te koboya na kolinga Ye. Lisusu, soki tozwi kondima ekoka, makambo na mokili na molimo mikosalema, maye makoka mpenza te na mokili oyo na mosuni, mpo été Nzambe Akozala na biso.

Ntoma Polo ayebaka ba Sekele na Mokili na Molimo

Na 2 Bakolinti 12:1 kino likolo, Polo alimboli makambo maye na mokili na molimo na kolobaka ete, "Ebongi na ngai komikumisa, ekozala na litomba ten de nakoleka kino bimononeli mpe bimoniseli na Nkolo." Ezalaki mpona makambo na ye na kozala na Paradiso kati na Bokonzi na Lola na LLikolo na Misato.

2 Bakolinti 12:6 elobi ete, ""Soko nakolinga komikumisa nakozala elema te pamba te nakoloba sembo. Nde nakotika te été moto akanisela ngai te bobele mpona yango ekomona ye mpe ekoyoka ye kati na ngai." Ntoma Polo akutanaka na makambo mingi na molimo mpe azwaka bimoniseli na Nzambe, kasi akokaka koloba makambo nioso te oyo ayebaka likolo na mokili na molimo.

Na Yoane 3:12, Yesu Alobi ete, "Soko nasili koloba na bino

mpo na makambo na mokili mpe bondimi te, bokondima boni soko nakoloba na bino mpona makambo na Likolo? Ata sima na komona misala mingi na nguya na miso na bango moko, bayekolo na Yesu bakokaka te kondimela Yesu na mobimba. Bayaka na kozwa kondima na solo kaka sima na bango kokutana na lisekwa na Nkolo. Sima na wana, babonzaka bomoi na bango mpona Bokonzi na Likolo mpe kosakola na Sanza Malamu. Na lolenge momko Ntoma Polo ayebaka malamu mpenza mpona Mokili na molimo malamu mingi mpe akokisaki mpenza malamu mosala na ye na bomoi na ye mobimba.

Ezali bongo na nzela mpona biso koyoka mpe kososola bikamwa na mokili na molimo lolenge Polo azsalaka? Ya solo, ezali. Na yambo, tosengeli kolikya mpona mokili na molimo. Kozala na mposa makasi mpona mokili na molimo etalisi ete tondimi mpe tolingi Nzambe oyo azali molimo.

Mokili na Molimo Iye Izanga Suka Italisami kati na Biblia

Kati na Biblia tokoki komona makomi mingi likolo na mokili na molimo mpe ba ezxperince na molimo. Adamu akelamaki lokola ekelamo na bomoi, oyo ezali molimo na bomoi, mpe akokaka kosolola na Nzambe. Ata sima na ye, ezali na basakoli mingi ba oyo basololaka na Nzambe mpe tango mosusu bayokaka mongogo mpenza na Nzambe. (Genese 5:22, 9:9-13; Esode 20:1-17; Mituya 12:8). Ba tango misusu, bange babimelaka bato mpona kopesa sango na Nzambe. Ezali mpe na makomi likolo na bikelamo minei na bomoi (Ejekiele 1:4-14),

Kerubi (2 Samuele 6:2; Ejekiele 10:1-6), ba mpuda mpe ekalo na moto (2 Mikonzi 2:11, 6:17), ba oyo bazali na mokili na molimo.

Mai monana ekabolamaki na biteni mibale. Mai ibimaki kati na libanga na nzela na mosali na Nzambe, Mose. Moi mpe sanza mitelemaka mpe mitikalaki bisika moko na nzela na libondeli na Josue. Eliya abondelaka epai na Nzambe mpe akitisaki moto na Likolo. Sima na ye kosilisa misala ma ye nioso na mokili oyo, Eliya akamatamaki na likolo kati na mopepe. Maye oyo izali ba ndakisa bisika wapi mokili na molimo italisamaka kati na mokili oyo.

Na konakisa, kati na 2 Mikonzi 6, tango mapinga na Alama bayaka kokanga Elisa, mosali miso na molimo na mosali na Elisa Gehazia mifungwamaki mpe amonaka ebele na mbalata mpe na makalo na moto mpe mizingaki Elisa mpona kobatela ye. Daniele abwakamaka kati na libulu na kosi na mayele mabe na baninga na ye ba minister. Kasi atikalaka kozwa likama moko te mpo ete Nzambe Atindaka muanje na Ye mpona kokanga monoko na ba kosi. Baninga misato na Daniele babatelaka bondimi na bango mpe babwakamaka kati na moto makasi iye izalaka mbala sambo koleka momesano. Kasi moko te kati na bango azikaka.

Muana na Nzambe, Yesu, mpe azwaka nzoto na baton a tango Awaka na mokili oyo, kasi Atalisaka makambo na mokili na molimo izanga suka, na kokangama te na bosuki na mokili na mosuni. Asekwisa bawa, Abikis ba malady kilikili, mpe

Atambolaka na mai. Lisusu, sima na lisekwa na ye abimelaka na bayekoli na ye mibale ba oyo bazalaka na nzela na bango na Emaus (Luka 24:13-16), alekaka na efelo nan a ndako mpe amonanaka kati na ndako mpona bayekoli wana bazalaka kobanga Bayuda mpe bamikangelaka kati na ndako (Yoane 20:19).

Yango ezali oyo tobengi teleportation, elekelaka espace physique. Etalisi biso ete mokili na molimo elekelaka ba limite na tango mpe espace. Ezali na espece na mosuni na bokeseni na oyo na biso tokomonaka na miso na biso, mpe Azalaka kokende elongo na espace oyo na molimo mpona komonana na bisika mpe na tango Ye Alingaka.

Bana na Nzambe ba oyo bazali na citoyennete na Lola basengeli kozala na posa na makambo na molimo. Nzambe atikaka baton a lolenge eye baleka na mokili na molimo, lolenge Aloba na Yelemia 29:13. "Bokoluka ngai mpe bokozua ngai wana bokoluka Ngai na mitema na bino mibimba."

Tokoki kokota na molimo mpe Nzambe Akoki kofungola miso na biso molimo tango tolongoli bosembo na miso na biso moko, lolenge na biso moko na komonela makambo mpe makanisi tokomisa sembo, na likolo na kozala na posa eye.

Ntoma Yoane azalaka moko na bayekoli zomi na mibale na Yesu (Emoniseli 1:1,9). Na mbula 95 A.JC, akangamaka epai na bato Domitianus Empereur na Roma mpe babwakaki ye kati na mafuta na moto. Kasi akufaka te kasi bamemaka ye na esanga na Patmos kati na mai monana na Agee. Kuna akomaka buku na Emoniseli.

Mpona Yoane kozwa emoniseli na mozindo, asengelaki kozala na makoki na yango. Makoki ezalaka ete asengelaka kozala bulee na kozangaka mabe na lolenge moko te mpe azala na motema na Nkolo. Akokaki kokitisa mozindo na ba sekele na Lola na lisungi na Molimo Mosantu na nzela na mabondeli makasi miye mipesamaka na motema petwa mpe bulee mpenza.

Lola mpe Lifelo Mizalaka Mpenza

Kati na mokili na molimo ezali na Lola mpe na Lifelo. Kaka sima na ngai kofungola egelesia Manmin, Nzambe Alakisaka ngai Lola mpe Lifelo kati na mabondeli na ngai. Kitoko mpe sai nayokaka na Lola ekoki te kolimbolama to mpe kotalisama na maloba.

Na ekeke na Boyokani na Sika, ba oyo bayambi Yesu Christu lokola Nkolo na Mobikisi na bango moko, bazwaka bolimbisi na masumu na bango mpe lobiko. Bakokende naino na Nkunda na Likolo sima na bomi na bango na mokili. Kuna, bakofanda mpona mikolo misato mpo komikokanisa na mokili na molimo, nde sima bakokende na bisika na kozela na Paradiso kati na Bokonzi na Lola. Tata na kondima Abalayama azalaka ye na bokambi na Nkunda na Likolo kino komata na Nkolo na Lola, yango tina tomonaka makomi kati na Biblia été mobola Lazalo azalaka 'na esika na Abalayama'.

Yesu Ateyaka Sango Malamu na milimo kati na Nkunda na Likolo sima na Ye kopema pema na Ye na suka na ekulusu (1 Petelo 3:19). Sima na Yesu koteya Sango Malamu kati Nkunda na Likolo, Asekwaka mpe Amemaka milimo nioso kuna na Paradiso. Wuta wana, milimo oyo mibikaka bakofanda na bisika na kozela na Lola oyo izali na suka na Paradiso. Sima na esambiseli na Ngwende monene na Pembe ikosila, bakokende na bisika na bango na koingela moko moko na Lola, kolandana na etape kati na kondima na moko na moko mpe bakobika kuna mpona libela.

Na Esambiseli na Ngwende Monene na Pembe, oy ekosalema sima na koleka na baton a nse na moi, Nzambe Akosambisa misala nioso na moto nioso oyo abotamaka wuta kokelama, ezala malamu to mabe. Ebengami Ezsambiseli na Ngwende Monene mpo ete ngwende na esambiseli na Nzambe ikongela mpenza ete nde ikomonana lokola mpenza pembe (Emoniseli 20:11).

Esambiseli oyo moonene ikosalema sima na bozongi na Nkolo na mipepe mpe na mokili, mpe sima na bokonzi na nkoto moko ikosila. Mpona milimo mibikisami, ikozala mpona esambiseli na makabo, mpe mpona ba oyo bazali te, ikozala esambiseli na etumbu.

Bomoi sima na Kufa mpona Milimo Mikobikisama Te

Ba oyo bandimelaka Nkolo te mpe ba oyo batatola bondimi na bango kati na Ye kasi babikisama te bakokamatama na na batindami mingi na Lifelo sima na kufa na bango. Bakofanda na bisika lokola libulu monene mpona mikolo misato mpona kobongama na kozala na kati na Nkunda nan nse, bisika wapi bakozwa etumbu na bango kolandana na masumu na bango.

Nkunda nan se oyo ezwami na Lifelo ezali monene lokola Lola, mpe ezali na bisika mingi mpona kofandisa milimo miye mibikisama te.

Kino tango esambiseli na Ngwende Monene na Pembe isalema, milimo mizali kofanda na Nkunda na Nse na kozwaka bitumbu na lolenge na lolenge. Bitumbu wana misangisi koliama na banyama mike mike to banyama, to kobetama na batindami na Lifelo. Sima na esambiseli na Ngwende monene na Pembe, bakokenda soko na libeke na moto to mpe na sufulu kopela moto (iye iyebana mpe lokola libeke na sufulu kopela moto) mpe bakozwa etumbu mpona libela (Emoniseli 21:8).

Esambiseli ezali soko libeke na moto to na sufulu ikoki te komekama na bitumbu kati na Nkunda na Nse. Moto na Lifelo izali moto na kobanzama te. Libeke na sufulu kopela moto ezali kutu mbala sambo moto koleka libeke na moto. Ezali mpona bato oyo basalaka masumu makoki kolimbisama te lokola, kotuka mpe kotelemela Molimo Mosantu.

Nzambe Alakisa ngai libeke na moto mpe libeke na sufulu. Bisika mizali na suka te mpe mitondisamaki na eloko moko lokola londende oyo italisamaka na bisika na mai kotoka, mpe bato bakokaka komonana malamu te. Basusu bakokaki komonana na ba tolo na bango, mpe misusu bazindisamaki kati na Libeke na ba kingo na bango. Kati na Libeke na moto, bazalaki komilela mpe konganga, kasi kati na libeke na sufulu kopela moto pasi elekaki makasi été bakokaka komilela te.

Tosengeli kondima été mokili oyo imonanaka te izalaka mpe kobika na Liloba na Nzambe mpo été tokoka solo kozwa lobiko.

Lolenge Moi mpe Sanza Mikesanaka na Nkembo

Kolimbola likolo na nzoto na biso sima na lisekwa, ntoma Polo Alobaki ete "Ezali na nkembo na moi, mmpe nkembo mosusu na sanza, mpe nkembo mosusu na minzoto; mpo monzoto ekeseni na monzoto mosusu na nkembo" (1 Bakolinti 15:41).

Nkembo na moi etalisi nkembo epesamelaka ba oyo balongoli masumu na bango nioso, babulisami, mpe bazalaka sembo na ndako mobimba na Nzambe na mokili oyo. Nkembo na sanza etalisi nkembo iye ipesamaka na ba oyo naino bakokisi etape na nkembo na moi te. Nkembo na mnzoto epesamaka na ba oyo bakokisi ata moke nan se na nkembo na sanza. Lisusu, lokola monzoto ikesanka na monzoto mosusu, moto nioso akozwa nkembo ekesana mpe lifuti, ata soki moko na moko akoki kokota na bisika moko na kobima na Lola.

Biblia elobeli biso ete tokozwa nkembo ekesana na Lola. Bisika na koingela na Lola mpe mabonza mikokesana kolandana na lolenge yolongoli masumu, na bisika nini tozali na kondima na molimo, mpe lolenge nini mlende tozala mpona bokonzi na Nzambe.

Bokonzi na Lola izali na bisika mingi mipesama na moto na moto kolandana na etape kati na kindima na moto na moto. Paradiso ipesamaka na ba oyo bazali na etape kati na kondima na nse koleka. Bokonzi na Liboso ezali likolo na etape na Paradiso, mpe Bokonzi na Mibale na Lola izali malamu kolela na liboso. Na Bokonzi na Misato na Lola ezali na mboka na Yelusaleme na Sika bisika Ngwende na Nzambe ezali.

Lola Ekoki Te Kopimama na Elanga na Edeni

Elanga na Edeni ezali bisika na kitoko mpenza mpe bisika na kimya ete bisika na kitoko koleka na mokili ikoki te kobanda na kokokana na yango, kasi Elanga na Edeni ikoki tea ta kobanda na kokokana na Bokonzi na Lola. Esengo oyo eyokanaka kati na Elanga na Edeni mpe oyo eyokanaka na Bokonzi na Lola mizali mpenza na bokeseni mpo ete Elanga na Edeni ezali na likolo na mibale mpe Bokonzi na Lola na likolo na misato. Ezali mpe mpo ete ba oyo babikaka na Elanga na Edeni bazali bana na Nzambe na solo mpenza te ba oyo balekela nzela na koleka nan se na moi.

Toloba ete bomoi na mokili ezali ezali bomoi kati na molili izanga pole moko, nde, bongo, bomoi na elanga na Edeni izali lokola kobika na mwida ya petrole, mpe bomoi na Lola ezali lokola kobika na minda makasi na courant. Liboso na ampoule esalema, basalelaki minda n mafuta, oyo ezalaki na se. Kasi ata bongo, mizalaka mpe na motuya. Tango bato bamonaka minda na courant mpona mbala liboso, bakamwaka mpenza.

Esi etalisama ete bisika na bika na kofanda na Lola mikopesamela bato kolandana na bitape kati na kondima mpe mitema na molimo bakolisaka na tango na bomoi na bango na mokili. Mpe, bisika na bisika na kofanda na Lola ikeseni na mosusu mpona nkembo mpe esengo ikoyokanaka kuna. Soki tomato likolo na etape na kobulisama kaka na kozala sembo na ndako mobimba na Nzambe mpe kokoma na mobimba moto na molimo, tokoka kokende kati na engomba na Yelusaleme na Sika bisika wapi ezali na Ngwende na Nzambe.

Yelusaleme na Sika, Libonza na Motuya Koleka Ipesamela Bana na Solo

Lolenge Yesu Aloba na Yoane 14:2, "Na ndako na Tata na Ngai bisika mizali ebele," ezali solo na bisika mingi na kofanda na Lola. Ezali na engomba na Yelusaleme na Sika oyo efandisaka Ngwende na Nzambe, bisika ezali mpe na Paradiso, oyo ezali bisika indimama mpona ba oyo bazwi kaka lobiko.

Engomba na Yelusaleme na Sika, oyo ibengamaka mpe 'Mbka na Nkembo', ezali bisika na kitoko koleka kati na bisika nioso na kofanda kuna na Lola. Nzambe Alingi moto nioso azwa kaka lobiko te kasi baya kati na mboka oyo (1 Timote 2:4).

Moloni akoki kaka kozwa masango na motuya mingi te kati na elanga na ye. Lolenge moko, moto nioso te oyo azwi koleka na baton a nse na moi akoki kobima lokola muana na solo na Nzambe oyo azali kati na molimo ekoka. Bongo, mpona ba oyo bakokaka na kondimama te mpona kofanda kati na mboka na Yelusaleme na Sika, Nzambe Abongisa bisika mingi na kofanda kobanda na Paradiso kino Bokonzi na Liboso, na Mibale, na Misato na Lola.

Paradiso na Yelusaleme na Sika mikesana mpenza, mingi na lolenge moko ndako moke na pamba na kekele ikesana na ndako na mokonzi na mboka monene. Kaka lolenge baboti bakolinga kopesa makambo na motuya koleka epai na bana na bango, Nzambe Alingi biso tokoma bana ba Ye na solosolo mpe tokabola biloko nioso elongo na Ye kati na Yelusaleme na Sika.

Bolingo na Nzambe isuka te kak mpona baton a lolenge moko boye, ipesamaka epai na ba oyo nioso bayambi Yesu Christo. Kasi bisika na kofanda na Lola mpe mabanza, mpe etape na bolingo na Nzambe ipesama mikokesana kolandana na etape na moto na moto na kobulisama mpe na bosembo.

Ba oyo bakokende na Paradiso, Bokonzi na Liboso na Lola, to Bokonzi na Mibale na Lola, balongoli mosuni kati na bango nioso te, mpe bazali mpenza bana na solo na Nzambe te. Kaka lolenge bana na solo na Nzambe. Kaka lolenge bana mike bakoki kososola nioso likolo na baboti na bango te, ezali pasi mpona bango basosola motema na Nzambe.Bongo ezali mpe bolingo mpe bosembo na Nzambe ete Abongisa bisika na bisika mpona kofanda kolandana na etape kati na kondima na moko na moko. Kaka lolenge moko izalaka malamu na kozala na baninga na lisanga moko na moko, ezalaka malamu mpe esengo mongi mpona baton a Lola kosangana na ba oyo bazali etape moko kati na kondima na bango.

Engomba na Yelusaleme na Sika ezali mpe elembo ete Nzambe Azwi ba mbuma na kokoka na nzela na koleka na baton a nse na moi. Mabanga na motuya na moboko na mboka etalisi ete mitema na bana na Nzambe ba oyo bakokota kati na mboka mizali kitoko lolenge na mabanga mana na motuya. Bikuke na mangaliti mitalisi ete bana wan aba oyo baleki na nzela na bikuke wana bakolisi molende kaka lolenge nyama na mangaliti isalaka mangaliti na molende.

Na lolenge bakoleka na nzela na bukuke na mangaliti, bakobanza tango na kokanga mitema na bango mpona kokoma na Lola. Tango bakotambola na ba balabala na wolo, bakobanza ba nzela na kondima bazwaka na mokili oyo. Monene mpe decoration na ba ndako ipesamelaka moto na moto mikobanzisa bango na lolenge nini balingaka Nzambe mpe lolenge nini bapesaka nkembo na Nzambe na kondima na bango.

Ba oyo bakoki kokota engomba na Yelusaleme na Sika bakoki komona Nzambe elongi na elongi mpo ete babongoli mitena bango na oyo na petwa mpe kitoko lokola kulusutala mpe bakomi bana na Nzambe na solo. Bakosalelama mpe na banje ebele mpe bakobika kati na esengo na seko mpe na sai. Ezali mpenza bisika na kokamwisa mpe na bulee koleka makanisi nioso na bato.

Kaka lolenge ezali na ba buku na lolenge na lolenge, Lola mpe ezali na ba buku na lolenge na lolenge. Ezali na Buku na bomoi oyo ikomama ba nkombo na ba oyo babikisami. Ezali mpe na buku na souvenir, oyo ekomi makambo makoki kosepelama mpona libela. Ezali na langi na wolo mpe ezali na bilembo na lokumu mpe na bakonzi na mboka likolo na couverture na yango, nde moto akoki na pete ete buku oyo ezali na motuya mingi. Ikomi na motuya likolo na moto nini asalaka likambo nini na situation nini, mpe biteni na motuya mitiama mpe kati na video.

Ndakisa, ekomi likolo na bisika wapi Abalayama abonzaka muana na ye Izaka lokola mbeka na kotumba; Eliya kokitisa moto na Lola; Daniele kobatelama kati na libulu na kosi; mpe baninga misato na Daniele kozwa likama moko te kati na litumbu na moto mpona kopesa nkembo na Nzambe. Nzambe Akopona mokolo moko na motuya mpona kotalisa makambo kati na buku epai na bato. Ban aba Nzambe bazali kolanda Ye na kosepela mpe bazali kopesa nkembo epai na Nzambe na masanjoli.

Lisusu, kati na engomba na Yelusaleme na Sika bilemba ebele mikozala kosalema, kosangisa bilambo mikozala na kosalema epai na Nzambe Tata. Ezali na bilambo ipesamaka na Nkolo, Molimo Mosantu, mpe lisusu na basakoli lokola Eliya, Enoki, Abalayama, Mose, mpe ntoma Polo. Bandimi basusu bakoki mpe kobengisa bandeko misusu mpona kosala bilambo. Bilambo mizali suka na bisengo kati na bomi na Lola. Izali bisika na komona mpe kosepela bofuluki, bonsoli, kitoko, mpe nkembo na Lola na ngonga moko.

Ata na mokili oyo, bato ba mikembisaka malamu koleka mpe bamisepelisaka kati na kolia mpe na komela kati na bilambo minene. Ezali lolenge moko na Lola. Kati na bilambo na Lola, banje basepelisaka na nzela na ba mabina mpe muziki. Bana na Nzambe bakoki koyemba mpe kobina na miziki mpe lokola. Bisika itondisami na mabina kitoko mpe ba nzembo mpe koseka na esengo na bato ebele. Bakoki kozala na masolo kitoko na

Kurudishwa upya kwa Roho

bandeko kati na kondima na kofandaka bisika na bisika, to mpe bakoki kopesa mbote na ba tata na kondima ba oyo balikyaka komona. Soki babiangami na elambo epesama na Nkolo, bandimi bakomibongisa na makasi na bango nioso lokola basin a libala kitoko koleka na Nkolo. Nkolo azalali mobali na bison a libala na molimo. Tango basii na ibala na Nkolo bakomi na ekuke liboso na chateau na Nkolo, banje mibale bakoyamba bango na komikitisa na bisika na bisika na ekuke iye izali kongala na minda na wolo.

Bifelo na chateau mibongisama na mabanga ebele na moyuya. Likolo na efelo mibongisama na ba fololo kitoko, mpe bafololo mana mazali kopesa solo na malasi kitoko mpona basin a libala na Nkolo ba oyo bawuti kokoma kuna. Na lolenge bazali kokende na chateau, bakoyoka makelele na ba nzembo iye ikosimbaka ata mozindo na milimo na bango. Bazali koyoka esengo mpe malamu nan a makelele na masanjoli, mpe basimbami na mozindo na matondi na bango, na kokanisaka bolingo na Nzambe oyo Atambwisi bango na bisika wana.

Na lolenge bakotambola na balabala na wolo kino na ndako monene na chateau na Nkolo na lisungi na bange, mitema na bango mitondisami na posa. Na lolenge bakopusanaka pene na ndako monene, bakoki komona Nkolo oyo abimi libanda mpona koyamba bango. Na mbala moko miso na bango mitondisami na pinzoli, kasi sasaipi bazali kokima epai na Nkolo mpo ete balingi nokinoki kokutana na Nkolo.

237

Nkolo Ayambi bango moko na moko na elongi na ye etondisama na bolingo mpe mawa, mpe na maboko maye mifongwama makasi. Ayambi bango na koloba ete, "Boya! Basin a ngai kitoko, boyei malamu!" Bandimi ba oyo bayambami na Nkolo bakopesa matondi epai na Ye na mitema na bango nioso. Nakolobaka ete, "Napesi yo solo matondi mpona kobengisa ngai!" kaka lolenge na ba oyo bakokabolaka mpenza bolingo na bango, bazali kotambola loboko na loboko elongo na Nkolo na kotalaka awa mpe kuna zinga zinga na bango, mpe bazali na masolo na Ye ete balingaka mingi kobeta awa na mokili oyo.

Bomoi kati na engomba na Yelusaleme na Sika, na kobikaka na Nzambe Misato, itondisama na bolingo, kosepela, mpe sai. Tokoki komona Nkolo elongi na elongi, kozala na esika na Ye, kobenbuka elongo na Ye, mpe kosepela makambo mingi elongo na Ye! Bomoi na esengo nini ezali! Kosepela esengo eye, tosengeli tokoma Bulee mpe tokokisa molimo, mpe lisusu molimo ekoka oyo ekokana mpenzampenza na motema na Nkolo.

Na yango, tika nokinoki tokokisa molimo ekoka na elikya oyo, tozwa lipamboli na makambo nioso kotambola malamu na biso mpe tozala na nzoto malamu lolenge milema na biso mikofuluka, mpe na sima topusana penepene na koleka na Ngwende na Nzambe kati na mboka na nkembo na Yelusaleme na Sika.

Mokomi:
Dr. Jaerock Lee

Dr. Jaerock Lee abotamaka na Muan, Province na Jeonnam, Republique na Koree, na 1943. Na ba mbula na ye ntuku mibale, Dr. Lee anyokwamaka na ba bokono kilikili mizanga lobiko mpona ba mbula sambo mpe azalaka bobele kozela kufa na elikya moko te na lobiko. Kasi mokolo moko na tango na sima na malili makasi na 1974 amemamaka na egelesia epai na ndeko na ye muasi mpe tango afukamaka mpona kobondela, Nzambe na bomoi na mbala moko abikisaka ye na bokono na ye nioso.

Kobanda ngonga akutanaka na Nzambe na bomoi na nzela na experience wana kitoko, Dr. Lee alingaka Nzambe na motema na ye nioso mpe bosolo, mpe na 1978 abengamaka azala mosali na Nzambe.. Abondelaka makasi na kokilaka mingi mpo ete akoka kososola malamu mokano na Nzambe, akokisa yango malamu mpe atosa Liloba na Nzambe. Na 1982, abandisaka Egelesia Central Manmin na Seoul, Korea, mpe misala mingi na Nzambe mizanga suka, kosangisa ebele na miracles, bilembo mpe bikamwa, mizalaka kosalema kati na egelesia na ye wuta.

Na 1986, Dr Lee azalaka consacrer lokola Pasteur na Assemblee Annuel na Yesu egelesia Sungkyul na Korea, mpe mbula minei na sima na 1990, mateya ma ye mabanda kobima na Australie, Russie mpe na Philippine. Sima na tango moke ba mboka mingi koleka mikomaka kozwa mateya na nzela na Companie Na Diffusion na Far Est. Station na Diffusion na Asia, mpe Systeme na Radio na Washington.

Mbula misato na sima, na 1993, Egelesia Central Manmin eponamaka lokola moko na Mangomba 50 eleka na Mokili" na Magazine na ba Bakristu na Mokili (America) mpe azwaka Doctorat na Bonzambe na College na Kondima na Bakristu, Floride, America, mpe na 1996 azwaka Maitrise kati na Mosala na Nzambe na Seminaire na Theologie na Iowa, America.

Wuta 1993, Dr. Lee abandaka kopanza evangelization na mokili mobimba na nzela na ba croisade ebele na mikili na bapaya ata na Tanzanie, Argentine, L.A, Balitimore Cite, Hawai, mpe New York mboka na America, Uganda, na Japon, Pakistan, Kenya, Philippine, Honduras, Inde, Russie, Allemagne, Peru, Republique Democratique na Congo, Israel mpe Estonie.

Na 2002 andimamaka lokola mosali na kolamusa bato na mokili mobimba mpona mosala na ye na nguya makasi kati na ba croiadе ebele, na biklo bapaya na ba journaux minene kati Koree. Mpe mingi mingi croisade na ye na Madison Square Garden, bisika ekenda sango koleka na mokili mobimba. Molulu mitelemaka na ba mboka 220, mpe na

Croisade na ye na 209, iye isalemaka na(ICC) Yerusaleme atatolaka ete Yesu Azali Messia mpe Mobikisi.

Mateya ma ye malekaka na ba mboka 176 na nzela na satellite kosangisa GCN TV mpe atangamaka moko kati na zomi na bakambi na Influence na Bakristu na 2009 mpe 2010 na magazine na Bakristo ekenda sango na kombo IN Victory mpe Agence na ba sango Telegraphe na Bakristu mpona ba diffution maye na misala na nguya mpe bokambi ma ye na mosala na Pasteur.

Kobanda sanza na mai 2013, Egesia Central Manmin ezali na lisanga eleki bato 120,000. Ezali na ba Branches 10,000 na ba egelesia na mokili mobimba kosangisa ba branche domestique 56, mpe koleka ba mission 129 mitindama na ba mboka 23, kosangisa America ya ngele, Russie, Allemagne, Canada, Japon, Chine, Inde, France Kenya, mpe mingi koleka.

Na mokolo na kobimisa buku oyo, Dr Lee akoma ba buku 85, kosangisa ba choeud d'ouvres lokola Meka bomoi na Seko Liboso na Kufa, Bomoi na Ngai Bondimi na ngai I &II, Sango na Ekulusu, Bitape kati na Kondima, Lola I &II, Lifelo, Lamuka Yisalele!, mpe Nguya na Nzambe. Misala ma ye mibongolama na ba koto eleki 75.

Makomi maye na Bakristu mibimaka na The Hankook Ilbo, The JoongAng Daily, The Chosun Ilbo, The Dong-A Ilbo, The Munhwa Ilbo, The Seoul Shinmun, The Kyunghyang Shinmun, The Korea Economic Daily, The Korea Herald, The Shisa News, and The Christian Press.

Sasaipi Dr. Lee azali mokambi na ba organization mingi na ba missionnaires mpe ba association. Ebonga na ye esangisi: President: Lisanga na Mangomba na Kobulisama na Yesu Christu; Presidentt, Mission na mokili mobimba Manmin, President lelo na Asociation na, Bokristo na Mokili Mobimba mpona Bolamuki na Molimo, Mobandisi mpe President na conseil d'Administration GCN; Mobandisi mpe President Reseau na Mokilimobimba mpona Ba Mingganga na Bakristu (WCDN); Mobandisi mpe President na Conseil D'Administration na, Seminaire International Manmin (MIS).

Other powerful books by the same author

Heaven I & II

A detailed sketch of the gorgeous living environment the heavenly citizens enjoy and beautiful description of different levels of heavenly kingdoms.

The Message of the Cross

A powerful awakening message for all the people who are spiritually asleep In this book you will find the reason Jesus is the only Savior and the true love of God.

Hell

An earnest message to all mankind from God, who wishes not even one soul to fall into the depths of hell! You will discover the never-before-revealed account of the cruel reality of the Lower Grave and hell.

Tasting Eternal Life Before Death

A testimonial memoirs of Dr. Jaerock Lee, who was born gain and saved from the valley of death and has been leading an exemplary Christian life.

The Measure of Faith

What kind of a dwelling place, crown and reward are prepared for you in heaven? This book provides with wisdom and guidance for you to measure your faith and cultivate the best and most mature faith.

www.urimbooks.com

www.ingramcontent.com/pod-product-compliance
Lightning Source LLC
LaVergne TN
LVHW021807060526
838201LV00058B/3264